THE MONSTERS OF ST. HELENA

THE
MONSTERS
OF
ST. HELENA

———

BROOKS HANSEN

FARRAR, STRAUS AND GIROUX

NEW YORK

Farrar, Straus and Giroux
19 Union Square West, New York 10003

Distributed in Canada by Douglas & McIntyre Ltd.
Printed in the United States of America
First edition, 2003

Illustrations: (*p. 1*) Map from *Carte Générale de l'Afrique*, by Eustache Herrisson, 1828; (*p. 7*) *Sancta Helena*, Langenes, 1598; (*p. 15*) *Saint Helena*, Lieut. R. P. Reade, 1817; (*p. 59*) *The Briars*, from *Views of St. Helena* by T. E. Fowler, St. Helena, 1863; (*p. 113*) *Goa*, unattributed, 1646, from the Collection of the New York Public Library; (*p. 161*) *Jamestown, from the Road to the Briars*, engraved by Finden from a drawing by E. S. Blake, 1830; (*p. 227*) *St. Paul's Church*, from *Views of St. Helena* by G. W. Melliss, London, 1857; (*p. 267*) *The Column Lot, Sandy Bay*, from *Views of St. Helena* by G. H. Bellasis, John Tyler, London, 1815.

Library of Congress Cataloging-in-Publication Data
Hansen, Brooks, 1965–
    The monsters of St. Helena / Brooks Hansen.
        p.   cm.
    ISBN 0-374-27019-8 (alk. paper)
    1. Napoleon I, Emperor of the French, 1769–1821—Fiction.   2. Saint Helena—
Fiction.   3. Emperors—Fiction.   4. Exiles—Fiction.   I. Title: Monsters of Saint
Helena.   II. Title.

PS3558.A5126 M66 2002
813'.54—dc21

2002023433

Designed by Jonathan D. Lippincott

www.fsgbooks.com

1   3   5   7   9   10   8   6   4   2

FOR MY FATHER

CONTENTS

DRAMATIS PERSONAE

ST. HELENA, C. 1530

Fernando Lopez, first resident of St. Helena
The white cockerel, his companheiro

ST. HELENA, 1815

THE "WHITE" ISLANDERS

William Balcombe: official purveyor to Bonaparte's suite,
owner and patriarch of the Briars
Margaret Balcombe, his wife
Jane, his eldest daughter, sixteen
Betsy, his second child, fourteen
Alexander and Nicholas, his sons, nine and six
Mr. Virgil Phineas Huffington, tutor to the Balcombe boys
The Reverend Richard Boys, senior chaplain
The Right Reverend James Eakins, former chaplain
Colonel Mark Wilkes, acting Governor of St. Helena

The Hodgsons, Mr. Willie Doveton, the Leggs, Millicent Legg,
Lt. Gov. Skelton, Miss Mason, Mr. J. Hammond,
Mr. Saul Solomon, Mrs. Bagley, Miss Wilkes

THE "COLORED" ISLANDERS

Sarah, nanny to Betsy and Jane
Toby, the Briars' gardener
Alley, a servant at the Briars
'Scilla, the Balcombes' cook
Sam and Charles, fourteen and fifteen, Mr. Balcombe's help in town
Marie, Quinto's mother, and a maid at Mr. Pourteous's Inn
Quinto, Marie's son, a basket weaver
Minnie, the Jamestown madame
Timu, a free black chicken farmer
Lotte, Alley's mate and helper at Country Church
Martin, a slave at Mr. Breames's farm
Oliver, a slave at Mr. Haywood's farm

THE ENGLISH

Admiral George Cockburn, charged with custody of Bonaparte
Dr. Barry Edward O'Meara, Bonaparte's physician
Lieutenant Henry Wood, 53[d] Regiment
Officers Stokes, Owens, and Pollard
Lieutenant Commander Thomas Chilcott
Tom Pipes, Admiral Cockburn's Newfoundland dog

THE FRENCH

Napoleon Bonaparte, prisoner and former Emperor of Europe
Count Emanuel de Las Cases, Bonaparte's principal amanuensis
His son Emanuel de Las Cases, fifteen, assistant to his father
General Baron Gaspard Gourgaud
Henri Bertrand, Grand Marshal to General Bonaparte

Fanny Bertrand, his wife
Marquis Tristan de Montholon
Albine de Montholon, his wife
Tristan, his daughter
Jean-Gabriel Marchand, the Emperor's valet
Ali St. Denis, the Emperor's valet
Cipriani, the Emperor's steward
Pierron, the Emperor's chef
Lepage, pastry chef

WINSTON-KUMAR'S SHADOW PUPPETS

JohnSree, King of the Portingale
Esta, his Queen
Dagama, the explorer
Poklemmit, the high priest
Dabakur, Viceroy of Nirindi
Hidalcao, the Moor King
Pulatecao, an impetuous Moor Prince
Rasalcao, the wily Moor Prince
Guards of Benastarim
Fernando Lopez
Mateus, Prince of Ethiope and brother of PrestaJohn
The family bound for Lisbon
The three sailors, Galinha, Figuero, and Bao-niya
Campanero
The Javaboy
Captain Tehera

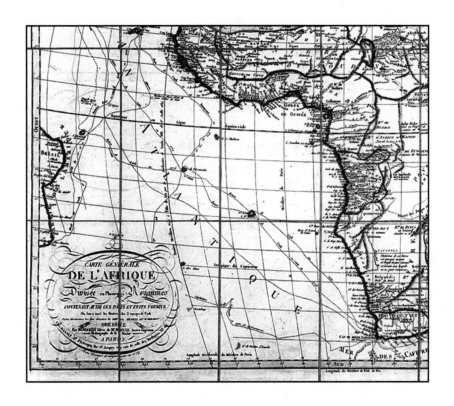

THE ISLAND

Sixty million years ago the plates beneath what we now think of as the South Atlantic Ocean buckled slightly, sending up a range of fiery, spewing volcanoes, while at the same time giving way to an even more cataclysmic flood, so deep and wide that it eventually swallowed the furious mountains entirely. Or almost. In time, two or three high peaks did manage to crest the waves, and by far the loneliest of these is the setting, and the subject, of this history.

For tens of millions of years she called, gasped, and raged alone, heaving countless flows of molten lava down her jagged face, to cool and calcify and be covered over. She sputtered fire, brimstone, ash, and magma, all unheard, unanswered, until finally she fell silent, leaving to the sky a hard, unyielding visage, etched by lava beds, cinder and vitrified stones, basalt spikes, bright red clays, and boil-pocked limestone.

Eight miles across, ten miles east to west, she was bounded on all sides by towering russet-colored walls, within which lay an endless tumult of pinnacles and valleys, ravines, gullies, rivers, cataracts, and springs. A high spine arched through the middle, curling from her southern to her eastern coast, while to the north lay a broad, flat plain, 4 miles wide, extending all the way to her easternmost bluffs

before plunging 600 feet into the ocean again. A few stray rocks surrounded her, ranging in size from obelisks to battleships, but otherwise she stood alone, the nearest next ascension 700 miles away to
the north; the nearest coasts, 1,140 miles to the west, 1,800 miles to
the east.

Her only two companions, then, were the sea and the sky, which
swept over and by, always in the same direction, from the southeast.
And over time they did bring life, tucked inside the scales of fish, the
smooth skin of migrating seals, carried in the beaks and wings of
seabirds, and sometimes on the wind itself, and drops of rain. So this
barren rock, this death mask of a lonely, lonely goddess, gave rise
here and there to pockets of verdure, luxuriant blankets of ferns and
mosses to soften her interior summits. From the silt that settled on
the lava rock and the fertile dust to which it patiently pulverized, she
grew a veil of redwood and ebony trees. She grew gumwood trees
and cabbage trees as well and took on spiders, snails, worms, crabs,
and wirebirds, which all, to live upon the features of her chiseled
face, developed in particular to it, so that the caterpillars who lived
there were not quite like any other caterpillars to be found anywhere else; the snails were not like any other snails; nor the crabs,
the turtles; nor were the trees like any other trees.

For seven million years she was this way, growing wild, unob-
served, and without memory. There were no predators or prey. All
creatures that found the island fed upon the island. Seals and sea
lions drowsed on her beaches, turtles inched along and slept in their
shells, while wirebirds nested in the gumwood trees and plastered
the coastal rocks in glaring white guano. Ferns bobbed in the
breezes, the flaxen meadows rolled, while nameless rivers tumbled
into the salty sea.

Then one day, the 12th of May, 1502, a sailor high in the crow's
nest of a Portuguese galleon sighted her, a hulking silhouette on the
horizon. Returning from another campaign beyond the African
Cape, the ship was part of a small armada led by Commodore João
da Nova Castella, who had just made a name for himself defeating
the treacherous Zamorim in Calicut. Sailing low and slow from all

the booty in their hulls, da Nova's fleet scented fresh water on the island and turned. One account has it that they were rebuffed at first. A ship was lost in the landing, and men, but finally the fleet prevailed and that same day stamped the island sand with its first human footprint.

Finding no one there, da Nova's men filled their casks with water, and scattered lemon seeds in the valley where they'd landed, in case any sailors should come this way again. For this same reason, they stood the hull of the broken galleon at the foot of the valley and fixed a cross to its prow, to serve as a chapel. Then they left one more gift as well: a name.

Not Commodore da Nova's, as would have followed precedent. Perhaps the island was too austere, or perhaps he blamed her for the loss of men. Perhaps he simply knew she was a she, but rather than give his family name, the Commodore christened her according to the day she'd been sighted, which his faith devotes to the sainted mother of Constantine the Great, and finder of the true cross at Jerusalem:

Helena.

West Zyde.

Moro groß

Aqui na õ ha fundo

Aquada Velha

Aqui naon acham fundo

Miguirgem em 4.

Nõort Zyde.

B. de S. Elena

Abriæs

Ribiera q Vein do paimar

Ribiera dagoa

P. do esparável

Alberta

Pomar

Occidens

Aqui podem surgir

Ylheo quadrato

Y. as dos Gatos

Ribiera dagoa

Ribiera dagoa

Ribiera dagoa

SANCTA HELENA

Paon da Sucar

Legoa

Mert   dies

ST. HELENA

LOPEZ

C. 1530

"Cocorrico!" the cockerel crows. *"Cocorrico!"* Time to rise.

The sun is still low, well beneath the ridge. The sky is a half-lit lavender, but the man can smell that the air is clear again and crisp.

"Cocorrico!" the cockerel calls again.

"Cocorrico," the man replies more quietly.

He crawls out of the grotto and looks up. The rains have passed, at last. Often he can avoid them—it tends to rain and shine in pockets—but for the last two days, clouds have cloaked the island, and the rain has punished it. He has had to stay beneath the shelter of his grotto, he and the cockerel. They've contented themselves with gobbled songs and weaving. His baskets are all fixed.

But now the cockerel is back up in his roost, crowing proudly. The man takes a shovel he's fashioned from a dead tree limb and up-turns some earth for his friend, his companheiro, who hops down and pecks gratefully at the helpless worms. The man takes out some strips of fruit to dry on the line, and uses a beach shell to drink the rainwater from his barrel. Bland. He prefers the water of the springs and creeks, the ribeira, because they carry the silts of the island.

He starts up a trail, which he has worn by habit, to see how the rains have treated his garden. The cockerel follows. The patch is still mud and puddles, but not too deep, and the soil drinks quickly here, once the sun is up. He grows wild celery, several different parsleys, sorrel, basil, fennel, aniseed, mustard, and radishes. Flowers too. The chickweed and geraniums are still asleep, safe inside their own embrace, but they can feel the coming warmth. They know the day is on its way and loosen their petals. The man sits and waits while the sun ascends, the light hues up the ridge, and the day's first shadows slant out from under the rocks and trees. Soon all the herbs and flowers are awake and open. The man feels the warmth upon his shoulders and stands back up.

With the sun behind them, he and the cockerel descend again, their shadows sliding over the mud, the stumps, stones, and moss. The man pays no more attention than his companheiro. He passes through a small grove he planted himself. Most are orange trees, but there are fig too, date, and pomegranate. On the far side stands a fat spotted goat. The man picks the ripest two figs he can find and tosses one over. It rolls right up to the hooves. The goat leans down to sniff, and the man moves on, as does the cockerel, jealously resettling his white wings.

They can hear the waterfall long before they can see it, roaring down at the foot of the ravine. The stream is swollen up the banks and running fast. The man follows it all the way to the ledge, as close as he can get. The water looks like undulating glass, sliding over the smooth black, then spilling down a hundred feet, exploding into a snow white mist, the outer edge of which has caught the morning rays: a band of magenta, edged by yellow, edged by white, edged by blue. He descends, using stones and brush for stairs. The cockerel chooses not to follow. He'll wait up here.

There is a pool at the foot of the fall, where the stream can roil a moment and gather itself before starting down the stones again. The man enters slowly; the water is cold. Waist deep, he removes his shirt, then his ragged pants. The wirebirds cackle down from their perches. The man lowers himself and moves nearer to the fall, his clothes drifting and billowing around him like ghosts. The water is coming down too heavily to stand beneath, but he slides his head under the surface and listens to the muffled, steady roar. Happy.

He'll see if he can find the seals.

Shoulders numb, he collects his clothes and climbs back out of the water. He wrings his pants and puts them on but hangs his shirt on a branch to dry. Most likely the seals will be all the way over on the southern bay, but that is too far, and lately the man has seen them sunning over on the flat rocks beyond the lemon orchard, which is nearer by.

His friend the cockerel rejoins him farther down, and the stream leads them most of the rest of the way, dodging back and forth through the ravine. As they climb the final ridge before the valley, though, the man stops suddenly, as if a musket ball had skittered against the rock beneath his feet.

Voices.

The cockerel gobbles, but the man shushes him quiet.

> *Já cá está o tiro liro liro lé*
> *Já cá está o tiro liro liro ló*

He only has to climb ten feet to see the valley, a flat spearhead lying between its too-sheer slopes. The lemon trees are bunched down at the far end; beyond them is the water, and in the water, the swaying masts of three groaning galleons, flying the red and green flag.

He had not known because of the rains, but there they are, and skiffs bobbing at the shore. He peers down through the fanned green petals of a fern, back into the lemon trees. He can see the sailors now, not far from the chapel-prow, their hands shuffling through shiny leaves.

> *Já cá está o tiro liro liro, ó amor,*
> *tiro liro liro abre a porta,*
> *e ó branca flôr.*

Open the door, O white flower.

Then another voice, much closer, calls. "Dom Fernao! Dom Fernao, venha cáá!" Dom Fernao, come out!

He scrambles back.

"Venha cáá ver o que lhe trouxemos!" Come look what we brought you!

He runs—as fast as he can without giving himself away. Too fast for the cockerel, who knows better than to follow. His friend is going to hide, going where they will not find him.

He'll take the high wood. It's longer, but quicker. He stays above the ravine until he's well past the waterfall—that's one of the places they'll look—then he crosses over. He follows the northern tine of the creek, and it leads him in beneath the towering, majestic canopy of redwoods.

The rain continues there, the last beads of water only now finding their way down the limbs and needles, dropping and patting the forest floor, soft as coins on a quilted bed; the man hardly hears. He does not pause to feel the pleasing give of the cool black decay beneath his feet. He passes by a constellation of insects hovering above the bog, whirling within itself but not moving; he does not notice. Or the gentle dance of ferns, bowing over them like calming, shushing hands. He will go as far as he can, as fast as he can. Then he will wait.

It takes him the better part of the day. He marks his progress by the number of creeks he has to cross. This side of the island they descend from the great peak like mangled wheel spokes from a single hub. He passes over seven; then the eighth he follows back out of the wood.

The island's highest peak is to his right, blocking out the late-day sun. Before him is her longest descent, leading down to a single opening in the southeastern walls, where there is the beach, and the black pools, and the red and silver fish. A finger-width to the right, he can see the salt white spikes. They are all over the island, like bolts thrown down from heaven, but these are a family here—a mother, a father, and then their children, standing white and swaddled in the distance.

He uses them as his guide as he climbs down the great ridge. He chooses the shallowest slopes and goat paths he can find, but it's still a slow descent. He falls three times. The soles of his feet crack through and start bleeding, but he does not stop until he reaches the beach and the bay.

He walks out to the water, ankle deep, just far enough to feel the descending sun against his back. He sinks his feet into the fine soaked sand and bows his head to rest, to breathe, but then he stops short. There in front of him, his own shadow stretches long and clear against the shallow water. All day he has been running, running from the men, he thought, but no, this is what he has been running from, and this is what he finds: the monster, with its posture low and bent, its left arm stopped abruptly at the wrist, its right hand missing the balance of a thumb, its head gruesomely smooth and round, as if permanently wrapped in bandages.

He turns away, but now the sun is waiting for him, and there at his feet he can see it even more clearly, the monster's reflection captured in the water and the low, golden light. The face looks back at him: gaping and featureless, except for the scars, the soft dead, unburnably dead white that will never reconcile to the tan of his cheek or forehead.

He will not eat tonight. The freshwater pools are up on a shelf of black lava stone which juts from the nearby cliffs. He bathes briefly among the red and silver fish. They swim between his legs, but he will not look. He climbs up farther. There are little caves inside the cliffs. He crawls inside the deepest he can find. He tucks himself into the corner like a wingless bird and waits. He does not even sleep. He sits in the hissing dark and, for one long night, feels his scars turn back into wounds again.

Morning comes, and with it, some relief. The sun returns and paints the cliffs gold, and he knows that the men have gone. They have taken what they need, and now the winds will sweep them back to Lisbon.

He returns the way he came, over the great ridge and through the high wood, but more slowly. Dusk is falling fast by the time he reaches the grotto. From around its great marled shoulder he sees the blue blot of his white shirt, hanging on the line, the shirt which he left by the cataract. There beside it, five saplings lean up against the stone, their roots sacked and tied. He does not know what kind, another pomegranate maybe. Down at the foot of his water barrel are more gifts, bound in leather satchels. One is filled with rice, he knows; another, biscuits; another, salt. The others hold seeds, but again he'll have to plant them to see what fruits or vegetables they'll yield. He peers inside the little hollow where he sleeps and sees they've left another tin of matches on his skillet, safe and dry.

A rustling sounds from the direction of his garden, and here is his companheiro, clucking through the brush, squawking out angrily at him. Where has he been? Why does he run so far? The white bird struts around him, turning circles and flaring his wings as if he might start stabbing at his ankles, but the man tells him, "Shshsh-shshsh." He reaches into the satchel of rice and scatters a handful on the ground. The cockerel forgets his anger in an instant. He begins pecking at the grains, one by one, and Fernao Lopez is forgiven again.

PART I

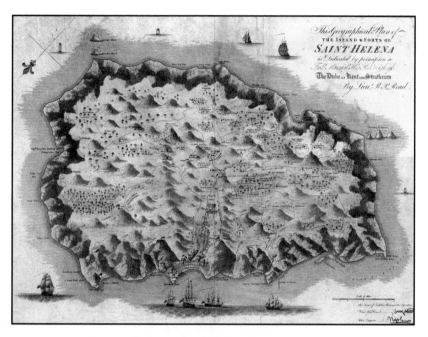

Baby, baby, he's a giant,
Tall and black as Rouen steeple,
And he dines and sups, rely on't,
Every day on naughty people.

CHAPTER ONE

OCTOBER 12-14, 1815

———

Betsy—Teatime—Toby

October 12—An alarm gun fires on Ladder Hill, and though it is a mile away, Betsy jolts.

"Hold still," says Sarah, lips gripping the pins in her mouth. "You're gonna get stuck."

"I don't see why they have to do that. I'm sure it woke up Father."

Sarah doubts that but doesn't say.

They are out on the veranda of the bungalow, and Betsy is wearing a ball gown intended for her sister, Jane, who is sixteen, two years older. There is no upcoming occasion, but the fabric came in a few days ago, and Sarah, who serves as nanny to both Jane and Betsy, needed someone to stand inside; Jane is off somewhere, reading to their brothers.

"But this isn't how I'd have mine," says Betsy. She is looking down at the collar and the brown silk. "Mine would be blue, in the first place"—a good choice, as blue will show better against her hair, which is a tangle of blond curls. "Royal blue, like Miss Wilkes's. And I want it not like this, so high, but down from the shoulder, and with white flowers."

Sarah shakes her head.

"Why not?"

"Flowers wilt, get dirty."

"No, but listen—made of paper. I saw in Solomon's shop. You can make them out of paper. And mine would be white flowers, like the Briars."

Sarah sucks her teeth in objection, but Betsy does not notice, or care enough to stop.

"And I bet when there is a ball, she won't even dance—Jane. She doesn't like it. I'd dance. You know who they say is the finest dancer?"

Sarah does not answer. They say Mrs. Wilkes, the Governor's second wife, is the finest dancer on the island, but Betsy does not answer herself either, for just now she notices there are two men descending the lane that leads down from the inland path. It's hard to see them in the speckled light beneath the banyans, but they are officers, in red, no doubt come to see her father.

Sarah removes the needles from her mouth and stands as they come upon the lawn.

"Ma'am. Miss."

Betsy says nothing.

"Mr. Balcombe in?"

"He is," says Sarah.

"He's resting," says Betsy.

The Captain looks at her impersonally. "We have intelligence of some importance to communicate."

"I'll see if he's up, Officer." Sarah offers a slight bow as she leaves.

The men stare straight out while they wait, almost as though Betsy weren't there, but they can't help glancing around at the property. All visitors do. The house itself is not so much, an Indian bungalow with a small upper story. It is the setting which is so exceptional. To the east is a nameless but no-less-proud precipice; to the south looms Peak Hill; westward the land falls off just as dramatically, making way for the stream and cataract. Coddled there, safe and cool, their home sits in a lush green pocket of trees and flowers—pomegranate, myrtle, shaddock, fruit trees of every imaginable kind, and a gated garden with more flowers than Betsy could possibly name.

She observes the officers intently, squinting with one eye, waiting to see if they will look at her.

The lead officer tilts his head to the west. "Is that a waterfall?"

She nods.

"Keeps it nice and cool, eh?"

She nods, and just then Toby comes around the side of the house. Toby is the gardener, older than her father, and a Malay. He sees the officers but doesn't stop until he comes to one of the briar bushes, the one beside the front steps. He touches the petals of a flower and murmurs something to himself. He throws a handful of dirt in his basket and continues on to the gated garden.

"Primrose?" asks the second officer, nodding at the flower.

Betsy shakes her head with unveiled disdain. "Briar rose," she says. "That's our name, briars. *The* Briars."

The officer nods, and now Betsy's father comes out. He is in his coat, not disheveled, but awakened, plump and sleepy, with matted hair.

The first officer steps up. "We have intelligence of some importance to communicate."

Her father has gathered as much. He asks Sarah to bring some tea, then escorts the officers out to the pavilion, across the lawn and up the narrow path. He is still limping.

The pavilion itself is almost all windows, but perched too high on the knoll for Betsy to see. Even on her toes all she can make out are the tops of the men's heads.

"Whom is Father talking to?" Jane has come around from the side of the house, with book in hand, and Alexander and Nicholas on either side.

"Officers," says Betsy. "There must be someone coming. I hope it isn't Colonel Burton again."

Jane turns, and only now does she notice that Betsy is wearing her new dress and that the hem is dragging on the floor. She frowns, which is as much as Jane is ever liable to do, but just then the door barks open up at the pavilion again. The men are coming back. As they emerge from the narrow path, Betsy can see the officers look no different, but her father is blushing.

"Father, what is it?"

"Where is your mother?" He nods the boys to go find her, and the men ascend the veranda. Sarah comes out with the tea and pours them all cups while they wait, but Betsy still can't tell: Are they worried or thrilled?

"Who is it, Father?"

"Betsy." He notices her dress too now, loose and pinned. "Perhaps you'd feel more comfortable if you changed."

Betsy shakes her head, and now her brothers are back with her mother. The officers introduce themselves. Her mother is polite, but wary. She can feel it too: The men are keeping something very large. They all turn to Betsy's father, who clears his throat by habit.

"It seems the island is expecting a visitor," he says, with his usual flat smile. He clears his throat again. "Yes, it seems that Napoleon Bonaparte has been captured—"

Her mother lifts her hand to her mouth as if he had spoken the devil's name. Betsy herself can hardly follow what he says next, except that Napoleon Bonaparte, the cause of all war and strife, has been captured and is coming to St. Helena. They are bringing him here, to keep.

"But I thought he already was captured," she says. "I thought they had him in the Mediterranean."

"Yes." Her father refers the question to the officers. "Captain Dunbar may be able to explain better than I."

They offer the Captain a chair. All sit, except for the second officer, and Alexander, who takes Jane's lap. Then Captain Dunbar proceeds to tell them what he knows. It was true, Bonaparte had been imprisoned on a small island in the Mediterranean, called Elba. He stayed there for three months but then escaped with a small battalion of men. He landed on the southern coast of France and started marching up to Paris, but Betsy doesn't really understand this part so well. Captain Dunbar seems to say that on the way he'd recollected his army, or they'd been waiting for him, and by the time they got to Paris there were so many of them the Bourbons simply gave up.

"But who is this man?" says her mother. "What does he want?"

"Margaret." Her father shakes his head imperceptibly, then turns back to Captain Dunbar, who continues.

Bonaparte then took his army into Belgium, he says, but this is all more than they can fathom at once. Mrs. Balcombe and Jane have gone white. Even Captain Dunbar seems fazed by what he's saying. It was General Wellington who finally stopped them—General Wellington, who stayed here once, in the pavilion. He surrounded the French at a place called Waterloo and defeated them. Captain Dunbar said that Bonaparte was subsequently taken into British custody, and he would be arriving in Jamestown in a matter of days.

"But how could he do all that?" Betsy blurts. "How was he able to escape? And why weren't there people to stop him?"

Jane seconds the question, and once again Captain Dunbar is made to explain what he knows, from the beginning. He does his best not to excite their fears, but the harder he tries not to say it, the clearer it becomes: Napoleon Bonaparte is obviously a demon of some kind, or a sorcerer. How else could a man march all the way to Paris and there not be one person to stop him?

Betsy has imagined him since she was a little girl: a gangly giant in a black cocked hat, long arms and legs, and a little body like a spider. He had a great long nose and one eye in the middle of his forehead, shooting flame. She knows this isn't how he really looks, but as the Captain goes back over the story, she cannot help thinking of it, this monstrous spiderlike creature who'd cast a spell on all the French, and they had simply followed him, like the rats of Hamelin. Thank heavens for General Wellington. Thank heavens for England.

"But why here?" she asks.

The Captain looks at her. "It was decreed," he says.

He does not know.

Her mother asks where they plan to keep him, but Captain Dunbar does not know this either, only that the boat is on its way, with two men-of-war attending and a third coming from somewhere else. Fifteen hundred men, he says. In a matter of days.

"But don't they have to ask?" says Betsy. "It doesn't seem fair."

No one answers this. Her mother's hand is to her breast, and all the blood has gone from her face. Betsy has never seen her so pale. It would frighten her, but her father is lit pink.

He stands. "I should go tell Mr. Fowler," his business partner in Jamestown. Betsy can tell, her mother doesn't want him to go, but he isn't paying attention. He asks the officers to wait for him, then goes in to fetch his coat, not limping in the least.

———

October 13—Teatime. The island landscape is such that outside of Jamestown, the houses tend to be fairly widespread and hidden from one another. It requires more than a casual interest to go calling, but today there is much more than a casual interest, and as tends to be the case when the news is of such moment, the islanders seek out the members of their own particular station.

The higher-ups, who sit on the councils and run the militia, have gravitated to the Governor's mansion, Plantation House. These include the Governor himself, of course, Mr. Wilkes; the Lieutenant Governor, Skelton; the former island pastor, the Reverend James Eakins; the Hodgsons; the Sealeys; the Pritchards; and Willie Doveton. With the exception of the Reverend, all are senior Company men, the island being in effect the private property of the East India Company since 1673, when the British government first issued its lease.

The junior Company men, including Mr. Balcombe and his partner, Mr. Fowler, meet down at Mr. Pourteous's Inn with some of the town merchants and shipping agents—Mr. Solomon, the Wrights, Mr. McRitchie. The only one who is not a businessman is old Mr. Huffington, who is Mr. Fowler's uncle and not coincidentally serves as tutor to the two Balcombe boys. He sits a safe, and somewhat disgusted, distance from the conversation.

The rest of the Balcombes go see the Leggs, where the Alexanders and Miss Mason are calling as well. Over at Coffee Grove in Powell Valley, the wives of farmers Lambe, Hayward, and Bagley convene at Mr. Barker's, while the island doctors—Mellis, Shortt, and Baxter—congregate at Knoll House, with wives. The Reverend Richard Boys and wife are also present.

As disparate and stratified as the parties may be, all discussion revolves around the same obvious subject: the "beast," as Mrs. Shortt puts it, as does Mrs. Sealey, miles away. "Tyrant," "traitor," "plebeian," "Jacobin," "Muslim," "criminal," "devil," "monster." Their imminent guest is called many things across the twilit island, none kind, but why should they be? Napoleon Bonaparte may be as pure an embodiment of evil as nature has yet spewed into being. Had he not single-handedly induced the entire European continent to war, time and again, as well as England and ample tracts of the East? Had he not tried to rule the Christian world—and beyond? The Sealeys know this first hand. They lost a cousin in the Mediterranean. Mrs. Breame lost an uncle. Two, if you count Archie Dykes, her mother's half brother. They all know someone who has died, and all place the blame squarely on this man's vain, maniacal shoulders (all but Mr. Huffington, whose nephew died at Leipzig, fighting *for* la Grande Armée). "More blood on his hands than any man in history," Dr. Shortt opines, and no one disagrees.

But he is worse than that even. Over at Plantation House, Mr. Doveton—who is a man of no ill will, but who should know as he still returns to London once a year—has it on good authority that Napoleon Bonaparte deliberately poisoned an entire battalion of his *own* men while in Egypt, killed them off rather than bother bringing them with him in his shameful flight from the Turks. Mr. Pritchard confirms the story and is quick to add the scandalous beheading of the Duke d'Enghien, or, as he was called over at Coffee Grove, "Dungeon." Poor man, executed without a trial. Similar tales are told over at Knoll House: Here the prisoners are killed in Africa, and there is a connection implied between this and the fact that the culprit is supposedly now a Muslim, having converted while in Egypt, which comes as no surprise to the Reverend Mr. Boys.

At the Leggs', where the Balcombe women all sip their tea, they are more interested in "the escape." Miss Mason, who rides an ox, smokes a pipe, and lives alone, is telling them her version of the march to Paris. Apparently the Bourbons sent their armies down to meet him, but Bonaparte stood up in front of them and challenged them to kill him, anyone who dared. None did. The soldiers turned right around and joined him, in fact, and by the time he reached Paris the entire country was behind him again.

Tea is sipped. Heads shake in cozy disappointment with the French, and the Continent at large.

"But did he escape from Corsica or Elba?" asks Mrs. Alexander.

"Elba," says Miss Mason, relighting her pipe. "Corsica was his birthplace. Elba was where they'd sent him after the Russian debacle."

"And what was that?" whispers Mrs. Robinson to her husband.

"The winter," Miss Mason reminds.

"Oh, yes. The winter."

Down at Mr. Pourteous's Inn, the concerns are decidedly more immediate and practical. How many people was he bringing with him? How many soldiers? How long is the port to be closed? They need to know, because they'll need to be prepared, take stock, set prices, but much the same as at the Leggs', or Coffee Grove, or Plantation House, there are no good answers. No one really knows anything for certain, but they've all grown so used to ignorance that no one thinks to question it anymore, or consider that it is precisely this, the profound deficiency of any good or timely information, which answers Betsy Balcombe's simple question, echoed everywhere this evening—why us? Mr. Sealey comes closest to saying it: "Because we're farthest."

The others know he's right, but there is an odd note of pride in the observation. Indeed, once the initial shock has worn off, once the lamps are lit and tea has given way to aperitifs, an almost upbeat quality sweeps over the various conversations. The islanders begin to understand, for all the terrors the Beast has wrought, and all the danger he no doubt brings with him, he will be bringing something else as well, something as pleasant as it is unexpected: significance. You see? Husbands turn to wives; their expressions suffice. Not *so* desolate. Not so remote. The wives concede, with postures slightly lifted now. They raise their teacups to their lips, breasts swelled over trembling hearts, quickened by the growing realization that their little island home, which heretofore could not have claimed a lesser hold on the world's imagination, was in a matter of days to become the object of its rapt attention. St. Helena.

The children feel it too. They take their teatime buzz out onto the darkening lawns, to share what they know and burn off their nervous energy. They run a little faster than usual, shout louder, tumble harder. Johnny Legg is smacked in the eye with a stick. Cries awhile but soon recovers. There are bigger things to think of.

Even among the practical businessmen there is an undue glint. Granted, the population is set to double. Prices will rise. The Company will be losing its sovereignty. Still, somehow, the prospect outgleams the cost. Old Mr. Huffington can see them each quietly taking stock: where they should hide their oil, the liquor, the accounts. Weather the next few months, and who's to say the prices should ever go down again?

It is finally more than he can stand to watch. He excuses himself, unnoticed, and returns to his little room just down the street, up on the first level, where if anyone but the maid had ever bothered to enter, they'd have seen: There on the bureau is an immaculate white bust of Napoleon Bonaparte, the First Consul and Imperator.

—————

October 14—The news, subject to various dilutions and augmentations, reaches most of the island underclass within a day. There are fifteen hundred slaves on St. Helena, who are most, but not all, black—from Africa and Madagascar. There are six hundred Chinese indentured laborers as well, to serve a free population of just over two thousand, including five hundred "free blacks."

Saturday morning the Briars' only groundsman, Toby—who is

not black, but a Malay—is at the back of the terraced garden, crouched among the little row of fruit trees that hide his hut from view. The oldest fruit-bearing trees on the property, they stand just outside the original fence—an orange tree, an apple tree, a dwarf peach, and another dwarf fig—and in a quiet corner of Toby's mind, he has always believed that they were planted by Lopez. Toby believes that he can taste it.

The little row hasn't been doing so well lately, though. The last cycle, worms crept in: the apples first, then the oranges. He is peeling one now to see if the rot is still there when a familiar sound, a distant clicking, turns his attention.

Alley. All Toby can see is the basket on his head, descending from the road, but he knows it's Alley from how fast it moves and how smooth. The basket glides beneath the garden slope, and a moment later he hears the kitchen door slam. The Balcombes' dinner has arrived for 'Scilla to cook.

Toby turns back to the orange. He pulls the two halves open, and there it is again. The middle is all black decay, as if a little flame had burst in the heart. Half the oranges looked this way. His worry now is the figs. They have been waiting their turn for weeks, months, sticky green bulbs, softening from within in clusters of six or seven. He has been washing the leaves in olive soap, but there's no way to be sure until they've ripened, which they have. They turned brown a few days ago and began dropping last night.

Toby is gathering a dozen or so into his basket when the gate at the far end of the garden clangs gently. Alley again. Toby stays in his crouch but waits. It's been two days since he's seen Alley, though their huts stand side by side.

And now he appears, moving swiftly but confidently, his white shirt hanging loose from his shoulders like a sail, his black torso boyishly slender but sinewed.

"Don't you look." He glares at Toby when he sees him. "Don't you look, Yam-stalk."

Toby rolls a fig out on the path. Alley stops in front of it, feels it with his toe, then turns to Toby. "What you smiling at?"

There is a large bottle stuffed down the top of Alley's pants, Mr. Balcombe's claret, from the cellar.

Alley shrugs; he's not afraid of Mr. Balcombe. "Blame the rats." He picks up the fig and starts digging in with his thumbs. "You hear about the monstah?"

Toby shakes his head.

"You stay too much inside this garden, Ra-Toby." Alley peers inside the fig and scowls. Not good. He flings the fruit away. "There's a monstah coming."

Toby tosses him another. "Seen Sarah?" Sarah is Alley's aunt, and only family on the island now. Both his mother and father are dead ten years.

Alley shakes his head. "What she want?"

"To know where you been."

Alley pauses and glowers down at Toby. "What did you tell her?"

"Tell her I don't know." Toby looks down at his basket. "I don't."

"That's right you don't." Alley tears open this fig and finds this one more to his liking. "Bony-Pah," he says, smiling again. "Bony-man. That's what they call him. They're bringing him on a boat." He pushes out the pink flesh and gnashes in.

Toby knows there's some truth in what Alley says. Something has stirred the Balcombes the last few days, ever since the officers' visit.

"Said he's going to be as tall as the steeple." Alley grins. "And he's got fire shooting out his eyes. Says Lotte."

Toby nods; Alley is going to share the wine with Lotte. "So you keep her safe, hunh?"

Alley's eyes snap into a playful glare again. "Maybe. Maybe no. And don't you talk to Sarah, else I sic Bony on you." The bottle slips, but he catches it and shimmies it back up to his hip. He tosses aside the fig skin and starts around to the huts.

Toby looks down at the scattered fruit; another falls, so brown and ripe all he has to do is squeeze it and the skin splits. The flesh is all pink until the center, but there again, the black.

Back by the huts, Alley's door claps open, and out he comes, now with the bottle in his hand and a blue horse blanket beneath his arm. He does not look back at Toby. He hops the fence and starts down the slope for the goat paths leading inland and wherever he's been spending his nights. Toby finally rises from his crouch and makes his way back to the garden shed for more olive soap; he does not mind. Better that Lopez keep an eye on Alley than grow another good fig.

CHAPTER TWO

OCTOBER 15

—◆—

The Emperor and his suite

Evening. Roughly thirty miles out to sea, in the Captain's dining room of the HMS *Northumberland*, Napoleon Bonaparte is seated at one end of the Captain's table. At the other end sits his escort and keeper, Admiral George Cockburn; between them are the principal members of the prisoner's suite, all of whom have volunteered to accompany His Majesty on this latest chapter of his glorious and tapestral history: the Further Exile.

Their arrangement, subject of daily change and ongoing controversy, is as follows:

Mme. de Montholon	Grand Marshal Bertrand	Count de Las Cases
Napoleon Bonaparte*		Admiral Cockburn
Dr. O'Meara	General Gourgaud	Marquis de Montholon	Mme. Bertrand

The woman to Bonaparte's immediate left, Madame Albine de Montholon, is wife to the "Marquis" across from her, who is no

---

*Bonaparte's two valets, Marchand and St. Denis, stand to the immediate right and left of his chair and back a half step.

Marquis at all, but a spendthrift and a gambler, here escaping debt. At thirty-one, Madame Albine has managed to maintain her looks. Her pale, almond-shaped face is accentuated by the crop of her thin black hair and at the moment bears an expression of unmistakable self-satisfaction. She has made good use of the journey; witness her place; witness the relative banishment of her only female competition, Madame "Fanny" Bertrand, the Grand Marshal's wife. A blonde, and slightly too tall.

Madame de Montholon leans in to His Majesty and with half-descended lids starts the conversation on a sensitive subject, deliberately and for her own personal amusement. "So tell us. How were the day's dictations?"

The Emperor tilts the question to Count de Las Cases, who, at fifty, is the oldest among them, most wizened and diminutive, and who has made it his primary purpose to serve in whatever way possible the cause of His Majesty's memoir.

"Extraordinaire," he replies. "His Majesty grows more and more precise. I am amazed." He pinches a smile the Majesty's way that gives way to an adoring gaze; the others have taken to calling him "Rapture."

"Well, but it stands to reason, does it not?" Madame Albine answers. "Once one has begun . . . to remember . . . more and more begins to come, yes?"

"Yes, but the detail," says Las Cases. "This very afternoon, in fact, His Majesty was telling a most remarkable story of his experience as 'Sultan Kebir.' "

General Gourgaud abruptly straightens. Youngest in the circle, most vain and lonely, he clears his throat to object, but no one seconds, so Las Cases turns to Dr. O'Meara to include him in the reference. "While His Majesty was in Egypt, the natives there were given to call him Sultan Kebir—literally, 'Father of Fire.' "

O'Meara nods appreciatively, demonstrating precisely why he, who met His Majesty only three months ago aboard the *Bellerophon*, has managed to become the latest *homme de l'Empereur*.

Las Cases then proceeds to tell the Sultan story, in English, for

the benefit of the doctor and the Admiral. It seems a tribe of ma-
rauding Arabs infiltrated one of the towns that the French had taken
and wantonly murdered a peasant, or fellah. Outraged, Bonaparte
gave orders that the criminals should be pursued into the desert and
hunted to their death. The local sheikhs, hearing this, went to him.
"Sultan Kebir," they said, "what game is this? This tribe can do you
ten times more harm than you can do them. And all for the death of
a lowly fellah? Was he your cousin?" The Emperor replied (and here
Las Cases offers both the French and English translations): "More
than my cousin. All those I govern are my children. My power is
given me only in order that I may ensure their safety."

The table nods in approval, all but Admiral Cockburn.

"Which hearing"—Las Cases flourishes to his conclusion—"the
sheikhs all bowed their heads. 'Oh, that is very fine! You have spoken like the prophet.' "

The Marquis de Montholon here begins to laugh, thinking this
must have been the purpose of the story, but no one else is finding
humor. He raises his glass. "To the Sultan Kebir."

All drink, except for Bonaparte, and Gourgaud, whose agitation
is finally more than he can abide. When the glasses are set down, he
sits up and for a second time clears his throat. "Votre Majesté"—he
speaks in French—"I don't mean to be a pest on this particular subject, but again, am I wrong to think we had come to an agreement?
It was my understanding that Count de Las Cases was to be hearing
only of the liberation of Italy, that the Egyptian campaign would
come under the purview of the Grand Marshal, and that matters
pertaining to the First Consulate would eventually be confided to
me. Was this not the agreement?" He looks to Las Cases, then to
Bertrand for support, but Bertrand offers none. It is true, they have
so agreed, but Bertrand desires no alliance with Gourgaud. He
would sooner share his canteen with a camel. Than any of them,
save Fanny. Most of the time.

The Emperor lightly shrugs. "The subject came up."

"Of course," says Gourgaud, "and in no way would I want to
impinge upon the free flow of Your Majesty's thinking. I only worry

that when he does come to Egypt, which shouldn't be too much longer, I wouldn't think"—he directs this to Las Cases—"I'd hope that the Grand Marshal doesn't find it . . . a plundered field." *Un champ pillage.*

"No one is plundering anyone's fields." Las Cases swipes peevishly at the table. "I can assure you, General Gourgaud, His Majesty has more than enough in his mind to provide for three more scribes. For ten! However"—he leans around to look at Bertrand—"if the Grand Marshal would like my notes—"

The Grand Marshal is saved the embarrassment of having to refuse this offer by the entrance of Monsieur Cipriani, the Emperor's steward.

"Oui?" says Bonaparte.

"Sa Majesté voulait être averti au premier aperçu de l'île." Cipriani turns to Cockburn. "Ze island. We see."

Napoleon rises and leads them up.

They have all been at sea for three months, stopping only once, at Madeira, to pick up provisions. Three months of cards, reading, competing, nitpicking, and waiting. Finally they are in sight, and yet they know so little of the place they've been sent there is more dread than anticipation as they now ascend the stairs and one by one step out on deck.

Dusk is settling. To the right is night; to the left, day. Most of the crew is there, looking off the starboard side. Cipriani opens a place along the rail, and the suite peers out. They can barely discern—the clouds have collected around the distant island like dust about a chair leg—but the outline peeks through. A hard gray stone, cresting the endless sea.

They are silent. Las Cases's face has curdled. De Montholon lets the slow breath of a punctured, flat balloon.

"And what makes her a saint again?" his wife asks quietly. "Helena?"

O'Meara answers. "She's supposed to have found the true cross, at Jerusalem."

Madame de Montholon sniffs. "One could build a fortress from all the pieces of that cross."

"And so they have," her husband murmurs.

Madame Bertrand is doing her best to keep a brave face. It was only seven days ago she squandered all favor when in a fit of pique, she made a dash for the rail of the ship. She by no means would have thrown herself over, but still the moment helped tilt opinion back in Madame de Montholon's favor. It was now Madame Bertrand who was thought to be the wild-tempered one, which is absurd. Madame de Montholon is not only much more prone to tantrums, she is vulgar and goading. Madame Bertrand grips tight to the rail.

Her husband, the Grand Marshal, stands straight and tall beside her, but his attention is turned sidelong to the Emperor, who is at his station beside the third cannon, hand upon the barrel. This is the same place and pose he has assumed at least once a day every day of their journey, looking out at the endless sea. Finally the horizon has yielded their destination. His face admits nothing but calm.

The sight elicits something similar in Bertrand. He has been with the Emperor from the very beginning. He was in Italy and Egypt. He fought beside him at the Danube, and at Leipzig, and has acted as his Grand Marshal for over two years now. He was with him on Elba as well, which is to say he has served His Majesty in the field and at the negotiating table, and as such has had the opportunity to witness firsthand the dual nature to which so many have ascribed his success: the rare capacity both to inspire and to administrate. Bertrand has noted a difference between the two, however. Curiously, the Emperor is far more subject to his emotions, to tantrums and insults, in the political arena. In the midst of battle he was serene. When a gambit failed or a bridge had been destroyed, he did not waste a moment on frustration or recrimination, nor did he panic. In fact, it is the Emperor himself who has observed that if for some reason he were thrown from a third-story window, he would not flail his arms on the way down. Rather, he would look about himself calmly for a place to land. This was true. And this is the expression Bertrand observes now, a stillness which derives not from the slowness of the Emperor's reflex, but the speed. Or so he hopes.

The Emperor removes his hand from the barrel of the cannon now. All take note. He turns to O'Meara, who is standing nearest him. "I'd have done better to stay in Egypt," he says quietly, then turns and makes his way down to their dining room again.

As soon as he is gone from sight, Las Cases removes the cahier from his pocket and hustles up to the doctor. "What did he say?"

O'Meara shakes his head as though he hadn't heard.

Las Cases moves to de Montholon. "What did he say?"

De Montholon rolls his eyes. "That he will have a closer view in the morning." He turns to Madame Albine, takes her arm, and together they make their way to the stairs.

Las Cases does not believe the Marquis, but makes the note in any case.

CHAPTER THREE

OCTOBER 16

—⊸⊸————

Two new proclamations, Longwood is chosen—Mr. Huffington—
Lieutenant Wood—Quinto

Jamestown awakes to the sight of the ship, hovering a half mile out in Jamestown bay, and two new proclamations posted on the kiosk down by the marina.

The first, issued by his Royal Highness the Prince Regent, acting in the Name of His Majesty, states officially the Honourable Court of Directors' decision to detain Bonaparte on the island of St. Helena, and furthermore warns "all inhabitants and other persons on this island from aiding and abetting . . . the escape of the said General . . . and to interdict most pointedly the holding of any correspondence with him."

The second is a notice of curfew. No one shall be permitted outside his (or her) house between nine at night and daylight the following morning unless in possession of the parole for the night. "It is distinctly to be understood by the inhabitants," the notice goes on, "that this ordinance is in no respect intended to interfere with the customary intercourse of hospitality and that every proper facility will be given to any respectable inhabitant who may intend to return home at a later hour than nine o'clock, by application to the field officer of the day."

Bonaparte will not be coming in just yet. Throughout the morning, select islanders are boated out to the *Northumberland*: Governor Wilkes, Mr. Pourteous, Mr. Solomon, all to see after their most immediate needs. Admiral Cockburn accompanies them back to shore. Then he and the Governor meet Lieutenant Governor Skelton in the Castle, the clean white, but still aptly named, government offices at the foot of Main Street, to discuss where the prisoner should be housed.

The Governor's first thought is to offer the guest rooms at his own estate, Plantation House, which traditionally plays host to dignitaries and guests of state. Admiral Cockburn reminds the Governor that General Bonaparte is not a guest of the state and that he has brought a larger coterie with him than anyone was anticipating: twenty-four, including children and help. The inns in town would do for now, but eventually they'll have to find a compound of some kind, preferably isolated, where they all can stay together.

The men ponder. Wilkes suggests Miss Mason's farm out beyond Tobacco Valley, or Colonel Greentree's. It is the Lieutenant Governor who first mentions the property up on Deadwood Plain, Longwood. He owns it himself, having purchased it several years before from the former Governor, General Beatson. Mr. Skelton's hope had been to convert the structure into a summer residence, its having been a stable for cows originally.

"Cows?" asks Cockburn.

"Yes. General Beatson had wanted to farm them, but the cows never took to the land. Mrs. Skelton and I had thought it might make a nice retreat when the weather gets too hot. . . ."

Cockburn waits. " 'Had thought'?"

"Well, but the wind," says Skelton sheepishly. "It never stops."

"The cows were right."

"I'm afraid so."

The three of them head up to Deadwood Plain that afternoon.

———◆———

At half past three o'clock Mr. Huffington and his two pupils, Alexander and Nicholas Balcombe—nine and six, respectively—

stand at the wide turn on Side Path. Mr. Huffington has ended the day's lessons early in order to bring the boys down.

He stands between them, stooped with age, the inward curl of his spine accentuated by the cut of his coat, whose collar climbs so high up his neck it is like a black crown surrounding his head. It is like a creature about to close its throat on Mr. Huffington, and the creature, knows everyone who has had the chance to speak to him recently, is dementia.

From their present landing they can see Jamestown in its entirety, from its inner tip all the way to the far end, the chapel, the marina, the bay, and the boats.

"The one in the middle, I'd suspect." Mr. Huffington lowers the telescope from his eye and hands it to Alexander. "Observe the guns."

Alexander looks through the eyepiece, more interested in the telescopic mechanism than in the object it sights, which he can hardly tell from the other ships that come to anchor. "Why don't they bring him in?" he asks.

"Waiting for reinforcement," says the tutor, thinking the patience they're showing is more a measure of their fear than power. The wind buffets him momentarily, and Huffington nods, yes. They know. They know the spirit he unleashes.

He nudges Alexander with his wrist. "Say them. Again." He takes back the telescope and hands it down to little Nicholas.

After a deep, burdened breath, Alexander answers, "Liberty."

Mr. Huffington pinches the younger one's shoulder to make sure he hears it too and won't forget. "And?"

"Equality."

"Of?"

"All men before the law."

"And?"

"The emancipation from prejudice."

Mr. Huffington pinches little Nicholas again. "And? Most important."

"The abolishment of privilege," says Alexander.

Huffington pinches Nicholas a third time before taking the glass back to look through the lens himself.

The boat sways, self-satisfied. The fools, he muses, thinking they can bridle what's inside, the greatest man of his age. They simply don't understand: Someone must come first. Someone must come and be prepared to meet resistance, and small minds, and cowardice, and accept the consequences. If the cause is right. But here they give no thought to cause, only how their lives will be disrupted. "How will the island fare?" "How much will the lamp oil cost?" They haven't the sense to see that finally this pointless little outpost, this overpriced brothel, this needless, worthless, feckless floating fleck had met its destiny; it was hovering out there right now, out there in the middle boat, like a lightning bug in a jar.

———

The boat on the left, in fact. The middle boat is the HMS *Ceylon*, just arrived from the Cape Verde Islands to deliver another three hundred men to the cause.

At 0900 hours, just before curfew, eleven of them kneel in a circle, down by the bunks. Nine midshipmen, one Captain, and one Lieutenant, named Henry Wood. Thirty years old, handsome, and entirely bald, Lieutenant Wood sets his clear blue eyes on a space approximately six inches in front of Captain Marshal's knee, trying with all his might to behold the face of Jesus Christ, and speaks the same words he's spoken every night since the *Ceylon* received its orders:

". . . we ask Thy help in keeping Thy will, and remembering Thy sacrifice. We ask for Thy blessing upon all the good people of St. Helena, the men and women, and especially the children. And finally, Father, we pray through Jesus Christ for the immortal soul of General Bonaparte, that he might find salvation, that he be reconciled and led to true repentance and stand before all as a shining monument of your infinite grace. Amen."

"Amen," the circle replies.

———

Not long before midnight Marie lies in bed next to Quinto, her son. It has been a long day, and Marie is very tired, but Quinto has rolled onto his side. He is in the position he always takes before he rises and goes on his sleepwalks.

Quinto is ten years old, and her only child. He was born the year after she moved down from Mr. Haywood's farm to town, to work at the Summers' House, a brothel. The fifth son of a Portuguese sailor who sired seven that spring, Quinto is nearly blind, and quiet, and his bones haven't grown straight, all because of a fever he suffered when he was a baby. Bitten by a spider.

Even so, his eyelids are shining as the balls search and roll underneath. What does he see? she wonders. Trees that aren't there. She takes his hand. His fingers are all covered in calluses, hard and smooth around the nubs and knuckles.

He begins to murmur slightly.

"Quinto?" she whispers.

He falls silent again. His lids rest.

They went around to Rupert's valley today, to gather reeds. Miss Mason let them use her cart, but it still took all morning just to get around Bunker Hill. Quinto sat in the back, the same as always, saying nothing, seeing nothing, his legs dangling from the edge like knotted ropes. They spent the whole afternoon out on the bluffs, Quinto leading them, feeling among the fronds and blades, Marie following next to him, serving as his crutch, collecting everything he wanted in the flower basket he made last spring. They filled the basket four times before Quinto let them go, and they didn't get back until after the five o'clock cannon. Marie had to leave the ox down by the chapel for Miss Mason, then walk Quinto all the way home to the valley's inner tip. She gave him his dinner, washed his face, his hands, and his feet. Then she had to go to Mr. Pourteous's, where she has been working for the last six years—paid. The inn has only seven guests at present, but they stayed late, talking about the prisoner on the boat. She didn't leave until after ten, which is why she took Bridge Street home, because it's faster, even though it takes her behind the Summers' House.

Minnie was out on the back porch. And her fat boy, Trey, leaning back in the chair.

"You hear?" Minnie waddled up to the porch rail when she saw
Marie coming, like a bulldog that smelled meat. She leaned into the
rail, bow-legged, square-hipped, frog-mouthed. "T'ree boat." She
held up her last three fingers. "T'ree full boat, enh? You still pretty
nuff. Enh?" Trey smiled in his chair, but Marie just passed by as if
neither of them were there, and Minnie gave up with a swipe.

Quinto was asleep when she got back. All the grasses they picked
today were hanging in the windows and spread out across the floor to
dry. She washed her face and lay down. Quinto turned, and though
she tried to stay awake, she took his hand and fell asleep herself.

She awakes with a start, to the cool of the bed beside her. Her
heart quickens, but steadies; tired of this panic, and it's still dark out,
he can't have gone far. The grasses in the window stir, and she can
see the trail he's left in the dirt.

He is only in the middle of the road, just beyond the reach of
the olive tree's moon shadow, and he has her fruit sack with him.
The town lies down before him, asleep between the steep walls
of the valley, which are a dull gray in the starlight, barren and
stripped of life. Marie has often thought it looks as if the houses had
first been built on the opposite slopes, to peer at one another from a
comfortable distance, but that one night, with a single sleepy shud-
der, the island had dislodged them from their places and they'd all
come tumbling down together, like white rubble in a gutter.

She touches Quinto's head; she strokes his hair. "Come on,
Quinto. Come back in."

He resists her at first. He closes his shoulder.

"Come on, Quinto. No trees." She tugs his elbow and he turns,
and she guides him back to bed.

CHAPTER FOUR

OCTOBER 17

———⊶⊷———

*Mr. Balcombe's report—The family departs, then the slaves—The arrival—
The island dreams*

Betsy doesn't know why they keep waiting. They still won't bring
Bonaparte to shore, but yesterday they named her father official purveyor to the prisoner's suite, so he got to go out to the ship this morning. It is all Betsy has been able to think about. He left for town at
nine o'clock. He does not appear again until late afternoon.

The moment she sees him, she runs. All the children do, and surround him on the lane. "Did you see him?" "Was he there?" "What
did he look like?" They tug at his arms; he does not resist. He answers patiently, No, he did not see him.

Why not? Where was he?

He was in his quarters, says her father. He did meet several members of his suite, though, who were very nice, very pleasant.

When are they bringing him?

Tonight, he says. Sundown. "But where is your mother? She
should know, the Admiral may be staying in the pavilion." Betsy can
tell he is very proud.

"And has anyone seen Toby?" he asks. "Is he in the garden?"

Betsy nods; he's always in the garden.

"I need to speak to him as well," her father says. "It seems that
General Bonaparte likes chicken."

Chicken?

—◄◼◼◻◼◼►—

The monster likes chicken. That's what Mr. Balcombe said, and Mr. Balcombe wants to know how hard it would be to start a coop, and where might they put it, and how much would they need, because Mr. Balcombe doesn't want Bony having to buy his chicken in town, or from Timu.

Toby doesn't favor the idea, but he told Mr. Balcombe the truth, which is that there's no reason they couldn't raise chickens if they wanted. There used to be chickens at the Briars, for eggs. As soon as Mr. Balcombe leaves, Toby heads down to the creek for fresh water. On his way he notes a space just down the slope from the kitchen garden. There's shade, and it's downwind. And he supposes it's a good thing knowing Bony prefers chicken to naughty children.

He returns just in time to see the Balcombes starting into town, to witness the arrival. They're dressed in Sunday clothes, the girls in their waistcoats and bonnets, the boys with their hair combed and parted, subdued by nerves and uncertainty. Mr. Balcombe hands out the lanterns at the top of the lane, and they quietly turn left.

As soon as they're gone from view, Sarah and 'Scilla step out from the far side of the bungalow. One is the plump mango, Sarah; one is the twig it grew from, 'Scilla. Sarah is stuffed inside a pink short coat that will never again button, but that she still wears because it has a matching bonnet. 'Scilla, who is the Balcombes' cook and has no teeth, is in her flower dress and white gloves.

They see Toby too, but they do not assume he's joining them. They stand and wait patiently and say nothing. 'Scilla chews. Sarah greets him with her eye, and he bows, as he always bows. Then he takes up his buckets and starts back for the garden.

He passes Alley halfway down the pomegranates, coming fast in the other direction. "Toby-Toby-Toby, you're not coming?" Even Alley has dressed for the occasion; he has his shirt tucked in. "Come on, Javaboy. Put on your shoes. It's the monster!"

His eyes are bright, his smile broad and white, but Toby shakes his head. "You see the monster, you bring him here."

—⟪∿⟫—

The walk from the Briars down to Jamestown is a mile and a half and takes the better part of an hour with the light descending and Alexander and Nicholas running out ahead and back again.

Betsy has made the trip hundreds and hundreds of times, more than she likes to ponder. The halfway point is marked by a cactus that's shaped exactly like Poseidon's trident. St. Helena's filled with hidden figures like that, lurking hands and faces, like an earthbound galaxy of constellations. There's hardly anywhere one can go and not be reminded of some legend or other, Lot and Lot's wife, Turk's Cap, Sugarloaf, Fairyland. But every time she passes the prickly trident, either coming or going, she thinks of the first day she ever saw the island. She was six. She remembers being on the boat and looking up at all the steep cliffs towering above their masts. One of the passengers pointed to a high crag and said it was the profile of a giant Negro. Betsy had never seen a Negro. She didn't know what they were supposed to look like, but the man said that when the breakfast bugle sounded, the giant Negro was going to come down from the cliff and devour them all. She had been terrified, but when they finally came ashore, there had been a real Negro there, who helped take them to the Briars. He carried her up Side Path on his head, in a vegetable basket. He sang an air as he walked, and at one point along the way he set her down to rest. Did she like her nest? he asked. She remembers his great wide smile, and that her father paid him for his kindness. But what was the song, she doubts she'll ever know.

They've come to the final turn now; they can see the town. The houses look blue in the descending light, but all surrounding them are thousands of drifting flecks of gold, from the lanterns of all the people who've come down to see. It looks as if the entire island is there. An anxious, excited murmur rises up, and the boys run out ahead. Betsy's mother tells them to slow, but they've already caught up with the line of people headed down. Miss Mason, Mr. Forbes, Mrs. Alexander.

They overtake the Dovetons at the top of Main Street. Betsy's parents pause to greet them, but Betsy sees the Leggs in front of Mr. Mason's tobacco shop. Millicent Legg is her best friend, so she runs ahead, and they remain at each other's side the rest of the way. They've never seen so many islanders all at once. This was more than came down for fireworks. Even the servants have come, dusky women and children, elbow to elbow with the Hodgsons and the Wilkeses, and on every corner is a red-coated sentry. Mr. Breame is waiting in front of Solomon's, telling Mr. Snipe that a boat had been sighted, coming in from the *Northumberland* at this very moment. Betsy calls back to tell her parents, who are only now pulling away from Mr. Doveton.

The crowd grows thicker and more excited as they near the promenade. People are jammed against the rail, but Betsy's father says they'll be taking Bonaparte to Mr. Pourteous's Inn, so the Balcombes and the Leggs climb up onto the theater steps, right across the way.

The crowd surges down on the promenade, and the torchlight jitters. The boat has arrived. A Captain shouts an order, and all the soldiers clear a lane. They face each other, a red fence with bayonet pickets, leading from the marina all the way to the front steps of Mr. Pourteous's Inn. For a moment they're all just waiting; Betsy assumes the boat must be having trouble docking at the pier, which is never easy with the swells. People have had to wait overnight sometimes before the water lets them on, but now a cheer goes up. They've made it, and Millicent takes Betsy's hand. The people down at the rail lean over to get a better view. He still has to make his way up the two embankments, but the crowd is strangely quiet now, as if they were watching a Bengal tiger being carried up in a cage.

They surge again when he reaches the promenade. The Captain barks another order, and all the soldiers turn about and face the people, who pull back in fear and offense—this is *their* island, isn't it?—but the space is won, and now Millicent squeezes Betsy's hand. There they are.

Three men. Betsy isn't sure at first which one he is. The one on the left is an English Admiral; she can tell by the sashes on his uniform. On the right is a taller Frenchman, but it's the one in the middle she can't take her eyes from, the shorter one, wearing the cocked hat from all the paintings. He is wearing a dark surtout with the collar turned up so she can't see his face at all. More clear are all the people gawking at him as he passes, leering over the soldiers' shoulders, a slave child looking up from under a red-sleeved elbow, wondering who and why.

He is very close now, though. He keeps his head tucked and moves briskly—she doesn't blame him—but as he reaches the steps of the inn, something glints upon his chest; a shining diamond—or a medal, it must be—catches the torchlight and winks at her. Then he climbs the stairs and enters, and that quickly it's over, what they all have come to see. The tiger is safe inside.

The people don't know quite what to do now. They look at one another, dumb. Those with hats remove them. There is Mr. Pritchard looking back at Betsy, his face a blank. Up on the porch of the inn, Mr. Pourteous closes the door, and out of respect to him, the people turn away. Or most of them. A light comes on in an upstairs window.

"There," says one, and the crowd sweeps around like a wave of tub water. A curtain is drawn.

"That was him," says another. "The hat."

And now a second light has come on in the room beside. The crowd swings around again, but too late; they cannot see.

"But he's not going anywhere."

"That's certain."

The soldiers have yet to move. The slave child is up in his mother's arms, then Betsy feels her father's hand on her shoulder. It's time to go.

They start back with the Leggs. All the people are headed back. A line of boys chases through, but otherwise there is a more trudging silence now, almost a sadness, as though the fireworks didn't really explode.

The crowd splits at the end of town. Half take Ladder Hill, half Side Path, and funnel back to their houses and huts and cottages, as quietly as streams, only flowing in the wrong direction, up.

An hour later, Jane and Betsy are in their beds, separated by a standing lamp.

"Do you think he's asleep?"

Jane turns away. "I don't know."

Of course she doesn't, and Jane would never guess, but Betsy can't possibly go to sleep so soon. Every time she closes her eyes, all she can think of is him, lying on top of his covers, with his collar turned up, and only the clear whites of his beady eyes showing out from under the black shadow of his hat.

⸻

The island dreams. More nightmares than usual among the children. The ones there always are, of wild boars trampling them and gnarling on their little bellies; of giant flying creatures with taloned legs, swooping down, plucking them by their collars, and carrying them away, to shred and feed the yearning beaks of their creature-kin.

But there are others too, newer dreams. Of valiant boys in night-time battles; dark skies lit by smoke and cannon fire; ships creeping forward toward the fortress walls, while the boys light bales of hay and throw them down from their turrets. In the fast-descending fire-light they can see the ships' sails, bearded with arrows. One dreams the boats are giant porcupines. One girl hides inside a church, terri-fied of being found, till Johnny Legg comes in and points her out, and she is dragged away to some dreadful, unimagined fate. A burn-ing boat, standing in a square. In one, it isn't a boat that's burning. It's Jamestown Chapel, and everyone is trapped inside, while the flames lick up the windows. One dreams he is a fish upon a chop-ping block, and all the soldiers have gathered to watch the men in black hoods scale him. A severed hand trembles in a basket, be-side a quiet thumb. The chapel valley filled with trees again, calmly shushing.

CHAPTER FIVE

OCTOBER 18

‑‑‑‑◉‑‑‑‑

The Governor, the "freebooters," and the Reverend Richard Boys—
Betsy's sighting—The Emperor's ascent—Luncheon at Longwood—
The Briars is chosen—The Russian quiz

The sun is just cutting through the early mist, and Governor Wilkes is drinking the last of his morning coffee outside on the Castle terrace. Just across the way in front of Mr. Pourteous's Inn, a light scattering of townspeople is milling about in hopes the prisoner will soon emerge. To the left, Wilkes can hear another boatful of sentries docking at the pier.

Admiral Cockburn mentioned last night that General Bonaparte wanted to go see Longwood today. He asked that five horses be made available. Governor Wilkes personally selected Bonaparte's mount from his own stable, a black pony named Hope, and brought her down from Plantation House first thing this morning.

At a quarter past the hour of nine the front door of the inn opens. First to emerge are the two valets, then the tall fellow, Bertrand, then Cockburn, then finally Bonaparte. He is nattily dressed for the occasion, in a coat of bright green silk, bedecked with medals, but his manner remains simple and direct, as Wilkes has previously observed. The valets bring the horses around, and they all mount quickly. Hope behaves herself quite well, and the five of them start up Main Street without occasion. The onlookers stand a respectful distance away. Wilkes can hear the soldiers calling orders down by the water, and for a moment, standing there with his coffee in hand, the Governor enjoys an inexplicable moment of almost cocoonlike contentment.

But only a moment. As he looks back up the street, he sees that the five horsemen are just now passing Mrs. Bagley, who is moving with far more determination, and speed, headed directly for him with a firm, set jaw.

"Governor?"

Worse, the Reverend Richard Boys is now standing beside him. Boys is the new island pastor, having taken over last fall from the Reverend James Eakins. It was the Council's hope that a younger, fresher pastor might revive a parish that almost all agreed was beginning to slump. Unfortunately, Boys proved himself a man of brittle nature. No doubt his intentions were good, and his belligerence a measure of dedication, but the Reverend's sermons are entirely too pointed in nature—all but naming certain individual members of the congregation—and the ongoing feud with his predecessor, Mr. Eakins, is likewise unendearing, particularly in light of the fact that the chaplains' chosen form of combat is by letter, through the Town Council. Mr. Wilkes was called upon but two months ago to order an official moratorium on any further correspondence between the two, direct or indirect.

"Good morning, Reverend."

"Governor." The Reverend's smile is, as always, snipped by an impatient underbite.

"Looks as if we've a lovely day in store."

"Perhaps." He pauses in case Wilkes might have something to share with him. He hasn't. "I take it you haven't spoken to the Council yet?"

"I spoke to them just yesterday. With regard to what, Reverend?"

Boys sniffs, despite the Governor's good humor. "Well, I spoke to Mr. Skelton. I gather he hasn't had the chance to communicate it to you. What I had suggested, and what I would greatly appreciate your taking under advisement, particularly in regard of recent circumstances, was that the Council issue a new order mandating attendance at Sunday service."

"A mandate?"

"Yes."

It is only the Governor's acquaintance with Boys that advises him not to think this a joke. "Do you mean among the slaves?"

Boys smiles again, but still without a trace of humor. "As I'm sure you know, Governor, attendance already is compulsory among the slaves."

"Oh, yes. Well, no, I suppose Mr. Skelton hasn't had the chance to mention it to me, but we can certainly bring the matter up tomorrow."

"Do. I think it's most important at times like these that the community stay rooted."

"Of course." Wilkes looks down longingly into the bowl of his coffee cup, as if were a black pool he could jump into and disappear. "No, it's a point well taken, Reverend."

"I'd be happy to speak to the Council myself."

"No, that won't be necessary." He looks back up to find Mrs. Bagley now upon them. "Why, Mrs. Bagley, good morning."

She offers not a twitch of greeting. "I trust you've heard."

Wilkes shakes his head.

"About all the disturbances. Last night."

"Disturbances?"

"Singing. Howling. Same as always." She looks at the Reverend. "Like a pack of wolves."

The Reverend nods, of a knowing suspicion. She is referring to the "freebooters"—runaway slaves. They are a problem as old as the island and always a good bet to crop up in times of flux.

"Where exactly?" asks the Governor.

"The cliffs. But I'm sure they're everywhere."

The Reverend agrees, this underscores his point.

"Well, I'm sorry," says the Governor. "I know it can be disruptive—"

"My worry isn't the noise, Governor. My worry is they're thieves."

"I understand. I'll have Colonel Sealey look into it." Wilkes directs their attention to the promenade, where the newest battalion of soldiers is just now ascending. "Fortunately it looks as if we'll be battening down the hatches."

Mrs. Bagley snorts. "Soldiers are the solution to nothing, Governor, save a glut of gin."

The Reverend nods. He couldn't agree more.

Betsy is the first to see him, not surprisingly. She is out on the lawn with Jane, and should be doing her lessons as well. Instead she is trying to fold flowers out of white paper, for the gown she intends to make with Sarah. She can't quite remember the pattern, though, when a butterfly happens by and distracts her.

"Jane, look. Look."

Up at the top of the banyan lane a party of five horsemen is passing, climbing the road that wraps around the hillside. Jane remains intent upon the page.

"Jane, it's him!"

"Who?"

"Him. Look. His hat." She points. The third in line is wearing the cocked hat and a green coat. "Mother!"

Her mother is already coming out, in fact, to make sure she's working.

"Look!" Betsy points, and her mother goes still. Riding single file, the five men look almost like a serpent slithering up the road. "Where are they going?"

Her mother shakes her head. "Sarah? The binoculars." Sarah is already on her way, but it is too late. They've disappeared behind the shoulder of the hill.

It is a five-mile climb from Jamestown to Longwood. Bertrand made the same trip yesterday with Admiral Cockburn, but for some reason it seems much longer today, perhaps because there are five of them, not just two. At a walking gait they make their way up a narrow mountain path which sometimes is, and sometimes isn't, bordered by low, crumbling walls. It leads them up and down, through a landscape of fantastic variety, around countless hills and precipices, past rolling meadows, fences perched on distant hillsides, jagged peaks, sudden bursts of life and color: a bungalow nesting in white flowers; a low, geranium-slathered vale, where the dip in the road is so severe they have to dismount their horses just to pass.

Bertrand watches the Emperor, who gives little indication that he minds one way or the other. He has not said a word, but his eyes are alert, gauging the military possibilities, no doubt, if only by instinct. How quickly could a battalion get over there? Sweep around that shoulder and meet up with the left flank? The open spaces are few and far between, though. The hills are steep. Battles here would consist of roadside ambushes, thinks Bertrand, quicker gambits. The Russians would do well, or the Turks.

The final leg of their journey, the road wends them to a tired white house called Hutt's Gate, then up onto a broad, windswept plain well named Deadwood, studded with tree stumps and little else. There is a low stone barn with a carriage out front and two eucalyptus trees off to the side. A mile up, the 53^{d} Regiment has already begun setting up a barracks, in plain view. And the same as yesterday, there is a constant, ear-ruffling wind.

The Lieutenant Governor and his wife greet them out front, then invite them in for a brief tour. Again, Bertrand is surprised at the ease with which he accepted it yesterday, the brazen contempt which informed the decision to install the Emperor here. Five dank and musty rooms, one attached to the next with no apparent design or forethought. The floor is riven with rat holes, some so large that Bertrand can even see the sag in the rug. Admiral Cockburn points to where the new rooms will be added, where they might put a garden or a hedgerow, but no discussion of windows, or verandas, or what flowers and vegetables might grow can disguise the insult. The Emperor is fully aware, but for the moment appears more concerned by the visible creep of mildew up the corners and drapes.

When they return to the first room, a table has been set out, with tea. They sit on warped, mismatched chairs, and pretend to be polite. Mrs. Skelton is an attractive woman, in fact, with a luxuriant head of black hair, a small face of delicate features. She speaks French well enough to make conversation and helps her husband explain something of the plain's history. There once had been a great forest here apparently, of ebony and redwood trees, until the English discovered that the bark could be used for tanning leather. They decimated the wood, which never grew back because of all the goats. All that remained was this, says Mr. Skelton, without a hint of shame.

"How long do you expect it will take," asks Bertrand, of the Admiral, "before the extensions are completed?"

"The Governor says they've got good workers, and our men are fairly efficient."

They turn their ears to the sound of the new barracks.

"Weeks?" Bertrand presses.

"Yes, I should think. At least."

"And until then?"

"Well, the rooms at the inn are open."

"In town?"

Bertrand looks at the Emperor, whose calm is more a show of his appreciation—to Bertrand, for representing his interest here—than a reflection of his feelings, which remain veiled, if thinly. He has told Bertrand he finds the Admiral boorish. He does not think him worthy of the assignment.

As soon as the cups are empty, the Emperor stands, and the Skeltons see them all out. They both wait upon the carriage road until the Emperor has led the party down and out of view. Then they prepare to leave themselves. They take their plates and cups and saucers—or their servant, Thomas, does. He sets them in the carriage trunk and starts them down the same primitive road, to get away from Deadwood Plain as quickly as possible.

—⁂—

The clopping silence is even more grim during the descent. Now even the spectacle of the landscape has dulled. All these fells, the dips, the distant hills, which on the way up at least enjoyed the benefit of introduction, have taken on the first tarnish of familiarity. Yes, these are the hills, the ditches, the brush which they will see again and again, the dip where they must dismount their horses and walk them past the low vale of geraniums. How many more times?

Worse, each hoof step brings them closer to town, where even now the locals are doubtless gathering to catch another glimpse. And night is still hours away. The sky above is a hazy, pale gray.

With less than a mile to go, however, the Emperor stops his pony. Just down the slope, at the foot of a curious tree line, sits that bungalow again, snug in its floral nest. And there is a family out front, looking up at them, through binoculars.

"Whose is this?" asks the Emperor.

"Mr. Balcombe," says Cockburn. "Did you not meet him on the boat?"

The Emperor shakes his head, turns his pony, and leads them down.

⸻⁂⸻

"They're coming here!" Betsy lowers the binoculars. "They're coming down the road!"

It's true. Jane and her mother can see as well. The Admiral's party, which the three of them have been watching from the moment it reappeared, snaking back down the inland road, is now descending the banyan lane.

"Jane." Her mother speaks calmly and without looking away from the coming guests. "Go see if your father is feeling any better. And fetch the boys."

"I'll go," says Betsy, as much for the excuse to leave as to be helpful.

"No, Betsy. Stay. We'll need your French."

The two of them wait there on the veranda as the horsemen approach. It is Bonaparte himself who leads. He rides in the peculiar French style, with his feet thrust forward. The others stop on the lane, but Bonaparte walks his jet black pony directly onto the lawn. Its hooves cleave deep into the turf, but Betsy does not take offense, oddly. She has never seen anything, or anyone, so noble and imposing. His saddle and housing are a crimson velvet, embroidered with gold. His coat is a shiny green silk, resplendent with medals. But it is his expression that entrances her. He looks at them both directly, his features perfectly cold, immovable, and yet prowling behind them is something she instantly recognizes: play.

He yanks the pony to a halt and removes his hat. "Good day, Madame."

Her mother curtsies slightly.

His footmen come and attend his dismount. The other two, the same ones who escorted him to Mr. Pourteous's, have descended as well. Both stand a good head taller, but it does not matter, he is clearly the one in command.

Betsy's mother invites them into the parlor, where Jane, the boys, and now Betsy's father all join them. Bonaparte sits in one of the rattan chairs, her father's. Her mother, then Betsy and Jane follow. The men remain standing, even the boys.

"I see only so much of your island"—he tries his hand at English, then reverts—"mais je constate déjà que votre propriété est admirablement située."

Her mother understands well enough to know he is complimenting her home; she thanks him. But Betsy is still amazed at how different he is from what she pictured. He is round, not dark, and his features are almost delicate. His skin is soft and pale.

They speak briefly of Longwood, the house where he will be staying—it is not ready for some reason—and at one point he looks straight across at Betsy. His clear blue eyes catch hers, and she sees it again—he smiles. He has a very sly smile, but it lights the pallor of his face like a lamp. And this light seems to light the room.

"Where will you be staying in the meantime?" asks her father.

The Admiral answers—Mr. Pourteous's—and the General's face goes dim again.

Her father sees too. "Well, certainly you are welcome to stay here," he offers. "We've another house, just beyond Hutt's Gate."

Betsy scowls, she hates that house, and Bonaparte reacts in turn. "Non, non. Je ne voudrais pas vous déranger d'une telle façon," he says—he would never pose an inconvenience—"mais je vois là-bas qu'il y a une autre . . ." He points behind him, in the direction of the tea pavilion.

Betsy happens to know her father has already promised the pavilion to the Admiral, but the Admiral says nothing.

"Well, I'm not sure the space is adequate," her father says obligingly, "but certainly I can take you up, to see."

The General does not need to; he has already made up his mind. He glances over at the other Frenchman, the tall one, and the decision is made.

The others—the tall one, the Admiral, and the two footmen—leave soon thereafter to get his things. Only General Bonaparte remains, so Betsy's father offers to tour him about the grounds. The whole family comes along, Betsy most important, for her French.

"C'est un grenadier?" He points to the pomegranate trees as they walk down the shaded lane to the garden. "Je n'en ai jamais vu pousser à cette taille!" He has never seen them so tall.

They enter the garden gate, and he starts asking about the plants and flowers. Betsy knows only so much, but they come upon Toby near the fishpond, and her father introduces them.

"Yours is the jardin?"

"The gardener," says Betsy.

Toby removes his hat and smiles. Aside from Betsy's mother, Toby may be the most commanding figure at the Briars, especially inside the garden, but he looks back at the General now as he looks back at everyone, with a gentle, distant, squinting smile, as if a low sun were peering over the General's shoulder at him.

"And what do you grow?" asks Bonaparte, trying his English. "What is this? Say the name."

Toby shows him a magnolia, some camellias, and an unusual buttercup which the General seems to like a great deal. He says his first wife, Josephine, kept a beautiful flower garden at their home outside Paris. He asks Toby if he grows vegetables as well, and Toby tells him which ones—potatoes, onions, tomatoes, lettuces, fennel, beans, peas—and General Bonaparte is interested in this as well, though he can't disguise the fact that he doesn't seem to have a taste for vegetables. When Toby mentions yam, the General grimaces.

Her father leads them on. The General continues to be very curious, and his curiosity continues to set them all at ease. Betsy tells him the English names of all the fruit that grows in the orchard: Orange? Yes, of course. Lemon, of course. Fig? Yes. Mango, yes. Guava, yes. He is very impressed. They pass through the myrtle grove, and she points out the various vines which climb the trunks and fences. When they come to the fence which runs nearest the house, Betsy shows him the cluster of prickly pear that runs alongside. "On dirait un match de tennis fou?" she asks. *Doesn't it look like a mad game of tennis?* The General peers intently, but he does not quite see it.

By the time they finally make it back to the house, her father's gout is acting up again, so he heads in. Her mother excuses herself as well, calling the children in to come and leave their guest in peace, but the General keeps Betsy. His valets have set out two chairs on the lawn, the Windsors. He asks that she sit with him, and they converse in French.

"So, Mademoiselle Betsee, where did you learn to speak so well?"

"My father took me to London when I was six, and we had a French nanny."

"And here, who is your teacher?"

"My mother. And father."

This does not satisfy. "Your mother and father are very fine people, to be sure, but they are not teachers. You must have someone who can instruct you in mathematics, and history."

His hair is so fine, she thinks, and silky. Like an infant's. "We had a tutor, Jane and I, but she left."

"This is not good. You will be ignorant." He sits up straight. "What is the capital of France?"

"Paris."

"And Italy?"

"Rome?"

He thinks. "And what is the capital of Russia?"

"Petersburg now. Moscow formerly."

"Very good." He pauses, slyly. "But do you know who set it on fire?" He leans in toward her, and his eyes glower. "Qui l'a brûlé?"

She sits back. "I do not know, sir."

Then they soften just as quickly. He smiles. "Yes, you do. You know very well that it was *I* who set Moscow on fire." He puffs his chest out like such a silly bird she cannot help herself.

"Oh, no, now I remember. It wasn't you. It was the Russians who burned it, to be rid of the French."

She is correct, and so he sits back with a half smile, conceding defeat. For now.

PART II

THE BRIARS

CHAPTER SIX

OCTOBER 18-20

—⟪ᒐ⟫—

The Pavilion, &c.—Timu farm—Mr. Huffington meets the Emperor—
"Masquerade"—Mesdames de Montholon & Bertrand

October 18—It takes the remainder of that day for the new guest's belongings to be moved from Jamestown—or in certain cases, all the way from the *Northumberland*—up to the Briars. The road from Jamestown is a narrow one, too narrow in certain stretches for a cart, so his things have to be carried up one by one: the iron campaign bed, the nécessaire, the silver washbasin and the ewer, a terrestrial globe, a celestial globe, the marble bust of Napoleon's son, the King of Rome. All of these and much more must ride the shoulders, heads, and backs of slaves and sentries, the mile and a half up Side Path, then down again along the banyan-shaded walk, across the lawn, and up the little stone path which ascends the rocky knoll on which the Balcombes' teahouse, the Pavilion, sits.

The dimensions are modest, twenty feet by fifteen feet, with a loft which has been divided into two small rooms. By dusk the main floor looks like the annex of a small museum. As well as the beds and tubs, there are several framed portraits, chess and backgammon boards, a telescope, a set of white muslin curtains, a tea chest, boxes of plates, decanters of eau de Cologne, books, maps, and countless other ornaments and sundries—snuffboxes, watches, miniatures.

Count de Las Cases has come as well, to continue the work on the memoir, as has his son, Emanuel, fifteen years old. The two valets, Marchand and St. Denis, will be staying at the Briars as well, of course, as will the steward, Monsieur Cipriani.

Following a simple chicken dinner, Bonaparte and Las Cases descend to the bungalow of their host and as a courtesy join the family in the drawing room. Noting the spinet in the corner, the Emperor teases Betsy. In French, he says, "Of course you are too young to play yourself."

In French, she replies, "I can both sing and play."

"Please sing then."

She does, to Jane's accompaniment. She stands beside the piano, lifts her chin, and sings.

> Ye banks and braes o' bonie Doon,
> How can ye bloom sae fresh and fair?
> How can ye chant, ye little birds,
> And I sae weary, fu' o' care?
> Ye'll break my heart, ye warbling birds,
> That wanton through the flow'ry thorn,
> Ye 'mind me o' departed joys,
> Departed never to return.
>
> Aft hae I rov'd by bonie Doon,
> To see the rose and woodbine twine;
> And ilka bird sang o' its love,
> And fondly sae did I o' mine.
> Wi' lightsome heart I pu'd a rose,
> Fu' sweet upon its thorny tree;
> And my fause luver staw my rose,
> But ah! he left the thorn wi' me.

Betsy's voice is like her appearance: fundamentally pretty, and licensed by this to a sometimes wanton disregard for the correct. The

Emperor is duly impressed. "But this is the prettiest English I have ever heard."

"It isn't English," she says. "It's Scottish." Ecossais.

"Ah, I thought it was too pretty," he says. "English music is vile, don't you think? The worst in the world. Do you know any French songs? 'Vive Henri Quatre'?"

No, she shakes her head, and so the Emperor stands. His shimmering green coat and decorations are a reminder of what she has already forgotten: Here stands the former Emperor of all Europe. Here is the monster who beheaded an innocent Duke, insulted the Pope, and poisoned his own men.

He begins to hum, without accompaniment. Betsy cannot recognize a note, but then come the words.

> *Vive Henri Quatre*
> *Vive ce roi vaillant*

He bobs his knees and then begins a kind of strut over toward the piano, with one hand delicately raised to shoulder height.

> *Ce diable à-à quatre*
> *À le triple talent*
> *De Boire et se battre*
> *Et d'ê-être vert galant.*

He brings with him the faint scent of eau de Cologne. When he reaches the piano, he touches it once, then turns and starts back, singing the second verse more boldly and with a puffier chest.

> *Chantons l'antienne*
> *Qu'on chant'ra dans mille ans;*
> *Que Dieu maintienne*
> *En paix ses descendants*
> *Jusqu'à-à ce qu'on prenne*
> *La lune avec les dents.*

He comes to the end of the song at precisely the moment he reaches his original position. He turns to her. "What do you think of that?"

"I couldn't hear the tune."

Las Cases comes to the rescue. "Of course, it's difficult when one has never heard it before."

The Emperor looks at Betsy to see if she accepts the Count's explanation. With a simple purse of her lips, she refuses. He would like to go and pinch that cheek, and he will, but not yet.

Upon their return to the Pavilion, the sleeping arrangements are settled. The Emperor prefers his own camp bed with the floss silk mattress—it has been with him since his days at the Élysées—but the frame of its green taffeta curtains is too tall for the lofts, so he will have to remain on the main floor. Las Cases and his son will take one of the rooms upstairs, and Monsieur Cipriani the other. The only problem then is that the main floor proves drafty. The Emperor is highly susceptible to sore throats and toothaches, so Marchand and St. Denis do what they can, stuffing rags around the sashes and erecting blockades with screens and paintings. Eventually the air is still enough, the flame of his bedside candle stands straight, and everyone can retire.

The lofts upstairs are cramped and stifling. Las Cases's son has to sleep on a mattress on the floor, but his father will hear no complaint. Crowded quarters are a small price to pay for the privilege of sleeping at His Majesty's residence, and so near his bed they can actually hear him turn and shift.

Marchand and St. Denis cannot. The last to lie down, they sleep outside, draped across the threshold of the Pavilion like a pair of faithful dogs.

—⟶⟨⟩⟵—

October 19—Toby hardly ever leaves the Briars anymore. It has been years, in fact, since he last hitched up Lewis to his cart and

climbed the lane of banyans. Lewis is an ox, and not quite as unaccustomed as Toby. Alley uses him when the inland roads are passable,
but once again Alley is nowhere to be found, and even if he were,
Toby wants to do this. He wants to see Timu. He fills a basket with
seven yams and the ripest mangoes he can find, as gifts.

Timu's farm is over in Church Land, which lies on the other side
of High Knoll. As a bird flies, it isn't far, but Helena permits no simple routes by foot or hoof. Toby knows that he is close when he
passes Country Church and the road slants right. The pine trees turn
into oaks, he can hear the drone of gobbles and grubbing chicken.
He can smell the droppings, too.

Timu is just closing the gate to the pen when Toby and Lewis
enter into the low canopy. A free black now, Timu used to run the
coop at Mr. Breames's, where Toby worked when he first came.
Now Timu sells his chickens in town and serves the country steads
from Thompson's Wood all the way around to Sandy Bay. He has
clients in the Governor, the Reverend, and Mr. Pourteous. Their
business affords him the land he farms his chickens on, a slouching
house, four rooms, a stove the size of his gut, and a gut the size of
his stove.

He does not recognize Toby at first. Normally when he sees
Lewis and his cart, he sees Alley too.

"Who's this? Java?" He squints, smiling. "Javaboy?"

"Java-old-man." Toby climbs down with the basket of yam and
mango, and Timu comes out to greet him, wiping his hands and
smiling broadly. They have not seen each other in ten years, at least.
Not since the death of Winston-Kumar.

"And look what he brought." Timu takes up a yam and sniffs it.
"And the mango—that looks good. Toby-Toby. Welcome."

His head seems larger, thinks Toby. His lower lip too. His hair is
more gray, and the skin around his eyes and temples has gone dark
purple like an eggplant, but it is good to see Timu.

"Lew thirsty?"

Toby nods, and the two of them start over for the pump. Beneath
the gnarly outstretched arms of the oaks, Timu's farm is all dappled

shade. The fallen leaves crunch beneath their feet. The captive chickens cluck from behind the fence pen. Toby can barely see them through the lattice of gathered sticks, the browns and whites of the feathers and waste. A dozen cats, at least, prowl the ground outside, stalking through the fallen leaves, cleaning themselves in root caves, and up in the limbs as well.

"So why are you here?" asks Timu.

"Need chicken."

"Could have sent Alley for chicken."

"For a coop."

Timu stops; the dead leaves hush, then his eyelids knowingly descend. "Ooh." He smiles. "For the monster. That's right, I heard you got him. 'Bony.' "

Toby nods, and Timu's laugh bubbles up from deep inside his very round belly. Toby misses Timu's laugh, the readiness for joy.

"Good man, Bony," he says.

Timu doesn't doubt. He starts them walking again. "And good man Bony, he likes chicken."

Toby nods.

"Mr. Fowler know?"

Toby shrugs. Mr. Fowler is Mr. Balcombe's business partner.

"Fowler don't know," says Timu. They've come to the pump. He hangs the bucket. "So how much? How hungry is Mr. Bony?"

"Say, two a day."

"To eat?"

Toby nods.

"Gonna get fat, eat two chicken a day." Timu glances at his own gut; he knows.

"Bony's got friends."

Timu doesn't doubt. He starts the pump. "And how long is Bony gonna be there?"

Again Toby shakes his head, he doesn't know. "But then he goes to Deadwood, and we still feed him, I guess."

Timu nods. He is less put out now; Deadwood is a long way. The well water starts coughing out. "No small thing, keeping a meat coop."

Toby agrees.

" 'Cause I can get Mr. Balcombe two a day."

Toby shakes his head. This is not a negotiation.

"So you know about the rats?" asks Timu.

"Got a cat."

Timu grins. "Better be a big cat." Timu nods in the direction of a prowling Burmese, with high rolling shoulders and a low searching head. "I tell you, they spend a lot of time looking out for themselves. What about the fence?"

"Bamboo."

Timu nods and stops the pump. The bucket is full. He takes it by the handle and starts them back for Lew. The chickens cluck at them from behind the fence, but Timu is calculating; his breathing turns thick and nasal.

"And the coop?" he asks.

"Hay."

This does not seem to be Timu's first choice, but he doesn't say. They give Lew his water and sit down at Timu's outside table. Timu wipes his face with his large fat hand, smearing it with sweat—just as he always has—then makes his offer. Thirty-four birds for now. Eighteen full grown, sixteen pullets, and some chicks. He decides to give him three different kinds—Sumatra, Cornish, Guinea—but just the thirty-two to begin, to see how they take. Toby agrees.

"How long you need to build the coop?"

"Three days."

"And you get Alley to help with the fence?"

Toby agrees. It would be good for Alley to help build the fence.

———

Mr. Huffington had to wake up at five o'clock this morning to start the walk from town and be on time at the Briars. He has had to start earlier and earlier each day because of his hip, which has grown considerably worse since his spell in August. He is told he fell; he doesn't remember. Dr. Shortt has prescribed a medicine for the pain, but the hip has not been the same. Mr. Huffington has had to rely

on his cane, so much so that now his right wrist and elbow have begun to ache and swell as well.

But he is on time. Just as he has every day for the past three years,
save Sundays, Mr. Huffington appears at the top of the Briars Road
at the very moment the ten o'clock cannon fires. He cannot hear it
so well anymore, but he can feel it, trembling the earth and quivering up his bones, right there as he comes to the intersection—this
most "trivial" place, he likes to joke to the boys. *Tri-via*—where
three roads meet.

The only difference this morning is the two red-coated sentries
stationed at the first banyan, who stop him and ask him his business.

"Tutor," he says gruffly, "to the Balcombe boys." They let him
pass.

He is hardly surprised by their presence. There is bound to be
more security about the island—another boat, the *Bucephalus*, arrived just this morning—and the Balcombes' home is better appointed than most to host visitors. Mr. Huffington assumes that one
of the English officers has taken up residence in the house—perhaps
Admiral Cockburn himself.

Yet as he descends the path, he can see through the windows of
the pavilion how cluttered it is inside. He glimpses the silhouette of
a bust in the far window; it's a child's head, but still he feels a glimmer of recognition. There is even something in the air, in the
crackle of the trees and shimmer and shush of the neighboring
cataract—like giggling children who cannot wait to tell their secret.

He will not be distracted from his purpose, though. Dutifully and
very much in pain, he rounds the house to the schoolroom. The
boys are waiting in their chairs, backs to the one window in the
dank and deliberately bare den beside the kitchen. Mr. Huffington
takes the books from the one shelf and thunks them down on the
table, the same as every morning.

Their lessons last three hours, measured by three turns of an
hourglass: first geography; then mathematics; then Latin. At the first
turn of the glass, Sarah enters with a pot of tea and a plate of biscuits. He asks, "Quis est novus hospes?"

She looks at him.

"Dans le pavillon."

She understands the last word well enough. "Bonipah," she says, and Mr. Huffington's heart pounds out its vindication. He knew it. He addresses Alexander this time. "Quis est in portico?"

It is a simple enough question. "General Bonaparte," the boy replies.

"Bony." Nicholas giggles.

Mr. Huffington's eyes well. Something small within him suddenly expands, a blooming flower. "And you have met him?"

Alexander nods, and Mr. Huffington reaches out to take his hand. Nicholas removes his from the table.

The remainder of their morning session passes in a blur. They are translating Virgil, but Mr. Huffington will need reminding several times of where they are. In the end he will set aside their books entirely and recount that fateful moment back in the year 312—October 28, in fact; the anniversary approaches—when at the "red rocks" just north of Rome, a vision appeared to the greatest conqueror of his day, of a giant cross glowing in the sky, bearing the inscription "Hoc Vince." Conquer by this.

Unfortunately for the boys, Mr. Huffington narrates the incident in a stunningly accurate approximation of Eusebius's Latin, though deliberately excising all mention of the visionary's name. When he is finished, he turns to Alexander. "Et quel est donc le nom de ce 'conquistador'?"

The boy looks at him, helpless.

"Qui est-ce qui fonda Constantinople? Oui, oui, Constantinople? Qui est-ce?"

Alexander ventures, "Constantine?"

"Oui, c'était Constantine!" Huffington turns to Nicholas now. "Et quel était le nom de sa mère?"

Nicholas actually knows this. He sits up and answers, pronouncing the name as the islanders do, with the emphasis on the penultimate syllable, and a hard e. "St. Hel-EE-na."

"Oui, c'était Hélène," repeats Huffington, and with that, calms.

From some vestige of his tutorial instinct, he understands that this should conclude the day's lesson. The boys bolt outside while Huffington follows at his more hobbled pace.

As he rounds the side of the bungalow, he can see the sentries still standing up at the top of the road, but there is something uncomfortable about their stance, like a pair of sighted deer. Mr. Huffington turns the corner to see the huntsman now, standing on the lawn. It is Him, the bust on his bureau become flesh. There are two others with him as well, but Huffington hardly sees them, his focus is so rapt. The color, the green silk of his coat, and the posture, one knee bent, one straight, shoulders back. And above all, the eyes—witness to the greatest triumphs and most crushing defeats—eyes which have scolded Popes and Kings, and which possess a second sight as well, of something much larger. What must be.

The great man turns. First he glances over at the two boys, who are frozen at the steps of the veranda, shy. He smiles. "You learn, eh?" He taps his temple. "Good, good. And this is your teacher?"

He looks over at Huffington now. Their eyes meet, releasing such a sudden burst of adrenaline through the tutor's aged frame, he swoons. His knees buckle. But for his grasp upon the cane he would surely crumple to the ground.

"Monsieur!" calls the Emperor, concerned, but Huffington catches himself just in time to turn his stumble into a bow.

"Pardon, Votre Majesté."

He does not look up to see the Emperor again. He bows more deeply, to show both his respect and his balance, then turns and starts off upon the lane. He can feel their eyes upon him, so he focuses on simply staying upright and keeping his pace. There is pain, but the pain does not matter. He wills it away and ascends the hill. When he comes to the two sentries, he does not even acknowledge their presence. They do not exist.

—⚏—

As soon as they are satisfied that the ghostly old man is stable enough to make it up the hill, Las Cases and the Emperor start for the garden. All morning they have been cooped up inside the pavilion, conducting their dictations out of view, but now some fresh air is in order.

No sooner do they enter the garden gate, however, than they are ambushed by the two Balcombe daughters, carrying flowers. Both are dressed in the unbecoming fashion of English girls—a high white skirt, bodice, pantaloons. The elder, who is taller and darker, is reasonably quiet and deferential. The younger one, on the other hand—the blonde, with all the tangled ringlets and sprouting bows—is entirely too familiar.

"Vous n'êtes pas supposé de voir!" she says—her French is atrocious as well. "Fermez les yeux."

The Emperor graciously closes his eyes.

"Présentez vos mains."

He holds out his arms, and she loads them down with all the flowers that she and her sister have gathered.

"Maintenant ouvrez les yeux."

He opens his eyes again. "Ah." He sniffs the blossoms. He is remarkably kind. He asks what sorts of flowers these are, and the girls answer—some common roses and a few more rare species that the Count has never heard of. His Majesty hands them over for Las Cases to carry, and together they set off, all four of them.

The Briars' garden is roughly three acres long, two acres wide, with various tiers and terraces. As they make their way around the outermost path, the girls pillory the poor Emperor with questions, the blond one in particular, flitting around him like a butterfly: Does he have a palace in France? How many palaces does he have? Are there towers? Has he ever slept in a high tower? Does he think it's more restful to sleep in a round or square room? And when she is not asking inane questions, she talks of nothing that His Majesty or Las Cases can possibly follow, as it all concerns islanders they've never met. More than once she strikes the Emperor on the arm.

This continues for the balance of the walk, once around the outermost path. The Emperor remains stately and obliging throughout, then when they reach the point where they first met, the girls finally take their leave, backing away behind a dense white-rosed shrub, then screaming and giggling away.

The Emperor waits until they are safely out of earshot before speaking. "I feel as if I have stepped into a masquerade ball."

———

October 20—The two ladies of His Majesty's personal suite, the Mesdames de Montholon and Bertrand, are, for the third time in two days, browsing the shelves of Mr. Solomon's shop.

"Quelle boutique ridicule!" mutters de Montholon. *What a ridiculous store this is.*

"Enfin, c'est une ville ridicule!" answers Madame Bertrand. *A ridiculous town.*

They are standing before a collection of Chinese fans. As ridiculous as Mr. Solomon's may be, the Mesdames are resigned to the fact that it is the only shop in Jamestown worth exploring, trading in a random mix of clothes, fabric, hats, gloves, plates, jewelry, linens, snuffboxes—whatever Mr. Solomon can find that bears even the faintest gleam of the Continent, or Britain, or anywhere but here. To the island residents, no doubt Mr. Solomon's represents a slender crack in their window on the world, a life-sustaining breeze. To the Mesdames Bertrand and de Montholon, sniffing their way up and down the shelves, the window might just as well be painted shut.

"Did you hear the rats again?" asks Madame Bertrand. "They kept Hortens up all night."

"I am well aware," De Montholon intones; the walls are thin at Mr. Pourteous's Inn. "Was General Bertrand able to find out anything about when we'll be permitted to leave?"

Madame Bertrand mournfully shakes her head as de Montholon takes up a white paper fan with painted cherry blossoms.

"It is beyond comprehension," she says, snapping it open to inspect. "No accommodation has been made!"

"No."

"Is this the hospitality the Count was speaking of, I'd like to know? I could spit. I could spit into this fan."

"From Peking," comes the mellifluous voice of the proprietor, Mr. Solomon. He is standing behind them, his unctuous smile giving no clue as to whether he has been listening. Madame de Montholon doesn't care.

"It's very quaint," she says, switching to English.

"We've more behind the counter, if you'd like to see."

"No. This will be fine. Êtes-vous prêtes à partir, Madame Bertrand?"

Madame Bertrand grants. They will be back tomorrow. Mr. Solomon conducts them to his ledgers and completes the transaction, Madame de Montholon's second of the day. She bought a pair of gloves this morning.

Alas, the problem, as both the Mesdames already know, is that to put Mr. Solomon's behind them is to put the town in front of them. They step out to a depressingly uniform row of cream white buildings, all with the same flat fronts, extending for one meager mile through the heart of the valley, from the promenade all the way up to where walls finally snip it off.

The walls. Madame Bertrand can hardly bear looking at them, yet they are impossible to ignore, so high and flat and looming.

"Oh, this heat," says de Montholon, brandishing her newest purchase.

"It has nowhere to go."

The Mesdames have two choices: either inland to the left— though there is clearly nothing there (they cannot even get a carriage up the road!)—or to the right, back to the inn, the peeling gazebo, and all the sullen children. They must decide quickly, though. The longer they stand in any one place, the more attention their presence is liable to stir. Already the posted sentries have noted their position.

"It was a prison, you know," says de Montholon, granting the inevitable and starting them back to the inn. "The island, I mean. The Marquis was speaking to Dr. O'Meara, who said he'd been told that the first man ever to live here was a criminal of some kind, sent here by the Portuguese."

Madame Bertrand is not surprised. "Do we know what he did?"

"No. I don't think we do. An absolute wretch, he sounds like. The Marquis says they 'scaled' him. Have you ever heard of such a thing?"

Madame Bertrand shakes her head but doesn't like the sound of it.

"It means they sliced off his ears."

"Oh, Madame, please."

"It's true. And his nose."

"Madame, stop," says Bertrand, and she is being quite serious. The combination of this heinous description and the very real presence of this terrible canyon, grinning at them, is beginning to make Fanny Bertrand queasy.

"But then sending him here"—Madame de Montholon presses nonetheless—"with nothing but a few slaves and goats." She glances up at the valley walls. "Poor goats." She lifts her chin. "Oh, look. Our friend again."

It is Dr. O'Meara, headed their way and once again pretending to be surprised, though clearly he has been sent to fetch them.

De Montholon's welcome is suitably arch. "Dr. O'Meara."

He removes his hat, undaunted. "Une autre surprise agréable!"

"Quelle chaleur!" *This heat.* She fans.

"Et ça continue." *Still.* He offers his elbow, and the valley walls close in on Madame Bertrand.

"We were just talking about the first man ever to live here," says de Montholon. "The criminal."

"Ah, yes," says O'Meara. "Mr. Lopez."

"Have you any idea what was his crime, Dr. O'Meara?"

He ponders. "I don't."

A plump bonneted woman with a very small mouth approaches from the opposite direction. They have passed her several times already. The bonnet nods. The small mouth smiles politely, and Madame Bertrand is very nearly overcome. To be here for His

Majesty, she accepts, even to be deposited here for some unknown crime—at least it might serve justice—but the idea of actually *choosing* to live here . . . The poor woman passes by and Madame de Montholon sniffs lightly; she is apparently thinking the very same thing. "Le mariage, c'est une malédiction," she murmurs under her breath as if Dr. O'Meara will not hear or understand.

Marriage is a curse.

CHAPTER SEVEN

OCTOBER 21–22

—◀▥ʃ▥▶—

The coop, &c.—Las Cases meets Mr. Huffington—
The Reverend meets Lieutenant Wood, &c.

October 21—Toby has chosen the spot he initially sited for the coop, a hundred yards or so down the slope from Sarah and 'Scilla's cottage. There's a flat half acre, with ash trees for shade.

Toby builds the coop himself, out of hay and lumber. He has enlisted Alley to help with the fence. Yesterday they dug the trench, and today Alley is planting the bamboo poles, one right up next to the other. "I'll put up the fence," he says, grinding the tips as deep as they'll go, "but I don't tend the chicken." He sniffs the reason why.

The birds arrive midday, and Mr. Balcombe comes down soon after, to make a count. Toby hasn't finished the coop just yet—the roof isn't covered, and Alley has a way to go—but Mr. Balcombe still looks pleased when he sees all the chickens. Toby has them penned up in a small circle of hay bales.

"These are getting more precious," says Mr. Balcombe. He plants his cane, and it scissors to a stool. He opens his wastebook, and Toby counts them for him—the hens, the capons, the brooders, the chicks. Mr. Balcombe writes all the numbers twice, on facing pages.

"And how long before we're ready to serve the General?"

It's hard to say, but Toby does his best to estimate. The pullets would be ready in a month or so, if all went well. The chicks would take three, but Toby can tell Mr. Balcombe doesn't care to calculate.

"So when again?"

"They grow? Two months. Till then we keep buying from Timu."

Clearly Mr. Balcombe had been hoping for sooner but shakes off his disappointment. "Two months it is. Good man." He tears out one of the pages he's made and gives one to Toby, so they can keep track of gains or losses.

"And how much longer will you be needing Alley?"

Toby looks over, and Alley quickly resumes grinding the poles in place. "Till he finish the fence."

"Good man." Mr. Balcombe unplants his cane and heads over to speak to Alley himself.

With an escort of two leery brooders, Toby takes the crate of chicks inside their section of the coop so they can get used to the smell and the light. He has built a small open wall around them, made of garden stones, with a coal stove in the middle, to warm them at night. He'll keep the smallest ones in a gunnysack and hang it from a beam. For now he just sets them down on the hay, to wander or sit side by side, as they choose. Their down is still soft and silky, but warm inside, with little beating hearts no bigger than a bean.

No small thing, said Timu.

Alley finds him there not long after, still crouched among the chicks, though a few more of the hens and capons have come in as well, to assess their new accommodations.

"See that, what you done?" He glowers in; his lean black shadow looks like Arjuna scolding Togog. "Mr. Balcombe sees me planting the fence, take me for a worker."

"You show them," says Toby.

"Says I gotta help with Bony's house. You know how far they put Bony's house? Up?" A pullet struts in as well now, sleek, lean, with houndstooth black-and-white feathers. "Get me one of those, I tell you."

"Where the fence?" asks Toby.

"The fence, the fence. You'll get your fence." He turns and leaves, with a playful spit. But he goes to finish. Toby looks down at a white mother hen, and she agrees: Good for Mr. Balcombe.

—◦◦◦—

By mid-afternoon it is far too hot and stifling up in the Pavilion loft for Las Cases's son, Emanuel, to work, so he and his father have taken a desk and chair out onto the Balcombes' lawn. Just as he does every day, Emanuel is copying the Emperor's dictations onto larger paper, and in a clearer hand than his father's, to present His Majesty at the outset of the next day's session.

Las Cases himself is more concerned at the moment by the presence of the two sentries, now stationed on the low path which runs alongside the house. They moved down from their previous post just yesterday, effectively confining the Emperor's dictations to the Pavilion, which in its present state of clutter is hardly conducive to clear thought and expression. This morning's session, in which His Majesty tried to revisit the Battle of Tagliamento, was an utter waste, and so the Count is steeling himself, preparing to go ask the two soldiers if they might find a less conspicuous station. He has in fact just begun his descent when his son cries out from behind.

Las Cases turns to see the top dozen pages of Emanuel's finished stack flying free of the table. A breeze has swept down the inland slope and is gleefully dispersing the day's work in aimless white swings and loops. Two pages in particular seem intent on escape, tumbling across the grass in the direction of the eastern valley. Indeed, all that stands between them and their freedom is the previously unseen progress of the Balcombe tutor, Mr. Huffington, just now emerging from the far side of the bungalow, and with perfect timing. The fleeter of the two pages wraps itself around his cane, causing its partner just enough apparent hesitation for the old man to clamp it underfoot.

"Don't move!" cries Las Cases, already hustling over.

The old man obliges, holding his position exactly until Las Cases arrives to collect the fugitive sheets.

"Thank you, sir. Thank you."

"Lessons?" the old man asks, nodding up at Emanuel, who is hurriedly gathering the other pages from the lawn.

Las Cases shakes his head, plying the first page from the shaft of the cane. "No, they are His Majesty's."

The old man looks more closely now, at the page still trapped beneath his foot. The top line reads: ". . . allowing the French Princes to remain in the Prussian territories, to which the French . . ."

Las Cases can tell by the sudden flare in the old man's eyes, he understands.

"C'est les mémoires?"

"Oui," says Las Cases, tugging the page free.

The old man looks up at Emanuel again. "And the boy copies."

"Oui."

The expression on his face turns very nearly lascivious. "Privilegium magnum et grave."

Las Cases pauses. *A great and grave privilege*, the old man has said— in Latin. He must have scented something. There was a time, during the emigration, when Las Cases was himself a tutor and taught classics. It's not a part of his past that he would ever openly acknowledge, but he is too proud not to pick up the glove. He replies, "Iuveni quidem. Ita est. Nobis omnibus, quamquam tota res non favet." *For the boy, yes. For all of us—if not the best of circumstances.*

The old man understands. His eyes slant over at the lurking sentries and simmer with contempt. He says something else—this time in Greek. Las Cases's Greek is not so fresh, and he rather finds the old man's crypticism curious. Fortunately, Emanuel is now near enough to have heard. He tells him the old man wants to know how far along they are.

Las Cases looks back at the tutor and once again is reassured, for the first time gleaning in an English eye what he deems a proper respect for the significance of his undertaking. He is about to mention all the work that lies ahead for the Generals Bertrand and Gourgaud, but then he stops. Who is to say?

"L'histoire commence à peine," he replies. *The story is just begun.*

The old man bows. "Alors, plus d'interruptions." He bows to Emanuel as well and starts off along the lane.

Finally, thinks Las Cases, a discerning Englishman.

———

October 22—It has been raining at Country Church ever since the service ended. Reverend Boys is back in the small office to the right of the altar, already at work on next week's sermon. The steady pebbling on the roof provides a soothing backdrop, measured by the languid stroke of Lotte's broom out among the pews, lilting toward sleep.

Another gust of wind rattles the window, and Boys lifts his pen from his paper. Lotte seems to have lifted her broom as well, and now she appears through the doorframe, returning it to the storage room on the opposite side of the church.

"Miss Lotte?"

She turns, tired.

"Where did you leave them?"

"By the door," she says, referring to the myrtle leaves. Reverend Boys does not know why, but the congregation up at Country Church has taken to scattering myrtle leaves among the pews. It's the slaves, he knows from where they sit, and they've been doing it for years and years apparently, but they left quite a mess today.

He watches Lotte. She is moving very slowly, hand to her back, elbow crooked. There's almost no doubt in his mind.

"Miss Lotte. May I have a word with you?"

She starts over slowly, the floorboards aching beneath every little step. An exquisite creature, in her way—small, a very clear mulatto complexion, with large black eyes. It's a wonder he hasn't had to speak to her before this.

"Sit."

There is a chair by his desk. She takes it with understandable caution; there's no good reason the Reverend should want to speak to her. She perches on the edge of the seat with her elbows on the rest.

"Miss Lotte, it is not of some vain desire to admonish that the church should seek to look after its flock. You are a member of the congregation, as valued as any other."

As she nods, her eyelids waver slightly, her eyeballs roll. He speaks up.

"As such, we would know if you had married. We would bless the marriage, and if such a marriage were to bear fruit—should you be graced with child—then we would bless that child, and baptize it. You understand that?"

Again she nods.

"However, should you find yourself—"

At that moment the flame of the candle on Boys's desk flickers, and the great door out in the main room of the church cracks open. They have a visitor. Annoyed, the Reverend excuses himself to go see who.

It is an officer, one of the island's new guests, standing down at the foot of the aisle, dripping, hat in hand.

"Yes? May I help you?"

The officer crosses himself before starting up. His head is reverently low, so Boys can see that he is quite bald, yet the nearer he comes, the younger he seems. "Are you the Reverend Mr. Boys?"

Boys nods warily, and the young man proceeds to introduce himself. He says that he is Lieutenant Wood, of the 53^{d} Regiment, but it is not his rank which impresses so much as the disarming earnestness of his expression. He says that he attended service in town this morning, in hopes of meeting him there, and that the assistant chaplain, Mr. Saunders, had directed him up here.

"You came all the way through the rain?" asks Boys.

"It wasn't raining in town." The young Lieutenant smiles at his own misfortune.

Back in the office, Lotte's chair creaks, and the Lieutenant realizes that he and Reverend Boys are not alone. He looks around. "Oh, I'm sorry, Ma'am, I didn't mean to interrupt."

He introduces himself again, and Lotte is as confused as the Reverend by the young Lieutenant's manners.

"Really, I just wanted to introduce myself," he says. "We've a number of men in the regiment who meet for prayers, and I expect it's something we'll be continuing on the island."

Here Boys is given to wonder if he isn't being made the butt of some joke and that there aren't a sniggering band of soldiers waiting outside the window, yet the Lieutenant's eyes are so remarkably blue and intent, so determined and innocent, he is inclined to take him at his word. "Well, we've a group that meets on Wednesdays and Fridays," he says, "at my residence across the road there. Anyone who's so inclined is free to come."

Wood nods. "I think I can promise you at least twelve new men. This Wednesday." He seems ready to take his leave. He looks back in on Lotte to bid his farewell when he suddenly cocks his head. "Is that a leak?"

Boys turns and listens. All he can make out is the rain on the roof, lifting slightly, but the Lieutenant points across to the storage room. "In there." Boys listens again, and he can hear it now, a more insistent tapping coming from behind the door.

"It is," says the Lieutenant. "Would you like me to take a look? And you can finish. I can tell I interrupted."

The Reverend stammers. The truth is, he'd rather the Lieutenant didn't go rooting about. The storage room can be something of a mess, and he hasn't gotten around to organizing it as well as he'd like since taking over for the Reverend Eakins, but the Lieutenant is already on his way, pausing to cross himself before continuing on to the door.

The tapping grows distinctly louder when he opens it. He turns back and nods brightly, and Boys is left no alternative but to trust him. He returns to his office, and to Lotte, now having all but forgotten what he'd been saying.

Her posture reminds him, and her tired eyes, but the young

Lieutenant's interruption appears to have unnerved her as well. "I don't want to keep you, Miss Lotte. I'm sure you've other things you need to do. What I wanted you to understand is that any child born of marriage we would welcome, and baptize." He looks straight at her. Her face is a telling blank. "But you are not married, Miss Lotte."

She shakes her head.

"No. You are not. In which case, should it come to pass that you found yourself with child, that child would have no father in the eyes of the church. That child we could *not* baptize. You understand that?"

She nods.

"And you would want for your child to live within the church."

"Yes, Rev'ren'."

"Well, so would the church." He sits back. "So does the church." He glances to the window. "It looks as if the rain is letting up. Perhaps you should take advantage."

He walks her out. They both can hear the Lieutenant in the storage room as they pass. They can see him, in fact, ascending the ladder to the small loft space. The Reverend feels another twinge of violation, as does Lotte apparently. She looks back over her shoulder as if the young officer might disturb a sleeping ghost or dragon.

No howl or growl attends, however, and so the Reverend sees Lotte to the door. The myrtle leaves are in a single pile to the side. He thanks her for collecting them, but they say no more. He has made his point, and alas, he suspects her silence only confirms his fears. As Lotte makes her way out into the brightening afternoon, on listless, heavy steps, the Reverend looks down at all the gathered leaves—a long diamond shape and thick like leather, though without the earth to feed them, they become like paper. Would that all the untamed forces on the island could be burned so quickly.

"Reverend?" The Lieutenant has emerged from the storage room now. He has a crate in his arms. "I found these." He brings them down the nave to the last pew: Books of Common Prayer.

"Yes?"

"Do you think I could borrow them?" the young Lieutenant asks. "I'm sure we've some men who'd appreciate them."

Once again the request is so unprecedented Boys doesn't know quite what to say. "But do take care," he says.

"We will. I won't let the men write their names." He smiles, un-requitedly. "I put a bucket underneath the drip. It's not too bad, but if you'd like, I could come back when it's dry and see what I can do about the roof."

"No, thank you, Lieutenant. We've got people for that."

"Of course," Wood defers. "And I moved the puppets."

Boys pauses. "Puppets?"

"Inside the bench. Balinese they look like."

"Ah, yes," says Boys reflexively. He knows of no puppets.

"I slid them over to a dry wall."

"Good. Thank you, Lieutenant. How many books is it, then?"

The Lieutenant counts, eleven in all, but Boys doesn't really listen. At the door they exchange a few more words about the prayer group, then the forthright young Lieutenant makes his way back to his barracks, crate in arm.

The storage room turns out not to be as cluttered as Boys expected. Some spare chairs with torn seats and busted rungs, candlestands, a second lectern, but the space is relatively clear and passable. The bucket is over in the corner; he can hear it better than he can see it, catching the drips with loud plunks and splashes. The chest that the Lieutenant spoke of stands safely away, square against the far wall. Boys takes a candle from the sconce and holds it close.

A very plain box, but well made. The sides and slats all are clean and flush. The lid is slightly warped from water damage, with a simple clasp lock. He lifts it slightly, and out wafts the smell of must and leather.

Shadow puppets, just as the Lieutenant said. Flat cutouts, each mounted on a slender spine of bone, stacked the height of the box. Boys passes the candle over, and a shifting web of shadows cascades down through limbs and elbows, slender bones and noses, crooked legs and leering eyes. There could well be a hundred of them, arched figures with arched smiles, all painted with elaborate costumes, and embroidered with lacelike slits and fine incisions. Not all are human. There is a church, a galleon ship, what looks like a large pine tree, a white chicken, all designed by the same clever hand. Indeed, the Reverend must resist the dazzling lure of craftsmanship, though it's hardly unlike the devil to cloak himself in spangling garments. Boys has little doubt these are a vestige of the Reverend Eakins's tenure, a forgotten confiscation whose presence here he does not appreciate, if only because of their overtly pagan stench. He is inclined to throw them out. He would, in fact, if he could be certain they were not the rightful property of some absentminded island merchant. Balinese, indeed.

He closes the lid again. He takes hold of the chest by its side straps and drags it across the floor to the ladder, then he lugs it up, swinging and barking against his shins and the steps. He heaves it up onto the deck of the loft. More books, hymnals. He shoves the chest over against the inside wall and covers it with a stray blue horse blanket, just to make sure that no one will find it.

—◆—

Lieutenant Wood delivers the men their prayer books after dinner. They kneel in a circle, and Wood reads several selections: from the Order for Evening Prayer, a prayer for the Queen Majesty, a prayer for the Royal Family, a prayer for the clergy and the people, and finally the prayer of St. Chrysostom, "that when two or three are gathered together in thy Name thou wilt grant their requests." The request at question is the same as the officers have made every night for the last three weeks: that Bonaparte be reconciled to the Lord and that his soul should find salvation.

Still, when Wood lies down to bed, his mind turns back to the puppets. He has been thinking about them ever since leaving Country Church, and one of them, in particular, the one which had been torn. All the other faces were turned in profile, with exaggerated, grotesque expressions, either round and bulbous noses, or with very fine, slim features. But this one's face had been torn and stitched over. This one hadn't the long thin nose. What one saw were the eyes, and the eyes were much more gentle than the others, and downcast; both tender and reconciled, as Wood imagines Christ's upon the cross; as a gardener upon the earth, perhaps; as a man on his wife. Oh, how Lieutenant Wood misses his Louise.

CHAPTER EIGHT

OCTOBER 23-24

—⁓‿⁓—

Toby and the Emperor—Betsy's pantaloons—The first formal dinner—
The servants' dinner—A letter of complaint—Betsy tours the Pavilion—
Mr. Huffington picks up his laudanum

October 23—It is dawn, and once again Toby feels the difference he cannot name. He is sitting out on his door stoop with a cup of black tea, as he does every morning. The gate at the far end of the garden is closed and locked. He is the only one inside. Alley did not come home last night.

The early mist is not so thick. The slate path leads from Toby's stoop up and over a small ivy-covered hump and past the four fruit trees—the orange, the apple, the peach, and the fig—and he can see well beyond, the garden receding by paler and paler shades of blue: The yellow of the poppy is blue; the pink of the briar rose, another blue. And all the leaves, the stalks, and blades are heavy with dew, waiting for the sun to come and warm them dry and open them. The same as every day, yet there is something different, something raw and tender, like the throat of a child who has been weeping and can't remember why.

The roosters will be coming today. Timu is sending two after lunch, and Toby will have to go chaperon, to make sure there aren't any fights and that the eggs are safe, but it isn't that.

In the distance he can hear the waterfall and the minor birds calling to one another, falling silent. If they know the answer, they aren't saying. This difference, it is almost like a dream he can't recall, except it can't be that because Toby has not been dreaming. He isn't sure for how long, but every night now when he lies down and closes his eyes, it is as though someone had come and tied a scarf around his eyes, a tight black scarf which remains there all night long until he wakes.

And maybe that is all it is.

"Tobee?"

He turns. A voice he does not recognize is whispering his name.

"Is Tobee zere?"

It's coming from behind the hedge of Chinese rose, the other side of the garden fence. Toby can see the white silk socks and low black shoes of the monster. "Musser Bonipah?"

"Is this Tobee?" He leans forward.

Toby rises and starts over.

Bony has been up for a while already. The skin around his eyes is puffy and pale.

"Good morning, Tobee."

"Morning, Musser Bonipah."

They bow, and Bony points in the direction of the gate, muttering something in French. He wants to come in. Toby nods, he understands. He starts down, and Bony follows. Side by side they make their way on separate paths, divided by the fence. One walks like a pheasant, upright, chin high; the other is more ducklike, with shorter, balanced steps, but their pace is the same, while the various trees and shrubs and prickly pear pass between them.

They meet down at the far end. As Toby unlocks the gate, the monster attempts English. "Sometime I wake before ze ozeur."

Toby nods, he does as well, and lets him in.

"Good man, Tobee."

The monster then proceeds up the path on the right. He seems to know where he wants to go.

They pass by a low bed of teaberry, bordered all around by a family of large spire-shaped succulents. They look like enormous pinecones or artichokes, so hungry for the sun, they've pulled their root stalks from the ground. And at certain times of day, late in the day, their separate gazes all will seem to converge on a single spot, twelve feet above the center of the teaberry. Toby knows it's only because of the path the sun takes overhead, and the alignment of the trees, but still they look like a circle of swooning maidens, gazing at their invisible idol. But it is too early now. He has yet to show, and so they rest.

"Jovi-bara," says Toby, introducing them.

"They should be more modest," says Bony, pointing to their roots, which look like bustles, it's true.

Not much farther along, he finds what he has been looking for, the little grape arbor. It shelters a space just large enough for two black iron chairs and a matching table, with a tile top. More gaping succulents surround the brick border, these ranging in size from roses to lettuce heads. Bony points at one of the largest. A tan spider has built a web between the stiff fronds of an agave.

"These are no poison?"

Toby looks more closely, sees the pale brown belly, and shakes his head. Bony takes a seat.

Toby leaves him there with a bow. He must go get his hat—it's time to feed the chickens—but he takes the low path back to the gate, so as not to disturb Bony and the weaving spiders.

As he exits the garden, he can see over at the pavilion, a faint trail of smoke rising up. The lamps are on as well; the others are awake. Toby locks the gate behind him, so the monster can rest.

—⁓⁓—

"Ah. Mademoiselle Betsee!" She finds him out by the goat paths. Already the way he says her name sounds familiar. "Êtes-vous sage? How are your lessons today?" She shrugs. He likes to pretend he cares about her lessons, but he really doesn't. In fact, he's much more concerned by her pantaloons. "Why these pants?" He looks down at them with a sour expression. "You look like a little boy. If your parents aren't going to grow your brain, they should . . . Ils devraient vous enseigner comment faire pour se bien présenter." *They should show you how to present yourself.* He flicks at her hair. "C'est déshabillé. How is le petit Las Cases going to see how pretty you are?"

"I don't care."

"Of course you do. You are going to marry him some day."

"I am not. He's boring and ugly."

"He is not ugly, and he will be"—he can't think of the word, he rubs his fingers and thumb—"dear."

"Rich."

"Yes, rich. He is going to be very rich."

"How do you know? He doesn't seem very rich."

"Because. I telled you! I am dictating my memoir. I put souzand francs in his fazeur's pocket, and he knows dis."

She tells him he was going to have to put a lot more than a thousand francs in his pocket if he is going to be rich.

"Et alors! How much? 'ondred souzand. Plus qu'assez pour une simplette effrontée comme vous."

Simplette effrontée. She isn't sure, but she thinks he just called her a saucy simpleton.

"Et vous, vous mangez des grenouilles," she says. *You eat frogs.*

He grants, it's a point well taken.

————◊————

October 23—This evening the first formal dinner is held at the Briars. The de Montholons, the Bertrands, General Gourgaud, Count de Las Cases, of course, and Dr. O'Meara all are in attendance. There is no suitably equipped kitchen on premise, so the Emperor's chef, Monsieur Pierron, prepares the meal in town, in Mr. Pourteous's kitchen—calf's brains, mutton, potatoes, and onions—all of which will have to be walked up to the Pavilion.

The guests, who all are still staying at Mr. Pourteous's Inn, start up an hour or so ahead of the food, and though they are not as yet accustomed to a walk of such length, or pitch, there is no denying that the island assumes a softer, greener quality as one passes beyond the valley.

Indeed, when they finally come to the banyan lane and can see the Briars down below, it hardly needs saying that the Emperor has done well for himself. That is his due, of course, but still, to see the property from this height, in increasing shades of blue and black, nestled safely among her countless leaves and blades, needles, fronds and petals, all dancing gently in the breeze, the light within the glassed pavilion dancing cozily, while a whisper of silver gray smoke ribbons up from the neighboring bungalow, the impression of the descending guests is both distinct and mutual: Fuck Las Cases.

They pay their respects at the main house first. The Balcombes receive them in the little parlor, and they are perfectly gracious. Protocols are observed. The women do not sit until after the Emperor. The men remain standing throughout. Mr. Balcombe offers drinks—gin and wine—but the suite declines, taking their cue from the Emperor, who seldom indulges. After a quarter of an hour of pure politesse, Monsieur Cipriani enters: "Votre Majesté, le dîner est servi."

The Emperor leads the suite up to the teahouse. The light is descending, but the two sentries are clear in view, over by the corner of the bungalow. No one deigns to look. Rather, as they come upon the narrow path, the Emperor pauses to ask Madame de Montholon, does Mrs. Balcombe not resemble the empress Josephine strikingly? Madame de Montholon doesn't really think so, but knows enough to agree—*absolument.*

—————

Toby heads down for dinner at Sarah and 'Scilla's not long after the French have been served. 'Scilla has a flat stove and a table beneath the eaves where they eat. Tonight Sam is there as well—one of the boys who works for Mr. Balcombe in town. He helped carry up Bony's dinner.

"Is Alley coming?" asks Sarah.

She knows the answer, but still she asks. Toby shakes his head. "But they give him dinner up at the house, I think. At Longwood."

Sarah nods to thank him for the effort, but she is not consoled. 'Scilla then comes out, scowling, with bread and bowls. She always scowls now, since she lost her teeth, but there's no doubt her frown has been deeper since the French came.

"Where is Charles?" asks Toby. Charles is the other boy who works in town.

"Still at Mr. Pourteous's," says Sarah, "coming with the dessert. And best be quick. That Bony eats fast."

'Scilla sniffs. "Tsy-aomby-aomby," she murmurs, which is a name of the wild, man-eating beast of Madagascar, the "Not-Cow-Cow."

Toby takes a seat, disagreeing gently. "Good man, Bony."

'Scilla sniffs again and sets out four wooden bowls. Mr. Balcombe allots them twelve rashers of salt pork per week. He sets no formal limit on the fruit that Toby can pick from the trees or the vegetables he pulls from the kitchen garden, and for this he is considered a kind master. Tonight they have guava, pomegranate, and, as always, yam. They sit four in a row with their backs to the house, looking down on the bamboo fence of the coop. Sarah bows her head, and the others follow.

"Bless us, Lord," she says, "for these Thy gifts. Bless Mr. Balcombe, for sharing them with us. And bless St. Helena, for giving us her fruit and bounty and watching every step. Even Alley."

'Scilla sniffs, "Amen," and they can begin.

―――

"So this is the infamous treatment for which we are reserved!" The splay of the Emperor's fingers expresses his confoundment.

Las Cases cannot help remarking the presence of the rest of the suite has had a distinctly poisonous effect upon His Majesty. He has been very much at ease the past few days, without them, but here they are, and from the moment they took their seats around the table, they have proceeded to do nothing but complain, with no regard for the far more profound suffering of His Majesty. They remind him not only of his situation but of his powerlessness to do anything about it, to address their petty grievances, and now his food is growing cold. He has hardly touched it.

"This is the anguish of death!" he says at one point, so spurred. "If I were so hateful to them, why did they not get rid of me? A few musket balls in my heart would have done the trick, and at least there would have been some passion in the crime!"

The table does not hide that they are stung by the suggestion, but no one disagrees.

"The only reason that I am provided for at all is because of you and your wives. I'm sure I'd receive no more soldier's pay otherwise."

Again, none can dispute. He takes fuel from a bite of potato.

"But it is the monarchs who surprise me most of all, how they can permit the sacred principle of sovereignty to be violated in my person. Do they not see that they are, with their own hands, working their own destruction?" A gulp of watered wine. "I entered their capitals victorious! What if I had harbored such resentment, what would have become of them? They treated me as a brother, and I was, by every meaningful measure: the will of the people, the sanction of victory, of the church, alliance, and blood. Do they think the people will not see this?"

No one ventures an answer. Only Grand Marshal Bertrand has the courage to address the Emperor's understandable outrage. "I'm sure I speak for the table when I offer my sympathy and support for Your Majesty's grievances. I agree they should be heard, both by the governing authorities here on the island and by Europe as well. I would only suggest that we remember the Emperor's dignity and character and to that end make sure that any complaints or objections that we express are understood to issue from ourselves and not the Emperor."

All agree, His Majesty included. "By all means. I must command or be silent."

———

October 24—Just after breakfast, a Captain Desmond of the HMS *Redpole* pays a visit to the Briars, offering to carry any pertinent letters to England; the *Redpole* is scheduled to embark the next morning. The Emperor promptly dictates the following to Las Cases, while Captain Desmond waits.

The Emperor desires, by the return of the next vessel, to receive some account of his wife and son, and to be informed whether the latter is still living. He takes this opportunity of repeating and conveying to the British government the protestations which he has already made against the extraordinary measures adopted against him.

1st. That Government has declared him a prisoner of war. His letter to the Prince Regent, which he wrote and communicated to Captain Maitland, before he went on board the *Bellerophon*, sufficiently proves, to the whole world, the resolutions and the sentiments of confidence which induced him freely to place himself under the English flag.

The Emperor might, had he pleased, have agreed to quit France only on stipulated conditions with regard to himself, but he disdained to mingle personal considerations with the great interests with which his mind was constantly occupied. He might have placed himself at the disposal of the Emperor Alexander, who had been his friend, or of the Emperor Francis, who was his father-in-law. But, confiding in the justice of the English nation, he desired no other protection than its laws afforded, and renouncing public affairs, he sought no other country than that which was governed by fixed laws, independent of private will.

2d. Had the Emperor really been a prisoner of war, the rights which civilized governments possess over such a prisoner are limited by the law of nations, and terminate with the war itself.

3d. If the English government considered the Emperor, though arbitrarily, a prisoner of war, the right of that government was then limited by public law, or else, as there existed no cartel between the two nations during the war, it might have adopted toward him the principles of savages, who put their prisoners to death. This proceeding would have been more human, and more conformable to justice, than that of sending him to this horrible rock; death inflicted on board the *Bellerophon* in the Plymouth roads would have been a blessing compared with the treatment to which he is now subjected.

We have traveled over the most desolate countries of Europe, but none is to be compared with this barren rock. Deprived of everything that can render life supportable, it is calculated only to renew perpetually the anguish of death. The first principles of Christian morality, and that great duty imposed on man to pursue his fate, whatever it may be, may withhold him from terminating with his own hand a wretched existence; the Emperor glories in being superior to such a feeling. But if the British ministers should persist in their course of injustice and violence toward him, he would consider it a happiness if they would put him to death.

The sky has been gloomy all day, but Betsy still goes to look for him in the garden. "Hallo?" she calls. "Hallo? Bony?" She starts up the path to the grape arbor. "Bony? . . . Où êtes-vous?"

She stops short, seeing Toby over by the fishpond: no shouting in front of the flowers. "Have you seen him?" she whispers as loud as she can.

Toby shakes his head, and she races back to the front lawn and up the path to the Pavilion. Monsieurs Marchand and St. Denis are nowhere to be seen, so she goes right in.

He is sitting at a small table near the back.

"Hallo."

He does not answer. He is concentrating on what is in front of him, a small tin box perched above a candle flame.

"Qu'est-ce que tu fais?"

She walks right up to the edge of the desk. He is making wax impressions of coins. There is a whole pile beside him, most of which show his profile, facing right. They have made his chin very round, which it is, but he looks almost Roman. "Napoleone Imperatore E Re—1811." At the moment he is trying to set one down in the soft wax, his fingers flared like two pink crabs guarding a jewel.

There is another tin box on the table, a bonbonnière with little black pellets inside, licorice. That's why his teeth are so dark. She reaches for one, but his hand flashes over and slaps her wrist. "Shshsht." His fingers resume their pose around the coin, and very gently he sets it down in place. "Voilà." She can see now, this coin shows two standing figures that are most definitely dressed as Romans. One is of him again, resting his hand on the shoulder of another, who is down on one knee: "François II À Urchitz le IV. Decembre MDCCCV."

He looks at her. "So? Ça va?" He slides the licorice toward her. She takes one, though she doesn't really like licorice.

"This is a very nice room for a ball, you know."

He looks about and shakes his head. "Too small." He stands.

"It isn't, though. If you took away all the trunks and quelques choses. And you wouldn't have to invite the whole island."

He starts her down a makeshift aisle of trunks and "quelques choses." She has seen most of it already: his nécessaire, his washbasin, which stands on folded necks of three golden swans. But here is something new, a collection of snuffboxes, set out on a tray. All are made of gold and some enamel. One has the initial L; another, JN; another, E; another, N with a crown floating above. And there is one that is larger than the others, and also made of gold, with a diamond-bordered portrait of the Emperor in the middle, though not a very handsome one.

"You like?"

"Comme ci comme ça."

He guides her over to a lacquered chest, which she can tell is from Asia because the corners turn up like her pagoda.

"Open."

She does, and right away she knows it is the most extraordinary and beautiful thing she has ever seen: an entire Chinese city, with buildings and temples, squares, all carved from ivory. There are even little Chinese men and women on the street.

"Canton," says the Emperor, as proud as if it were the city itself. Betsy is too in awe to answer. They've even carved all the people to look different.

"When I was Emperor of France," he continues, "I grew tea in Switzerland that tasted so much like China tea even the Chinese could not tell the difference. It's true. And I made sugar out of beets. Do you know why?"

She shakes her head, still gazing.

"So that France would not have to rely on any foreign produce."

With that, he closes the lid on the ivory city and ushers her along to the next desk, which displays a service of six plates. The outer rims are all decorated in gold against a dark blue base, surrounding painted illustrations of his great triumphs. One is of Egypt, she knows, because of the figures decorating the rim and the hieroglyphics. Another is titled *The Bridge of Arcola*, where he appears very young and dashing. His hair is longer, and he is wearing a sash around his waist. He is looking back over his shoulder, and there is a flag above his head. Another plate is titled *Leipzig*, which strikes her as odd. The Battle of Leipzig was a great victory for the Allies, she happens to know. She looks at him.

He pats his paunch. "I was slimmer then."

She doesn't mind his belly; he's slimmer than her father. She turns back to the plates, the Egyptian one. It looks as if he is inside a pyramid. He is sitting on a table, surrounded by at least a dozen turbaned men on the floor, who are all looking up at him like apostles.

"Is it true that you tournee Turk?" she asks.

"Tournee Turk?"

She can't think how else to put it. She means "became a Muslim," and he understands well enough. He sees no harm.

"We were in Egypt," he says.

"So?"

"I always adopt the faith wherever I go."

"But that doesn't really count then."

He shrugs, perhaps so. "But religion is for women and priests. I am a soldier. A soldier's faith is battle." He looks at her, eyes twinkling with pride at the turn of phrase. He gestures to the service. "Would you like one?"

"Of the plates?" She looks down at them. She can hardly believe he is offering, even if he is just showing off. "*The Bridge,*" she says, pointing to the one where he has the long hair and the sash. She can tell from his expression that she has chosen well. He wanted this one.

"Very well," he says. "*The Bridge* is yours."

"Really?"

"Take, but now I must go check on the coins."

"Thank you!" She is already clutching it to her chest. "Thank you, Your Majesty." She curtsies. It is the first time she has done so, or called him Majesty, but it happens so quickly she hardly notices. Before he can change his mind, she races off all the way back to her room and hides the plate in her bureau, underneath the pantaloons.

⸺⊸⊷⊶⸺

Mr. Huffington has to make a brief stop at J. Hammond's tobacco shop before heading home, to pick up the medicine that Dr. Shortt has prescribed him for his hip. Laudanum.

"Three vials, please, Mr. Hammond."

"Yes, sir, Mr. Huffington. And all is well?"

"What's that?"

"All is well? You have everything you need?"

"Don't need much, Mr. Hammond."

"I didn't mean to suggest—"

"The vials, Mr. Hammond. The vials, I need!"

Mr. Hammond excuses himself to check downstairs, but Mr. Huffington is not alone. The tobacco shop is a fairly popular place this time of day. No fewer than five patrons are there, comfortably propped against their usual bars and stools, puffing their chosen leaves and confabulating. Mr. Huffington won't lift his eye to see who, but he knows the voices.

"I heard them," says Mr. Alexander. "*Boom, boom, boom!* I said to myself, that can't be ten already. Wasn't ten. Was quarter past nine."

"Quarter past. That's right." McRitchie.

"Warning shots, gentlemen." And that is Mr. Pritchard, as always pretending he knows best. "Not offensive."

"If you're in the boat, I'll wager they sound offensive."

"Warning shots, Mr. Alexander. The boat had entered the Road."

"Was she American?" asks a gruff-voiced woman: Miss Mason, clamped upon her pipe.

"That's right. Coming from the Cape and needing water, that's all."

"But they dumped their water. I heard." And that's Knipe, the Fowlers' doctor. "Colonel Greentree said they were sending boats back and forth all morning. Greentree went out to take a look, said a jolly told him they'd dumped their tanks just to see if they could come ashore and have a look. Apparently, we keep him in a cage on the pier."

"Did they let them in?" asks Alexander.

"They did not."

"But what about the water?"

"They brought the water out, cask by cask."

Chortles and guffaws—"well served, well served"—giving way to a galling silence, wherein all can puff their smoke and enjoy the unearned privilege of their island status. A truly noxious air, the combination; it travels straight to Huffington's hip.

Where in ages is Hammond with those vials? He thumps his fist against the glass counter and only then does he notice, in regard of his own clamor, the image underneath the glass: It is His Majesty, and a rather passable likeness, looking straight back at him from the top of a deck of playing cards—

"But they're letting in the company boats," McRitchie asks, sounding a more characteristically pitiful note.

"Oh, the company boats, yes. And the men-of-war . . ."

—He is seated on a throne draped in coronation robes, with a laurel crown and scepter, and looking out with such firm intent—

"Mr. Huffington?"

"Eh?"

It's Mr. Alexander, asking about some nonsense. "I was saying, I'm sure *you* know . . . what they were serving the other night up at the Briars. Calf brains, yes? Four. I don't mind the brains"—he turns to the others again—"but that's four mutton, gone."

Mr. Huffington can hardly bear to look at him, suffer the image of so petty an interest. He turns back to the playing cards, where the Emperor is still glowering back out at him with such a clear eye, such a firm intention, Mr. Huffington is inclined to think that they have been put here for this very reason, that he might see them—

"When's the *Newcastle* due?"

"Three weeks."

—that he might look into the Emperor's eye and hear the Emperor's voice: *L'histoire commence à peine.* The story is just begun.

And here are the vials, at last. Mr. Hammond is back and handing them over, discreetly bagged. "Are you interested, Mr. Huffington?"

Huffington has no idea what he is asking. "In what? Be clear."

Mr. Hammond taps the glass to indicate the cards beneath. "Looks a bit like Mr. Stewart, wouldn't you say? The cobbler?"

"I know very well who Mr. Stewart is, Mr. Hammond." He squints down at the image again. It looks nothing like Mr. Stewart.

"That's the last deck, if you're interested. We can put it on your—"

"Cards are for idle hands, Mr. Hammond. No, thank you." Mr. Huffington swipes up the brown bag and clambers out the door as fast as his three legs will carry him.

CHAPTER NINE

OCTOBER 25–27

———

The Emperor's daily routine, &c.—He meets Miss Legg—He ponders Toby—
The children of the suite visit the Briars, America, &c.—Mr. Huffington's dream

October 25–26—Despite the clutter hemming in their lives—or
more likely because of it—the Emperor and his suite have, by their
second week at the Briars, established a fairly fixed schedule to see
them through the day.

His Majesty rises every morning between five and six. Those in
the lofts upstairs sleep on, but Marchand and St. Denis are already
awake and know the sound of His Majesty's first stir. Marchand pulls
the green drapes of the campaign bed and lets in the light, such as it
is. The early mornings are normally shrouded in mist.

St. Denis has prepared a cup of black coffee from the dwindling
reserve of beans they've brought with them on the *Northumberland*.
His Majesty's normal preference would then be to bathe—he suffers
a mild but chronic infection of the urinary tract, which only immer-
sion really helps ameliorate—but his tub is already up at Longwood,
and he is accustomed to going without, from his time in the field.
He sips his coffee and dresses—just his bottom half at first, white
trousers and white silk socks.

There is no space inside the Pavilion to shave, so the valets have
carried his silver washbasin outside, to the far, protected side. The
water has been drawn from a nearby stream and heated by open fire.

St. Denis holds the mirror. Marchand attends with towel and blade. He is both careful and swift, and His Majesty's beard is not thick, so it doesn't take long.

A rubdown follows. The Emperor stands between them with arms slightly raised. St. Denis douses the pale and hairless skin of his torso with eau de Cologne, while Marchand scrubs it in with a soft brush. He does so vigorously but accepts it as part of the ritual that His Majesty will demand more. "Yes. Harder. Harder!" The Emperor's mood for the day can well be measured by the force of these instructions, and quite often it is to the sound of these grunts, slaps, and commands that the others upstairs awake.

"Yes, good! As if you were scrubbing a donkey!"

Once his skin is suitably pink and fragrant, His Majesty finishes dressing: a white shirt, red braces, and a long dressing gown that resembles a doctor's coat. He takes a brief walk alone, perhaps to the garden gate and back. He returns for a light breakfast of toast and sometimes jam. Las Cases attends, has his own cup of coffee, and when they are done, the two remove themselves to work on the memoir.

For now, and in large part because the sentries have chosen to maintain their post nearby the lawn, the valets have arranged a work space in the corner of the Pavilion. Las Cases presents His Majesty with transcriptions of the previous day's session. Yesterday they discussed the various letters that the Emperor discovered upon his return to Paris just last March, professing loyalty to the departed King. His Majesty had been surprised at how many were written by his own supposed supporters and confidants, but he chose not to hold the authors accountable. From yesterday's transcript:

> "We are so volatile, so inconstant, so easily led away, that after all, I couldn't be certain that these people hadn't really and spontaneously come back to my service. In that case, I should have been punishing them at the very moment they were returning to their duty. I thought it better to seem to know nothing of the matter and ordered all the letters to be burned."

The same as every day, the Emperor makes his corrections and offers elaborations, and eventually they move on to fresh material. This can take them all the way to three o'clock, at which point the Emperor requires some time to himself.

———

"You'll see," says Betsy. "He is the least frightening man."

She is leading her best friend, Millicent, out to meet him. Millicent has been begging for an introduction ever since the French moved in, but now as they approach the garden, Betsy has to pull her along by the arm.

"Général Bonaparte!" She raises her chin above the gate, which is locked again. "Général Bonaparte! Hallo!" She rattles the irons, and now one of the valets appears—the handsome one, Monsieur Marchand.

"Mademoiselle."

"J'aimerais entrer," she says. She'd like to come in. "S'il vous plaît. J'emmène quelqu'un." She has brought someone.

" 'Oo is it?" The Emperor's voice barks out from the far end of the garden, with intended overferocity. He knows very well.

"C'est Mademoiselle Betsee!" she calls. "Laissez-moi donc entrer! J'ai quelqu'un à vous présenter."

An annoyed silence follows, then: "Come. Betsee."

Betsy turns to Millicent, who has hunched her shoulders all the way to her ears. "Stay here."

Monsieur Marchand lets her in, and she races back to the arbor. He is waiting for her in his chair, feet square, fists on knees. "What is this? Who have you brought? A woman?"

"A friend of mine."

"A girl." He does not hide his disappointment.

"Yes. Her name is Millicent Legg, and she believes you are a monster."

"I see."

"I wanted to show her that you are not. I wanted to show her that you are very kind, but you must behave."

The Emperor's hand is already lifted, summoning the guest. "Bring her."

Millicent is still cowering back at the gate, and once again Betsy practically has to drag her up the path. "You'll see," she says.

"But I don't want to anymore."

"Yes, you do," says Betsy. "Now come."

He is waiting in his chair, in much the same impatient pose. Betsy pays no mind. She stands between them very formally and begins.

"Mademoiselle Legg, permettez-moi de vous présenter à Sa Majesté l'Empereur, le Général Napoléon Bonaparte."

Dutifully he rises from his chair, and for a moment it seems he is going to be perfectly courteous, but just as he is about to bow in front of her, his eyes bug out. He juts his chin, sweeps the hair up on top of his head, and howls like a monkey.

Millicent screams and flees.

When she is safely away, the Emperor lets go of his hair, and his face relaxes to an expression of great self-satisfaction.

"That wasn't very nice," says Betsy.

He shrugs. "Mebbe she is right." He howls again, straight up like a dog, but Betsy is not impressed. "That's a Cossack war cry, you know. You should be very frightened."

She simply turns on him and goes back to console her friend.

———

Time and will permitting, the Emperor and Las Cases may hold another session in the late afternoon, followed by a brief stroll. They may choose to walk either along one of the lower paths in the garden or out among the goat paths or the orchards, where they are even less likely to be seen. The Balcombes have been receiving an unusual rush of visitors since His Majesty arrived, so the Count has tried to steer him clear of ogling eyes and pointless introductions.

The one person on the property whom the Emperor is always pleased to stop and talk to is the Balcombes' gardener, an elderly

Malay named Toby. The Count well understands the appeal. Toby is indeed an agreeable fellow, his expression and demeanor unfailingly courteous and pleasant, even oddly dignified. He and the Emperor speak to each other in simple sentences, with Las Cases's help.

"The Emperor would like to know, where is your home?"

Toby gestures to the back of the garden.

"No, but first, before."

"The naime?" says the Emperor.

"Java," says the gardener.

"Java."

"Java," Napoleon repeats knowingly. " 'Ow long ago?"

The gardener does not seem to know exactly. "Long."

"You were a man there? Near to a man?"

The gardener agrees.

"You 'ave fam'lee zere?" asks the Emperor.

The gardener nods.

"And 'ow you come 'ere? Zey capture?"

The gardener nods.

"And zey bring you 'ere?"

Again.

The Emperor is openly disgusted. "And Monsieur Balcombe, he buys you?"

Toby shakes his head. "Mr. Lysander. Mr. Balcombe hire me."

"He pays you?"

"He pays Mr. Lysander."

"C'est honteux." The Emperor clucks. *Shameful.* He gestures to Las Cases that he should compensate Toby for the conversation. Las Cases takes a napoleon from a small purse and gives it to the gardener, who notes the likeness to the Emperor and offers a squinted smile before pocketing the coin.

The Emperor and Las Cases then return to the Pavilion for dinner, which is still prepared down in Jamestown and carried up by servants. Other members of the suite may or may not join him. Either way, the Emperor eats quickly, as is his way, but even more so here as there is so little space; the sooner he is finished, the sooner Marchand and St. Denis can have their meal.

The evenings are open. Again, depending upon who has come to visit, they may read aloud from classical plays or fiction—the Emperor enjoys Rousseau and Florian—or they may play games. Las Cases concedes it is his one great failing as His Majesty's companion that he is hopeless at games. He does not know chess, whist, or piquet, and so the Emperor will sometimes descend to the Balcombes' to play with the girls and listen to them sing.

Preferably he will close his day with one last walk, and indeed, these are the occasions, when there are just the two of them, safe in the fold of dark and the night crickets, that Las Cases is most certain of his decision to come here and leave his wife and other children behind. How else would he ever know the exquisite joy and honor of hearing His Majesty's most intimate thoughts?

"What is this strange machine, the human?" he asked last night, as they were walking in the moonlight. "There is not one which truly looks like another, on the inside or out-. It is when we forget this that we are prone to commit our greatest sins." With a glance back in the direction of the little cottage at the end of the garden, he continued. "Had our friend Toby been a Brutus, he would probably have killed himself. Had he been Aesop, perhaps he would now be adviser to Governor Wilkes. Had he been a Christian man, he might have borne his chains in the sight of God and been grateful for them. But he is Toby, poor Toby, who endures his misfortune quietly, who stoops to his work and spends his days innocent and tranquil.

"Certainly it is a great leap from poor Toby to a King Richard, and yet the crime is no less offensive, for this man had a family, yes? His happiness, his liberty. It was a terrible act of cruelty and injustice to bring him here to suffer the fetters of slavery.

"Ah, but I can see you think that Toby is not the only one! My dear Las Cases, there is not the least resemblance between his suffering and ours. The outrage of our confinement may well be of a higher order, but we also command very different resources. We have been subjected to no physical hardship, and if we had, surely we possess spirit enough to frustrate our enemies.

"No, our situation may yet turn out to be a kind of blessing. The eyes of the universe are fixed on us. We are martyrs of an immortal cause. Our motherland grieves; glory mourns our fate as we struggle here against oppression. Why, one could even say there is cause for gratitude. Adversity was wanting in my career, and hardship carries with it a measure of heroism, does it not? And glory. Had I died upon the throne, cloaked in the robes of power, they would always claim this was my legacy, to rule from on high. But now, here, these trials will enable all to judge me without disguise."

—◁║)╭╮(║▷—

October 27—Today, for the first time, the children of the suite come visit the Briars. There are the three Bertrands—little Napoléon, Henri, and Hortens—and the de Montholon boy, Tristan, who is a girl. There is also an enormous Newfoundland dog named Tom Pipes, who belongs to Admiral Cockburn, who has come as well.

All arrive after breakfast and are shy upon introduction, except for Tom Pipes. He and the Emperor are the only ones who show any life. Monsieur Pierron has brought a plate of sandwiches, which the children eat quietly, but as soon as they are done, the Emperor decides to lead them on a tour of the grounds. Betsy and the boys come as well and listen politely while he shows off the garden. Everything that she has told him—or that Toby or her father has told him—now flows from his mouth as though he had made it up himself: how the giant succulents surrounding the sage all point at the same mysterious spot, how the stalks of the daylilies grow right up through the blackberry bush, "like hands through prison bars." He introduces them to Toby, then they all head out to the less cultivated areas, the goat paths and the cataract. He shows them how cresses grow along the banks, and as Betsy watches the children picking them, with the water tumbling down behind them, she is reminded of what an unusual place her home is, and that she is proud of it.

The children are much more relaxed now. They begin snaking in and out of the paths as they make their way back up to the house, and Betsy begins to feel slightly too old. She leaves them to their hide-and-seek and joins the Mesdames up on the veranda, having tea with her mother.

"So how many years?" asks Madame de Montholon.

"Seven years," replies her mother.

They are talking about how long the family has been here.

Madame Bertrand smiles politely, and all Betsy can think is how lucky she is to be so tall and elegant. "A Dillon," she has heard her say, as if they should know who the Dillons are. Betsy has no idea, but covets the earrings she is wearing, the way they fall against her long neck. Lapis stones.

"And does your husband ever speak of leaving?" de Montholon continues.

"Oh, someday."

The ensuing silence is broken by a growl in the distance. The Emperor is stalking the children out beneath the pomegranate trees, or they are stalking him, while in the foreground, frail Mr. Huffington hobbles by, tea in hand, headed for the cluster of gentlemen standing on the summit of the lawn.

"Quite remarkable," observes Dr. O'Meara. He, the Admiral, the Marquis, and Mr. Balcombe are all looking back down at the Emperor, who is swiping at the dirt like a bull now, snarling, measuring the trunk of a pomegranate, behind which hide three gleefully terrified children.

"But you were saying he comes from a large family," says Balcombe.

"Yes, five brothers and sisters. But even on the boat I found his spirits to be remarkably high. Didn't you think so, Admiral?"

"He has made the adjustment quite well, yes."

"Provided one believes he's made the adjustment at all," murmurs de Montholon.

The others turn. It isn't entirely clear that the Marquis meant to be heard.

"What was that, Monsieur?" asks Mr. Balcombe.

"I said, 'Provided one believes he has made the adjustment at all.' " He explains: "I don't think he quite believes it yet."

O'Meara clears his throat. He is already familiar with the Marquis's brand of provocation. Mr. Balcombe, unfortunately, is not.

"Believes what, Monsieur?"

"Why, that he is here," says the Marquis. "To stay. He has said to me several times he believes the British will soon realize their mistake. Or that there'll be a change of hands in Britain."

O'Meara and Cockburn cannot help a faint snigger at the idea—a change of hands. England is not France.

De Montholon would seem to agree. "Yes, and that the new ministers will rescind the order and let him go, provided he doesn't return to the Continent. This he concedes."

"Where would he go?" asks Balcombe, guileless.

"America."

"America?"

"Yes, yes." O'Meara enters impatiently. "He says he would go to America, but . . . he is only thinking aloud. Conjecturing."

De Montholon merely lifts his brow: his point precisely.

Mr. Huffington has finally reached them now, and Mr. Balcombe uses his entrance to try steering the conversation to safer, more diplomatic waters. "Mr. Huffington, welcome. You've met the Marquis."

He has; he bows. "You speak of America?"

"Yes," says Balcombe quickly. "Have you ever been, Mr. Huffington?"

The tutor shakes his head, another faded dream.

"I believe the Admiral has." O'Meara turns. "Just recently, in fact."

Cockburn acknowledges. Just last December, he took part in the burning of the capital, but before he can share his impressions—and he will—there comes another shriek of laughter from the shade of the pomegranates. The stalking beast has just been felled. Alexander is pounding him with little fists. Nicholas clings heroically to his legs—the serpent unto Athenodorus—while Tom Pipes bounds around them, lapping at the monster's face.

—⬤—

Mr. Huffington suffers a more restless night than usual. He took his laudanum before retiring, but he is still too infuriated by this Cockburn to sleep. Smug, small-minded criminal, vandalizing the globe wherever he goes. If Huffington were a younger man—if he'd only had the chance again—he'd have been there waiting, everywhere the Admiral chose to go.

The agitation doesn't help his hip. When the medicine wears off, the throbbing grows so intense he cannot sleep on either side. Even on his back, gravity pulls on the joint, urging the bones to unclasp and settle flat on the mattress like fossils. Near midnight he takes a second dose, which dulls his senses and suspends him in a disturbing hinterland between waking and sleep. He does not really fall away till dawn and then is visited by a vivid dream, disturbing only in the fact that it seems so real but isn't.

He is back at the Briars, emerging from another lesson. He comes upon the front lawn to find much of the suite standing about, the children too, looking down, but he cannot tell if they are amused or concerned. Through the thicket of stockinged legs, he sees what they are looking at, the Emperor lying flat. Huffington knows it's him because of the green silk coat. He pushes through to see the face, but it's covered by a blindfold, a pillow beneath his head, a stone beneath the pillow.

Then little Nicholas leans down and tugs at the blind; he pulls it down and shows them it isn't the Emperor at all. It is Mr. Stewart, the cobbler, smiling.

Up at the top of the hill, at the "trivial" place, St. Denis and Marchand are pushing a wheelbarrow down Side Path. They are running, and Huff is beside them now. In the barrow is a coal sack, and from inside the sack, he can hear the Emperor's voice, "Allez, allez!" They are speeding him to Jamestown. They are secreting the

Emperor to the *Newcastle*. And Mr. Huffington is running alongside them as fast as when he was a boy. He remembers now, as if it were only a matter of remembering, he can run without pain if he runs fast enough. HE CAN RUN! HE IS PERMITTED TO RUN! and if he times his strides just right, and the balls of his feet touch down just so, then he can very nearly fly. Why, headed downhill he can, he can fly, if the wind is right. He lets it carry him upward, while the valets race on below with the wheelbarrow. He looks down at them, urging them on: "On, boys! On! Allez, allez! The ship is out ahead! The ship is turning! The ship is pulling anchor even now!" And as he sees their only hope turning in the bay, not even waiting, he looks back down at the struggling valets—so far to go, so far to go— and he begins to fall. He has gone too high; he cannot really fly. Not this well. Not really at all. He plummets.

He awakes in his bed just before he strikes the ground, but with such a sudden jolt, his hip would hardly know the difference. Twelve lightning bolts of searing pain shoot out in all directions from the failing joint, to every toe and fingernail. "Fool," he cries. "Old fool!" He whimpers and soon forgets. The pain is just too much, and his mind returns for consolation to its fury with that demon savage, Admiral Cockburn.

PART III

GOA

CHAPTER TEN

OCTOBER 28-29

—◆—

Winston-Kumar's puppets—The Queen's harangue, &c.—
Betsy dines with the Emperor, &c.—Toby's sleepless night—
The Conquests of Affonzo Dabakur, &c.

October 28—At the first chill breath of evening Toby heads down
to the coop to put the chicks in their bag for the night. Even as he
passes 'Scilla and Sarah's cottage, he can sense an unusual calm in the
air. There is no sound coming from within the bamboo fence. He
slides the slate stone from the gate and steps in to find the grounds
entirely still and quiet. The hills are barely a silhouette; the sky is
only lavender. For some reason the chickens don't care to watch.

Not wanting to disturb them, Toby rounds to the far side of the
coop. The chicks are all gathered inside the little stone turret he
built them, waiting beneath the gunnysack, which hangs limp above.
Soon they'll be grown enough to sleep out in the open—he'll use a
drawer from the cellar—but for now he sets them down at the bottom of the sack, one by one, nestled in beside one another. As he
lights the stove, the little birds chirp their good nights, while inside
the main space of the coop, there is a curious contentment to the
quiet. Not so much as a stray shift or cluck.

Toby ducks his head in. The hens are all perched in two rows,
along the two perching poles. Only the nearest notes his entrance.
She offers a scolding glance, but Toby can tell by the way she turns
her head away, she is hiding something. They all are. He leans in farther and looks back around at the near peak.

All he can see is a shadow at first, a dark shape four hands high, propped upon the second pole, but even in that glimpse he knows, as clear as if the thing had dropped into his lap. He knows the slope of the shoulders, the stumped arm, the tilt of the head. It's Lopez, and now he understands the question he has been asking every morning. What is not here is here in front of him now. Or its puppet is, and for an immeasurable moment Toby is still, locked by the conflict between his elation—as if something gold within him had been awakened and were rising—and his fear—as if a basket of snakes had been toppled over.

"Who found you?"

His eyes have adjusted to the dark now. He can see the slender bone upon which the hard leather cutout is mounted, he can see the warp in the leather, and he can see the eye. It is looking over Toby's shoulder, as if to answer him. He turns, and there in the corner is the rumpled blue of Alley's blanket, swaddled around what looks like a bundle of kindling, but Toby knows better.

He lifts the hem just enough to see the buckskin boots with steely spurs. He sees a beetle-back hat, and just like that, the little sun inside Toby turns cold.

He moves quickly. He takes Lopez down and wraps it inside the blanket with the other puppets—four or five, he did not see exactly. One of the chickens gobbles her objection, but Toby pays no mind. He tucks the blanket under his arm and starts back up to the garden.

He must take care, but he must keep moving, too, and make sure no one sees or wonders at the slender bones sticking out the end of his bundle. He hustles through the garden gate and up the main path, with his head low and his eyes searching all around.

His arm is aching by the time he reaches his cottage. He dumps the blanket onto his chair, but before he can catch his breath, he sees two more familiar shadows waiting for him in the twin windows: the King and the Queen—JohnSree and Esta. She is more clear because the sky is behind her, and still bright enough to pierce all the embroidery on her face and robes, and pronounce her silhouette: the long sharp nose, the gangly arms and slender fingers for pointing and thrusting and smacking her husband, the King.

Then, just as if he'd willed it, the right arm flicks, and there comes a deliberately high and strident voice: "That is some kingdom there, of PrestaJohn!"

The arm flicks again, and Alley's face appears beside her, grinning broadly at him through the open window.

"Where did you find them?" asks Toby.

Alley pulls back. This is not the reaction he had been expecting. "What you care where? Here."

"Where is the others?"

Alley is confused. "You want the others, I can—"

Toby shakes his head. "You take them back."

"Mora-mora. I'm not taking them back." Alley peers at him and tries prying a smile. "You're like 'Scilla."

" 'Scilla knows?"

"No." Alley pauses. He is not used to seeing Toby like this, so cowed; it makes him angry. "What you so scared of? This?" He swipes in the direction of the tea pavilion and Bony. "Or what they do?"

"Shsht," Toby hisses. He is not frightened of Bony, or the redcoats. "The puppets," he says, "should not be spread."

"Well, I'm not taking them back." Alley pushes away from the window. "Dig a hole and bury them." He wanders off, but Toby can still hear him talking. "Burn 'em, what I care . . . old Yam-Stalk . . ."

Toby did not mean to drive him off. He knows that Alley only meant to please him. And Toby is pleased—that is the strange part—he is thrilled, but too nervous to enjoy. He calms only when he looks at the King and the Queen, because they are so familiar: John-Sree and Her Serenity, Esta. She looks back at Toby with her arched smile and crooked back. And now he hears another voice, deeper and more nasal, and coming from inside his mind.

> Oo-oh, most lovely, beautiful,
> and pleasing to the ear,
> Queen Esta.

Toby smiles. Winston-Kumar's voice, or one of his voices; Winston-Kumar, whom Toby never knew so well, but whose eyes were most like his, and whose skin, and who, when he smelled sweet cassava, would be reminded, too, of the old island where they both came from; Winston-Kumar, whose passing Toby still grieves, though he is dead for fifteen years now, buried out beneath the yew tree at Fairyland.

Winston-Kumar was a dalang. Ombiasy is what the blacks all called him. He was the one who made the puppets, cured the leather, cut the designs, painted them, and gave them life, with lantern light and all his voices. He was the only dalang on St. Helena, but that was enough. St. Helena was not as old as the island where Toby and Winston-Kumar came from, so there weren't as many spirits with stories to be told. Nor was there as much time to tell them. Only when the masters went off dancing, which happened once a season, then all the slaves who could would find their way to Mr. Doveton's barn to watch Winston-Kumar and his brother, Henry, perform.

Toby was still working for Mr. Breame back then, as was Timu, with his barrel chest and his pick of women, like Alley. Together they would walk down to Sandy Bay. With the light descending, Mr. Doveton's barn looked like a giant shadow lantern down at the bottom of the slope, and they could hear the voices inside as they descended, and the clanging of Henry's makeshift gamelan—not the same sounds that Toby heard when he was a boy, but close enough that when he heard, and when they stepped inside, he could feel himself breathe deeper.

The air was always thick with the smell of hay and spiced cigarettes, the smoke catching the lantern light and suspending it, blue. Depending on what time of night it was, there might be a dozen slaves there, watching, or four dozen, all sitting or standing in a great circle around the edge of the space. Oliver was always there, from Maldivia, the Burnham twins from Mount Pleasant, all the children from Miss Mason's. The Chinese brothers. They came and went throughout the night, as they were able, but Henry and Winston-Kumar never stopped till dawn.

And it was just as any dalang at home would do. They set a great white sheet in the middle of the barn, stretched tight across a wooden frame. There were no gamelan instruments on the island, so Henry made do with copper pots, spoons, bells, and a fiddle he strummed on his lap. Winston-Kumar knelt beside him, with the pinewood chest just to his left. That was where he kept the puppets, and also he would use the sides like a drum, tapping out rhythms as the shadows made their entrances and exits. They danced and squabbled, staged great battles, sang laments and spat, and when their parts were done, Winston-Kumar would plant them upright in the soft wood of the banana tree logs that supported the frame, the good characters on the right-hand side, the bad ones on the left. And the only light in the room was the oil lamp behind Winston-Kumar, which cast the shadows of all the players, and the moths flitting around the flame, as big as birds. The children sat up front, always on the shadow side. The adults were free to choose their places.

The only real difference from when Toby was a boy were the stories. These were not about the Pandewa brothers, or their cousins the Kurewas. There was no Judistra, or Bima, no Arjuna or Kumbekama. Winston-Kumar's tales were about the slave named Oliver who led Kedgwin's army up to Prosperous Bay. They were about Lot, the siege of Sugarloaf, and Edmund Halley. But of all the stories Winston-Kumar told, the most important by far were those of Fernao Lopez, the greatest of the island spirits, other than Helena herself. He was her groom, some believed, and they worshiped him especially because he had lost his home, too, and then he found it here on St. Helena.

But he never would have found her at all, or even had to look, if the skinny, screeching Queen now propped in Toby's window had not long ago come pestering her husband, King JohnSree.

I

"I have read the letter!" she would cry, holding the parchment in her slender hand. "The letter you would not let me see. I have found the letter! I have had my mistress read it me, and now I know! I know why you would not let me see."

Then she would slide up to her husband's ear. "That is some kingdom there of PrestaJohn. Some kingdom, yes. How many kings beneath his crown, do they say? Seventy-two! Three score and a dozen more! And when he sits to dinner, did you read? How many bishops does it say are there with him? Twelve bishops, sitting on his right. And thirty more archbishops on his left. Oh, that is some kingdom there, belongs to PrestaJohn."

"Is no small t'ing, no," replied the King.

"No small t'ing? It say all men and beast is ruled by him, from Amazon Queen to serpent to snail. Even the monster ants that dig gold— What is this?"

"I don't know."

"—the monster ants that dig gold, they are there, and the fish that bleed the purple, these are ruled by him as well."

"Yes," the King admitted wearily.

"And all precious stones and perfumes, they are possessed by him, did you read? His scepter is made of emerald. The magic pebble which gives light, restores sight, and makes the holder so he cannot be seen, PrestaJohn possess this pebble. He possess the Sea of Sand, the fountain of youth, and all the fish of wondrous savor. The underground stream whose sands are in themselves gems, this stream is his. They say he wears a salamander robe which is washed in fire—"

"I never understand."

"No, but you would like this robe, yes? And you would like it too if when you would go to war, thirteen crosses precede you in chariot, made of gold and stud with jewels, and each of these is followed by ten thousand knights and hundred thousand footmen—for this is what they say."

"Yes, is most impressive."

"Most impressive. And there are no poor in Presta's kingdom! No thief, no flatterer, no miser, no lie, and no vice."

"If the letter is to be—"

"And his throne, did you read? They say it sits on a pedestal twelve flight high, with a great mirror on top, so large it sees all that happens in his dominion, all plot and conspiracy."

"Yes, would be very nice throne."

"Yes, I think. And to be served by seven king at once. And sixty duke, and three hundred sixty-five counts. And to clean the sewer, a king. And to dress him, a bishop and a king. To make his bed, another bishop, and another king. To brush his horses, the archimandrake and a king. And to cook his dinner, he got an abbot and a ki—"

"Yes, yes, my sweet, I see." The King would finally stop her. "I know, is some kingdom. And you are not, believe or not, the first to think of finding it. I am tempted many times myself to go and look, as was my father, and my father's father, but . . ." And here the King would grow uncomfortable. ". . . but is very far."

Far, the King continued, and also hidden behind the empire of the treacherous Moor, the mere mention of which would cause his crown to tremble. He said the Moor were like a "giant wall of fire rising from the desert sand," and that it would not be wise for the Portingale to try passing through. "For what good is the scepter to the cinder?"

The Queen was not patient with her husband's cowardice. She would summon the sea captain Dagama and make him tell the King—*again*—that he had discovered a way around the Moor.

"The coast is long," Dagama would explain. "The coast it go and go, but if you follow far enough, it sweeps you round, and there you come to Indi."

"You understand?" the Queen would caw. "You go the way Dagama go, then you don't have to pass through fire. And maybe you find your PrestaJohn, and the river of jewels, and all that other stuff."

The King did not question his brave and humble Captain, but still he was not sure. First he had to speak to his friend and adviser, the high priest Poklemmit, who in appearance was more like Togog, more ogrelike, with a bulbous nose, a beetle-back hat, with white tufts of hair puffing out the sides. Poklemmit looked like the Reverend Eakins, the island pastor before the Reverend Boys—and he acted like the Reverend Eakins too, pretending with words to all the grace and beauty he lacked in person.

Poklemmit knew of PrestaJohn. He had read the letter too. He knew of all the bishops and archbishops who were said to sit at the Presta's dining table. He knew of the salamander coat, the mirror, and the river of jewels. Above all, he knew about the crosses which were said to precede the Presta into battle. And so when JohnSree now explained to him how this Dagama had found a way around the Moor, Poklemmit was most intrigued.

"If he is there, or something left behind, then we should go and look."

"But what if he is not?" asked the King, still nervous. "What if there is only more . . . Moor?"

"Then they have taken what is his," replied Poklemmit, doubt-less. "And we should have it back."

"Ah-haaaaaa!" the Queen cried gleefully, scrambling to her husband's ear. "You hear what your friend say? Why do you wait?"

"I do not wait." The King would sigh. "Go build the boats."

And Henry would start clanging on his copper pots, and rattling his spoons, the clamor of the boats being built—the fleet of mighty *karak*—and all the children would join in, imitating with a nasal whine and clicking tongues.

. . . *kara-kara-kara-kara-kara-kara-kara-kara* . . .

Toby rises at the sound, the memory of the sound, and takes the King and Queen down from the sills. He sets them on the chair with all the rest, wrapped inside the horse blanket; then he goes to dinner. Sarah and 'Scilla will be waiting.

—◁▦▷—

"Come," says the Emperor to both Betsy and Jane. "Eat dinner with us." He means in the Pavilion.

"But we've already eaten," says Betsy.

"Then you will watch me."

They do. Monsieur Cipriani serves chicken again, which the Emperor eats twice as fast as the two Las Caseses.

"Why is chicken the only thing you ever eat?" asks Betsy.

"All I eat is not chicken." He chews. "I eat many things." He drinks. "It is you Eenglish who only eat rosebif and plum pudding."

"That's not true."

"Yes. And jeen, to drink. Jeen, rosebif, and plum pudding." He looks across to Las Cases and winks.

"At least they're not frogs," she says, and she thinks of the picture she has, cut from a newspaper, of the Frenchman with an empty spoon and frog on his nose.

The Emperor merely smiles as Monsieur St. Denis clears his plate. "Creams?" he asks.

Neither of the Las Caseses has finished his main course, but Monsieur Cipriani appears with a silver platter heaped with dessert creams. Betsy made the mistake a few days ago of complimenting Monsieur Pierron's creams, and the Emperor has been forcing them on her ever since. "These are the one you like, yes?"

"I told you I'm not hungry. I ate."

"You didn't eat. Now sit. Eat the creams." He sets two on a plate and slides it in front of her.

"But I don't want any."

"Yes, you do. These are the ones you say you like."

She clamps her lips.

He huffs at her stubbornness and looks to the boy. "Emanuel, show her. Eat." He hands a plate to Emanuel, who obediently eats a cream.

"See? They are very good."

"I'm sure they are quite delicious," says Betsy. "I just don't want one now."

He clucks his tongue and turns to Emanuel. "She is going to be trouble." He means when she and Emanuel Las Cases are married, which makes her even angrier. He smiles. "Mais elle est bien jolie quand elle est si têtue, n'est-ce pas?" *But she is very pretty when she is being so stubborn, isn't she?*

Emanuel says nothing. He doesn't know what to do.

"Come," says the Emperor. "Kiss her."

"He will not," says Betsy.

"Yes." The Emperor likes the idea. "Stand."

Emanuel stands.

"Now go around. Show us how you give the girl a kiss. Show her."

Poor Emanuel is frozen, but Betsy doesn't care. She glares at him.

"Do it!" commands the Emperor. "You will do this for l'Empereur. Emanuel, go. Donnes lui un petit baiser." *Give her a kiss.* Emanuel looks over at his father, who nods that he should do as the Emperor wishes.

"Yes, right here." The Emperor taps his own cheek to show him where.

Emanuel starts around the table.

"He'd better not," says Betsy, but Emanuel is now standing beside her. The Emperor taps his cheek again, and Emanuel obeys. He closes his eyes and leans forward. Betsy is appalled. He puckers his thin little lips. No sooner do they graze her cheek than she strikes him, open-handed and square across his face, so hard his forelock falls. Las Cases bolts up in his chair, but before he can respond, the Emperor roars with laughter, clapping his hands.

"Ah, Emanuel, now you see who is the true Emperor."

Emanuel's face is burning red, but the Emperor is more concerned with Betsy's hand. He takes it and looks at the palm. "Êtes-vous fait mal?" He should kiss it, she thinks, and he looks as if he might, but he does not.

"It's fine."

"Good. Now, we go play whist."

She is still very angry at him as they make their way down to the main house. He leads them, single file. Betsy is at the back of the line, then Jane, then the Las Caseses, then the Emperor. When they come to where the pathway narrows between two stony embankments, Betsy decides to act. Before she can think twice, she shoves

Jane, who falls into the Las Caseses, who both stumble into the Emperor, who barely catches himself from falling over, but he still looks ridiculous. Betsy laughs, just as loud as he did, but clearly the Count doesn't think it's so funny. He grabs her by the arm and turns her abruptly against the embankment. "Young lady, you are a rude little hoyden!" His fingers are digging in.

"Ow," she cries. "You're hurting me."

The Emperor can see that Las Cases has been too rough. "Here, don't cry." He takes Las Cases by both elbows. "You may hit him."

Betsy does not waste the opportunity. She rears back and pounds him in the shoulder.

"There," says the Emperor. He lets go, but she is not finished. She lands another blow on Las Cases's other shoulder, then a third. She rears back again, but before she can swing, Las Cases runs away out onto the lawn. She chases after him, much to the Emperor's delight, landing punches as she goes. She finally corners him up against the embankment and wales her fists at him, stopping only when she grows tired.

"Very good," says the Emperor. "Enough. You must know when your opponent has surrendered."

Las Cases has surrendered, but she adds one more blow for good measure, and she can tell it hurt. He is still rubbing his shoulder as they proceed to the bungalow to play their game of whist.

———

Toby said nothing at dinner about the puppets. Hardly a word was spoken, but for Sarah's asking yet again if Alley slept at home last night, and Toby's saying he isn't sure, though he thinks the answer is no.

As usual, he has poured himself an evening tea to take back with him and lit himself a cigarette of dried banana leaves. Its amber tip is a lazy firefly, floating back through the black womb of the surrounding hills to the little cottage on the right, at the far end of the garden.

The blue horse blanket is as he left it, on the chair with Winston-

Kumar's puppets inside. Toby sits on his bed, a simple mat laid on flax. He sets his tea down on the floor. He lights his oil lamp, which illuminates the blanket, which sits still in its chair, its shadow wavering gently on the wall.

Toby watches it, his arms upon his knees, moving only to lift the thick spliff of banana leaves to his mouth. The shadow trembles like a restless, impatient heart, and Toby knows whose it is; he can hear his voice, as clear as if Winston-Kumar were standing in the corner.

You there!

A deep, commanding snarl. And if Toby closes his eyes, the figure appears just as clearly, with his long, sharp beard, his spurs, his hat the shape of a diamond on its side.

Men of Cochim, tell me, who among you knows this?

And he would hold his cross out like a sword, while all the huddled men of Cochim looked and shook their heads.

Then tell me—who among you knows the metal which it's made from?

And he would press the cross against the sheet to show them—gold.

"*Aaaah, yes.*" All the huddled Moor of Cochim would smile; *this* they recognized. They would point and nod, unaware that Dabakur was now lifting the cross even higher above his head, so that he could bring it down that much harder, and bludgeon their heathen skulls with it, and smite them dead.

Toby rises. He does not want the puppets inside. He takes them out onto his stoop. He looks at the orchard beyond the fence, but why? And what did the Briars do that they should have to hide these stolen spirits? There is a nail beneath the eaves outside where Toby sometimes hangs his fruit to ripen and keep safe from the ants. Tonight he hangs the blanket there with the puppets cradled safe in-

side like baby chicks, as if by suspending them there, touching nothing, their stories cannot reach him.

He returns to his bed and lies down, hoping sleep will come—
come quick and tie its scarf around his eyes. But Toby's ears are too
wide open. The orchard trees are shifting in the breezes, and he can
feel the puppets swinging out beneath the eaves, as if his hut and
they were balanced on the same long limb. He is meant to listen
tonight, he knows. The damp night air sweeps through the coarse
wool; it curls around their slender limbs and lace, and carries their
memories through Toby's open window and into his room—their
rhymes, their screams, their cheer, their song; it carries the chimes
and clangs and clatters of Henry's gamelan, and the shadows come
drifting in as well, to float above his head and fall like incense all
night long, not letting Toby sleep, not letting him wake, not until
he remembers everything of how it happened that the noble Dom
Fernao came to be punished so.

II
The Conquests of Affonzo Dabakur

JohnSree and his Queen sent many Captains around the Cape to
see what they could find and fill the bellies of their boats. There
was Dagama, of course—the one who found the way—but there
was Dakunha as well, and Danova, Tehera, and many others who
found great success in the distant kingdoms of Nirindi—of
Mozambique and Calicut, Cochim, Calayat, Coulau, and Ormuz.
But of all the men that JohnSree sent, there was one more fierce
and determined than all the rest, who wore a long, thin beard and
buckskin boots with steely spurs, and who never forgot: The King
and his high priest, the holy of holies Poklemmit, had not asked
the Captains just to find them treasure; they had asked them to find
an empire. So when this brave Captain arrived in all the wondrous
distant kingdoms, always the first thing he did was ask the people
there if they had ever heard of PrestaJohn, or of the cross to which

he prayed (for how else did they come by their riches, he would wonder to himself, than by stealing them from the once great Priest-King?). And when the people there would shake their heads and say they did not know, and they had never seen this cross, this one most determined Captain made them pay. He punished them as he would a liar, a thief, or a traitor. He set their boats on fire and cast them all adrift. He toppled their temples, looted their homes, and maimed their horses. And when he returned to his King and Queen to show them all the many treasures that he'd found, he always promised them one more: that he would find the Presta and see his kingdom restored. So pleased were the King and Queen by this, and by the riches he brought with him, they sent him back with yet more boats, with bigger bellies, and they named him Viceroy of Nirindi, the great and fearsome Affonzo Dabakur.

> Who where 'er he go,
> the skies all black and smoky grow,
> and soon the sea run red,
> from all the Moor blood that he shed.

It was not long, of course, before word of the brutal Portingale reached the ear of the great Moor King, Hidalcao. He understood that this Dabakur was a menace, so he called together all his Princes and all their armies from all across the empire—the Turks and Rumes as well. They met in a city on the water called Goa, and there made plans how they could meet this fiend, and all those who followed him, and drive them from Nirindi for good.

But here they only showed they did not know the man whom they opposed, for when Dabakur heard this, that all the armies of the Moor had gathered together in one place and were plotting against him, he did not turn and run as so many would have. Nor did he go and plunder the other defenseless cities, as many of his Captains urged he should. Instead he called together his own men and bade them to prepare to go to this place, Goa.

"But it is all their armies," the frightened Captains warned.

"Why, they outnumber us as one by ten, and they have seen our ways. We cannot take them there."

Dabakur only shook his head. "How the coward does not hear himself. If Goa is where they gather, then Goa is where we go."

But he told them he did not want the doubters coming with him, or the faint of heart. "You give me only men of faith," he said, "who feel the Lord's eyes burning on their back, and they will be enough."

So the doubters stayed behind. Dabakur took with him only the bravest and most loyal of his Captains: Camelo, and Rabelo, Lopez, and da Silva, and all the men who followed them. Together these few set sail for Goa, and for the fortress which protected it, called Benastarim, and though they were outnumbered and thrown back at first, they soon returned and struck down the wall. They stormed the streets and drove out all the armies waiting there, including the Turks and the Rumes. And when those fearful Captains back in Cochim heard this—that Dabakur and his loyal band had taken the city—they cursed their cowardice and envied the ones who had gone, for they knew their names would live forever, as heroes, as the men who had taken Goa from the treacherous Moor: the brave Camelo, and Rabelo, da Silva, and Lopez.

And now that Goa had been taken and was safe, Dabakur set about repairing her. And on the third day following his triumph, as his men were clearing the fallen stones from the great city wall, one spied a shining trinket buried in the rubble. Dabakur was summoned, and when he saw, he took the trinket and held it up. "A sign," he cried, showing them. It was a little copper cross.

> Which our Lord hast planted here
> for us to find! A sign, so that we may know,
> and whosoever doubts, that we may show:
> was once another kingdom here.

Then, as he held the little cross high above his head, his inspiration turned to fury. "Now, go you, and find the Moor remaining! Search the streets, search the houses, search every well and cupboard, and take them to the temple where they pray!"

And it was done. All the streets and houses, all the cupboards and every jar were broken in search of the Moor, and when they were found, they were taken into the greatest of the temples, every last man, woman, and child, until there were six thousand there, all crammed inside.

"Now bolt the door!" cried Dabakur.

And it was done. The door of the temple was bolted shut.

"Now put the torch unto this place, and guard it well, till every seed inside is burned!"

And this was done. The Portingale put their torches to the temple, and as the flames took hold and all the Moor inside began to wail, Dabakur held high his little cross and proclaimed, "The kingdom which was buried here is born again this day in Goa."

But his own men could barely hear him, as could the slaves in Mr. Doveton's barn, so terrible was the howling of the Moor, trapped inside the blazing mosque. . . .

Toby can hear them even now, and it isn't just the sound of Henry's gamelan. It is their voices crying, all as one, deep inside the cricket hum outside and all the shivering trees—the wailing, burning Moor. Toby wishes he could shut his ears. He wishes he could rise and take the blanket down, but it is as though the night were pinning him to his bed, holding him in its shadow and making sure he hears—the awful cries Lopez brought here with him and stuffed inside the trees and caves, so they'd remember too, and all who listened and all who knew: the sound of his faith failing. And it does not stop, it will not stop, it did not stop, even at the giddy cry of the high priest Poklemmit, Holy of Holies.

"Gather round," he'd call, from his perch atop the eight-step pedestal, gleeful at the news of the Portingales' success . . .

all sheep of the flock,
And listen to the news the winds have brought,

of how our fearless Captains meet triumph on triumph.
Now whenever you doubt, you think of them,
and how the Lord doth favor those of constant faith,
how He doth guide the fate of those who never question
and give their life to him. . . .

They gathered at his feet, and so he told them, to the distant cries
of the burning Moor, how Dabakur had been emboldened by his
victory at Goa, to continue his search for the Great Priest-King. As
soon as he was sure the fortress walls were strong again, and that
the men he left behind were true enough and brave enough to
protect her, he set sail again and led his little fleet around a second
cape, unto a world of countless unknown islands: Sumatra, Campar,
Ceylon, and Java, Cambaya Narsing, and Malacca—"the golden
kingdoms of the east," he called them, "where everything desirable
in life, they have there in abundance." Dabakur was amazed by all
he found, and just as he has done in the Nirindi, he then did in the
Far-. He asked among the people there, the Kings and the fishermen
alike, if they knew of PrestaJohn, and when none could say yes, or
account for the wondrous gems and treasures they possessed, he
spilled their blood into the seas surrounding, so fast and thick that
the other Kings of the nearby islands were soon rowing to his
conquered shores and kneeling at his feet with offerings of peace.
They brought him golden cups and swords, bells, lances, elephants
and iron lions, seamstresses, scarlet and velvet crimson. One even
brought a bracelet said to protect its wearer from ever bleeding.
    "And so you ask yourself," Poklemmit posed, as the distant
howls only now began to die away . . .

    what better proof our Lord is true,
    than that so few should go so far,
    and win so much from so many.
    Let us give thanks to the Lord our God
    for the favor He has shown:
    Thou art the Captain, Thou the Counselor.

Thou that doth strike fear into our enemy,
and maketh them to flee the glory of Thy Name. . . .

And finally the Moor were silent.

Yet all was not entirely as well as Poklemmit told the flock, for though it was true that Dabakur had met with much success in the golden kingdoms of Farindi, much treachery was taking place in his absence back at Goa. From the moment he sailed away, in fact, the Moor King Hidalcao was scheming his return, and by the wiles of two Princes—first the impetuous Pulatecao and then the clever Rasalcao—the Moor had retaken Benastarim, the fortress which stood across the bay from Goa and was meant to protect it. It was even said that some of Dabakur's own men, the noble Portingale whom he had chosen to protect the city, had since crossed over the bay to join with them.

When Dabakur was told all this, he left Farindi at once, for there was nothing in all the world he cherished so much as Goa. Goa was like his only child. So he packed up all the gifts that he'd been given—the wooden castles on the elephants' backs, the palanquins, the iron lions, the scarlet, the bracelet, the velvet, and the seamstresses—and set sail. But he was not three days into his journey when, off the treacherous shores of Sumatra, the false gods stirred a storm and threw his fleet against the rocks. Dabakur's own boat, the *Flower of the Sea*, was smashed to splinters. All the gifts—the elephants and wooden castles, the palanquins, the iron lions, the scarlet, the bracelet, the velvet, and the seamstresses—sank down to the bottom of the sea, and it seemed that Dabakur was surely lost as well, but as it happened, the Cross God had not yet withdrawn his hand from his faithful servants, for the great Commodore was thrown upon a floating mast and rescued by another *karak* in his fleet, and even as his Captains pleaded with him not to, he entered back into the storm and saved the least of his men from the furious waves.

With his remaining ships, he then returned to Cochim, and when the people saw him there, they were amazed, for they had thought him lost as well. They called for a great celebration, but all Dabakur wanted was to know about his precious Goa, how did she fare?

At this, the Captains bowed their heads and told him what a woeful winter it had been, that since the fall of Benastarim, the Moor had been pounding the city walls with their guns, and that a length had just now fallen. And they said the Moor had blocked their gates and ports

> so they cannot get their bread in Goa.
> They cannot get their oil.
> And the children hath grown deaf
> from cannon roar.

Now Dabakur was much distraught. "Then go," he said. "Go to Goa now, and tell the people I will be there soon."

At this the gamelan bells would ring, the beads would hiss the joyous call of all the Goans celebrating the return of their savior. *Hhhhhaaaahhhhhhh*—they let out a cry so high and resounding it rose from the streets of the city, carried across the harbor, over the fortress walls of Benastarim, where two shivering guards stood in a cannon turret.

". . . What is this noise? Coming from the city?"

". . . It is a howl. Did we take the streets today?"

They listened to the bells and beads. "But it don't sound like howl. . . . It sound more like . . . joy."

"But what they got for joy in Goa? Got no food."

"Got no oil."

"Got children deaf from cannon roar."

"Yeah, what they got to sing about?"

Hhhhhaaaahhhhhhh.

". . . Got no wall."

"And their Dabakur is dead, is lost at sea."

The first guard paused. "You hear *dead*?"

"You don't hear dead?"

"I hear only lost. . . ."

The bells and beads kept on, as all the Goans cheered across the harbor, and the two guards turned to each other slowly, not shivering now from cold, but trembling from fear.

Dabakur wasted no time. As soon as he entered the city, he gathered together his Captains and told them his plan. The fortress of Benastarim was half surrounded by water, half by land. So he would divide his men—"half to boat, half to boot." The boots would stay in the city, to guard the streets and await his word. The boats he would lead across the harbor that very night, to barricade the fortress on the water side.

But as the men were taking their final meal before the launch, a letter was delivered from King JohnSree and given straight to Dabakur. It said how pleased His Highness was to learn that the great Commodore was still alive, for in him resided all the hopes of the Portingale, both in the Nirindi and the Far-. But was it wise, he wondered, to place such stock in this one place, Goa? Was it worth the losses they were sure to suffer, just to have it back?

When Dabakur finished reading the letter, his men all asked, what did their King say? Dabakur told them: "that you are his pride and the pride of all Portingale, who pray for us tonight." And he put the letter away so no one would ever know of His Majesty's uncertainty. "Now let us go."

The first to see the fleet approaching Benastarim were of course the two guards in their turret.

"Hoy," said the first, peering into the darkness. "Is some black upon the blue."

"Waves," said the other.

"No . . . There . . . A sail . . . And another . . . And another. Do you not see?"

The second guard now peered and nodded. "Turn the cannon."

And they turned their cannon, which had been pointed at the city walls all winter long, and aimed it down at the twelve silent shadows now creeping through the water toward them. And they fired—

Boom!

—the gamelan roared, and—*crash!*—their shot smashed down into the waves surrounding the black fleet. None of the boats was struck, but the archers of the Moor were summoned by the blast. Now they appeared beside the guards, in turrets of their own, and seeing the dark shadows out in the distance, they stretched back their bows. The cannon roared again—*ka-boom*—and the archers flung the arrows into the sky. Like a flock of herons, they pierced the moon and fell down on the Portingale fleet, which was staggered this time but not stopped. Still they kept creeping closer to the stony walls of the fortress.

So again, the archers and the gunmen loaded up their weapons. They even turned the greatest of their cannons now, the Giant Basilisk, whose massive barrel reached out over the wall like a giant black arm, and—

BOOOOOOM!

—the gamelan thundered. Another flock of arrows went sailing through the air, behind another flight of stone and shot, and this time the great ball from the Basilisk did smash into the flank of a boat, which then began to sink. The armies of the Moor all stood and watched to see if this would stop the fleet, but all they heard was one proud voice, crying out, "Stay with the Captain! Stay with the boat, and we shall find you!" And still the shadows kept creeping closer. The lead in fact was just now sliding its prow underneath the floating gate which surrounded the fortress.

And now the army of the Moor did not wait. They sent another frantic spray of arrows down through the smoke. Every spear that they could find, and every stone and cannonball, they rained down on the dauntless Portingale. They lit trusses of straw and threw them from their turrets to show where they should aim, but it was no use. By the falling light they could see the Portingale decks were pitted by shot, their sails were bearded by arrows like a porcupine's back, yet one by one they kept sliding underneath the gate, till all eleven—all but the one which the Basilisk had sunk—were hovering just outside the fortress walls, so close their hulls were bumping and nuzzling the stone.

And only then, when the Moor's guns had finally gone silent and their quivers were empty, did Dabakur return to the city, back across the harbor. The people of Goa all lit their torches down at the pier to welcome him. The fidalgos brought him a cross as well, and a mare beneath a canopy, and he led them up to a chapel called Cabayo. On the way it began to rain, and Dabakur offered his canopy to the cross. Then he and all the people prayed, giving thanks to the Lord for the courage they had shown and would show. And when the prayer was done, a messenger came to tell them that the Moor had quit the fortress, slipping out the landed side, and now were waiting in the field.

"Then let us at them," urged his Captains. "We cannot let them run out back, these cowards who have been stealing our food, our oil, who make our children deaf from cannon roar. Let us go and meet them and have our day."

It was not Dabakur's first choice to do this. He thought it best to take the fortress now, but seeing the hunger in his Captains' eyes, and the righteousness, he acceded. That very night he led his foot soldiers out onto the field beneath the moon. He made his camp by a lone jambu tree and sent his men out in columns, and when the Moor awoke at dawn to find themselves surrounded, they quickly withdrew back into the fortress.

But Benastarim was their prison now. They had spent their arrows, their shot, and their stone. The fortress was nothing but a shell inside a vise, clamped on one side by the tattered fleet and on the other by their restless, vengeful foot soldiers. Dabakur had only to strike one blow upon the fortress wall, and Rasalcao hoisted the white flag.

Again, the eager Captains pleaded with Dabakur not to let the Moor give up so easily. They wanted their revenge, but this time Dabakur would not be persuaded. He said, "The lives of all the infidel inside the fort are not worth a single drop of Portingale blood." So he sent the Moor Prince his conditions for surrender: that all the Moor and all the armies that had come in their support should abandon the fortress at once, taking with them only the clothes on their backs; that they should leave behind their bows, their cannons, their horses; and finally that they hand over the renegades. Dabakur had not forgotten.

Rasalcao accepted these conditions, all but the last. He could not hand over the renegades, he said, as he was forbidden by faith to deliver any man over to certain death.

"By his faith!" spat Dabakur when he was told. "Then tell the Prince by mine, I have no intention on the lives of these men."

Rasalcao accepted the Portingale's word, and so began to pull his men from Benastarim, but so many had come and gathered there in the year that Dabakur was away, it took two days for them to clear the fortress, even with the help of the Portingale boats, rowing them to shore. But finally they were gone, and all the people of Goa, who had endured so many months beneath the enemy guns, now gathered in the city square to celebrate. And Dabakur appeared before them, but not to gloat, not to rejoice, or even to pray. Instead, while all the people of Goa stood by watching, he called for the renegades to be brought out before him.

The throng pulled back, and out stepped the cowering band, wincing at the people's spit and scorn. They pleaded to Dabakur for mercy. They had been wrong. They had been weak. In the name of the cross they begged for forgiveness. But Dabakur did not hear them.

"Show me the leader," he said.

And now the renegades parted and withdrew, leaving one man there, a figure of noble bearing, with a high, straight posture and a slender nose like Arjuna. But his wrists were bound.

"Down!" cried Dabakur.

And the nobleman fell to his knees, while at the far end of the scrim, there now appeared the shadows of two black-hooded giants, wielding sabered swords.

"One year!" bellowed Dabakur, glowering down at the leader of the renegades. "One year I am gone. What wretched dog cannot wait one year for his master to return? What wretched dog would

so soon take bread from another master, drink from the bowl of
another master, sleep in the bed of another master and his mistress?
Your heart is made of sand! It blows and blows. You are like the
river which follows the easy path. You are like the fish who turns
and turns in the bowl and does not remember where he has been!"
He then signaled to the two black giants. "Scale him."

One took hold of Lopez.

"First, the hair."

The gamelan screamed, and the two black giants began tearing
at the nobleman's head, while over the top of Winston-Kumar's
scrim would fly handfuls of hay that the children would catch and
put in their hair.

The nobleman knelt before them, bald and bleeding.

"The thumb," said Dabakur.

The one black giant took hold of the nobleman's hand and held
it on the block, while the other raised his sabered sword and—
thunk!—over the top of the scrim, a carrot would fly into the lap of
one of the children.

"The hand," said Dabakur.

Then the black giant would set the other hand against the block,
the sword would rise again and—*thunk!*—over the top of the scrim
would fly a hand of sugared ginger, down into the lap of another,
luckier child.

"The ears," said Dabakur.

The giant would take hold of Lopez's head again, while the
other flashed a sword—*sling-sling*—and over the top of Winston-
Kumar's curtain two sections of dried apricot would drop into the
laps of the luckiest children yet.

"The nose."

The sword would flick again, and—*sling!*—with an upward slice
a turnip would fly over the top of Winston-Kumar's curtain, down
into the lap of the least lucky child.

"Behold!" cried Dabakur, and all fell silent, the children and the
gamelan too, as Dabakur himself took hold of the nobleman's collar
and hoisted him up for them to see: his fish, dangling helpless and
in agony, shorn of hair, of thumb, and hand, and face.

"Can you hear me, Dom Fernao? Now you are free to go. The people have no further use of you, but know that all who look upon you now, or all who ever will, will bear witness of these wounds, and know what thou hast done, and all thou hast betrayed in the name of the infidel." Then he held him up again, to show the people, and the children, one last time. "Let us not forget Fernao Lopez."

Toby opens his eyes. It is as if the weight which had been pressing down on him all night had been lifted. For fear it might descend again, he sits up quickly. It is still dark outside. He rises from his mat weary but determined. He goes to the eaves and lifts the puppets from the hook, then starts down through the garden to the gate.

But he cannot help the voices. Even as he makes his way along the lane of pomegranates, the puppets whisper in his ear. Like a coin which must spin out before coming to rest, they remind him of the end and how the great Dabakur was finally vindicated.

The renegades were punished for three more days; then once again all the people set about restoring their precious city. And once again it was as the men were rebuilding the fallen length of wall, with all the fidalgos and corazones standing by, that a strange little boat slid up to the port. It was shaped like a green and red slipper with a pointed toe. Inside were two women and two men, one of whom was a black, who stood and spoke to them.

He said his name was Mateus and that he had come on behalf of his brother, the King of Abyssinia, Lord of Ethiope. He said his brother was aware of all the victories that the Portingale had won since finding their way around the Cape and that none had pleased him more than the rescue of Goa. For this, his brother, the Lord of Ethiope and Abyssinia, wished to extend his thanks and praise, to express his hope that his own children might be wed to the children of the great King of all the Portingale, and to offer, as token of his admiration, a gift, which Mateus presented in a small casket made of gold.

The fidalgos sent for Dabakur, who alone was permitted to accept gifts on behalf of the King. Mateus repeated to him all that he had said to the others, then offered Dabakur the golden casket. Dabakur took it and opened it, and when he saw what was inside, he asked Mateus, "Tell us, what is your brother's name?"

Mateus told him, "PrestaJohn," and Dabakur knelt down. Then all the Captains knelt as well, as did the fidalgos, the corazones, and even the fishermen, who knew not why. From his knees, Dabakur gave thanks to Prince Mateus, saying he would take this casket back to Lisbon himself and deliver his King the good news: that PrestaJohn was found, and sought his brotherhood, and offered as proof of his faith this most precious gift on earth, which he called the Vera Cruz.

The Queen would not be pleased when she finally opened the gift of this, the greatest Emperor the world had known—the once-almighty Priest-King of the East, ruler of seventy-two kingdoms, who had once possessed a river of jewels, a salamander coat, and a mirror which saw all. All these treasures he had known, and what did he give them for their sacrifice?

"A splinter of wood." She slammed the casket shut. "Pleh!"

Toby descends into the Balcombes' cellar by the outer stairs. In the second room, there are two racks of bottled wine beside a cupboard 'Scilla uses for preserves. The bottom shelf is clear. Toby slides the puppets in as deep as they'll go, still wrapped in Alley's blanket. He slides some jars in front, then latches the cupboard door. For now, he thinks, until he can find a better place. Then he returns all the way back to his hut and his bed, to sleep the one remaining hour before dawn.

CHAPTER ELEVEN

OCTOBER 29–NOVEMBER 1

———————

The return of the suite—Betsy's day, mother's scolding—
General Gourgaud meets Mr. Huffington—Officers Stokes, Owens, and Pollard

October 29—By day eleven of his stay at the Briars, it is clear that
the Emperor's brief respite from the smothering presence of the
suite—the rest of the suite, that is—is coming to an end.

The process has been a slow but steady one, which Las Cases has
observed with varying degrees of apprehension. First, the Emperor's
two chefs, Pierron and Lepage, moved up, Mr. Balcombe having
come to the realization that the previous arrangement—whereby the
Emperor's meals were having to be cooked in town and carried up
Side Path atop the heads of slaves—was perhaps not the best-laid
plan. He has outfitted Pierron and Lepage with a small atelier on
premise, a tent with a wood-burning oven, the minimum they require. Monsieur Lepage's nonetheless spectacular desserts and pas-
tries have lured the two Mesdames up from the valley, almost daily
now, to complain about the inn, the flies, the townspeople, or the
latest infestation in sentries. On the matter of the girl they remain
conspicuously quiet. They are plainly jealous.

More significant, the Grand Marshal is now coming daily as well,
in the afternoons, to begin work on his appointed portion of the
Emperor's memoirs, that concerning the Egyptian campaign. It
brings Las Cases no relief, having to relax his grip on the Emperor's

recollections, but his eyes have been failing him. He has been finding it increasingly difficult to work both a morning and an afternoon session, and truth be told, if he'd had his pick of whom among
the others he should have to share His Majesty with, he'd have chosen the Grand Marshal. He is the truest, the most loyal, and certainly
the most calming influence.

Unfortunately, when General Gourgaud learned that Grand
Marshal Bertrand had begun his chapters and was now enjoying
daily audience with the Emperor, he went straight to Admiral Cockburn and requested permission to move from the Inn to the Briars.
He apparently offered to live on the lawn if he had to, as the Admiral seems to have called his bluff. A tent arrived today, gift of the 53^d
Regiment. It is in the marquee style and has been erected—by the
Emperor's valets and under the direct supervision of General Gourgaud—directly in front of the Pavilion. It is in fact connected to the
door.

October 30—Betsy's day began with another quarrel about her lessons. The Emperor came down midmorning to inspect her work, as
is his habit now. She hadn't done any, and she doesn't believe he really cares so much, but he stole away with her journal and showed
the blank pages to her father. "Mais elle ne fait rien travail!" *She
never does any work!* Her father wouldn't have cared either, except
that the Emperor seemed to, so he said Betsy had to finish her lessons before noon, some translation which she has yet to look at.

She went to Millicent Legg's instead, and Millicent told her that
Admiral Cockburn had announced he was going to host a Garrison
Ball in Jamestown on the twentieth, three weeks away. Millicent
wasn't sure yet that her father would let her go, but Betsy is. She
would get the Emperor to ask him, and her father would say yes. So
she and Millicent got Millicent's nursemaid, Louise, to pierce their
ears, but Louise did a very poor job of it. Betsy's lobes began to swell
and burn on the long walk home.

When she finally gets there, the Emperor is out on the lawn.

"I'm still angry," she says, referring to his tattle-taling earlier.

He does not care. "Then you cannot join us on our walk."

"Who?"

"General Gourgaud and I."

General Gourgaud is absurd and boring and full of himself. Still, Betsy goes along. They climb up to Peak Hill together, and there she starts making fun of Bony's hands again, even though she really thinks they're quite beautiful. At one point she tells him, "They don't even look strong enough to hold a sword." For some reason this prompts General Gourgaud to draw his own sword right there.

"Voilà! Le sang d'un 'aingleeshmahn'!" he says, and he shows her the stains at the tip. The blood of an Englishman.

"Put it away," says Bony, displeased. "It's in bad taste to boast in front of ladies. Besides, here is a sword that Mademoiselle Betsee can admire." He shows her his. The handle is gold, fleur-de-lis, and the sheath is tortoiseshell, studded up and down with bees. It looks more like a jewel than a weapon.

"May I?" she asks. He grants, and she pulls it out. It's much heavier than she expected. The tip swings down and bounces on the ground, but then she lifts it up with two hands and points it straight at him, the tip aimed right between his eyes. "Now you'd better say your prayers because I'm going to kill you!" She takes a quick swipe, Gourgaud gasps like a woman, but the Emperor doesn't mind. He just steps aside. She is only fooling.

She is very tired when they finally get back, and her ear is hurting again. Bony pinched it when they said good-bye, on purpose, and she just wants to go to her room and lie down, but when she comes around to the front of the house, she sees her mother is on the veranda, waiting for her. Betsy can tell she is due for a scolding, just from the way her mother's mouth is set; the hair on her upper lip always looks much thicker when she's angry.

"Sit."

Betsy does, with a sigh.

"You should be aware that certain members of the suite have been expressing their concerns at the manner in which you have been treating our guest."

Las Cases, she thinks, the little worm. "But *he* doesn't mind."

"It isn't our place to venture what the General minds or doesn't mind. He is a guest here and, as such, is due respect—more, I fear, than certain members of the suite believe that you have been extending him."

They were just jealous. "I'm not doing anything—"

"The Count tells me you were running around the garden with the memoir."

"I was only fooling. I wasn't going to do anything with it." He hadn't let her in the gate. Betsy begins laughing right there in front of her mother, but she can't help it when she pictures how he looked, stamping his foot. "Retournez! Retournez donc, ou je ne serai plus votre ami!" *Come back, or I will not be your friend!*

"I don't think they find it so amusing," her mother says.

But *he* does, she thinks. She wishes she could make her mother understand that it was all *him*, the way he teases her and smiles. He is the one making her do it. But her mother would not understand, so Betsy doesn't even try. "Why do you call him General Bonaparte?" she asks instead. "That's not what the French call him."

"Well, the French are mistaken. Now, do you understand what I have been saying to you? About your behavior?"

"Yes."

"I don't want to hear any more about you."

"No, Ma'am."

"Now, what have you done to your ear?"

Betsy tells her—it was dumb Louise's fault—and her mother goes to get some iodine. Betsy can hardly fathom Las Cases, though, telling on her like that. She looks up to the Pavilion. The lamps have been lit. They're probably having dinner already. She sticks her tongue out at them. All of them. Him included.

The Briars' newest resident, General Gaspard Gourgaud—youngest, loneliest, and most sensitive member of the Emperor's suite—has decided to busy himself this morning by cutting an imperial crown into the turf that bridges the two halves of his marquee. This way anyone wishing to see the Emperor will have to pass over the image. He has drafted Monsieur Marchand for the task, as he has a good eye and renders well. St. Denis is also there. They both are down on their knees, snipping the design into the grass, while Gourgaud stands over them, arms crossed.

"It's too small." He shakes his head in aimless dissatisfaction. "It must be bigger. What about the border? Could we make an extra border?"

Marchand supposes. With handfuls of dirt he begins outlining another, wider border when a crooked shadow suddenly falls in his light. Gourgaud looks up to find it's the old gentleman he has seen hobbling about the property, the children's tutor.

"Monsieur," says Gourgaud, "s'il vous plaît. The light."

The old man sees and steps aside, but in- rather than out-. He looks down at the crown with a curiously admiring expression, then notes the camp bed and the bureau. "Vous venez donc vous installer en permanence?" *You've come to stay?*

"Oui," says Gourgaud abruptly. He appreciates the old man's French, but there's something odd about him, a desire to please which ill suits a person of such advanced years.

"One can't help being moved," he says, still in French, "by the loyalty of the suite—yourself, the Count—"

Gourgaud responds abruptly with such a loud snort he surprises himself, but it's true. The Count. The Count's only loyalty is to his own pocketbook and reputation. "There is no lack of self-interest, I can assure you." He nudges Marchand's rump with his foot. "No. Still wider. So that three people could walk over it." He takes some dirt from Marchand's sack and demonstrates the desired width. "Like this."

"How long have you been with him?" asks the old man.

"The Emperor?" Gourgaud stands back, pleased by the question. "A long while. Since Spain," he says, which is true, if misleading. There have been lapses.

"Were you with him on Elba?"

Gourgaud pauses. He was not, in fact, and this remains a sensitive subject between himself and His˙ Majesty. During that particular episode, the ten months that His Majesty was enduring his Mediterranean exile, Gourgaud was serving as an officer in the army of the newly restored Bourbons, having contacted them shortly after the disaster of the Russian campaign.

"I was not on Elba, no," he says. "I was with His Majesty in Spain, however. And Austerlitz. And Russia." He pauses. "At Brienne I saved his life."

It isn't clear the old man heard this, but Gourgaud nonetheless proceeds to tell him of the incident, which both Marchand and St. Denis have now heard at least a dozen times. It was during the long trek back, the agony of which Gourgaud assures the tutor words could not express. The freezing cold had been bad enough, but also they were under constant attack from roving bands of Cossacks.

"During one such skirmish, fortune placed me in open view of His Majesty's position, such that I could see one of these barbarous fiends sneaking up on the Emperor from behind, with his blade raised, murder in his eye. There is no doubt he would have killed the Emperor right there had I not the instinct to fire my gun and stop him." Gourgaud's voice falters here, as usual, at reference to this, the finest thing he has ever done or will do, whether he actually did it or not. He looks at the old man, eyes welling.

"But you were not on Elba?"

Gourgaud straightens. "No."

"Were any of you?"

The young General is confused, and off-put. "I don't know. The Grand Marshal?" He waves the question away, though it is absurd for him to have appended even the faintest note of uncertainty to this answer. Of course Bertrand was there, as were the two gentlemen kneeling in front of them.

"He's the tall one?" the old man asks.

"Yes, the tall one," Gourgaud snaps. He's had quite enough of this interview. "But the Bertrands owed him, you understand, after all the gifts he'd lavished on them at their wedding."

Silence. The old man nods at him vaguely, then with a slight bow makes his way. Gourgaud turns back to the crown in the grass, where Marchand and St. Denis are still busy snipping away, their two derrieres pointing up at him, like faintly wagging fingers.

—————

November 1—There has been a miscount of beds up at the Hutt's Gate quarters, so half the unit of light infantrymen who were supposed to have moved inland yesterday are still at the town barracks, doubled up with the three hundred fresh bodies just in from the HMS *Ceylon*.

At 2100 hours, or 9:00 p.m., Minnie, who runs the pub at the Summers' House, sends over three girls and a bottle of gin. Twenty minutes later the girls return with six soldiers. They use a pair of curtained rooms in the back.

Scenting their activity, a slow but steady trickle of soldiers wanders down. The girls can manage one every ten minutes or so. By ten o'clock there is a backup. Minnie does her best to pacify the men with gin and the promise of more girls on the way, but there are no more girls.

In the case of Yeomen Pollard, Owens, and Stokes, the combination of alcohol and unfulfilled expectation has turned them restless. Halfway through their second fifth, Stokes suggests they move on and see if there aren't any other watering holes in town. Minnie notices and meets them at the door.

"Here, I tell you. No lie. All the way up Bridge is a girl you like. Got a olive tree in front. All a mess on the ground."

Stokes nods.

"You tell her Minnie send you. Minnie no steer you wrong."

The yeomen are dubious, but at that moment one of Minnie's girls staggers out from behind her curtain, holding the hem of her dirty white peasant dress in a bunch between her legs. She is bleeding. Minnie curses at her and turns to the men. "No good, that one. Up at the olive tree, you like. Marie."

For the half mile walk up Bridge Street, it seems the only sound

in all Jamestown is the yeomen's boots and the half pint of gin swish-
ing in Stokes's bottle. Near the end of the lane a lone parakeet
screams, Stokes answers with a howl, and Pollard taps him on the
elbow. They've found the olive tree, the ground all smudgy and
stained underneath. A little white cottage crouches behind—one
window, a Dutch door, with the top half opened and a large headstone propped up against the bottom.

The three men stand in the middle of road, bracing themselves.
Stokes takes a coin from his belt and tosses it. It rings against the
stone. "Hey!"

Nothing.

Stokes motions for Owens to do the same. A second coin rings
against the stone. They wait, all three staring into the blackness
through the window. Still nothing. Stokes gives his gin another
swish and is about to call out when Pollard quiets him with his hand.

He nods. A figure is coming to the door, from within, a glowing
brown against the black. It bumps against the bottom half, but the
headstone keeps it shut. The figure stills. Skinny, shirtless, with
cropped black hair, looking out at them with no expression at all.

"Marie?" whispers Owens.

"It is a boy," says Pollard.

"Boy?" He sees. "Boy . . . what's your mum's name?"

The boy says nothing, just keeps looking straight ahead.

Stokes takes offense. "You hear me, boy?" He advances.

"Peter, stop," says Owens. "Stop. He doesn't know you're there."

Stokes yields two steps from the door, still confused.

"He's asleep."

Stokes squints. "Is that right?"

"Fast."

Stokes takes another step closer but holds his lantern up to the
window now, looking in; the boy still doesn't move. "Doesn't look
like Mum's home."

Owens and Pollard both nod. Just as well, they've lost their
mood, but Stokes looks back at the boy again, swaying like a reed in
the doorframe. Stokes sets down his gin and sticks his chin right up

to the boy's. He waves his hand before his eyes and smiles. "Out cold."

"Yep, let's go."

Stokes backs off, and the three sailors start away again, down Bridge to see if the queue at the Summers' House is any shorter.

Marie doesn't arrive home until after midnight; some of Bony's suite stayed up late in the sitting room. She can see that someone's been there, though, and there's little question what he wanted. There is a bottle of gin on the stoop and two coins lying at the foot of the headstone.

CHAPTER TWELVE

NOVEMBER 2-3

—◆◆—

The marionette—Toby cleans the coop, &c.—
The Emperor's suggestion to Bertrand—Betsy's punishment—Betsy's dreams

November 2—Betsy and Sarah went into town this morning to look
at fabric for Betsy's gown. The Admiral's ball is still a month away,
and Betsy has yet to ask her father if she can go, but she has mentioned it to the Emperor, and he knows she has been looking forward to it. She chose a bolt of royal blue silk, exactly as she had
wanted, then she and Sarah stop in at Solomon's on the way back.

She isn't looking for anything in particular, but up at the desk
Mr. Solomon is showing Mrs. Knipe a new toy he just received. It's
a marionette of the Emperor. It doesn't look like him. It is tall and
gangly, with a large nose, but she knows it's him from the cocked
hat. This was how she pictured him before.

The puppet is suspended before a small staircase, each step of
which has the name and shape of a country painted on it. "Italy,"
then "Austria," then up and up; "Spain," "Egypt." They're the
places he was supposed to have conquered, or tried to conquer. Mr.
Solomon shows them there's a button at the base, and every time
you push it, the string pulls the puppet up another step. The top
three steps are "Russia," then "Elba," then "Waterloo," except that
when the puppet reaches "Waterloo," it automatically comes tumbling down over the top and lands in a gangly clump on a small gray
blot called "St. Helena."

"That's very clever, isn't it?" Mrs. Knipe smiles, but she doesn't seem interested in buying.

Mr. Solomon turns to Betsy. "Miss Balcombe?"

She knows she shouldn't, she knows her mother would disapprove, but it's so silly-looking—the marionette—it's so hideous and stupid she wants to show it to the Emperor. He would think it's funny.

She carries it herself, back to the Briars, in a box. Sarah has the blue fabric in a basket on her head, but when they finally come to the banyans, she sees Monsieur Marchand out on the front lawn and bolts from Sarah's side. "Où est-il?" she calls. "Où est-il?"

Monsieur Marchand points her to the garden. She runs all the way, but the Emperor and Las Cases are just leaving as she comes to the gate.

"Look!" she says, holding out the marionette.

"What is this?"

"It's you. See?" She points to the hat and all the countries, but he is confused. Finally she can't stand it any longer. She takes it back and shows him how it works. She makes the puppet climb all the way up the ladder, then tumble down onto St. Helena.

The Emperor looks at it a moment, the jumble of limbs, but he doesn't smile. He doesn't do anything, and Betsy feels instantly ashamed. She didn't mean to hurt his feelings. She only meant to tease him and show him what she thought before, but his posture goes very stiff, and she doesn't know what to do. She takes the toy and runs back to the house. She is already crying by the time she reaches her bed.

Stupid, stupid, stupid.

—————

Toby heads down to feed the chickens at the end of the day. He has his wheelbarrow, a bucket of water, a bag of scratch, and a bag of grit. He can already smell the waste as he passes behind Sarah and 'Scilla's cottage, and he can see 'Scilla out back. One of Bony's cooks, Piran, is showing her again how he wants her to kill the chickens. She's not supposed to cut the heads off anymore. She is supposed to slit the necks twice and hold the birds upside down in a cone. Piran is demonstrating. Toby can't see the blood—the stream is too thin and black—but he can hear it, running into the bucket like milk.

'Scilla doesn't seem to be paying very close attention, though. With her deep-set eyes, it's difficult to tell, but Toby's sense is that she's looking at him. This has been his sense for the last few days.

He slides the stone from the bamboo gate and announces his entrance with a few clicks. The chickens scatter, grays and reds, high tails and stubby tails. Some run outside, some stay, to perform their leery, bobbing dance for him, catching him with one eye, then the other. Is he the one with the net or the grain?

The grain. He scatters some across the litter, and the birds go instantly to work, scratching and pecking greedily, all but the broody hens, who only guard a circle of feed and wait for the chicks to come over and have their share.

Toby goes to change the water in the coop but once again finds the ground surrounding the trough is filthy with waste. He cleared it out just the day before last, but it looks as if the hay needs changing again. He heads back out to get his barrow and sees Mr. Balcombe coming down from the bungalow with his cane and his book. Piran is scalding one of the birds now, swirling it around and around like a ladle in a pot of boiling water, while 'Scilla has already started plucking the other, her bony hands jabbing at the carcass, while the small feathers float down around her.

"Toby." Mr. Balcombe plants his stool cane right beside the barrow and takes a seat. "I've come to see how we're doing."

Toby nods. "Doing very good, Mr. Balcombe."

Mr. Balcombe glances around, mildly concerned by the presence of the birds outside their pen. "And this is safe? They won't run free?"

Toby shakes his head, though at the moment two of the more curious hens are bobbing their way up the slope to see what 'Scilla's up to. Piran flops their scalded coop-mate on the table in front of her.

"So tell us, how are we coming with the number?" Mr. Balcombe opens his book and consults the slate he posted on the fence. "Are these the one's we've lost?"

Toby has been marking them. "And the ones they eat."

"I see." Mr. Balcombe makes a note with his pencil as two quick hacks sound up the hill; 'Scilla has cut off the dead chicken's head and neck. Piran is leaving as two more feckless hens trot up the hill. Toby still isn't sure, but 'Scilla's shaded eyes seem trained on him, even as she slices up the sternum of the plucked chicken. He wonders, Did she find the puppets, then, looking for a jar of apricots in the cellar?

Mr. Balcombe claps his books shut. "You haven't seen Alley about, have you?"

"He's not at Longwood?"

Mr. Balcombe shakes his head. "I believe he told them he was helping with the General's coop."

Toby isn't surprised. "He brings the rooster up from Timu's," he says, which is true enough, though it accounts for only one day so far.

Mr. Balcombe doesn't press. "If you see him, tell him I expect him to keep going up. They're expecting him, and the sooner General Bonaparte is settled in, the better."

"I'll tell him."

"Good man." Mr. Balcombe stands. He has to give an extra tug on the head of his cane to uproot it from the ground. "There we are."

He starts back up the slope, his books now up-to-date, but 'Scilla is still glowering down the slope at Toby, even as her hands keep pulling at the gizzard of the open chicken. Three more hens have gathered around her, watching as she works the liver and lungs. One takes a peck at a fallen entrail; it whips around like a long, wet worm. Toby shakes the bucket of mullet, and they all turn abruptly—more familiar food—and start bobbing back down the slope in their helpless, armless strut.

He opens the gate and ushers them in. He doesn't look at 'Scilla, but he can hear her—*sling, sling*—resharpening the knife, and he can feel her eyes casting shadows on the back of his neck.

—⊶⊷—

The Emperor and Bertrand are out beneath the grape arbor. They've spent the better part of the afternoon speaking of Egypt, but the Emperor closes the session by drafting a new letter of grievances on behalf of the suite. Provisions at Mr. Pourteous's Inn still are not what they could be.

He is in the midst of requesting more lamp oil when he goes suddenly silent. Bertrand cannot tell if he is collecting his thoughts or letting them drift.

"When did you last see the house?" he asks finally. "At Long-wood."

"Yesterday, Your Majesty." Bertrand has been going every other day to check their progress. "It looks to be another few weeks."

The Emperor sighs his impatience. Then, as though it were an idea just now occurring to him, he nods back in the direction of the Balcombes' bungalow. "And what do you think of the idea that we might purchase the house here, the Briars?"

Bertrand is confused. "The Balcombes' home, Your Majesty?"

"Yes."

"But what of the Balcombe family?"

"They have another house. I am not suggesting we inconvenience them any further, but they have another, and we would pay."

Bertrand is still slow to answer. "But your accounts have been frozen, Your Majesty."

"I am aware. No, *you* would purchase it. And I would pay you back."

Bertrand now pauses as though to ponder the question, though he is far more concerned by His Majesty's apparent grasp of the situation—or lack thereof. "It's possible," he says.

"And Toby as well," the Emperor adds.

"Your Majesty?"

"The gardener. He is a slave, you know."

"Your Majesty wishes to purchase one of the Balcombes' slaves?"

"And set him free, yes." He gestures to the Grand Marshal's pen. "Put it in the letter. With the rest."

He waits, and waits some more, until he actually sees the Grand Marshal resume writing.

——————

Just before dinner Betsy's mother has asked to see her in private, out on the veranda. Betsy already knows why.

"The Count came to speak to me today," she says, pressing her lips and not looking at her. "He was very upset. He said that this afternoon you deliberately mocked the Emperor."

"I didn't mock him."

"He says you showed him a toy of some kind, a marionette."

Betsy is silent.

"Do you still have it?"

She nods.

"Bring it to me."

Betsy does not protest. She knows her punishment is a fait accompli. She retrieves the puppet from the top of her armoire and brings it back out to her mother, whose cheeks flush instantly with anger and shame. "Betsy." The muscles in her jaw flex. "You will learn."

Betsy doesn't care what she has to say. She already has learned. She wishes she'd never even seen the stupid puppet.

"You will spend the night in the cellar."

Betsy can hardly believe her ears. "The whole night?" She had been made to spend hours down in the cellar, as punishment, but never a whole night.

"The General has been very kind to you, Betsy, and you are not being very kind to him. Perhaps a night in the cellar will make you see."

"But that's not fair."

"It isn't fair that we should have to say things to you over and over again, things you know very well. You take liberties, and it must stop."

"But what about the rats?"

"They won't bother you if you don't bother them."

Her mother says nothing of Betsy's punishment at dinner. Betsy hopes she might have forgotten but knows she hasn't. The family repairs to the parlor afterward, except for the boys, who go to bed. Jane reads. Her mother sews. Her father works on his books. Betsy just sits on the sofa, dreadful and bored, wishing the Emperor would come down or that she could go up to him. He wouldn't be so mean and cruel and cold and boring and brutal as her mother.

When the clock chimes nine, her mother looks up from her frame. "Betsy, get your things." Jane just keeps reading, and Betsy can tell she knew all along. And her father too.

She meets her mother at the cellar door, in her nightgown and slippers. She has her blanket and pillow as well, and her mother permits her a lantern and a book, *Héloïse*.

Her mother leads her down to the foot of the stairs but no farther. "Sarah will come for you in the morning," she says. Then she climbs back up, lifting the hem of her dressing gown. She doesn't even turn to look at her, just closes the door and hooks it from the outside.

Betsy will never forgive her for this, she has already decided. She sits on the third stair. She won't even give her the satisfaction of going up and pleading at the door. She'd rather remember her mother did this to her, all because she has no idea about him and what he likes, what he is like.

The cellar is divided into two rooms, with wooden ceilings, posts, beams, and brick walls. The far room is for unused furniture and other things they don't need. This one is for the wine. She can only barely see the rack by the lantern light. And a cupboard beside. She doesn't even want to look at the far wall, or the floor, because she knows they are there: the rats.

Then suddenly her heart stops. A sound. A gnawing, crumpling sound in the corner. The nearer of the wine racks is an arm's length from the stairs. Betsy reaches, breathless. She has to jam her shoulder through the banister posts, but she is able to get her fingers around the neck of a bottle and pull it out. She takes a second as well.

Then she listens. Silence. She raises the bottle up over her shoulder because she knows they're out there. She can feel them, looking right at her, standing up on their hind legs. Another moment of pounding silence passes, then something moves, something over in the corner, and Betsy hurls the bottle out into the blackness. It shatters against the wall. She can hear the wine seeping over the bricks. A shadow darts out from behind the cupboard, and she throws the second bottle, which does not shatter but merely thunks and rolls.

"I hate you!" she shouts. "Hate you!"

She is small enough that if she curls up, she can fit her entire body on a single stair. She lies down, but more out of desperation. She isn't tired. She looks at the flame in the lantern and begins to cry. The light splits into grainy rays. The tears spill down into her ear. Her ear hurts. She hates her mother, and she hates herself as well, for being so stupid and cruel and thoughtless as to have shown that horrible puppet to the Emperor, her friend. And she can't imagine she'll ever get to sleep down here. Not with them out there, looking at her, scurrying back and forth along the edges, nesting in the cupboards. . . .

III

In Betsy's first dream she and her whole family are part of a long caravan of pilgrims, headed for the city. They are walking along a road in a dry, desertlike place; she thinks it must be Egypt, though there are no pyramids. And they all are very sad for some reason, and weeping; Jane and her mother are, but Betsy doesn't know why yet.

The road they're on passes by a distant set of tombs, or catacombs, where all the beggars live. There is one standing at the roadside. His face is covered in rags. Betsy's mother thinks he is a leper. "Get away," she says. She pulls them all over to the far side of the road, afraid, but when her father sees the man, he is more angry, which isn't at all like him. He isn't very like him.

"Put down your hand," he says. "Do you think only of yourself? When you see these people passing by, and see how they are weeping, do you not ask yourself why? Or do you think only of what they can give you? The General lies at bay," he says, "gravely ill, awaiting death."

Betsy cannot believe her ears. The General? Bony? Is that why they are crying, because he is sick? But why didn't he tell her?

They come to the city, which isn't so different from Jamestown. It's much bigger, but it has a pier and a marina where all the people are gathered. And there is a ship at bay. It's very far away, but Betsy can see they've come too late. There is a smaller boat rowing to shore, and he is in it. They've laid his body on a bier, and all the people are weeping and trying to console themselves.

But when the boat comes near, Betsy is confused because it doesn't look like him. He is much older-looking. He has a long gray beard and a velvet cap and stole. And he is wearing buckskins and boots with spurs, which he would never wear.

They cover him in a black pall and carry him to the church on their shoulders, and the church is all draped in black. They lay the bier down before the front stairs, which are marble. The Reverend speaks. He says they should not be so selfish as to grieve. If the Lord has called the General, then there must be a terrible war raging in heaven, and He needs His greatest warriors fighting for Him. "But we should not fear for ourselves," he says, "because as long as we have his bones, the city will be safe."

Then they slide his body inside the steps and close him in with marble.

IV

Her second dream, she is aboard a boat. It's the boat her family first took to St. Helena, except they have left from the city where they buried Bony, so Betsy is still very sad, but she is also parched. Everyone on board is because they've been at sea for a good while, and she is down belowdeck, alone, looking for something to drink, when she comes upon a cabin full of animals—goats, chickens, pigs, pheasants, and partridges—some in cages, some not.

She enters in, because she thinks they must have saved some water for the animals. There is a barrel at the far end, but when she comes to it, she sees there is a filthy man crouching in the corner, and she becomes very frightened. It's the beggarman from the catacombs, the one whose face is wrapped in rags. Betsy wants to scream, but her throat is too dry, so she pulls on the tail of one of the animals—a pig or a goat—who starts screaming. All the goats start bleating, and her parents come rushing in. When her mother sees the beggarman, she is horrified.

"We have to have him thrown overboard!" she says. "And all the animals as well."

But her father tries to calm her down. He tells her no. "This man isn't a leper. He is the traitor, and the reason he covers his face is to hide his shame." And he turns to the beggarman and says, "Show them. Take the wrappings from your face and show us, or we shall have to throw you overboard, and all the animals."

So the beggarman begins unwrapping his face, unwinding the rags, and finally Betsy realizes who it is. It's Fernando Lopez, and she is very excited, because she has never had a dream about Fernando Lopez. This is her first, so she tries pushing her way through all the people so she can see him, but now the room is filled with other passengers, as well as all the animals, and she can't get a very good view. All she can see is the look on her mother's face—she looks ill—and the people are all gasping. "It *is* him." "It *is* him."

And some of them are angry. "Throw him over," they say. "Let him drown." But others are saying no, because he's been punished already, and the General set him free.

"Then give him a boat," they say. "He's bad luck." Aye, bad luck, bad luck, all agree. But Betsy still can't push her way through.

She's desperate just to see his face, just a glimpse before they all decide, but then there comes a loud thumping from above. They're stamping their feet up on deck; they've sighted the island. Fresh water ahead, drinking water. St. Helena. They keep stamping their feet . . .

. . . and that is when Betsy awakes, to the sound of Sarah's sandals, clomping down the cellar stairs to get her. It is morning.

PART IV

JAMESTOWN, FROM THE ROAD TO THE BRIARS

CHAPTER THIRTEEN

NOVEMBER 4-6

———

*A spider—Tragedy in the coop—Betsy is forgiven, and educated—
The distant beetle—Toby meets Quinto—The Grotto—Huffington's vow—
The shrine*

November 4—Just as the Count had feared, the reemergence of the suite—or the reencroachment, better put—has had a clearly debilitating effect upon His Majesty. He is not sleeping well; Las Cases can hear him turning through the night. He is rising later in the morning and has as a result dispensed with much of his prebreakfast ritual. No solitary walk, and the rubdowns administered by Messieurs Marchand and St. Denis are more brief, owing as well to the finite reserve of eau de Cologne that St. Denis managed to smuggle from the Continent. His Majesty does not head out until after breakfast now, and then it is in his white dressing gown. If he puts on his uniform at all, it is not until later in the day. The dictations continue, of course, they being His Majesty's one constructive purpose. There is a small grape arbor at the back of the garden he has chosen to make his office. To spare his eyes, Las Cases has had a canvas spread over the top of the trellis to keep the sunlight from raining down on his pages and ink.

It does not keep away the spiders, though.

"I asked him his motive." His Majesty taps the table between them, as an unseen tan belly, native to the island, descends on her thread and stops at the level of Las Cases's liver-spotted pate.

He scribbles, " 'What . . . is . . . your . . . motive, sir?' "

"Was it religious principle?" His Majesty continues. "If so, then why was he there? I did not force him to become Counselor of State."

"Hardly."

"He had sought the position, eagerly, and as a favor. He was the youngest—"

" 'You . . . are . . . the youngest . . .' "

"He had no other claim on the position, save as heir to his father's services, and I told this to him. 'You took a personal oath to me! You permit your religious feelings to let you violate this oath? This is a crime, sir.' "

". . . 'a great crime, sir.' "

" 'If your purpose had only been to murder, then we could stop you with manacles, but this . . . conspiracy to influence the public mind—this is like a trail of gunpowder.' "

"Well said, Your Majesty. 'A trail . . . of . . . gun—' "

The spider ascends, unimpressed.

———

November 5—Toby goes down to check on the coop first thing after his tea. The chickens know his tread by now, and this morning the ground is muddy from last night's thunderstorm. They all begin clucking as he nears the gate, but so loud today—greedy birds. He slides the stone aside and enters, but he's not two steps in when one of the larger hens, a nasty longtail, comes charging at him. She opens her wings and begins shrieking and pecking at his shins until finally he is forced back out. He closes the gate again and peers in through the slats.

It looks as if all the hens are out and acting nervous—pacing back and forth, but not interested in food, their skinny legs and pronged feet amuck with mud. Something has upset them. Toby looks over at the coop, but nothing seems amiss. Then he listens. He doesn't hear the chicks, not so much as a chirp, and now he sees that one of the bamboo poles over on the far side of the pen is slanted, and another has fallen.

He tries entering again, and this time the hens let him in. With scolding clucks and grunts they follow him over to the coop, sponging through the mud, the wet feed and waste. Toby goes straight to the nook he built for the chicks, the stone turret, and the stove. The morning light slants in to show the floor all scarred and strewn with feathers. The gunnysack still hangs from its hook, but limp, the bottom gnawed through. One of the hens ducks in through his legs to make sure he sees: Up against the base of the turret, there is a long black lump, lying stiff. It's a rat, innards spilling from its middle like little dead worms.

⸻

Betsy apologized the day after her night in the cellar. She didn't tell the Emperor about the dream—she barely remembers it anymore—but she still felt awful about the marionette. In a way she is glad it happened, though, because she thinks she understands him better now. His situation is no different really, trapped here among rats, and she wanted him to know that she understood now, that it is dreadful the way they are treating him, and if she'd really been at all considerate, she'd have known how hurtful it was to show him that stupid toy.

She meant to say all this. What she ended up saying was that she'd only wanted him to see how silly it was. "It doesn't even look like you."

"Yes, and this is the important thing." He pinched her cheek, as always a bit too hard.

They have since resumed their walks. And she has been able to spend more time with the Mesdames Bertrand and de Montholon. The Emperor likes to ask which one she thinks is the more beautiful. Betsy thinks they both are quite beautiful—the way they carry themselves especially, their style. And she grants that Madame de Montholon's looks are more exotic, and lovely in that way, but if she

had to choose, she'd say she prefers Madame Bertrand. She is so tall
and graceful. And blond. And she is slightly kinder to Betsy, even
offering to superintend her lessons.

"No, Your Majesty is absolutely correct," she says, eyeing Betsy's
attire. "The pantaloons are a problem."

"And the hair," says Madame de Montholon.

"Do you see?" The Emperor turns to Betsy. "How else is the little Las Cases going to see?"

Betsy need only scowl, and Madame de Montholon seconds her
objection. "What about Gogo?"

"Oh, no," says Betsy. "I don't like him."

"You don't like my savior?" The Emperor turns to the Mesdames. "Yesterday he saved my life again—from a ferocious bull."
Un taureau féroce!

"A cow," says Betsy. Une vache. "And it was all the way on the
other side of the field."

"Well, I'm sure it will be a bull at dinner," says Madame de Montholon. "In any case, I'm of the impression that the Baron's atten-
tions may be spoken for."

The Emperor sits up. "Really? With?"

"Miss . . . Wilkes, is it?"

Betsy confirms the name. "Oh, she is very lovely. I think she's
the prettiest on the island."

"Who is this?" asks the Emperor. "What? Why have I not met
her?"

"Governor Wilkes's daughter," says Madame Bertrand.

"By his first marriage," adds Betsy.

"And Gourgaud likes her?" asks the Emperor.

Yes, the Mesdames nod.

"She likes him?"

This they cannot confirm.

"But she is too good for him?"

The women nod.

To Betsy: "And you're too good for him?"

She nods.

"Which is why we must do something about these pantaloons."
The Mesdames both agree, with sips. High time.

——◦○◦——

November 6—From the parlor of Mr. McRitchie's home at Alarm
House, the road to Longwood is a barely discernible, and markedly
flat, line slicing through the top of a nameless peak a mile away. Mr.
Balcombe stands at the window, looking out, his squint pinched by
apprehension. He is here primarily on business—Mr. McRitchie
stocks lamp oil, and Mr. Balcombe is seeing if he can negotiate a
deal on behalf of General Bonaparte's coterie—but at the moment
he is more concerned by the distant road. Normally it sees very little traffic—a cart per hour, if that—but ever since the Arrival, there's
been a steadier stream of slaves and soldiers making their way up and
down, all day long. Because it is morning, the majority are headed
up, bearing lumber, bricks and mortar, paint, and puzzolana.

"Poor devils," mutters McRitchie, peering through the eyepiece
of his spyglass.

They are a line of ants to Mr. Balcombe, carrying the crumbs of
a picnic muffin up the hill. There is one in particular, though, that
has him concerned—not red, but black and bent, and moving at a
pace considerably slower than its more burdened comrades.

"May I?"

McRitchie hands over the glass. "Still a bit far to be sure."

Balcombe takes aim nonetheless and finds him—a beetle now,
but blurry. He spins the focus, just to make certain.

It is. Mr. Huffington.

"Dear, dear."

——◦○◦——

Timu knows what's happened the moment he sees Toby and Lewis
descending underneath the oaks. He barely looks up from his lunch,
chicken and biscuits. "Rats?"

Toby nods.

" 'Cause of mud?"

Toby nods.

"You have to drive those poles deep." Timu tosses the bone out into the leaves. The prowling cats trot over to inspect, and Toby sees there is a boy on Timu's porch. "How many you lose?" asks Timu.

"All," says Toby. "The chicks."

Timu hoists himself up from the table and starts back for the pens. Toby does not follow. The boy on the porch has yet to move or even glance in their direction. Ten years old or so, and serious, he is working on something in his lap, but Toby can't tell what yet. He starts over, and the cats scatter from his path.

Timu's porch is a wraparound, but narrow and not well kept, with busted teeth in the fence and rotting, warped planks. As Toby comes near, he is pleased to see Campanero leaning up against the wall beside Timu's front door. Alley must have brought it for him. The leather is warped, and the white paint flaking; still, it is a proud and jealous bird.

"Campanero," says Toby, now climbing the steps and smiling over at the boy. He is sitting out on the corner, cross-legged. His spine is curled like the handle of a teacup, shoulders closed, head tilted at an angle. He is weaving. There's a crosshatch of bamboo reeds in his lap, and behind him are two piles of finished baskets, spilling out on both sides of the corner. Toby can see now, the boy is blind. His pupils are turned up beneath his lids, his attention entirely with his hands, tucking, tightening, shaping the reeds, like a pair of birds, making a nest.

Toby quietly steps closer, to see the ones he's finished. They are of no single type. Their shape depends upon the grass that he has used, or the reeds. Some are round and stiff like pots, some shallow and softer, more like hats, with patterns woven in. There is one, almost hidden underneath the rest, made of straw. It's more a sack than a basket, deep and loose like the one the rats ate through the night before last. Toby picks it up.

"Good baskets."

Quinto does not respond; the hands keep on.

"You sell me this?"

No answer, other than to take up a new reed and bite off the tip to correct the length. Handsome boy, thinks Toby, though one wouldn't expect—with such deep-set eyes and slightly bucked teeth. His brow is strong and intent, as is the tilt of his head. Then Toby sees; there is a rope tied around his ankle.

"I'll buy this." Toby takes a coin from the purse that Mr. Balcombe gave him and tosses it into the shallow weave in Quinto's lap. Without missing a tuck, Quinto's hands sweep up the coin and slide it into his shirt pocket. The birds set a berry stem aside.

Timu is a while longer. Toby sits back by the steps, where Campanero can keep an eye on him. *Blegblegbleg.* That was how Winston-Kumar used to imitate the sound of his chicken feet shuffling, or was it his grandmother who used to tell of spirit chickens who stole rice for their masters, hiding it under their wings?

Blegblegblegbleg

Timu brings two crates back with him. He smiles when he sees Toby's new purchase. "Quinto sell you that?"

Toby nods. "Who is Quinto?"

Timu looks over, but the boy doesn't seem to notice or care. "Belongs to Marie."

Toby doesn't know Marie.

"They'll be staying here awhile, both." Timu sets down the crates. Two dozen more soft yellow handfuls are stirring inside. Toby opens his new straw sack, and Timu begins lifting out the little birds and setting them down at the bottom, like fruit. The fabric gives comfortably. Loosely. The weave is soft. The little birds chirp, but they don't mind,

"Bleg-bleg-bleg," says Toby.

Timu smiles. He recognizes the reference and glances up at Campanero. "You been to the grotto," he asks, "since Bony?"

Toby shakes his head. He hasn't been to the grotto for years.

"You should," says Timu, and he leaves it at that, lifting out three chicks at once now, coddled gently in the palm of his great black hands—and never safer, thinks Toby, for the moment.

V

The Grotto

The same day they came to bay, the Portingale sailors rowed Lopez into the island and left him there, alone. Most who know the story assume this was at Lemon Valley, but there are those who say it was Rupert's Cove, because it's easier to land there. Either way, Lopez found himself alone on an island unknown to him. He did not even know if there were wild beasts there, and so, as evening fell, he had to find somewhere safe, and the safest place he could find, according to Winston-Kumar, was a little cave at the bottom of a grotto, just barely large enough for him to fit inside. He dug out some of the dirt and laid down some grass for his bed, then he pulled a thorny bramble in front to cover it, and that is where he spent his first night, and many nights after that as well.

The Portingale fleet didn't stay long. The following day all the sailors came in in their boats to fill their baskets with fruit and their casks with fresh water. Some called out for Lopez, as they'd brought a few supplies, as much as they thought he'd need and they could spare. But hearing no reply, they left them in the shelter of a broken hull at the front of the lemon orchard: a barrel, some biscuits, a bag of rice, a skillet, a box of salt, and a tin of matches. Then they climbed back in their boats and returned to the fleet, setting sail that day for Lisbon.

⸺⸺

Mr. Huffington finally reaches Longwood a full seven hours after leaving Jamestown on this, his one day off. There he sees what he assumes everyone who comes this way must see: the grim, defeated plain, a long-since abandoned battlefield, swept clear of trees and dead soldiers. All that remains are two lonely eucalyptus and the cowering house. A checkerboard crew of red-coated soldiers and black-skinned slaves clings to scaffolding, hammering at the new frames, their wielding limbs etched against the gray-white sky. Over to the east, a barracks has been set up in plain sight. A row of sentries studs the hillcrest even now, rehearsing for the day the prisoner arrives.

Mr. Huffington starts north, for no reason he can discern and despite the pain in his hip, which is now verging on numbness. He is caked in mud and in terrible need of water, but there is a road running east of the house, a mucky, stony, mud-puddled half mile up the plain. Mr. Huffington follows it all the way to the end, from where he has a clear view of the immense stone turret that guards the island's northernmost face, the Barn, as it is called. As Mr. Huffington looks upon it, he notices something he has never seen before. He has a kind of vision, though he can't imagine he is the only one, the image is so unmistakable—because it isn't a great cross in the sky, or a descending light, or a burning bush. It's right there on the cliffs and as clear as if God's own hand had come down to render it: the Emperor's profile. The straight nose, the protuberant chin, the collar, even the eyes, hidden beneath the brim of his bicorne, staring out at the endless, prospectless sea and sky.

Can he be the only one who has seen? Or is this why Cockburn chose the plain, or the plain chose Cockburn? It does not matter, though, the seed of the conspiracy, only its significance, which to Mr. Huffington is crystalline. The sculpted cliff is an augury, awaiting its fulfillment, when the Emperor is brought up here and installed in the pitiful house behind him. If they are able to bring him here, he will never get off. That is the message. He will never leave this place, and here shall his visage acquire this same expression, of defeat.

And standing there, trembling in the mud, Mr. Huffington knows with an equal clarity what must be done. Such a man as this, who moves the world, who advances history, cannot rot and die here on this horrid isle. No, vows Huffington, with a rheumatic clench of his fist upon its cane. The cliffs out there will have to wait another eternity; the winds will have to carve another visage, of another king. But not Napoleon Bonaparte. And if Mr. Huffington is the only one to see it, then he must be the one to act. He feels it in his frantic thumping heart. At last his chance has come, and so long after he abandoned hope. Destiny is calling—not just to the island, or the Briars, but to him, to Virgil Phineas Huffington, and he will not fail it. He will not shrink. He turns his back upon the seaside bust and pledges his defiance. The Emperor will escape the island before they bring him here.

The journey back to Jamestown will be far more grueling than the trip up. What took seven hours to climb will require Mr. Huffington thirteen to descend, a path which is variously muddy, puddled, and treacherously inclined, up and down. Before he is done, Mr. Huffington will be passed by nearly all the workers at Longwood, soldiers and slaves alike, the majority of whom will, on seeing his spastic leg and smelling his urine-soaked trousers, offer their assistance, to carry him, summon a pony or an ox. Mr. Huffington will wave them all away with hostile swipes of his walking cane.

Jamestown will be asleep by the time he reaches it. He will need a half hour to walk the three hundred yards from the foot of Side Path to the back entrance of his nephew's house on Market Street. The flight of stairs to his room will take another full hour, at the end of which his foot will be numb, his hip screaming in pain, and the palm of his left hand shredded white and pink by the knob of his cane. He will collapse on his bed, a quivering pile of flesh, bone, wool, and excrement, his only solace the vial of laudanum that stands in arm's reach. This six ounces, which were to last him until January, will be gone within the hour and service a night of cold sweats, tears, and the dry weeping, not so much at the pain that is fast devouring Mr. Huffington's mind as for His Majesty's suffering, and the beneficence of Fate, for giving a dusty old man one last chance to make a difference in the world.

The grotto is not so far from the route that Toby must take back to the Briars. He follows the road past the Governor's house and turns right at the great red cedar tree just as he normally would, but when he crosses over the creek bridge, he pulls Lewis over to the side. He takes the sack of chicks with him and one mango—Timu kindly let him have one back—then climbs down the embankment to the creek, whose waters will eventually slide over the cataract that cools the Briars, a mile or so down.

For a long time it was a question where the grotto was exactly. All anyone knew was that it must be small and probably not so far from Lemon Valley. Winston-Kumar never said in his stories. It wasn't until a slave named Bernardo had a dream of finding a white shirt on Francis Plain; some of the children went to look for it, and they're the ones who discovered the little cave not so far away.

Toby comes upon the plain just past a gentle rapid. The bank gives way to a small meadow, bounded on the south by a little grove of willow trees and then a sudden limestone ridge that shelf by shelf climbs all the way from here to Diana's Peak.

The grove Toby remembers. What he does not remember are the tents to the north. There are a dozen or so, and cabins too, with a campfire in the middle, and men—soldiers, standing and sitting, drinking from tin cups. They don't seem to pay him much mind, though, not as he climbs up from the creek, not as he enters under the willows. They cast passionless glances his way, as they might a passing goat.

The willows aren't so large or so many, but bunched together, they enclose a breezy world of sifted sun and fallen catkins. Toby shuffles through, and the chicks stir contentedly at the bottom of their sack, all headed for the sudden rise of limestone on the far side. Toby's more specific guide is an old locust tree, whose roots grow right out of the crevices. Just to the left there, and tucked beneath the lowest ledge, is a small opening, the size and shape of a palm leaf, barely large enough for a man to crawl inside.

There is no thorny bramble—Lopez soon discovered there was no need—but in the small clearing between the willows and the rock, the ground is studded by a small collection of stones, chipped from the wall. They're arranged like seats around a stage, some as small as bowls, some as large as footstools, but all have a flat top, and all offer a gift of one kind or another: dried flowers, seeds, fruit, a tin of matches. Some rest in beds of myrtle leaf, which are supposed to keep the birds away, and may. The flies buzz in and out, showing Toby how far the gifts extend, appearing and disappearing well inside the dappled shade. He sees polished stones, and oranges, ginger, forks, and spoons. A skillet.

There is one close by, beside a drape of low braids—an offering of white briars and dried roses. Toby recognizes how the stems have been tied with three cords of hay. That's 'Scilla's knot, and beside it he sees the crumbs of one of Sarah's biscuits, surrounded by a small garland of leaves.

Toby sets the mango between them and kneels, once again facing the locust tree but not looking. The chicks begin to scurry when they feel the ground from inside their sack, but Toby's mind is clear. He bows all the way down till his forehead presses against the fallen leaves; never to forget, he prays. His eyes stay closed. The chicks protest with chirps and nips. The mango waits beside him, round, ripe, and patient. Toby stands. He swings the restless sack over his shoulder and starts back through the willows for the creek, not once looking around behind him. There is no need. They only leave him gifts when they know he isn't here.

CHAPTER FOURTEEN

NOVEMBER 7

—◆—

More complaints, the Grand Marshal's explanation, &c.—Toby's vision

"C'est absurde!" spits Madame de Montholon. "Passwords! How can we be expected to remember a new password every day? They know who we are. The whole island knows who we are. They would not be here except for us!"

The rest of the suite quite agrees. They are out at the far end of the garden, at the arbor, surrounding the Emperor, the women seated, the men standing, and all in an ill humor. It is hot. The walk was not pleasant.

"Was this not in the letter?" The Emperor turns to Bertrand.

"To Mr. Balcombe, Your Majesty?"

"Whichever."

"Well, I'm not sure that passwords are something that Mr. Balcombe is in a position to address."

"Who said they were?" Madame de Montholon snaps.

Bertrand remains calm. "Were we not speaking of recommendations to Mr. Balcombe?"

"We were speaking of everything! The entire situation! The fact there are no shutters in the Pavilion."

"Or drapes," Madame Bertrand slips in.

"The fact that we have to remember impossible passwords and

find whoever is the parole officer for the day. We are talking about the fact that the Emperor's bath is not even here."

"It's at Longwood, I believe."

"Well, what good is it doing there? And how long will it be before the house is ready?"

"I spoke to Admiral Cockburn. He—"

"He's a liar." Madame de Montholon flicks the air. "No, it's true. Mr. Balcombe is adequate. You're lucky to have him, but the Admiral, and Mr. Pourteous—perfectly useless."

"The bread," mentions her husband.

"Inedible."

"And the wine."

"The wine is not wine."

"The coffee is not coffee."

"That is absolutely true," Gourgaud joins.

"It's unconscionable," says Madame de Montholon. "We are being treated like prisoners!—like criminals!—when clearly the most dangerous person on the island is this old man, this tutor, Old Huff."

This prompts helpless chuckles from both Gourgaud and de Montholon.

"I'd sooner trust my children's education to a seal! It's no wonder they are so ignorant."

More nods of quite-agreement, excepting the Emperor, who once again turns to Bertrand. "But these are the same complaints which I put in the last letter, yes?"

"Some," says Bertrand, "but again, it is a matter of—"

"And if the letter had been delivered as I asked, then there is at least a chance that these problems would be addressed." He looks about, finding support. "But unless the Grand Marshal prefers that I take up these matters in person—which of course I am unable to do, as I am here in confinement—then I don't see how else these complaints can be properly posed."

"And I think we agreed"—Las Cases steps in—"letters are best."

"Yes, but only if they are delivered," the Emperor answers. "Perhaps I should entrust them to someone less negligent."

"It is not *negligence*, Your Majesty." The Grand Marshal's tone turns suddenly abrupt.

"If it is not negligence," replies the Emperor, "then what is it? Defiance?"

At this affront the Grand Marshal's forehead turns so red with rage his wife, Fanny, is overcome. She rises and exits the arbor, hand to brow. Though of stronger stomach (and actually enjoying herself), Madame de Montholon is obliged, as a woman, to follow, leaving just the men now.

"Tell me," says the Emperor, still addressing Bertrand, "if there was something you deemed inappropriate in the letter, then you should tell me, but that does not excuse delay, if only for the sake of the others."

Bertrand looks to Las Cases, who takes his meaning: The Grand Marshal would like to be alone with the Emperor. He gently clears his throat and leads Gourgaud and de Montholon from the arbor as well.

"Your Majesty." Bertrand recovers his composure, and with it, the proper note of subservience. "It is not that I defy Your Majesty's will or that I am negligent. My failure to convey all the suite's complaints has to do with their number—and the nature, I am afraid."

The Emperor waits, chin high.

"I think it legitimate to ask that the de Montholons be given more suitable lodgings—that a floor of the Inn be set aside for their use, for instance. I think it is clearly wrong, and an insult, that we should be made to petition in order to see Your Majesty. These are reasonable requests, but to pose them alongside certain others—"

"Such as?"

"Such as that you might purchase the Briars or purchase the gardener. Your Majesty, with all respect, I can anticipate the Admiral's response, and I think it would detract from the legitimacy—or the legitimate consideration of the other needs expressed—if at the same time we choose to ask . . . for the right to purchase the house."

Napoleon has been listening without apparent objection. "The suggestion was that *you* would purchase the house."

"On your behalf, and that you would live here."

"Did you ask?"

Bertrand is slow to answer, unaccustomed to seeing His Majesty so apparently oblivious of the facts of the matter. "I don't think it will be received in the same faith as the offer is made."

The Emperor nods. "Very good." He stands and abruptly starts them back out of the garden.

Bertrand is still troubled, uncertain what has been resolved in this last exchange, but as they approach the bungalow, the sight of the children playing on the lawn relaxes him. Hortens has a kerchief tied around her eyes and is staggering, laughing, blindly flailing at the others. There are Henri, Napoléon, and the Balcombes as well. When the blond girl sees the Emperor, she immediately runs over and tries to get him to play. "You promised!" She tugs at his arm, but he refuses. It is time for lunch.

Bertrand is hungry as well. The others have joined the Balcombes on the veranda for tea and cress sandwiches. When they see the Emperor's expression, high and satisfied, all take relief. They bow gratefully to His Grace as he climbs the stairs. Bertrand waits, so as not to let their veneration fall upon his shoulders and, in that moment's pause, feels a curious rubbing upon his leg, as if a cat were nuzzling his shin. He turns.

It is the most dangerous man on the island, according to the others, the tutor, looking particularly frail this morning, overdressed for the heat in his black wool cloak, and prodding him with his cane.

"Would you like to come up, sir?" Bertrand extends his elbow, but the old man seems uninterested.

"Warm enough?" he asks.

"Quite. Thank you."

The old man's eyes are dancing wild. His face is damp and ashen, except for the middle of his cheeks, which, if Bertrand is not mistaken, have been unsparingly rouged. "Coal is on the way." He twitches.

"Coal?"

"The eighteenth." The old man is trying not to smile. He may be trying to wink, in fact. "From Newcastle."

Bertrand isn't certain what to do. He nods. The old man lifts his cane—his wrist is trembling terribly—then turns and makes his way.

Only de Montholon has witnessed this exchange and welcomes Bertrand up the veranda steps with a glass of lemonade. "Pray tell, what are our orders today?"

——⚬——

Toby is one of those who have seen Fernando Lopez. Not the only one. There is Christopher, Mr. Pritchard's old footman; and Martin, who only heard his voice; and Winston-Kumar, of course. And it isn't only the slaves. Mr. Doveton was said to have seen him out by Sandy Bay one time. Still, they are a chosen few, and Toby is one of them. And that is why—he now sees, he now admits—when Alley found Winston-Kumar's puppets, he brought them straight to Toby; that is why 'Scilla has been looking at him so intently and so impatiently—not because she's seen the puppets in the cellar but because she believes that Lopez has gone hiding. Bony has driven him away—he and all the redcoats—and if there is anyone on the island who can find him, it's Toby, the "Javaboy." That is what she thinks.

Toby saw him only once, though, and it was a long time ago, back when he was still working at Mr. Breame's. He was bitten by a spider out in the tobacco field and became very sick. He was in bed for eleven days, so hot and cold that some feared he might not survive. Toby didn't know himself, or even if he wanted to, but that was when he saw beyond the shadows for the first time.

His body lay in bed, in the slave cottages at Mr. Breame's. His mind, though—and his mind's eye, and nose, and ears—all found themselves in Chapel Valley; only there were no houses or streets or even the church. Only trees, mostly lemon but some orange too. It was late in the day, coming on night, but the colors of the fruit were more rich and deep and glowing than he had ever seen, like little balls of sun, suspended among the deep green leaves. Their fragrance was the same, the air was more redolent, and the sound of the air, stroking the leaves. Toby was down among them, listening, smelling, gazing at the color, when he became aware that someone else was in the orchard. He was being watched. He turned, and there he saw him, twelve paces up the slope.

He was wearing a rag around his head like a turban and a loose beard which ran up his cheeks. His nose was two deep scars, black in the middle. His mouth was low and straight, comfortable in silence. He didn't have a shirt. His torso was lean but firm, his shoulders broad, retaining the posture of his noble youth. His right arm hung loose from his elbow, swaying for its lack of ballast. But Toby was looking mostly in his eyes, which were wide-set and sat high upon his cheekbones. They bore an expression of great gentleness, come by sorrows, without shame. He looked at Toby for only a moment, while the leaves swayed around them; then he turned away. That was all.

Toby has returned to that island many times since, in dreams, the old island, where there is no Jamestown, no Briars, and no roads; where Deadwood Plain is a redwood forest, and none of the fields at Sandy Bay are tilled. And he always knows that Lopez is near. He can feel him. But it was just that first time, when he was so ill, that he actually saw him, looked in his eyes for just a moment and understood: He was not going to die, not then anyway, but that when he did, it would be here on St. Helena.

CHAPTER FIFTEEN

NOVEMBER 8–10

—⚜—

The Emperor and the Greeks—"Respect the burden"—Campanero's wink—
Campanero—Mr & Mrs. Balcombe—Marchand's orders—
Miss Lambe and the prickly pear—The prophet speaks

November 8–9—"Another day done." The Emperor sighs, looking
up at the sickle moon. "I cannot bear to think how many years are
left to me. What a horror, to be old and useless."

It pains Las Cases to see him this way. "Your Majesty, if you
would permit the presumption of my suggesting?"

The Emperor so grants.

"It strikes me that Your Majesty has gone without exercise . . .
for quite some time now—on the boat, needless to say, but even
here—whereas before he led a life of great vigor and action. I wonder if it wouldn't be of benefit to include more exercise in the day's
schedule. Riding, perhaps. We have been provided horses."

The Emperor dismisses. "They would only follow," he says, referring to the guards. "I'd as soon not ride at all."

They walk on in silence, and once again the Emperor looks up at
the sky, the span of stars. "Do you think maybe the ancients had it
right?"

"How so, Your Majesty?"

"When they saw no further use in life, when all that was left was
the disgust and vexations of age, they ended it. I know it makes you
nervous to hear me speak this way, but you must remember, you, my

good Count, were raised in a conventional morality. Not I. I tell you, if I could be convinced that France was happy and at peace, that she no longer needed me, I would be perfectly prepared to take my leave."

The following morning before breakfast Las Cases goes and speaks to Captain Poppleton, the ranking officer currently appointed guard at the Briars, to ask about rules regarding riding. He makes no bones. He tells Poppleton that the reason the Emperor has not availed himself of the horses is that he assumes an escort might be forced upon him. Poppleton's silence is answer enough and sparks a tiny flare of outrage in the Count.

"He is not going to race off. Where would he go?"

Poppleton acknowledges his conflict. On the one hand, it's true, he has explicitly been asked to practice discretion and not do anything that the General or his suite might deem intrusive or offensive. On the other hand, his orders are fairly strict not to let the General out of his sight.

For now Las Cases decides not to labor the point, satisfied that the Captain at least recognizes the Emperor's frustration. When he happens to mention the exchange at breakfast, however, His Majesty is more annoyed than grateful.

"You should not have done that," he says. "I'm sure the Captain's orders are clear. We should not be asking soldiers to disobey their charge." The matter, it seems, is settled.

—⠿⠿⠿—

Betsy's mother is entertaining some guests in the parlor. Every day there's someone else: Mrs. Julio, the Ibbetsons, officers, all come to meet him so they can say they have. Today it's Mrs. Hamilton and a friend of hers from India, Mrs. Pravali. They have just come back from their introduction and are still atwitter. "He has such a bearing about him, doesn't he?" says Mrs. Hamilton. " 'Respect the burden.' "

"What is that?" asks Betsy. She makes them tell, even though her mother clearly doesn't want to. Apparently they'd all been walking along the inland road, the Emperor as well. They had been talking about who knows what?—which exact village in India Mrs. Pravali was from and what was her favorite Indian flower—when a pair of slaves came up the road in the opposite direction, carrying trunks and lumber. Her mother started scolding the slaves, which Betsy can hear her doing, telling them to step aside and make way, but the Emperor stopped her. "Respect the burden, Madame." Betsy can see exactly how he would do it, too, sweeping his arm in a deliberately grand fashion, directing the ladies to the side of the road to let the men pass.

"Such character!" Mrs. Hamilton now fans herself. "Such a countenance!"

Betsy doesn't find him until a while later. She mentions the incident, but he hardly remembers it. "With the Indian woman?"

"Yes, Mrs. Pravali."

He scowls. "I think she is one of the ugliest women I have ever met. Do you not understand? If you are going to allow people here to meet me, do you not think you owe it to me, as your guest—as your friend—to see that they are attractive? Why do you not invite the Wilkes woman? She is the pretty one, yes?"

"Yes."

"Why do you not bring me her? If you persist with such ugly people, then I can no longer allow you to introduce me to your friends."

"They're not our friends."

"Whoever they are. The people who think they can ask favors of you. To see me."

She nods. She understands. She will try to do better.

November 9—Alley appears midmorning today with one of the roosters from Timu's farm. It's the rooster's day to seed the eggs, as many as he can before sundown. Alley comes by the goat paths, as usual, with Timu's crate up on his head. It's the first Toby has seen him in over a week.

"You been at Longwood?"

"Some," he says.

The hens begin clucking nervously even before Alley enters the pen. They can sense what's in the crate, and the rooster can sense the hens as well. He starts beating his wings in anticipation, and Alley has to wrestle him to get him out. A fierce-looking bird, wiry and strong, with golden red feathers, a dark green tail, a long neck like a horse with a full red mane, except down at the base, where his hackle meets his breast, there is a distinctive white star.

"Campanero winking." Alley holds him up, smiling. "Timu said."

"You been at Timu's?"

"Some."

He sets the rooster down, and the anxious hens all back away. The Red takes a dozen aimless trots to shake off the indignity of being handled, then assumes a more studly strut. He eyes the hens, and as he moves in their direction, they flock away like blown leaves. Some not as fast as the others, though, and the Red has a keen eye for these, the wanting. He charges. The flock flees, but he runs right up the back of the nearest hen he can get his spurs on and begins humping.

Toby closes the gate. "Hungry?"

Alley nods, and together they walk over to the kitchen garden, a discrete but impressive tract, governed in tandem by Toby and 'Scilla. Alley isn't interested in much there, but Toby starts a sack for him. He adds some carrots, potatoes, and turnips, but Alley refuses the yam. "That's for you." Toby adds a few in any case.

Alley is more receptive out in the orchard. Toby starts a second sack—of orange, mango, cherimoya. To the intermittent crows of triumph vaulting from the distant bamboo pen, Toby picks the ripest fruit he can find and gives them all to Alley—grapes, berries, and figs as well. Alley saves some for later. Some he eats right there, and he sits for an early supper. 'Scilla serves him salt pork and some cider she's been saving. She even fries some bananas.

"Nice house you building him?" Sarah asks him.

Alley shrugs, the only one eating. "House is good," he says, devouring the bananas. "Where they put the house . . ." His eyes finish the thought.

"How much longer?" asks Toby.

Alley shrugs again. "He'll still be here awhile."

Down at the far end of the table 'Scilla sniffs.

With twilight falling and the bowls all clear, Alley and Toby go fetch the Red. They bring 'Scilla's net, but it isn't needed. The hens are all milling together at one end of the pen, the tousled hind feathers signaling the day's select. The Red is over at the far side, scarred and spent. Alley has no trouble dropping the net on him and returning him to the crate.

He leaves the way he came, by the goat paths, the fruit sacks slung over his shoulder, and the crate up on top of his head. Toby means to tell him he should be taking the roads now, not the goat paths, but Alley's too stubborn and quick. He moves off through the brush, rocking the weary rooster as he goes. Toby bets the bird is fast asleep already, blending with the black shadows of the cage, all but for the lone white star, winking at the base of his hackle.

VI

Campanero

Campanero came to the island the same way most of the slaves did, crowded in a pen at the bottom of a boat. But he was very young when they first took him, and no one could not tell him from the other birds, until one day his keeper, a sailor named Galinha, came down and discovered that he wasn't growing like the others.

"Look at you, these spurs and combs," he said.

Galinha didn't want a cockerel with the hens, not while they were still at sea, so he borrowed a crate from another sailor, and he put the young bird there to keep. Campanero could still see the other birds sometimes, and they could see him—how he was growing into a fine white cockerel—but that was as close as he ever came.

Then one day, as the boat came in sight of a tiny black island in the middle of the ocean, Galinha came down to feed the chickens with two of his friends, Bao-niya and Figuero, and the three of them were in the middle of an argument.

"Oh, the man is there," said Galinha. "And just like they say. No face and no hand."

"A ghost," replied Bao-niya, whose trade was spices.

"No ghost. No man," said the third, Figuero, who kept a nursery of fruit trees. "A lie. Is nothing on the island but lemons and water."

"Is so," said Galinha. "He sleeps in a straw bed and wears a white shirt."

"A white shirt, ha!" said Figuero.

"Which shows he's a ghost," said Bao-niya.

"No, I can show you," said Galinha, "and you will see. And you will give me one fig tree."

"One fig tree." Figuero scoffed. "Very well. And if you show me nothing, which you will, then you give me one of these chickens."

So it was agreed, and witnessed by Bao-niya, who still insisted the man on the island was a ghost but was too cheap to join the wager.

The ship dropped anchor, and all the sailors rowed into shore with their casks and baskets. They entered the orchard valley, and while they picked their lemons and oranges, Galinha sang:

> Hombre, hombre,
> Dom Fernao, don't hide.
> Let me have my tree.

But no man showed himself, and Figuero smiled.

Hombre, hombre,
show us you're not here,
and let me have my chicken.

Next they went to fill their casks at the streams, and again
Galinha sang,

Dom Fernao, Dom Fernao.
Come show yourself.
Let my children eat
figs and cream
figs and cream
figs and cream
in the morning.

But still there was no answer. And no answer either to the call of
Figuero, whose children wanted eggs instead.

So Galinha brought them to the grotto where the man was said
to sleep, and he showed them the bed of straw inside the little cave.

"A viper's nest," said Figuero, "is no proof a man lives here.
Where is the shirt? Where is the barrel?"

There was no shirt. There was no barrel, and finally Galinha
had to admit that he had lost the bet. When they got back to the
ship, he went to get Figuero his chicken. He chose the cockerel,
the white-feathered one he'd set aside, but when he brought it out
on deck to give to Figuero, Figuero would not take it.

"Ooooh, no," he said. "No cockerel. I want eggs before my
dinner."

"But we did not wager eggs," said Galinha. "Tell him, Bao-niya.
He said chicken."

"You said chicken, Figuero."

"Oh, no. No, no, no. I wager a fig tree. Even for a hen, this is
not fair. Now I have won, and you give me what I am owed!"

"A chicken," said Galinha, and he pushed the white cockerel
into Figuero's arms, but Figuero still would not have it. The two

began to push and shove, and in the middle of the scuffle, the bird went tumbling overboard and down into the cold pitching water.

"Oh, no, no!" cried Galinha. "Now go." He punched Figuero in the arm. "Jump and get him!"

"I'm not jumping. Is not my chicken," he said, and by then it was too late. The waves were pulling the cockerel back toward the island, while the ship was turning away. The sailors could only stand and watch as the white wings thrashed helplessly in the swells, which drew the bird ever closer to the treacherous black rocks of the island shore. The bird was surely doomed.

But then—"Look!" Galinha cried, and pointed. There on the rocks was the figure of a man, standing.

But Figuero would not even turn to see.

"Look!" Galinha cried again. "It is he!"

Bao-niya turned, and he too saw, the distant figure was diving into the water now.

"He is going to save the bird!" Galinha cried. "Look and you will see I am right. You can see his face."

So you could. The man swimming out to save the cockerel had no face, just scars and black holes.

"And look at the arm!" said Galinha.

He was right about this as well, for when the man reached out to take the cockerel in his arm, anyone could see there was no hand at the end of his wrist.

But Figuero would not even turn. "I see nothing."

"Because you do not look," said Galinha, now grabbing him and spinning him around, but by now the mysterious man had taken the cockerel back onto the island and disappeared behind the trees.

"Nothing," said Figuero.

"Not nothing," said Galinha. "Tell him." He turned to Bao-niya. "Tell him—was a man dived down from the rocks to save the cockerel, and he had no face, and no hand. Tell him. Was a man."

Bao-niya turned to Figuero. "Was a ghost."

"Did you see?" asks Mr. Balcombe. "Alley was here today."

He and Mrs. Balcombe are standing at separate windows in the parlor, looking out. Betsy and the General are on the lawn, in the Windsor chairs; the boys have just joined them. The boys too have grown quite comfortable with their guest. Alexander sits on the grass at his feet. Nicholas is twiddling the medals and decoration on his coat.

Mr. Balcombe looks over at his wife, to see if she heard. Her face is inert, grimly so. He suspects she is looking at Betsy, who is in turn looking at the General, smiling as she watches him request a knife of some kind from his valet, or a pair of scissors. It's a new smile for Betsy, one she seems to have learned from the General, that faint lift at the edge of her mouth, which recognizes the appeal of oneself to another. She watches as he snips an ornament from the breast of his coat and gives it to Nicholas. Alexander, two years older and more shy, awaits.

"Did you hear?" Mr. Balcombe asks again. "Alley was here."

Still his wife does not reply. Out the window the General takes the scissors to the opposite breast of his coat and cuts off something for Alexander.

"Did you speak to Mr. Huffington?" she asks, nodding over to the right, where Mr. Huffington himself is just now making his way under the shade of the banyans. They have been discussing a reduction in Mr. Huffington's hours, on account of his wavering health and the best interests of the boys.

"Oh," says Mr. Balcombe. "Yes."

By this, he means, yes, I shall, but before his wife can clarify, a small barrage of knees and feet comes thumping up the veranda steps. A moment later the boys are charging in to show the gifts that "Bony" has given them. Alexander's is a medal with an eagle on it. Nicholas's is a tiny bugle, made of golden silk.

Monsieur Marchand has set his easel out in open view and in that respect has only himself to blame. He is painting another picture of the Briars, just as he has made renderings of all the various residences where the Emperor has stayed over the years. This time he has chosen a spot on the northern side, three-quarters of the way up the incline that leads to the inland road. From here he has a good view of both the bungalow and the Pavilion, and he is also in position to track the impossibly slow progress of the Balcombes' tutor up the tree-lined lane to his left. The old man passes him by five steps, then stops and turns, to observe.

This is not the first time he has so paused. He did the same last week, when Marchand was down on the lawn painting just the Pavilion, but Marchand offers no objection, in expectation that as before, the old man will eventually turn and continue on his turtle's walk home. Marchand uses the moment to work on one of the less crucial portions of the tableau, the sky. He is sweeping a watery pale blue overtop the hills, when the old man actually mutters something. Marchand isn't sure what, though, not speaking English very well.

"Excusez-moi?" He turns. "Pardon?"

The man is ashen—even in the shade Marchand can see—withered and trembling, the dry sticks of an old frame barely supporting a dark wool cloak, the deathly black of which is enlivened only by its mud-caked and salt-stained filth. He is looking at Marchand with eyes possessed and eyes departed, and he speaks again, this time more slowly and clearly, enough for Marchand to recognize that this is not English. It is Greek, which Marchand understands far less well. Still, he feels compelled to meet the tutor's gaze, if only to hold to the thread by which the poor old man is clinging to life. He speaks a full paragraph of the long-dead tongue, inserts a mention of Monsieur St. Denis, then waits for his reply.

Monsieur Marchand isn't certain how, but at that moment he notices something gleam inside the old man's cloak, a burnished knob of some kind. The cloak quickly closes, and Mr. Huffington still awaits. Marchand nods vaguely, and the old man's blood seems to start running again. He bows with an aged elegance, then turns and restarts the long journey home.

Marchand rewets his brush, prays that that was not the handle of a dueling pistol in the old man's coat, and continues his painting.

What Mr. Huffington said was this: "The Newcastle [translated from the words "new" and "palace"] is due to arrive on the thirteenth. That evening after dinner the girl will persuade the Emperor to play the game. We need only make sure that Bertrand receives the ace of spades [translated, the "alpha" of "shovel"] and that St. Denis is ready with the cart. If this is clear, you need only nod . . ."

—⊸⊸—

November 10—Miss Lambe came by to meet the Emperor today, much to Betsy's delight. Miss Lambe is very attractive and, more important, takes care in how she presents herself. Today she is wearing a sky blue dress, lighter than the one Betsy has chosen, but it shows well against Miss Lambe's eyes and blond hair. She has a matching hat, her skin is alabaster, and she has on a pair of cloud white gloves that Betsy has been coveting for some time at Mr. Solomon's. Betsy escorts her out at once.

They find him in the orchard, and as always, his greeting is cheery. "Ah, Mademoiselle. Êtes-vous sage?" *Are you wise?* She introduces Miss Lambe, and the three of them take a brief stroll, during which the Emperor treats their guest to the usual peppering of questions: Where does she comes from? What does her father do? Where else has she been? He searches for some point of interest, some topic where he might dig in and surprise her with the depth of his knowledge and insight, but her answers are all so plain, he gives up shortly. Betsy leads her back to the veranda and deposits her there with Jane, excusing herself as soon as it's decent.

She runs back and intercepts him on the lane of pomegranates; he is headed in for the day as well. The low garden fence runs alongside to their left.

"So what did you think?" she asks. "Better?"

He shrugs.

"You don't think she is pretty?"

"Well, yes, she is very pretty, but she has the air of a . . . une marchande de modes."

Betsy isn't quite sure what this means, except that he is very difficult to please, and that she is also inclined to agree.

"But what of Miss Wilkes?" he says. "She is the one I am supposed to meet, yes?"

"Oui."

"So show me Miss Wilkes." He glances up, and his eyes suddenly roll in exasperation. Down at the end of the lane Mr. and Mrs. Thomas are greeting Jane and Miss Lambe on the lawn—Mr. and Mrs. Thomas, who have been begging her father to invite them over for the last two weeks.

"I cannot," says the Emperor. "I refuse."

The fence to his left is just above knee height. The Emperor grabs hold of the top of the post and jumps—nimbly, at first, over the crosshatch of the posts, but he comes down directly into a low splay of prickly pear. His stockinged calf is stuck by a pricker, and he falls back rump first into a much larger configuration of pads and needles.

He howls—a pair of birds quit a nearby branch—and everyone in earshot, Mr. and Mrs. Thomas included, looks over in alarm.

"Marchand!" He whispers his command. "And St. Denis! Vite!"

Betsy runs, pausing only long enough to curtsy hello to the Thomases; then she races up to the marquee to find the valets.

——

Las Cases has just returned from an extremely frustrating trip into town. First he could not find his preferred ink and had to make do with diluted island stock. Then he was confronted on the street by an officer whom he had *never* met, who proceeded to tell him that he had spoken to Captain Poppleton of the Emperor's need for exercise and that he wanted the Emperor—or "General Bonaparte"—to understand that while the Admiralty recognizes the General's desire for activity, and offers that he may have at his disposal as many horses as he likes, the fact remains that if he should choose to ride one, a sentry *would* be required to accompany him.

Las Cases expected as much, but the sheer pettiness of the order, the look of unyielding small-mindedness in the officer's eye, has been a burr in Las Cases's shoe the entire walk back. By the time he reaches the property, he is burning with indignation, and he can already see an audience through the new shutters in the Pavilion. It looks as if a good number of the suite were gathered inside. He stalks up the lawn, prepared to deliver his report, only to find the girl guarding the entrance of the marquee. "You're not supposed to go in."

He brushes past her.

"You're not supposed to," she calls.

There is a small gathering in the back of the room—Dr. O'Meara, Marchand, St. Denis, Gourgaud, Cipriani, all standing to the side of the Emperor's curtained campaign bed. Las Cases stops short when he sees that the Emperor himself is within, lying on his stomach. Dr. O'Meara is sitting on a chair beside with his medical case opened before him. The Emperor is not wearing any pants. The doctor is examining his left buttock.

"What's happened?" asks Las Cases.

Gourgaud answers. "His Majesty has suffered—"

"I fell," says the Emperor less ceremonially. "In the sticky bush."

"The prickly pear."

"Yes, what did you want?"

"I'm certain it can wait, Your Majesty."

"Clearly you came in here with something to say. What?"

Las Cases is at a momentary loss, but finally, if only in deference to His Majesty's command, he tries mustering up his indignation once again. "I just spoke to Captain . . . I'm not even sure of his name, but he said that he'd spoken to Captain Poppleton and that Your Majesty was correct. An escort would be required for any riding excursions."

The Emperor nods, annoyed that the matter has apparently persisted.

"It seems so little to ask," says Las Cases. "What do they fear, that you are going to dash off into the ocean?"

"Yes, a horse that swims," the Emperor jests. All chuckle, the Emperor included, though the bounce disturbs the work of Dr. O'Meara, who is still intent upon the little prickers in his patient's soft pale rump.

Las Cases is not entirely assuaged. "I am inclined to go back right now"—he simmers—"and tell them they may have their horses back."

The Emperor shakes his head, his wrist nearly grazing the floor with a calming gesture. "You are out of temper, Monsieur le Comte. We shall send the horses back, but tomorrow. It's best to sleep one night after the day's offense."

Las Cases bows his head, much as the Arabs must have bowed their heads before the Sultan Kebir, he thinks. He had spoken like the prophet.

CHAPTER SIXTEEN

NOVEMBER 11-13

⸺◆⸺

The mission thwarted—The Emperor's bijouterie; Betsy's apologia—
The body is discovered and buried; 'Scilla speaks

November 11—Mr. Huffington reminds himself at least a dozen times to remember to pause when he comes to the wide turn, to check the bay and see if any of the ships have arrived. He has been trying to do this every day, but nearly every day, when the moment comes, he forgets, such is his state of mind. He finished another vial of laudanum this morning, during the walk up to the Briars. Now he has none, and the pain which bolts from his right hip with each next step is so searing, so riddling it's all he can do to keep moving forward. Leaning as much weight on his cane as it will bear, he once again bypasses the wide turn, where even if he did remember to stop and look, he could not see; his eyes are tears.

As the day wanes, the eastern slope of Jamestown Valley is a glaring gold, while the west is a blue shroud. Huffington notes neither. His only two purposes now are to pick up more of his medicine at the tobacco shop and then to get to his room, where he can drink it down.

Mr. Hammond has not been expecting Mr. Huffington but knows very well when he sees him why he has come.

"Still not feeling up to snuff, eh, Mr. Huffington?"

"Not as well as I might, no." He slaps down his coin, and Mr.

Hammond does his part, for the third time this week slipping back into his office to fill another vial.

Huffington waits—alone this evening—chewing restlessly on nothing, while his eyes flick spastically about the shop, from stool to beam to window sash, unable to stay on any one thing until they snag upon the only image in all the world that could possibly hold them still: There beneath the glass of Mr. Hammond's front display case is the Emperor Napoleon, once again looking back at Mr. Huffington from the back of a deck of playing cards. It is the same picture as before—the formal Roman portrait, bedecked in emperor's robe and laurel—the only difference being that there are twelve of them now, four stacks of three decks each, lain down like fallen dominoes.

Huff taps the glass as Mr. Hammond returns. "When did these come in?"

"Just today."

"I didn't hear the cannon."

"It fired. Early. Are you sure you're well there, Mr. Huffington?"

"And the *Newcastle*? What's the date?"

"Saturday."

"No, the date!"

"Eleventh, Mr. Huffington. Are you—"

"But you said the thirteenth. You said it was due the thirteenth."

"Must have caught a wind. Mr. Huffington, are you well?"

Huffington looks back down at the playing cards, and his mind begins to reel faster than he can track. Four stacks of three decks. Twelve Emperors, twenty-four eyes all glaring back at him:

The story is just begun.

"But do they know?"

"Who is that, Mr. Huffington?" Mr. Hammond is looking at him with a kindly concern. "Did you want to buy a deck?"

Huffington checks the window. The light is fading fast. "Yes.

One." Be safe. "Two." Careful. "One." He reaches into his pocket and sets down another coin, the only one he can find.

"That's a handsome offer, Mr. Huffington. I'll have to—"

"Keep it. Give." He opens his hand. "Give." His wrist is trembling. His body and face have burst with sweat, but Hammond passes him the deck nonetheless. As it touches his palm, Mr. Huffington feels an electric charge, a shock of life which drives him straight out the cacophonous rattling door. He bustles down the steps, past the Mesdames de Montholon and Bertrand, who are just now ascending.

"It's here," he says. "Ici. Maintenant."

The Mesdames are lost.

Useless. "Agh!" He waves them aside. "I must deliver it." He pushes through them and makes his way up Main Street, as fast as his cane will carry him, headed for Side Path.

"Was that not a gun in his pocket?" asks Bertrand, without irony.

"Let us hope," replies de Montholon.

But this is too soon, thinks Huff. Much too soon. They are not ready. He cannot remember who has been told, and there is even a voice in his head, shaking its head, assuring him, no one. No one knows. You have failed again, Mr. Huffington. The chance has been offered to rise, and you have known of it, but it shall not be, and the fault lies with you, the one who understood.

But this is not true, he thinks. There is Marchand. Marchand was the key, and Bertrand.

Across the street, he can see the cobbler's shop, Mr. Stewart's. The shades are pulled. No lamps lit. That's a good sign. The cobbler gone. Yes, a good sign. St. Denis must have come and got him. Or Marchand, loyal Marchand. So perhaps they're there already, waiting. He just needs to get them the cards, and all will proceed from there. He lowers his head and starts the climb. If only one of the boys were there, he thinks, if he could borrow their legs for just a moment and run, run all the way, or fly.

"Mr. Huffington!" It is Mrs. Alexander, but Huffington won't even look. "Where, in such a hurry!"

"Can't," he says. "Can't talk. Good day."

"Mr. Huffington, are you all right? You look not well."

He waves the cane, no, and staggers on. He has come upon the first steep incline of Side Path. A searing pain shoots through his hip, down to his toe and through his arm to his elbow, but it does not matter. He cannot think of that. He must push on, up and up. That is the only thought he permits. Up.

He rounds the second shoulder and comes upon a pair of sentries headed down, their coats looming ahead like two red lanterns. His breath grows short. He must get by. He can feel his dueling pistol hooked to the top of his pants, digging in his thigh. He finds the cards in his left pocket and clutches them tight. The cards and the cane, that is all. He keeps his eye a step ahead, on the road, step by step, and he'll be fine.

"Sir," says one of the officers. "Sir."

Huffington sees only the gray spats above his boots, the glaring red of his coat, the blinding white sashes, crossed at the breast.

"Sir, are you all right?"

"Fine, fine, must be going."

"Can we help—"

"No," he barks. "No!" He buries his chin, holds tight to the cards in his pocket, and passes right between them. He can feel the muzzle of his pistol digging into his thigh. Trust in Marchand. And Bertrand. Just get them the cards in time, and make sure the Emperor receives the—

But then he is seized by horror. The ace. The ace! He hadn't even stopped to check, but wouldn't it be just like them, like dastardly Hammond, to keep the ace? Keep the ace and foil the plan.

He must make sure it's there. Of course it is, but if it isn't. If it isn't . . . what will it have been worth? He pulls the deck out from his pocket, but his hand is trembling so, and the cards are new and slick, his palm is numb. A wind kicks up, and they burst from his fingers like fireworks. They scatter and turn on the breeze and flutter down on the path, all fifty-two—but one. One flits down the bank, twirling down. He's certain it's the ace, the one he needs, and as he watches it descend, farther down than his hip would ever let him climb, he sees that he has failed and will not make it. The card is gone. And no one knows.

—⁓⁓⁓—

The Emperor didn't want to walk today. It's rainy, and he is still sore from his tumble in the prickly pear. He cannot sit comfortably, so Betsy does her best to distract him. In the bungalow parlor she brings him her pagoda. It is the most exotic thing she owns, the size of a dollhouse, lacquered red and black. Her father bought it for her in London when she was six.

She can't quite tell how impressed His Majesty is; enough, she supposes. He asks Marchand to bring down his bijouterie. It takes both Marchand and St. Denis to carry it, a great green trunk, which they set down on the tea table.

"Did I show you these?" he asks.

She shakes her head, and he opens the chest to reveal a very carefully arranged collection of trinkets and jewelry, framed pictures, cameos and miniatures, all waiting for their appointed walls or tabletops.

He takes out a small portrait of a young child, asleep.

"Mon fils," he says.

She looks more closely. She'd nearly forgotten he has a family, or a son, but the resemblance is very clear, in the bow of the child's lips. The picture shows him cradled in a helmet.

"Of Mars," says the Emperor. "This shows that he will be a great warrior, and this in his hand"—in the child's hand is a small globe—"this is to show he will rule the world." A banner of France waves over his head.

"He is very sweet," says Betsy.

The Emperor agrees and looks back inside the chest again. He now takes out a snuffbox, which also bears the image of the boy, kneeling before a crucifix. Above him is an inscription: "*Je prie le bon Dieu pour mon père, ma mère, et ma patrie.*"

"That's very sweet too."

She reaches in herself this time to take up yet another portrait of the boy, here with two lambs.

"This was given us by the people of Paris," says the Emperor. The little boy is riding one of the lambs and decking the other with flowing ribbons.

It's strange looking at him, though. Up to now she has been thinking of the Emperor only in relation to the people here—as their Majesty—not as someone's father or husband. She is jealous, in a way, and angry. Why did General Gourgaud get to come and be with him, and not his own son? She looks at the little boy's hands, and wonders if he'll grow up to have hands like his father's, with their delicate, tapered fingers and dimpled knuckles.

There is one more picture—Betsy's least favorite—a drawing of the boy with a woman, in a halo of clouds and roses.

"Is this his mother?" she asks, pointing at the woman.

"Marie Louise," he replies. "She would have followed me here, but they would not let her." He looks down at the image, but his eyes are so flat, and dead almost, Betsy is inclined to think this isn't true.

He removes another miniature now, and his manner instantly brightens. He speaks in Italian. "Era la dama la piu graziosa di Francia." Here was either the most gracious woman in all France, or the most graceful, Betsy isn't sure, but she knows very well who it is: his first wife, Josephine, the one he says looks so much like Betsy's mother. Betsy doesn't see the resemblance herself, but again, she can tell just by the way he looks at her—the way he smiles, to himself and to her—he cares much more for Josephine than Marie Louise. Betsy doesn't like Marie Louise. She wishes, for him, that Josephine could be here, if she were not dead, and his son too. But not Marie Louise.

"And now"—he takes out one more, an oval miniature—"I will show you the most beautiful woman in the world."

"Please."

He hands it to her. It's the size of her palm. She must hold it to the light. An almond face, black hair, with high, delicate brows.

"Who is she?"

"Pauline," he says. "Ma soeur."

Betsy nods. "She is very lovely, yes."

"Yes." He takes it back. "This proves you have taste."

The Wrights and the Mellises come for dinner that evening—just the parents, but Betsy and Jane are invited to join as well. There is no expectation that the Emperor will dine with them, but he does her father the kindness of descending from the Pavilion to meet the guests for drinks, though as usual he himself does not indulge.

Betsy enjoys watching him with the others, and the others with him. She knows very well what they've let themselves think—the worst things one could ever think of a person—yet look how quickly and easily he charms them. He greets them one after the next, focusing all his attention in turn: "You are a doctor? What do you practice? Where did you study? Do you find a difference between the maladies on the island and those on the mainland?" And he always offers his own brash opinion on whatever topic has arisen. "I don't trust intrusive treatments," he tells Dr. Mellis. "I believe in fasting and purgatives." He tells Mr. Wright, a lawyer, that "the law distorts truth and exults in the success of injustice." Of politicians, he says it's best that they be provincial in their mind-set and possess a "conventional conscience." Mrs. Mellis giggles like a girl. He refers to soldiers as "cutthroats and robbers," and Mrs. Wright gazes at him as though he were the apparition, or an angel, sitting there in their living room.

The matter comes up explicitly at dinner, long after he has said his good evening. "Quite astonishing," remarks Dr. Mellis, carving his mutton. "He doesn't seem the sort of man who'd . . ." He forks himself a bite and continues, with greasy lips. "Well, any of it, I suppose."

They all nod inanely.

"Yes, I must admit," says Mrs. Wright—quietly, of course. "Very charming. Very . . . easy. Or simple. Do you know what I mean?"

So they all pretend.

"Yes, but the eyes," says Mrs. Mellis, flashing her own. "Did you see how they look about, taking things in?"

"He certainly doesn't lack for opinions," says Mr. Wright.

"No," says his wife, "but still, the doctor is correct. Not at all what one would expect from . . . well, I suppose I'm thinking of Java."

They all nod again. Java. Betsy can't help herself. "What happened at Java?" she asks.

Her mother answers, "I'm not sure it's dinner conversation."

"Oh, do you mean the poisoning?" Betsy looks about at them. None answers. "Oh, I thought you said Java. You said *Jaffa*."

Her father clears his throat. "Yes, Betsy, but I think your mother—"

"Oh, but he had no choice." She clearly cuts him off. "The men were suffering from the Black Death."

The guests begin to stir uncomfortably. Mrs. Mellis dabs at her mouth.

"He took as many as he could," Betsy continues. "And as for the ones he left behind, he knew if they were still alive when the Turks got there, their heads would be cut off—"

"Betsy, please. Not at the table!"

"It's true. When one is far from home, one is obliged to adopt more stringent measures. He says so."

Mr. Wright smiles. "It appears you've a budding little general, William."

"And the same goes for the Duke d'Enghien," Betsy persists. "The Duke was plotting to kill him."

Dr. Mellis chuckles nervously.

"And surely one can take the life of one who'd do the same. It's only fair." She looks around at them again, but they simply sit there, stunned. "And he has read the Kor'an, and he says that it is sublime—"

"Betsy!" Mrs. Balcombe strikes the edge of the table. "You have finished your meal. You are excused."

Betsy looks at her mother, who is staring straight ahead at the tablecloth, mortified. Betsy rises and says nothing to excuse herself. She is happy to go and be done with them—*imbeciles*.

She goes to her room. He is just better than they. He has done more. He has lived more, seen more. She sits in the chair by her window and rests her head against the wall. She cannot quite see the pavilion from there, just the light shed from its window.

—∼◖◗∼—

November 12–13—At roughly 0900 hours Mr. Huffington's body is discovered, crumpled behind a rock on the side of the road, a quarter of the way from Jamestown to the Briars. The soldiers who found him notify the town coroner, Dr. Shortt, who renders a quick but reasonable judgment. The apparent proximity of the blast to his head, the pistol in Mr. Huffington's hand, the sheer unlikelihood that anyone else on the island could possibly have reason to murder the Balcombes' tutor all lead to one sad but simple conclusion, submitted that same day by Dr. Warden, that Mr. Huffington has taken his own life, felo-de-se.

As such, the body is ineligible for Christian burial and so is turned over to Mr. Fowler, nephew of the deceased, to do with as he sees fit. He and Mr. Balcombe arrive at the idea that it should be buried somewhere in the vicinity of the Briars, where Mr. Huffington passed his happier moments. Mr. Balcombe has in mind a site up near the top of the banyan lane, not far from the spot where Mr. Huffington would appear every day at the stroke of ten—there where the three roads meet.

The burial takes place the following morning at dawn, with little ceremony. Mr. Balcombe, Mr. Fowler, and the boys attend, along with two sentries and the boys from Mr. Balcombe's office, Sam and Charles. Alexander reads a passage from the *Aeneid*, thought to be one of Mr. Huffington's favorites, then Sam and Charles start shoveling the dirt.

—∼◖◗∼—

Toby observed the gathering on his way to and from the coop. He could see that the redcoats were digging a grave. He knew they buried a body. He was fairly sure it was the teacher's, judging by the Balcombe boys' attendance and the old man's pallor as of late. What Toby doesn't know is why it should be buried up by the road or why the hill and valley now seem to have a shroud upon them. He doesn't find out until dinner.

"Shot himself," Sarah tells him. "In the ear."

'Scilla begins shaking her head, chewing her gums restlessly. Toby agrees, it is not good, it is not wise, planting a body like that so near. They all must be more careful.

"You see him, you say," says 'Scilla, her *s*'s thickened by toothless gums. Still, Toby understands, she isn't talking about the old man's ghost.

He nods, he knows. "I look."

CHAPTER SEVENTEEN

NOVEMBER 14

—◦◦◦—

The Reverend at Francis Plain Camp—JohnSree's Invitation

Tuesday morning the Reverend Boys pays an impromptu visit to the military camp on Francis Plain. At last Wednesday's prayer group Lieutenant Wood mentioned there was a catechumen at the camp, seeking the baptismal rite. The candidate, a petty officer named Sifton, is not in when Boys drops by, unfortunately. The Reverend trades greetings with the acting quartermaster, Captain Sampson, of Thompson's Wood, and is struggling to take his leave from the apparently bored and lonely Captain when he notices, over on the far side of the plain, what looks like a slave emerging from the copse of willows and then descending to the creek.

"What was that, excuse me, Captain?"

Captain Sampson, in the midst of his disquisition on the local coffee bean, doesn't seem to mind the interruption. "Over in the trees, yes. We think it's a slave cemetery of some kind."

"A cemetery?"

"Yes, and a popular one."

Boys affects no great surprise, though he knows of no cemetery on Francis Plain, slave or otherwise. His first thought is that it might be a small nest of freebooters, but that wouldn't make much sense either, so close to a military camp. Also, he thinks he might have recognized the slave—Oliver, from Mr. Haywood's.

As soon as he is able to conclude his business with Captain Sampson, leaving notice of his schedule for the absent catechumen, Boys makes straight across the meadow to the trees.

The grove is a half acre, if that, and old, with a vaulted, braided canopy that sifts the southern light and flings a tiger print of shadows across the catkin-covered ground. The Reverend's focus is the far side, though, where the trees run up against an immense shelf of limestone. Boys can see already there is an arrangement of stones in the little clearing there, catching rare light. They're not headstones, though. As Boys comes closer, he can see they've been chipped from the lime and sit flat on the ground, like a set of little altars, each one with something different to offer—he has seen their like before— dried flowers, polished stones, bruising fruit. He is not surprised that some are set on beds of myrtle. He recognizes the smell now, from church. Their newly disturbing redolence gives bloom to an unsavory clove in the Reverend's stomach. This is a shrine, obviously, a pagan place of worship, whose object, to judge by the vaguely concentric arrangement of gifts, is located down at the foot of the limestone shelf, just to the left of a locust tree—a small black hollow. Nothing but a shadow.

A diving sparrow directs the Reverend's attention to a nearby gift, a muffin. Oliver's, it must be—it's so fresh—and as he looks down at it, already plucked and ravaged by scavenging birds, he begins to fill—partly with anger, partly with disappointment—that they still must seek the living among the dead. He even wonders if he should take the gifts himself, gather them up and discard them in the creek, but as he looks around to gauge the number, he now sees that the breadth of the slaves' devotion is far wider than he'd first thought. The stones are all throughout the grove, in fact, hidden under leaves and shadows, each one tendering its own special token or talisman. He passes candles, skillets, paper dolls, match tins, ginger, and the more he sees, with every deeper step inside, the more that anger and disappointment in his stomach churn into a kind of antic queasiness. He begins to feel surrounded and harassed, and as if the only thing to do were to leave. He must, and just as well, he thinks, not bother to disturb the space or clean it. For who is to say, if tomorrow's slaves should come and find their gifts were gone, they might not make a miracle of it, believe their offerings had been accepted?

Careful not to step on any hiding stone or trinket, Boys leaves briskly then, a spooked crow in his black chaplain's cloak. He even feels a chill against his neck, of that little hollow blowing gently, whisking him away like a bothersome fly . . .

VII
The Invitation

[Four shadows.]

THE KING

You could not find him?

TEHERA

We try, Most High. He hides.

THE KING

How big is this island, Captain Tehera?

TEHERA

Not big, Most Gracious Lord and Master, but high and low, and deep with caves and forests. More places to hide than we can seek, I fear.

THE KING

But you still believe he is there?

TEHERA

He is there, Most High. Somewhere.

THE KING

So you leave him gifts?

TEHERA

Gifts, my Lord?

THE KING

Saplings, seeds, pheasants. No?

TEHERA

Nothing we would not leave the island in any case—

THE KING

Biscuits? Rice? You are very kind to the island, Captain Tehera.

[Queen Esta joins.]

THE QUEEN

Who is very kind? What gifts are these?

THE KING

Those left Fernao Lopez, my Most Serene Queen.

THE QUEEN

Ooooooh, he I want to see. He is most intriguing to me. How hideous he must be! Is it true he has no nose?

TEHERA

So is said, Your Highness.

THE QUEEN

How disgusting. How grotesque that must be, a face with two black holes in the middle. And no ears too, is this true?

TEHERA

So is said, Most Serene.

THE QUEEN

Ooooooh, how repulsive! There was a cat we had here at the palace once, do you remember? The one who had no ears? What a hideous creature that cat was.

THE KING

Yes, I recall, my Queen.

THE QUEEN

And is it true about the hand as well, Tehera? That they cut one off, and then the other thumb. How terrible! I did chip the nail on my finger one time. I could not lift a cup.

THE KING

I recall.

THE QUEEN

And with no thumb, how is he to hold a stick? Cannot be done.

THE KING

Would not be easy, no.

THE QUEEN

So is he mad, then? Is his hair all wild and in knots?

TEHERA

So is said.

THE QUEEN

"So is said," "So is said." Have you not seen him with your own eyes, Tehera?

THE KING

No. He has not seen him. None of them has seen him. They only like to leave him gifts.

TEHERA

My Lord, I—

[Poklemmit joins.]

POKLEMMIT

You are speaking of Fernao Lopez?

THE KING

Ah, Most Holy Poklemmit, welcome. Yes. Lopez.

THE QUEEN

Who has his face cut off.

THE KING

For betraying his Crown.

POKLEMMIT

And forsaking his God. Yes, I know this one, to whom the sailors sing their songs.

THE KING

Songs too? Tehera, is this true?

TEHERA

Sailors sing of many things, my Lord. They sing of the bugs and fish.

POKLEMMIT

And virgin mothers.

TEHERA

My Lord. [He turns.] And my Most Holy, their interest is only in a mystery. In a man they cannot find.

THE KING

Then they should find him.

THE QUEEN

Yes, they should!

POKLEMMIT

Agreed.

THE KING

And they should see.

THE QUEEN

Oh, and see him, yes. His wild hair. His foaming mouth.

THE KING

His scars.

THE QUEEN

And what's in his eye? Oh, to see his eye. I want to see his eye!

THE KING

I want to see his eye.

POKLEMMIT

And I. I would like to see his eye.

THE KING

Then let us do. Tehera!

TEHERA

Yes, my Lord.

[A scribe appears.]

THE KING

When next you visit the island, and leave all the gifts which you would leave in any case, deliver this man this message: Say . . . "Dom Fernao. Your King and earthly master—"

THE QUEEN

And Your Queen.

THE KING

"And Your Most Serene Queen, Esta—"

[Poklemmit clears throat.]

THE KING

"And on behalf of His Most Holy Poklemmit, witness and counselor to the Lord, know: Crown and cross have heard thy story, know thy crime, and of the punishments which thou hast suffered for it."

[The Queen shudders.]

POKLEMMIT

Continue.

THE KING

"Dom Fernao, you need not hide or live in banished exile any longer. You may know again the fellowship of your brother. You may eat the fruit of your father's orchard, you may hear the laughter of your children, if you but confess your sins. Own what you have done, my kingdom's lowly son, and you shall be free again."

POKLEMMIT

Words well chosen.

THE KING

Take this letter, Tehera, and leave it with your trees and biscuits. Stay it by a heavy stone where he is sure to find.

TEHERA

I will, my Lord.

THE KING

We do not want our subjects living off alone—

POKLEMMIT

Not those who repent.

TEHERA

No, Your Holiness.

THE KING

We want them here with us.

TEHERA

Yes, my Lord.

POKLEMMIT

Where all may see how pure is their contrition.

THE QUEEN

How hideous is the punishment.

THE KING

And be told the reason why.

THE QUEEN

Take it, Tehera! Take the letter!

TEHERA

Your Grace is most moving, Most High, Most Serene, Most Holy. May word of your mercy spread throughout the kingdom, and the kingdom of our Lord, to serve as an example to all who hear it.

THE KING

So it is hoped.

POKLEMMIT

So it shall be.

CHAPTER EIGHTEEN

NOVEMBER 16-17

——◄◄◄ ∪ ►►►——

*Olav—Mr. Huffington's grave—Elijah—An apparition—
The de Montholon's foreplay—Lieutenant Wood encounters Alley*

November 16—Betsy is in a foul mood. She spent the morning at Millicent Legg's, and Millicent told her what everyone else seems to know already: The Emperor is *not* going to be allowed to attend the Admiral's ball, which seems perfectly absurd to her, since he's the only reason they're all here. She has been upset ever since, and it doesn't help that now, as she finally reaches the last turn for home again, tired and grumpy, she must pass by Mr. Huffington's grave and the reminder of his dead old body rotting in its coffin. She hurries past and down the banyans, straight to the garden.

"Was it you?" He acts as if he has been waiting for her. He is already sitting upright in his chair as she comes around the bramble.

"No. What?"

"Who has been stealing your father's wine." Marchand is there as well. "And bread."

"Who said?"

"Your father—he says that wine is missing. He is very concerned. He was asking Monsieur Cipriani."

"You didn't tell him?"

"That you are scared of rats? No. But I don't think you are the culprit."

He is hoping she'll egg him on, but frankly the topic no longer interests her. "Is it true you're not going to the ball?"

"This is true."

"Why not?"

"I have not been invited."

"But don't you think that's unfair?"

He ponders. "I think it might be unfair if I did go. Besides, someone must stay and guard the wine."

"Stop—"

"Yes, because I think I know 'oo is stealing it too."

"I don't care."

"You should."

She sighs. "Very well. Who?"

"Ol' 'Uff."

"Olav?"

"Ol' 'Uff. Ze teecher."

"Stop." She hits him.

"His ghost must eat."

Marchand agrees.

She hits him again. "It isn't funny."

"No, it isn't funny. It's true. His ghost must eat, must have some wine and bread, to remember what it was to live—"

She hits him a third time. "Stop it! Stop it or I'm leaving."

He stops.

——

Mrs. Balcombe has asked that Toby deliver fresh flowers to the tutor's grave site every day. Toby has decided to do better, that it will be easier and more useful if he simply plants a bed of flowers up there. He has chosen nasturtiums because they are hearty, they're not picky about their soil, and they seed themselves. Also, they're very fragrant, and something his grandmother told him about spirits was that they could still smell. Smell was like food to spirits. If Mr. Huffington was still lingering around, the fragrance of nasturtiums would make him feel better, send him on his way.

There is an orange thicket of them in the beds beside the fish-pond. Toby takes his shovel and wheelbarrow. As he passes by, the fish wander beneath the shade of the lily pads, nibbling on the tendriled plants at the bottom.

"You see him?" he asks.

They wag their slender bodies, no. You, Javaboy?

No. Toby wheels on to the nasturtium beds, but they shake their ruffled heads as well. All the flowers do, the camellias, the briars. The fruit trees he has asked especially, "Do you know where our friend has gone? The one who planted you?" The leaves shiver, no.

He unearths three of the larger bushes, leaving ample dirt around their roots, then wheels them all the way up to the grave site, along with a mulch sack, ripe with chicken waste. At the turn of the road he bows to the old man's stone, then takes up his shovel. He chooses a spot just down from the foot of the grave. The ground is soft. The sun will be ample.

As he digs their new bed, he speaks to the bushes, not in words. He gives them their instructions: to grow and open and clean the air up here. Some heads are drooping already, but he tells them no, he would be back up to make sure that they like the ground. After he has planted them and combined the soil with his mulch, he stays awhile to show the flowers his good faith. He crouches down beside them and smokes a cigarette while they get used to their new surroundings.

Rain is coming. A dark bank of clouds is headed up the valley, coming from the far side of the island, necklacing Diana's Peak. The bungalow and the pavilion stand straight and still amid the billowing leaves and bushes. The humid breezes sweep through like invisible hands, combing the Briars and the hillsides beyond, but they can't find him either.

Instead they find Alley, his white shirt flapping through the distant brush, and headed toward the coop. Toby doesn't know where he's coming from—Timu's or Deadwood Plain—or how long he intends to stay, but he rises quickly at the sight. He says good day to the nasturtiums, he'll come and see them tomorrow; then he takes up his barrow and starts down to meet up with Alley, tell him if he comes this late, he should spend the night. Mr. Balcombe has been more nervous lately.

—◁▦◁▦▷—

To *the Honourable Town Council.*

In regard of the recent proscription against any further correspondences between the current and the former Senior Chaplains, be it known that the following in no wise bears upon the controversies of the summer. It has come to the attention of the chaplain's off

There the draft abruptly ends, teetering above the page white, as it has since yesterday, stopped upon the very topic that moved the Reverend to take up his pen in the first place, the shrine on Francis Plain. He has felt uneasy ever since his Tuesday visit and has considered several different remedies, among them this: informing the island Council. Perhaps adding mention of the freebooters as well, just to lend some teeth to his concern. And yet he knows—he has written the Council so many letters in the past year—he knows he'll only stir annoyance and smug indifference. He might just as well tell them about the myrtle leaves or the puppets in the loft. The members of the Council, and the island authority in general, simply are not interested in the spiritual sustenance of the community. They do not see themselves as being subject to its fluctuations, or susceptible to its cancers, or if they do, it is a responsibility they are content to have delegated. Otherwise it is not their province.

He has thought of writing the Reverend Eakins as well, his predecessor, though he has been expressly forbidden to do so, and though, there again, he knows very well that Eakins would only construe some sign of weakness in it or accusation, in which case he'd not be incorrect. Boys does blame Eakins, absolutely, for not paying more attention to the pagan embers smoldering throughout the island, or doing more to stamp them out.

Thus it is his mind returns, as it returns each time he starts the thought, to one undying certainty: that he is alone in this, alone in his anxiety, and powerless alone to do much about it.

The Bible on his desk stand lies open to I Kings, chapter 18, as it has since Tuesday, there to remind him of Elijah's courage and conviction, when he challenged all the prophets of Baal on Mount Carmel and proved to them whose God was true.

> 37. Hear me, O Lord, hear me, that this people may know that thou art the Lord God, and that thou hast turned their heart back again.*

Overtop the book, the Reverend's open door gives view of the altar, standing heavy and dark in the middle of the church space. As yet no bolt of lightning has shot down through the steeple to consume it. But Boys will wait in faith and patience. And put the stubborn page out of its misery when next he builds a fire.

—⁕—

Betsy isn't the least bit tired. She lies in bed, wide-eyed. Her gown reclines upon the chair in front of the window. She finished folding all the flowers today, and Sarah has begun sewing them on. There will be forty-nine when she is done, but only a dozen have been sewn so far. They seem to glow against the blue of the silk.

She wishes he could see, see her in it. It isn't fair, their not letting him go, even though she thinks she's figured out the reason why. It's

---

*The passage continues:

> 38. Then the fire of the Lord fell, and consumed the burnt sacrifice, and the wood, and the stones, and the dust, and licked up the water that was in the trench.
> 39. And when all the people saw it, they fell on their faces: and they said, the Lord, he is the God; the Lord, he is the God.
> 40. And Elijah said unto them, Take the prophets of Baal; let not one of them escape. And they took them: and Elijah brought them down to the brook Kishon, and slew them there.

just as he said: It wouldn't be fair to the Admiral, because if the Emperor did go, then he would be the center of attention. Everyone would be looking at *him*, and going to meet *him*, and *he* would be watching them dance, not Admiral Cockburn. That's why.

A light breeze teases the collar of her gown. The flowers rise and settle again.

She supposes she could just put it on here, at the Briars. Her mother will tell her not to. She'll say she should wait till they get to town, at Mrs. Bingham's, as she and Jane will do, but Betsy doesn't care. What difference does it make as long as she's careful? She'll dress here.

A sound intrudes. It may have tried once before, but this time she really hears it. A voice, but a strange voice, coming from outside. The white flowers of her dress breathe in the dark light.

She rises. She takes the blanket with her to the window and looks out. Usually it's hard to see the lower vista at night, swallowed in the hills, but tonight the moon is so bright she can see the leaves and branches of every tree, the pomegranates and the myrtle. The ground is laced with shadows.

And there is the voice again, moaning, as if someone had fallen down and hadn't the strength to rise. She peers, and now she sees a figure out at the far end of the tree line. It's a human figure, silvery, and seeming to hover almost. She thinks of Mr. Huffington, and her breath catches in her throat. She has never seen a ghost, ever.

"*Bheeee*tsy."

She clutches the cover. Her ears begin to pound.

"Bet*seeee!*"

"Jane," she whispers, but Jane is fast asleep, and now the ghost lifts its arms and starts toward her, gliding through the lattice of moon shadow. If she could scream, she would, but she can hardly breathe.

The voice moans again from outside, but it's strange—it sounds so much closer than the body, almost as if it were coming from behind the rosebush.

"*I caaahme to steeeel the cheecken!*"

The figure is closer now. She can see it isn't glowing. It's covered in a sheet.

"Betseeee, it's meeeee, Ol' 'Uff."

"Who is that under there?" She knows very well who is speaking. He has even started laughing.

"Who?"

The ghost stops and lowers its arms. The Emperor is laughing harder now as the ghost starts backing away, then turn and runs. She can see his skinny legs and bare feet. It's Alley, the one her father has been so worried about.

"Stop it!" she says, speaking to the Emperor now, who is still laughing behind the bush. "It isn't funny."

"You scare away the ghost, Ol' 'Uff."

"Arrête! You frightened me."

He stands up now where she can see him.

"Tais-toi! Je te déteste!"

"Aah!"

"C'est vrai. Je ne vais pas vous laisser voir ma robe de soirée!" *I'm not going to let you see my gown!*

"Aaaah!"

"Betsy!" comes her mother's voice, from her room, hissing out her window. "Shsht! Think of others."

Bony steps out into the open and puts his finger to his lips in agreement. Then he marches off quickly. He's afraid of her mother too, and he has to go find Alley, she bets, and pay him for his services.

Another evening has come to a close at Mr. Pourteous's Inn. The dinner plates are dried and stacked. The brandy has been put away, and Tristan de Montholon climbs the narrow stairs to his bedchamber, slowed by the combination of drink, trepidation, and jealousy.

The suite was joined by the Wilkeses this evening: the Governor, the Governor's surprisingly charming wife, and the Governor's daughter, who, though unrelated to Madame Wilkes (she being the Governor's second wife), attests to the apparent consistency of the Governor's good taste. Indeed, the young Mademoiselle is far and away the most nubile woman on the island. This isn't saying much, but even in Paris she would fetch her share of suitors. Here, alas, the only candidate is General Gourgaud, who for this reason was seated next to her. De Montholon was across and two seats down, but even despite this handicap and the icy stares of Madame Albine, the Marquis did manage to score a number of jokes and held the young lady's eye for just long enough to be assured that—but for his obvious attachment—he could no doubt have won her from the likes of Gourgaud.

And yet there was the attachment, and English custom as well, which provides that men and women separate after dinner. The men retired to the smoking room, the women remained at table, so that was that until they said good evening, Gourgaud managing to synchronize his own departure with that of the Wilkeses, no doubt to get in one last clumsy boast.

De Montholon has now reached the door, treading as lightly as he is able, in hope his wife is asleep. The latch claps as he tries it, but it does not matter. Albine is wide awake, sitting up against her pillow.

"Mon cher."

"Alors. Qu'avez-vous à dire?" What has he to say for himself?

He assumes she is referring to his behavior toward the Mademoiselle, which was hardly inappropriate. He had only been charming. He is charming.

"Concerning what, my dear?"

"You heard Madame Bertrand, didn't you? Or were you too busy looking down the cleavage of the Governor Wilkes's daughter?"

"I'm not sure." He sits in a chair against the far wall. "What did Madame Bertrand say?"

"She said the Grand Marshal had found them a house."

"Hutt's Gate. Yes, I did hear that."

"So?" Her brows are the lifted wings of a murderous raven.

"So, what, my pet?"

"So the Bertrands are going off to their house, and we are staying here."

"My dear, it occurs to me that perhaps you have not seen the place at question, Hutt's Gate. I have, and I can assure you that it would not satisfy any of the cravings which find you so ill of humor. It is a miserable little cottage. If they want it, they are more than—"

"Worse than this, I find hard to believe. And at least the Grand Marshal is *doing* something on behalf of his wife and family."

"Madame, they are building rooms onto the house of the Emperor. We will be living there, in the house. As soon as it's finished."

"Yes, and won't that be delightful, with Las Cases, and Gogo and the Emperor."

"Madame, it will be better for us in the house. A little patience now will be rewarded. Trust me."

"Trust you. I trust you and look at me. Look at us."

"Would you rather be in Paris?"

"Yes, I'd rather be in Paris! The only reason we're not in Paris is because of you."

"Quiet."

"I'm not going to be quiet. I want to know, when are we getting out of here?"

"We have to be patient, but I promise you, the purpose of our coming is so that we can return free of—"

"When?"

"As soon as—"

"As soon as what? He's not leaving. You said so yourself, and how is he going to pay us? I happen to know his accounts are frozen. Madame Bertrand says."

" 'Madame Bertrand says—' "

Mocking Albine is never a good idea. Before he can finish, she picks up a saucer from the bedside table and rifles it past his left ear.

"Madame!"

"I don't care, let her hear! Let her know her mother wants to go. Her mother is miserable, because her father is a miserable gambler"—she scoops her earrings from the bedside table and whips them at the Marquis—"who drags his family to the middle of nowhere in hopes that Napoleon Bonaparte is going to pay him. Napoleon Bonaparte! He is a prisoner!"

The pillows come now, one after another. The Marquis lowers his head and beats his way toward the bed. He wrestles the Marquise down onto her stomach, covers her foul mouth, and mounts her from behind, as they have both recently come to prefer.

—⊶∙⊷—

November 17—Late Friday afternoon at approximately 1700 hours, Lieutenant Wood is returning from Prayer Group at the Reverend Boys's home. From lunch until now he and the other members, who number seven, have been praying, singing, reading, and praying some more.

He has his prayer book with him. Next week there will be a baptism for one of the new men. Wood will be acting as his sponsor and so is reading through the "Ministration of Publick Baptism to such as are of Riper years, and able to answer for themselves." More specifically he is reviewing the priest's instruction to the Godfathers and Godmothers when just ahead, and climbing up the rugged slope toward the road, he sees a young black.

Lieutenant Wood recognizes him from Longwood. He is one of those who have been helping carry up the bricks and lumber. Slim but strong, and with a pleasing and infectious smile, he would appear at the moment to be running a risk. There is a wiry red rooster in his arms.

"Hello," calls Wood, with a deliberate cheer. He waits on the road as the young slave climbs up to meet him, clearly frustrated by the delay.

"It mustn't be easy on your feet," says Wood, indicating the overland route the slave has chosen.

"Quicker," says the slave with an untrusting glare.

"Where are you bound?"

"Delivery."

"For?"

"Mr. Balcombe."

Wood looks him in the eye to gauge, but again with a determined effort to gain trust. "Mr. Balcombe lives in the other direction, doesn't he?"

The young black nods, and the red rooster stirs in his arms, scowling back at Lieutenant Wood.

"You have a name, son?"

The young black nods, as just behind him—what Lieutenant Wood had been hoping against—another officer appears from around the bend: Lieutenant Commander Chilcott, headed down from Hutt's Gate. The slave is unaware.

"Could you tell me your name?" asks Wood again.

The young man does not answer.

"Very good, then. I think you'd do well to hand over the chicken."

Wood reaches out in what he hopes is an open gesture, but the young slave pulls back. "Making a delivery!"

The sudden movement alerts Lieutenant Commander Chilcott, who pauses on the road. He begins reaching for his belt, but Wood holds up his hand for calm. The young black turns, however, sees Chilcott, and perceives himself to be surrounded. Suddenly, and without warning, he swings an open hand at Wood, striking him square against the side of the head, stunning him momentarily.

"Hoy, there!" calls Chilcott, but the young slave does not waste his advantage. He strikes Wood twice more, hard, with his fist. Wood falls, and now the black, seeing the second officer draw a pistol from his belt, leaps over the stone wall bordering the far side of the road and bounds down the embankment, the rooster still clutched beneath his arm.

Lieutenant Commander Chilcott, a veteran of the battles of Frenchtown, Fort Mackinac, and Waterloo, is an expert marksman. His pistol is loaded. He need only cock the hammer and aim. "Halt," he calls, but the young black shows no sign. Chilcott waits a moment to let the assailant clear the sprawl of a fern; then he fires. The thief drops instantly, but it is difficult to tell if he has been hit or merely tripped. The rooster goes tumbling, a flash of red, then rights itself to a nervous strut.

The thief lies still.

Wood is standing now.

"Are you all right?" asks Chilcott.

"Yes. Did you hit him?"

"Aye," says Chilcott.

They both look. The body has not moved. The rooster is hiding in the brush.

The two officers climb over the stacked stones and make their way down to confirm: Lieutenant Commander Chilcott's one bullet has drilled a clean path from the back of the young black's skull out through his left eye.

PART V

COUNTRY CHURCH

CHAPTER NINETEEN

NOVEMBER 17–19

—◦◦◦—

The Emperor is a cheater—Sarah is told—The burial—
Toby waits, a broken vessel, &c.—The Javaboy

November 17—The Emperor has asked Betsy and Jane to dine with
him this evening at the Pavilion. As usual, they eat chicken and
salad, and as usual, he finishes long before anyone else. The two Las
Caseses are there as well.

"Shall we retire to the parlor?" He asks this in particular of Betsy,
who is deliberately taking the longest. She tells him that her mother
has instructed her to chew at least twenty-four times per bite.

"Twenty-four!" He dispatches St. Denis to go light the lamps at
the bungalow. Betsy's parents are out this evening. "Please, come.
You are done."

"I'm not. I have two more bites."

"You're done. We'll play. Very good." He pushes himself up and
stands, tapping the table until she finishes.

Down in the bungalow it is agreed that they shall play whist. The
Emperor chooses teams: he and Jane versus Betsy and Las Cases.
Emanuel sits out, as he prefers to leaf through botanical books.

The players take their seats around the table, partners opposite
each other. Betsy makes sure the Emperor sees her displeasure at the
teams. Las Cases is a terrible player, but she is doubly determined.

"So we play to five," she says. "But what shall we play for? Something new." Usually they play for sugarplums, but the Emperor, sensing her resolve, agrees that there should be more risk tonight.

"But what have you to offer?"

Betsy tries to think, what has she that he would find valuable?

"I will tell you," he says. "If we win, you will give me the pagoda you showed me . . ."

Betsy doesn't like the sound of that, but then she wonders, could he possibly be wagering the tea chest with the ivory city of Canton inside? "Yes?"

"And if you win, I will give you a napoleon."

"One of the coins?"

He nods.

"That's not fair! The pagoda is worth much more."

He sits up, his eyes beaming at her impertinence. "What do you know? How can you say this? I could buy ten pagodas with my coin!"

"Not true."

"True!"

"Fine," she says. "It doesn't matter anyway, because Monsieur de Las Cases and I are going to win."

The Emperor takes up the cards. They play with one deck, a new set that Betsy's father bought for Alexander, with Napoleon himself pictured on the back. He begins to deal them out, but the cards spin across the table, too slick.

"This is no good. Monsieur le Comte, s'il vous plaît."

He hands them over to Las Cases, who takes the deck away to the side table by the window and begins dealing them alone, to tack up the faces and make them more playable.

While they wait, the Emperor turns back to the girls. "So, the Admiral's ball? How many days is it now?"

"Three," says Betsy. "It's Friday."

"And you have chosen what you are going to wear?"

"Yes," she says, and she wishes she could simply leave it at that, but she can't. "Would you like to see?"

No, he shakes his head, but in a flash she is up and racing off to her room to fetch it from her wardrobe. She runs back, holding out the gown as though there were a fainted woman inside.

"Là voici. Elle est belle, n'est-ce pas?"

He looks at it very seriously at first, then allows. "And how did you make the flowers?"

"Out of paper." She holds them up to the light, so he can inspect more closely.

"Bien conçue," he says. *Well conceived.* She lays the gown down on the chaise beside them, and he turns back to Las Cases. "Monsieur le Comte? Are we ready?"

Las Cases gathers up the pile and returns.

The rules are simple. It is a plain trick game with partners sitting opposite, no bidding. Betsy deals thirteen cards each, and since the Emperor is sitting to her left, he leads. As he sets down his card, however, she can feel his foot tapping underneath the table, trying to get Jane's attention. Betsy peeks down to make sure—he is a terrible cheater—and when she looks back up, he is plainly showing Jane his hand.

"What?" he says.

"Stop that!"

"Stop what?"

"Showing her your cards."

"She didn't see. Jen, did you see?"

Jane says nothing.

"I want a redeal," says Betsy. "Give me."

"No!" He clutches them to his chest. "I like my hand. Jen, don't you like my 'and? We like our 'ands. Now go." He looks to Las Cases for some respect. "Make your play."

Las Cases looks at his cards foggily. He clearly doesn't know what to do and finally takes so long choosing his play that the Emperor starts tilting back in his chair to peek at Las Cases's hand.

"Stop!" Betsy hits him in the arm.

"Ah! You are going to teep me."

"You're a cheater!"

"Betsy, stop," says Jane.

"He is a cheater. You are a cheater."

"You're a cheater," he replies.

This time she puts down her cards to punch him. His eyes bug out, looking at her hand on the table. "Look who is cheating now, showing everyone your 'and. Where is this pagoda? We win, Jen and I."

"You do not."

"We do. You cannot follow the rules. You put your cards down where Monsieur le Comte can plainly see. We ween."

"Stop—"

"Where is the pagoda?"

"Stop it. You are the worst cheater I have ever met."

"You are méchante. Where is the pagoda?"

"I'm not giving you the pagoda."

He glances over at the blue dress beside him. In a flash he leaps up, grabs it beneath his arm, and flees the bungalow. Betsy nearly topples her chair racing after him, but he still manages to close the door in front of her. She cannot make up the difference. She runs as fast as she can up the walk, but by the time she reaches the marquee, he is already inside the Pavilion. The door slams, and there are Marchand and St. Denis, waiting outside.

"He has my dress."

"Pardon, Mademoiselle," says Marchand. "L'Empereur s'est retiré pour la nuit."

"He has not, and he has my dress."

"No dress, Mademoiselle."

"Stop." She calls over his shoulder, "Let me in!"

There is no answer.

"Let me in!" she yells.

"Monsieur Marchand"—the Emperor's voice returns from within, with pretended fatigue—"would you please tell the young lady that we are trying to sleep?"

"I want my dress!"

"Monsieur Marchand!" They both can hear his bedcurtain being jerked closed.

"You're a cheater!" she shouts. "Cheater, cheater!"

She waits. Again, nothing.

"I'm coming back! I'm not forgetting. And you'd better not do anything to it."

From behind the curtain he blows his nose.

"You'd better not. I'm coming back!"

He replies with a long, loud snore.

—⬤—

November 18—Midmorning an English soldier, in his red coat and white sashes, descends from the inland road. On another day Toby might assume that he has come to relieve one of the sentries, to bring a message to Bony, or take his mail. But the crunch of his bootheels on the lane is somehow too clear. Toby stands to watch, and a sparrow flies out from one of the banyan trees, then darts back in.

Alley.

The soldier meets Mrs. Balcombe out in front of the veranda and speaks to her briefly. She goes inside and returns a moment later with Sarah, who is already in her hat and gloves. She and the redcoat descend the veranda together, then make their way back up the shaded lane, the redcoat three steps out front, Sarah trailing behind with her head low, her broad shoulders tight and timid, her hands already clasped.

—⬤—

The Reverend is notified upon his arrival at Jamestown Chapel just past noon. One of Mr. Balcombe's slaves, a young male who'd apparently been freebooting in recent weeks, has been shot and killed, resisting arrest while trying to steal a chicken.

Boys goes directly to Mr. Balcombe's office. Mr. Fowler is there as well, and another of Balcombe's slaves, Sarah, a member of the Country Church congregation. The body of the deceased is behind the office, lying in the back of a tobacco cart. The bullet's exit through the left eye socket has disfigured the face somewhat, but Boys can see well enough this is not a slave he knows—that is to say, he is not a parishioner.

"Sarah is family?"

"His aunt," replies Mr. Balcombe, both solemn and pleasant. It occurs to Boys that Mr. Balcombe has been having a difficult time of it, hosting Bonaparte, losing his children's tutor, and now this. One would hardly know.

"And had he been sleeping away?"

Mr. Balcombe shakes his head, uncertain. "He'd been helping up at Longwood. I'd asked him."

Boys understands. Clearly Mr. Balcombe has been distracted, and the slave was taking advantage. The question now is where to bury him.

"Where are the parents?"

"Oak Knoll."

Oak Knoll is a slave cemetery just in from Lemon Valley. Normally Boys wouldn't consider holding the burial there. He doubts very much that the slave was baptized (though this probably can't be confirmed, owing to the unreliability of the Reverend Eakins's records), and certainly he'd been living outside the church's embrace. In any other circumstance Boys would likely turn the body over to the family to do with as they pleased, but at the moment he sees no benefit in giving the slaves another cause to gather and perform ceremonies of their own device.

"Beside his parents' lot, then, without rites."

Balcombe nods. "When?"

"As soon as possible."

Mr. Balcombe goes inside to inform Sarah.

The Oak Knoll cemetery is an hour's walk, at a wood's edge just in from Lemon Valley and to the east. The body is transported by cart, covered with a tarp. Two workers from Longwood, infantrymen, meet them there, with a simple pine box constructed from spare lumber. One of the slave workers has led them down.

It takes the soldiers three-quarters of an hour to dig the grave, in which time a stone is chosen from the fence surrounding and chiseled with the appropriate dates and initials. Two more slaves appear in the meantime, from Longwood. Then, just as the infantrymen are climbing out from the hole, Lieutenant Wood arrives. Boys knows not why, but that completes the party: Wood, Mr. Balcombe, Reverend Boys, the two infantrymen, the three slaves from Longwood, and Sarah.

The box is laid on three coarse ropes. The infantrymen slide it over the pit and begin lowering it hand over hand. As it descends, Lieutenant Wood, unaware of Boys's decision, begins the prayer.

"Forasmuch as it hath pleased Almighty God," he says quietly, and to the muttered, halting accompaniment of the others, "of His great mercy to take unto Himself the soul of our brother here departed, we commit his body to the ground; earth to earth, ashes to ashes, dust to dust."

Boys clears his throat here to cut him off and thus omit the "sure and certain hope of the Resurrection to eternal life." The box has settled. The infantrymen coil the ropes, then begin shoveling.

Toby tries to go about his day as if he had not seen the redcoat come this morning. He feeds the chickens, changes their water, counts the eggs. He inspects the bamboo fence to see if the rats are digging any new tunnels. They are not.

'Scilla finds him out at the kitchen garden, watering the yam. "Where's Sarah?"

"I don't know."

"Where's Alley?"

He still does not look up at her. "I don't know."

He goes to check on the nasturtiums, up by the teacher's grave. He chooses not to take the shaded path for fear he'll see or hear the sparrow. He does not want to think of Alley. Whatever has happened to Alley has happened, and perhaps he is only hurt; perhaps he is in prison; perhaps it isn't Alley at all. Toby looks back down at the bungalow and the valley beyond, as if he might see him even now, bounding through the brush, his loose white shirt and gleaming black skin, but there is only the girl on the lawn, Betsy, pleading with Bony's servants to take her dollhouse. They are ignoring her.

Toby spends the rest of the day inside the garden, weeding and sweeping the paths. He doesn't see anyone until late afternoon. He is removing the tarp from overtop the arbor to let the grapes and grapevines breathe awhile when Mr. Balcombe finds him. He has a wood crate with him. "Ours, I take it." He sets it down.

Toby lifts the drape to meet the stunned black eye of Timu's red rooster. "No. Timu's."

"It *is* Timu's?" Mr. Balcombe straightens. The corners of his eyes wince, and Toby knows. Alley is dead. "We can return it tomorrow, yes?"

Toby nods. Alley is dead. He has been killed trying to return Timu's rooster, and because Toby has known in his heart all day, the blow is not as sudden as it might be, but it bends him; it starts a poison in him.

Mr. Balcombe leaves the bird there, but a gauze is descending around Toby. He is going numb with the knowledge—not just of Alley's death, but that he has known, that he has felt this coming from the moment Alley told him about the monster. He takes up the crate with the rooster inside and carries it back to the two cottages, but he hardly feels the handle digging into his fingers.

Alley's door is open. There is a tin plate on the far side, on the shelf beneath his window, a broken lantern on the frame, a crooked mat on a dirt floor. Nothing Alley wanted. Toby breathes. It doesn't even smell like him, and it is this, the absent scent of nothing-Alley, that gives Toby's poison a name: blame. Should he not have been more firm, telling Alley not to sleep away, to be more careful, at least while Bony was here? Was Toby not the one who asked him to help with the coop? Would Alley not be dead tonight?

But Toby must stop himself. It's not his place to say who lives and dies and when. Alley would do what Alley would do, and he is with Ilena now. Alley can see everything now, like her. Toby's place is to accept this and help Alley move on where he should—the same as with the teacher.

Sarah is back. She came back with Mr. Balcombe, but she doesn't come out for dinner. Sam and Charles are there, and 'Scilla. The four of them sit in a row, the boys chewing eagerly, though they can hear Sarah in her room, crying. Toby doesn't eat. He drinks black tea, and no one says a word, but 'Scilla's silence is clear enough, the fury and the accusation in every gnash of her old gums. If she would speak it, he would tell her: She should stop expecting so much from him. He is not Winston-Kumar, not a dalang or an ombiasy. He is not even the Javaboy. He is only a gardener who once got bitten by a spider.

"Where did they bury him?" he asks.

" 'Sides Tom and Alfreda," says 'Scilla: Alley's parents. "There'll be respects at Timu's."

The boys both nod as they spoon their meal. Respects.

"Monday?" asks Toby.

Sam and Charles both nod again. Monday is the night of the Admiral's ball.

Before he leaves, Toby scatters salt below Sarah's window, to keep her safe while she's so open with sorrow and grief. Then he checks the rain jugs. One is half full. He hoists it up to his shoulder and starts back to the garden.

He passes by the pavilion on his way, past the two redcoats posted in the shadows of the low path. They're standing straight up like pickets, though there's nothing much to see. The shutters of the pavilion are all closed. Only a dim light behind; Bony was feeling poor again today. Toby imagines all the servants and helpers, standing by nervously, boiling more tea, and for the first time he wonders if the others were right about Bony—'Scilla and the English. Bony doesn't look like a monster. He doesn't act like one, but everything surrounding him and everything that's happened since he came— Toby wonders if maybe the English did bring something black to the island, something ugly and wicked. And maybe that's why no one knows where Lopez is.

When he gets back to the two cottages, Toby takes the water jug to Alley's threshold. It's too dark to see inside now, but he doesn't need to. He lets the jug drop from his shoulder down onto the stoop. It bursts into shards and flowing water. The sleeping rooster rouses in its crate. "Shshsh," Toby whispers, looking down. The black rivulets trickle between the stones and seep into the dirt.

A broken jar and nothing more, thinks Toby. As is Alley. And this is supposed to help him with his grief.

He tries to sleep, but the black tea is still turning in his stomach, and the smoke is drifting in his head. Across from him there is his fruit basket on the floor, and there is his empty chair. No one has ever sat in that chair, ever since Toby has been here, but of all the people who might or might once have, the one that Toby sees is Winston-Kumar, who would surely prefer to sit on the floor, but who accepts the chair as offered, his slender, supple wrists on his knees, his head propped back on his neck, the fine, clear skin lying slack on his bones, and the smile that never leaves his eye. And it occurs to Toby that Winston-Kumar has been sitting there for a long while now, watching him and smiling—maybe since the puppets first appeared. But is he the one who has been tying the blind around Toby's eyes at night? Is he the one who has been guarding Toby's dreams?

But why? asks Toby silently. Why can't I see what I could before?

Winston-Kumar's smile remains. The basket yawns beside him.

Because I am not the Javaboy, says Toby.

Winston-Kumar's smile remains.

IX
The Javaboy

The Javaboy was the only other person ever to share the island with Lopez; the only one who knew all the places he hid. He came all the way from one of the golden kingdoms Dabakur had conquered, a little island called Java, which is where both Winston-Kumar and Toby are from, which is why the other slaves used to called Toby the Javaboy, when he was younger.

Like Toby, the Javaboy was taken from his home and his family by men he had never seen, who spoke a language he had never heard and who put him on a large ship bound for a land he had never been.

The boy was most unhappy, chained and hungry and crowded in. Then one night, when they'd been at sea for months already, the ship dropped anchor at a small dark island in the middle of the sea. The Javaboy did not care. He slid free, slipped over the rail, and swam to shore. The following morning the sailors found he was missing, and they went looking for him—in the orchard valley and the woods beyond, but the boy hid up in the limbs of a gumwood tree, and the sailors soon gave up. They took their fruit and water and sailed away again. The Javaboy was all alone.

Or so he thought. It wasn't long before he found the water barrel, the skillet, and the patch of vegetables, and not long after that he saw the monster who tended it, whose face was unlike any face he'd ever seen, made of holes and scars, and who had a stump at the end of one arm.

He was not a very friendly monster. He did not like to share the island. Any time he saw the boy, he would retreat into the bush. Sometimes he left out fruit, if he had extra, but always beside arrows in the dirt, pointing the boy to go away and leave him be.

The Javaboy did the best he could. He learned the monster's ways and tried to stay away, sleeping in a broken boat hull by the shoreline, cold and often hungry.

In time another tall ship arrived in the bay. When the boy saw the small boats rowing into shore, he went running out to meet them, waving his arms and begging the sailors to take him away with them again, but all the sailors wanted was to know about the monster. Had the boy ever seen him? The boy said yes. They asked if he knew the places where the monster liked to hide. Again the boy said yes. "Then show us," they said. "Take us to him."

The boy refused at first. He said the monster did not like to be bothered, but the sailors replied that if he did not take them to the monster's hiding places, then they would go again and leave him there, so finally the Javaboy agreed. He led a band of sailors— including their commodore, Captain Tehera—deep into the woods and hills. He showed them all the secret places he could think of, but they did not find him until they came upon the far side of the island, in the high caves where the petrels made their nests. The monster tried to run, but the sailors captured him and dragged him out upon the rocks and set him down at the feet of their Captain Tehera, who spoke to him, a beautiful song that the Javaboy did not understand.

"Dom Fernao" he called the monster. "Dom Fernao, why do you hide? Every year we come and call to you. We leave you gifts and letters from the King. Why do you not come and speak to us?"

The monster did not reply.

"Do you fear that we will take you? Do you fear your fate shall be the same as this Javaboy here?"

The monster still did not reply. He would not even raise his eye.

> Hear me, Dom Fernao.
> And know I speak the truth.
> Dabakur did punish you, it's true,
> but then he let you go. And so
> we would not take you from this place,
> unless you choose.
>
> But be it known, and this is just as true,
> that both the King and his Most Holy
> have ope'd their hands to you.
> They wish to see you, Dom Fernao,
> and hear you own what you have done.
> Until you do, I promise you,
> by every moon and every sun,
> by every ship that comes,
> and every song that every sailor sings to you,
> their hands await, and wait, and wait . . .

Then they left the monster there, kneeling on the rocks. The Javaboy led the sailors back to the valley of the broken boat. And because he had done as they asked and shown them where the monster hid, the sailors kept their promise. They took him back to their tall ships with them and sailed away to another land where he had never been.

CHAPTER TWENTY

NOVEMBER 20–21

—◆—

Leaving for the Admiral's ball—Leaving for Timu's farm—Maldivia—Respects—
The Reverend's vigil—Dom Fernao's confession—Denouement

November 20—The day of the Admiral's ball has finally arrived, and
Betsy has all but given up hope that she will have her blue gown in
time. She has gone to make her pleas to Marchand and St. Denis
again—it is the first thing she did this morning, before breakfast—but
their answers are the same as yesterday. His Majesty is still indisposed,
and there is something in the way they say it which has her very
nearly believing them. And if it is true that the Emperor is not feeling
well, then of course they do not care about her blue gown. So she has
resigned herself to wearing the white dress, the same as she wears to
church, and she will not have near as much fun as she expected.

As the day wears on, she can see more and more parties passing
by, up on the inland road, making their way to town to get ready for
the evening's festivity: the Pritchards, the Mellises, the Greentrees.
Jane tries consoling her, there will be other balls, and she knows it's
true—she'll get to wear her gown someday—but she had wanted
him to see it, and though it is not something she lets herself think
for long, she doubts very much that he will still be here when the
next ball is held, whenever that may be.

The horses are brought around at five. Two of the boys from her
father's office have been summoned up to carry down their various

ensembles in tin cases, though Betsy doesn't see the need. They can drag her Sunday dress along the road for all she cares.

Her father comes out in his blue coat with the high collar and the white cravat. "Betsy's first ball?" he says, trying to rouse her. He helps her up onto her pony, and she smiles wanly, for his sake, but he is aware of her disappointment. Her mother is, too, but will not mention it. She asks if they've forgotten anything. Of course they haven't. Her father says he'll follow on and meet them in town, and with that, the three women start off on their ponies, her mother in the lead, then Jane, then Betsy, who can hardly believe how little she cares, how unexcited she is. She'd cry if she were alone, and if she still weren't so angry.

But then, just as she is ducking underneath the shadow on the banyans, a door slams behind them. Marchand and St. Denis step out from the opening of the marquee, then his voice calls out, "Arrêtez-vous. Ne partez pas!"

It is the Emperor, running across the lawn with the gown in his arms. He looks very silly, in fact, his little feet scurrying beneath him. "Attendez donc!" *Wait, wait.* He does not stop until he comes directly to her side. "You weren't going to forget this, were you? I thought you were going to wear it." He looks at her innocently. She isn't sure what to say. If not for the others, she'd kick him, but now as he smiles, her anger melts, and she wonders that she could ever have doubted he would return her gown; knows, in fact, she never did, and that her pleas and tears were only her part in the roles they had chosen to play. His, now, is as Savior. He holds the gown out to one of the boys. "Take care, though." He points to one of the flowers near the shoulder. "This one was loose. I made sure Monsieur St. Denis stitched it tight." And so he has. The dress has been perfectly preserved.

Marchand helps the boy exchange the two dresses, the royal blue for the boring white, and for a second time the Balcombe women start up the bridle road, now with the Emperor walking beside Betsy like a footman. "You will be a good girl now and enjoy the ball. Mind you dance with Gogo."

She tsks.

"He will be only."

"*Lonely*," she says. "Yes, he will."

He walks them all the way to the top of the lane and there stops, not far from Old Mr. Huffington's grave.

"So?" He waits.

"So?"

"What have you to say?"

He's perfectly ridiculous, she thinks. "Thank you."

"You are welcome."

He bids them all farewell, wags a warning finger at the black boy to be careful, then pats the pony firmly on the rump and sends her off.

—

As soon as he sees the Balcombes are gone, Toby takes up the sack of fruit he picked this morning and starts down to the bungalow. He has been smelling 'Scilla's cooking all day, fried fish and turmeric.

Sarah and 'Scilla are not expecting him. 'Scilla is stripping the meat from the bone as he enters the kitchen, combining it with rice and basil in her largest wooden bowl. There is a pair of small sandals on the table as well, Alley's from when he was a boy, and a folded silk. Alley's hair and nails.

Sarah is waiting in a chair by the wall, with biscuits in her lap. "Is that fruit?" she asks, gesturing to the sack.

Toby shows them—figs and apples mostly. He sets them on the table, then crosses to the cellar door.

"No wine," 'Scilla calls down after him. "No wine."

"No wine," repeats Toby, descending.

He scatters the rats with a hiss. The preserves cupboard is still over behind the racks of claret. He knocks on the drawer to make sure there aren't any more inside, then opens it. He has to reach all the way to the back, past the cool glass of the preserves to the coarse warmth of Alley's blanket, just as he left it, with the puppets wrapped inside like a stack of cat skeletons.

Sarah straightens when she sees. She knows what they are from all the slender bones sticking out the end. "Ra-Toby, what are you doing with those?"

Toby gives the only answer that would silence her. "Alley found them." He looks over at 'Scilla, not knowing if she'll scent fady in their presence—taboo—but her eyes are sparkling beneath their bony hoods. She doesn't know what Toby means to do with them, but at least he means something.

She covers the bowl, and the three of them start out with their gifts—the silks, the puppets, the fruit, the food, and Alley's sandals. Shoulder to shoulder, they make their way down to the stables to wake up Lewis and hitch him to the cart.

Las Cases hasn't decided yet if he is going to the Admiral's ball. True, the Admiral's purpose in holding it has been to offer, on behalf of the island, a formal welcome to the suite; all received written invitations, even his son, Emanuel. In that respect, not to attend would be an obvious affront. On the other hand, to go and dance and greet the island in all its finery would be to indulge an equally obvious pretense for which the Count is not sure he has the stomach. He has decided to leave it up to the Emperor's health. If His Majesty seems well enough, Las Cases will consider going. If not, he will happily stay and keep him company.

Unfortunately, the Emperor's state is not entirely clear. He seemed better this morning, then more dreary at midday, so much so that Las Cases had assumed he would *not* be attending the ball, but now Monsieur Marchand has come to fetch him, telling him that the Emperor would like to see him.

He is standing up at the top of the road. The Balcombes have left, but His Majesty seems not ready to return just yet. Las Cases hustles up as quickly as he can, and as soon as he arrives, out of breath, the Emperor starts them down the road, which is curious only because the Emperor has never before ventured so far, without an approved escort. It seems a clear violation, but as there is no guard in sight, Las Cases follows.

"Shouldn't you be getting ready?" the Emperor asks.

"I should." Las Cases is still huffing and puffing. "But I wasn't sure I should go, Your Majesty."

"Of course you'll go. It will be a diversion, and who knows how many others there will be?"

This is true, thinks Las Cases. They stop. They have come to another lane descending from the road, leading to another small cottage nestled in the shadowed valley. The Emperor looks down with a curled brow. "Who is this, do you know?"

"Major Hudson, Your Majesty?"

"Hodgson, yes. 'Hercules.'" A warm golden light welcomes from within the home. "Shall we?"

For a second time Las Cases balks. As it is, they've strayed much farther than the terms of their captivity would allow, yet His Majesty seems either oblivious or to enjoy the breach. In any case, Las Cases feels in no position to protest. With a glance up the road to make sure they've not been followed, he starts down after the Emperor.

The incline is a deceptively steep and rugged one. They must go slowly and take care, particularly with the light descending. By the time they reach the more level slope, the door of the cottage opens and out comes a festive bouquet of islanders, headed for the ball. When they see the two strangers approaching and identify the first, they are suddenly, and rightly, stilled.

"I see your smoke," His Majesty says, in English. "I do not impose?"

"No, no." The paterfamilias, Major Hodgson, steps up. "Welcome, General. Allow me to introduce you."

He does so. Three generations are present. His own, represented by himself, his wife, and Mr. Doveton; the younger Hodgsons, who are ball bound; and finally the grandchildren, whom the Major and his wife have been drafted to look after this evening. Greetings are brief, exuberant, and somewhat awkward, but at length the younger Hodgsons peel themselves away, the children stay outside to play in the waning light, and the visitors are welcomed in.

Drinks are offered. The Emperor declines but urges all to sit, then proceeds to set the party at ease by his usual means—friendly and pointed interrogation. Another lovely home, he tells the Major. Maldivia. How did it get its name? How many people work the property? What do they grow? How long have they been there?

Major Hodgson—or Hercules, as some are said to call him—fields the questions well. The unofficial mayor of Jamestown, he does indeed possess an imposing presence, with large feet and hands, bushy muttonchops, eyebrows, and ear sprouts, but he conveys good cheer and openness. It is his wife who guards the most suspicion, behind tight lips and a plump face. She begins the conversation stiff and upright in her chair, hands folded in her lap, but His Majesty thaws her with compliments to the house, the property, and, most important, the grandchildren. "Very handsome." She softens enough to admit the real reason that she and the Major no longer attend the balls: Her feet are too small for dancing.

By far the most benign presence in the room is Mr. Doveton. Portly, he sits in his wingback like a giant egg, brandy in hand, and drowsy, contented eyes. A longtime islander—over thirty years now—he is an old friend to the Hodgsons, father of their daughter-in-law, Penelope, and here this evening principally to see the grandchildren. The Emperor inquires about his property as well, Mount Pleasant, which he has heard of. "Over at Sandy Bay," he says. "Near Fairyland?"

"That is correct," says Doveton, pleased by His Majesty's acquaintance. Again they speak of crops and personal histories. Mr. Doveton explains how and when he first came to the island, but Las Cases isn't paying very close attention until they come to the topic of England and travel. Mr. Doveton has apparently made a habit of returning to London at least once a year for the past two decades.

"I suspect there are still a few clubs where my name is known," he allows.

"More than a few," says the Major, raising his glass. "Sir Willie."

Mr. Doveton is a knight. The Emperor nods his respect, which Sir Willie gladly accepts.

"I must admit, though"—he now sighs—"I'm considering I might not go this year."

Mrs. Hodgson rouses with concern, as now a servant enters with the carafe of sherry.

"It is a very long way," Sir Willie explains, "and I've come to wonder if the reason I keep returning is out of respect for Mrs. Doveton," his dear departed, as previously noted. Mrs. Hodgson says a silent prayer. "She used to enjoy it so when we went back."

The Major understands. "It's true, the woman's thirst for civilization does outlast the man's." The downward cast of Mrs. Hodgson's eyes offer her endorsement, as does Sir Willie's nod. He extends his glass to the waiting servant.

"Which is why I think I may ask her permission to slow the pace a bit—thank you, Lawrence—now as I find myself rounding the bend, as it were."

Mrs. Hodgson clucks her tongue; he goes too far.

The Major seconds. "You've still some pink in your cheek, Willie."

"I grant, and thank you." He sits back. "I only mean to say that I've come to find it very reassuring, do you know? The permanence of the place." Here, for some reason, he seeks His Majesty's eye, as a confederate in years. "I'm not sure why it is exactly—the appeal of the pasture, I suppose—but I've come to take great comfort in knowing I've found the place I'll finally rest, that there will be no other homes, no other trees that one shall have to get to know, no other beds, or windows—"

It is at this moment, gods be praised, the front door bursts open and a weeping child enters, interrupting Sir Willie's ode. Just how much His Majesty has understood Las Cases cannot be sure, but for once he is thankful for the Emperor's linguistic deficiency, as no one else in the room seems remotely aware of just how exceedingly inappropriate are the sentiments now floating in the air, given their guest's obvious proscription from doing such things as choosing his final trees and windows.

As soon as the child has been calmed, His Majesty stands. "We are most grateful," he says. "But I am afraid we should not compromise the officers." He means the ones that they've escaped, though again the English seem oblivious. The Major offers them two ponies for the ride back, as the light is nearly gone, and the climb a steep one. The Emperor accepts, but that is the last word he says until he and Las Cases reach the Pavilion again—and a stilted, silent ride it was. "To the ball, Monsieur le Comte, I insist."

His Majesty's display of nonchalance is valiant and would likely persuade a man of less sympathy, but Las Cases can tell by the glaze about his eyes the Emperor understood quite well. If not for the demands of obedience, the Count would surely stay and keep him company. Indeed, he wishes they'd not ventured out at all.

—⦿—

Even before they descend under the oaks, Toby, 'Scilla, and Sarah can hear the voices and see the extra light sifting through the leaves. Two dozen guests are already gathered over where Timu usually stands his table, but the table has been set aside, and kerosene lanterns have been hung from the limbs of the trees. Beneath the largest, blankets have been spread, and some silks. Food has been set on the blankets—more fish, rice, breads, puddings, and fruit. Gifts have been laid on the silks or wrapped inside. Sarah offers the sandals and Alley's remains, the hair and nails. 'Scilla sets down the bowls and the bread.

Most of the others are eating, or they've already finished. The men are all sitting, on the ground, or on stumps, or on cords of wood. Toby does not see Timu yet, but there are Sam and Charles. And Oliver, whom Toby saw just recently picking up bamboo at Mr. Haywood's. He recognizes some others from Mr. Doveton's barn—the Chinese brothers; the carpenters, who've lost all their hair; the whole group from Miss Mason's, who are black, all Malagasy; James, who used to work for the Reverend Eakins; and Cornelia, the cook. And there are some he has never seen before—a circle of young men, also black—from Longwood, Toby guesses, or wherever else Alley had been going.

Quinto is there too, over on the far side of the lantern. He is leaned up against a woman with tired eyes and long dark hair, who must be his mother, Marie. They have their food already, but

Quinto is only eating grapes, holding a full stem against his cheek, his eyes, as ever, shrouded by his large brow, scrolling with the endless weaves and reeds and patterns.

One of the older women hands Toby a plate loaded full with three kinds of bread and lumps from every bowl in front of them, mostly rice, which is precious among the slaves. She shows him where there is water and where there is rum. The men from Longwood have a jug, and they are the ones talking loudest and most intently. Not angry. They believe too much in fate, and death is an honor to them. To die is to become an ancestor. Still, there is something restless in their tone, and aggressive.

Toby finds a clear space to sit, alone and away from the light, but he can still hear them, hissing about "Tsy-misarat," "Tsy-misarat." He gathers that is what they're calling Alley now, because calling him by his name, the name he had here, would be another fady. Tsy-misarat is in Oak Knoll, says one, and Toby knows the reason they're so interested is that they want to move his bones. This is something they will do, the blacks, wait till the flesh and blood are dry and move the bones out to the woods. But one of them—the tallest and skinniest, whose cheeks are as dark and round as plums— he says no, he waves his slender hand, they should not move him, because his mother and father are there at Oak Knoll too.

"Buried there," says another, meaning what if their bones were moved. "Who knows? Who knows?" They look around, for someone who might. "The boar won't come to you."

Toby averts his eyes so they won't see him. He wishes he did not have to listen either and be reminded of this. In many ways the blacks are not so different from the Malay. Winston-Kumar told him once their oldest ancestors were Malay, come in a boat from the golden kingdoms, and Toby believes it when he hears some of the words they use. But they are different too, the way they try to keep the dead and ask them all their questions. Toby respects the dead no less, but he was taught to let them go and look only to the oldest of the ancestors. It is the first you listen to. Not the last, like Tsy-misarat, Tsy-misarat.

He wishes he could shut their voices out, be more like Quinto, feeling only the smooth skin of the grape in his mouth. He takes a bite of bread, with ginger in it, and slowly starts churning his jaw, grinding the cake into a smoother and smoother meal, as if the same might become of the voices, that they'll blend into a single indistinct murmur. And so they begin, patient mash by patient mash, until a pair of feet come crunching up through the leaves and stop right in front of him.

"Javaboy."

Toby looks up. He can't tell who it is at first, until he sees the bangs on his forehead. It is Martin, who also worked at Mr. Breame's, and still does. The years have thickened him, though. As he sits down and turns his face to the light, Toby can see his skin is stubbled with moles, and his cheeks have fallen like one of Major Sealey's hounds, so his face cascades outward, from forehead to nose to chin; his clearest feature by far, most tender and fresh, the ample sacs beneath his drowsy eyes.

"Javaboy." They lift as he smiles and sets down a jug of water be-tween them.

"Martin."

Martin is another of those who says he has seen Lopez—or heard him, outside his window one night years ago, talking to Campanero. Martin's is not the most esteemed of claims, but sitting there with Toby seems to make the point: It is the two of them. That and the fact that they say so little. While the others whisper and scheme, and laugh and gossip, Toby and Martin trade sips from their jug and eat what they've been given.

Their plates are nearly clear when the guests on the far side of the silks and blankets begin to stir. Timu has appeared, his great, round belly catching the lantern like a low-slung moon. Toby is glad to see him, and relieved, though he can tell that Timu feels the bur-den too of what's happened to Alley.

He has brought a young woman with him, and she is the reason the guests all turn. Lighter-skinned, with a kerchief around her head, large eyes, and a small chin. Pretty. Lotte. Toby knows because he knows, and because of the way the others stand up when they see her. And he knows by the expression on her face as well—how sad she has been, how sad she is going to be—but she is smiling now, in the full glow of the lantern light, taking comfort in the others.

One of the guests steps forward, the eldest man from Miss Mason's farm, Ephraim. With eyes intent and focused on the silks, he begins to speak.

"The little bird says, 'I lay my eggs in a tree.' " His voice is clear but rasped, more by the intensity of his delivery than age; the phrases come fast and clear.

"The tree is toppled by the wind."

And Toby knows this poem.

> The wind is stopped by the wall.
> The wall is gnawed through by the rat.
> The rat is eaten by the dog.
> The dog is beat by the man.
> The man is struck by the spear.
> The spear is broke by the stone.
> The stone is covered over by the water.
> The water is walked in by the little bird.

"Aaaay," some sigh as he comes to the end. Some laugh. Lotte smiles in thanks and others bow as Ephraim steps back again. With that a flute begins to play. Another of Miss Mason's servants has brought a recorder. And another has brought a twelve-string guitar, made of bamboo and catgut, a valiha. The women's voices join, with more of a chant than a song. Toby doesn't understand so well what they're saying, but it's the rhythm that matters, and the hope that Tsy-misarat will hear.

Most of the guests are standing now, including Toby and Martin. Even Quinto; his mother pulls him up by his arm, though he stays back with the women. The men move in closer to the light; again, it's mostly the blacks. They start hopping to the rhythm of the strings, not quite dancing, shucking themselves to make room for whatever else might enter.

Toby is watching Ephraim. His eyes are clamped, and his tongue

is turning in his mouth as if he were tasting something. The chants
are growing louder, and Toby begins to feel the magic of their
joined voices filling the air beneath the oaks, but he is apprehensive
too. What words, what voice is Ephraim preparing to unleash with
that rolling, restless tongue?

Just then there comes a startling shrill cry from out of the shadows, so clear and loud the players pause a moment, as do the dancers.
The roosters have awakened. They see the light of something other
than dawn and want to join. Two more piercing cries come flying
overtop Timu's stick fence, and the guests all laugh. One answers
back: Sam. Sam shows he has a very handsome crow. He tucks his
arms like chicken wings to make it, and the others are inspired
enough to follow, bursting out with high-pitched whoops and broken hollers, which only rouse the roosters all the more.

The musicians have missed hardly a beat meanwhile. The thrum-
ming strings keep giving time, and the men keep taking it. They're
moving in their circle now, slowly, letting go with yips and hoots.
But it's Martin who steps up next. He takes a bold half step from
Toby's side, lifts up his chin, and lets out.

"*Cocorricooooo!*"

The others turn; they recognize.

"*Cocorrico!*"

It's Campanero's crow. The guests approve, and now a whole
slew of Campanero's crows go flying up through the oak limbs like
ten triumphant spears. Some of the guests begin the jealous cluck—
cluck-cluck-cluck. Some the walk—*blegblegbleg.* Sam starts strutting
around, wagging his elbows, and scratching the dirt with his feet,
while the tall plum-cheeked one is laughing aloud, stamping his feet
side to side.

Toby is relieved too. He prefers this, he isn't sure why, but then
his ears pick out one voice among them, calling out a strange word,
kalanoro. He can't see who, but it's an older voice, and he knows it
belongs to one of the blacks again, because this is the name they've
given Lopez. Kalanoro. In the midst of all the crows and thrums
and flutes, he keeps repeating it, like a lonely bird in a tree, but faster
and faster and louder and louder, until the others begin to quiet,

the players and the women too, to listen: "*Kalanoro-kalanoro-kalanorokalanorooooo!*"

Silence, even among the roosters.

Toby leans around Martin to see that it's James, who works for the former Reverend, humble James, standing in a semicrouch with his arms straight down and his fingers splayed, eyes closed and breathing heavy.

> . . . Let me have my tree . . .

He is singing the song of Galinha, the sailor who wagered Campanero. The others nod, approving. Come out, Dom Fernao, don't hide.

> Let my children eat
> figs and cream . . .

And now the valiha recognizes as well. It strums in, but at a slower, more insistent pace, and the women join.

> Figs and cream,
> in the morning.

Again, their voices charge the air and make it hum, none deeper or fuller than James's. The roosters sit and listen, while Galinha's plea fills out the golden pocket underneath the oaks, thickens the light, and caresses the leaves.

> Figs and cream
> figs and cream
> let my children eat
> figs and cream
> in the morning.

Toby looks for Quinto, but again his eye finds the tall young black with the plum cheeks. His dance has brought him around to Lotte, and this time when they sing of the children, he leans down and places his long, slender hands on Lotte's belly. The women let out sighs and laughter; how her face and her womb are glowing in the light. Even the roosters cry out, while the women keep singing.

> Figs and cream,
> figs and cream . . .

Miss Mason's cook, Cornelia, reaches out and touches Lotte's belly now, and so they begin taking turns, all of them, the singers and dancers alike. They come around to bless the unborn child, some with their hands, some with just their smiles, some with jittery bows and genuflections.

Again Toby looks for Quinto and this time finds him farther back and away from the circle. It's dark, but Toby can just see him through all the arms and legs. He is still safe beside his mother. He still has the grapes in one hand and her arm in the other, and his expression is the same as well, almost as if no one were there, except that down low, Toby can see that his right foot is brushing against the leaves, if only very lightly and to a distant, distant rhythm.

Toby moves back into the shadows himself. While the rest keep on, dancing and singing, taunting the roosters and blessing the child in Lotte's womb, he returns to the cart for Alley's blanket and the puppets. No one sees but maybe 'Scilla, maybe Timu, as he shuffles back through the dark of the unlit oaks, all the way to Timu's porch, up the aching steps and down to where the baskets are piled.

There is a pot of ivy hanging from the eaves. Toby takes it from its hook nail and replaces it with the puppets, still cradled in their blue horse blanket and entirely hidden but for the four slender bones sticking out the end.

—⁓⁓⁓—

Reverend Boys hears the roosters; his home is that close to Timu's farm. A sore throat was his excuse for not attending the Admiral's ball this evening, and it was his intention to go to bed early. He has long since finished supper and is in fact folding down the cover of his bed when the shrill crows muffle through his windowpane and lift his ear. And he would not normally think so much of it—perhaps that rats had found their way inside the coop again—except that earlier in the evening he did notice a number of the slaves headed in Timu's direction, against the tide of masters. He lifts the sash three inches, and now he can hear voices as well, singing in a strange nasal tone, and thumping. And right away he begins to feel that same queasiness he felt at Francis Plain.

He puts back on his slippers and his dressing gown, in consideration of stepping outside and listening from the road, but then he hears the laughter. He hears hands clapping and tells himself that they are merely dancing. Dancing with each other, while their masters do the same.

So he doesn't go outside, but he doesn't go to bed either. He takes his Bible and sits at the window, gripping the Good Book tightly in his two hands as he listens and waits and watches the clock.

The first of the slaves appears at quarter past nine, a quiet pair headed back on foot. It is too dark to see who, but Timu's has gone quiet, and more slaves soon follow on. He sees at least a dozen pass. The masters' carriages don't appear for another hour or so, but in a steadier stream, trundling back home from the ball, the women inside like wilted flowers. By eleven-thirty Boys can account for most of the islanders this side of Plantation House and assures himself that all are safe in bed by midnight.

—⋘⋙—

He's not so far off. Save for the natural night creatures and a few turning pages, there's nothing moving through the island but the winds, as they do every night, buffeting the cliffs at Sandy Bay, spilling up around Diana's Peak, and curling off on countless trails and secret passages. Some sweep across Deadwood Plain unimpeded, some eddy down the Briars' valley, or brush through the willows at Francis Plain, while others slip beneath the oaks at Timu's, stirring all the scents of the evening—turmeric and fish, spiced cigarettes, biscuits, cooked chicken, sleeping chicken, chicken droppings. The ducking breezes clear the air beneath the canopy and nuzzle the blue horse blanket hanging just outside Quinto's room, gently rocking them all night long, the King, the Queen, the High Priest, and Fernao Lopez.

X
The Confession

[Four shadows.]

THE QUEEN

He is here! He is here! Where is my robe and diadem? Bring them here, and my throne too. But not too high. Not too high. I want to be down close where I can see.

THE KING

What is all this noise? Esta, whom are you screeching about?

THE QUEEN

The monster! The man without the face, who lives alone on the island. Finally he has answered your letter.

THE KING

Fernao Lopez?

THE QUEEN

Yes. He spent the night in the Captain's house, but now he is here, come to the palace, to show his face! I cannot wait!

THE KING

This is most unexpected. Where is my scribe?

[A scribe appears.]

THE KING

Come, and write down every word most faithful. Make sure your quill is sharp and the well is full. Is full? Is sharp? Then bring him in.

[A drum begins to thump, and a familiar shadow appears on the right side of the scrim—of a hooded figure, the same as stood on the road outside Goa. The drum beats out his pace as he crosses to the foot of the King and Queen and kneels.]

THE KING

What is your name?

LOPEZ

Fernao Lopez, my Lord.

THE KING

Dom Fernao Lopez, prisoner of St. Ilena, the one to whom the sailors sing.

[The shadow is silent.]

THE KING

And are you the same who once did live here on noble land, a nobleman, of noble blood and station?

[The shadow nods.]

THE QUEEN

I cannot see! Make him take down the hood.

THE KING

Silence, woman! Dom Fernao, take down your hood, that all may see.

[The shadow removes his hood. The court gasps. The Queen pulls back in horror.]

THE QUEEN

Oh, how terrible. I never seen such an ugly face! Look at how miserable. He is like the earless cat we had!

THE KING

Silence! Tell us, Dom Fernao, why do you come now, after so many years of silence?

LOPEZ

The invitation of Your Maj—

THE QUEEN

Oh, it is terrible! To see him speak! To see the lovely words of Portingale spill from such a hideous face.

THE KING

Silence, woman! Dom Fernao, continue.

LOPEZ

At Your Majesty's invitation, to own what I have done.

THE KING

At last. And I am most obliged, because I must confess, I cannot understand what you have done, Dom Fernao. You are he who once did serve in the brigade of Affonzo Dabakur, is this not so? And who sailed with him around the Cape to search for the great Priest-King, PrestaJohn?

LOPEZ

I am, Your Majesty.

THE KING

And were you then among the Captains who helped rescue Goa from the Moor?

LOPEZ

I was, Your Majesty.

THE KING

And this was a very great victory for the Portingale, was it not, inasmuch as the Moor did outnumber you, as one by ten? And yet still, by courage and inspiration, you did defeat them.

LOPEZ

We did take Goa, Your Majesty.

THE QUEEN

Oh, look at him. I cannot bear, but I cannot take my eyes away!

THE KING

Woman, please! Yes, you did take Goa, Dom Fernao, but this is where I am lost. For then you were among the chosen few whom your great commander did entrust to keep the sacred city safe, while he ventured farther in his search.

LOPEZ

I was.

THE KING

But you did not do this, no? For when the Moor returned, just as Dabakur had feared they would, you did not fend at all but crossed over to their side to fight with them.

LOPEZ

. . . This is true.

[Gasps.]

THE KING

And is it true that you caused others to do the same?

LOPEZ

If I was the cause, I do not know.

THE KING

But you were their leader, were you not, and noblest among them? Do you not think that when they see their betters crossing over to the heathen side, they are bound to follow?

LOPEZ

I grant I was of noblest birth, Your Majesty, not that I was better, though I will own that some did answer to my command.

THE KING

And so it was at your command, they did raise arms against their own, so that when your leader would return, he should find his precious city lost, and the greater insult still: the sight of his own men, whom he had trusted, now hiding behind heathen walls and heathen guns?

LOPEZ

Yes, Your Majesty.

[Gasps.]

THE KING

How does this happen, Dom Fernao? Did you not take an oath? Did you not avow your loyalty? You betray your word, and your commander, and in this way, betray your King, who sits before you now. How does a man succumb like this, and forsake everything he knows?

LOPEZ

My faith did fail me, Your Highness.

THE KING

Say this again, Dom Fernao, and clear, if anyone has ears too weak to hear, how a man can spit so square upon his home, his family, his land, and the sacred Crown which protects them all.

LOPEZ

My faith did fail, Your Majesty.

THE QUEEN

Oh, how pathetic he is. Look how low and miserable!

THE KING

I would silence my Queen again, Dom Fernao, and yet I must agree, you do move us to pity. Tell us, then, how you regret your treachery.

LOPEZ

It has brought me here, Your Majesty.

[The shadow bows down, its head upon the ground.]

THE KING

. . . Very good. So turn and let the people see. Let them look upon you as they bear witness, how the Crown you once did scorn still finds the strength and grace to forgive you, according to its word. Your long and lonely exile is ended, Dom Fernao Lopez.

[Much applause.]

THE KING

The kingdom opens its arms to you and welcomes you again. You are free to return to your family and the land of your youth. Only tell us where you would go, and there you shall be taken.

LOPEZ

Your Majesty's kindness humbles me, but I cannot yet avail myself.

THE KING

What is this?

THE QUEEN

Look at him, stupid husband! Of course, he cannot accept. He is ashamed of how he looks, and of the sins to which his ugliness attest. Look. Does your forgiveness give him back his face? His hand or thumb? Does it smooth out these scars? The people will still look and see, and seeing, they will know.

THE KING

Hm. Is this so, Dom Fernao? Is what my Queen says true?

LOPEZ

I cannot know what others see, Your Majesty, but the wisdom and compassion of Her Serenity are most moving.

THE KING

But if what she says is so, then let me offer this: There is a house of friars on the hill, where they are bound by vows of silence and humility not to raise their eyes, or open their mouths to speak. I can assure you, the friars on the hill will not take notice of you or the scars which still betray you. Would you be with them, then?

LOPEZ

Again, Your Majesty's kindness is most humbling to me, but I still cannot accept.

[Murmurs of concern.]

THE KING

Would you test my patience so?

LOPEZ

I would not, but that I know I shall never be free till I confess before the cross as well.

THE KING

Ah, 'tis so. Was not my invitation alone. Then go. Go and kneel before Poklemmit. Then you will tell us where you would be.

[The gamelan plays, and Lopez is set upon a ship, which starts gliding to the right of the scrim, where even now there appears a great high cross, a flock of followers, and an eight-step pedestal, with the High Priest Poklemmit seated at the top. The ship stops, the gamelan falls silent, and Lopez is delivered to the foot of the pedestal.]

LOPEZ

Your Holiness.

POKLEMMIT

Dom Fernao Lopez, of whom so much is told.

LOPEZ

I cannot answer, Your Holiness, to all that is said of me.

POKLEMMIT

Then let me see if I am right, and you correct where I stray: that you did serve with Dabakur, and were among the valiant few who went with him to Goa, and took it from the Moor, though they outnumbered you, as ten by one.

LOPEZ

I would not attest to my own valor, Your Holiness, but I did fight with Dabakur at Goa.

POKLEMMIT

And yet, despite the victory was granted you and God's clear favor shown, you did, once left alone, cross over to the Moor. Did eat with them, and sleep with them, did bathe with them, and even pray with them.

LOPEZ

I did.

[Flock-wide gasps.]

POKLEMMIT

Woe to you, Dom Fernao. Woe. And am I right that you did cause others to follow you and thus expose their minds to heresy?

LOPEZ

I was not alone, Your Holiness, and I do own they followed me.

POKLEMMIT

Then, woe. Woe to you, Dom Fernao. A greater sin there cannot be, nor greater punishment to bear, for to a King a man bears but his life. To God he bears his immortal soul. Tell us how, Dom Fernao. Let the people know.

LOPEZ

My faith did fail, my Lord.

POKLEMMIT

Aye, did fail and cast you unto devils. But you were saved, Dom Fernao. You were found, and punished for your sin, and cast into the wilderness, to live among the lepers and the beggars. And only when Dabakur was called to heaven were you then found on a boat bound back for Portingale and cast upon a lonely island to live on in exile absolute. How long?

LOPEZ

I do not know, Your Holiness.

POKLEMMIT

But long enough to ponder and repent what you had done. Long enough to bring you here, to kneel and beg forgiveness.

[The shadow bows down, its head upon the ground.]

POKLEMMIT

People, observe contrition, for a sin so great, to betray not only one's commander and one's King, but one's only God in heaven. Observe how he has suffered for it. Let his sorrow and remorse shine forth to you, and witness to your neighbors that from his most private penance and exile, Fernao Lopez has been moved to come to us and kiss this ring. Ponder how great is man's hunger for forgiveness, and how great is the Lord's mercy that He should give it, even to this most wretched sinner. Dom Fernao, come.

[Lopez climbs the pedestal.]

POKLEMMIT

You do confess, then, that you have done amiss in aught, and willingly bear
penance, to aver the infamy of which you stand accused?

LOPEZ

It is my sin which brings me here.

[Lopez kisses the ring.]

POKLEMMIT

Behold! The hundredth sheep has returned to the flock, and there is
more joy in heaven for this today than for all the ninety-nine which never
stray.

[The oak trees shiver.]
[The people applaud.]

POKLEMMIT

Dom Fernao, your penance is served. You confess, and you are free, to live as
you would choose, in the Grace of Our Lord. You may live among the friars
on the hill. You may live among your family and make amends with them.
Tell us, with the arms of the Holy Empire once more opened to you, where
would you be?

LOPEZ

The island, Your Holiness.

[Silence.]

POKLEMMIT

Say again. I don't think I hear.

[Silence.]

LOPEZ

The island, Your Holiness. St. Ilena.

[Poklemmit lifts his head and looks across to the far end of the scrim, where King JohnSree has just been told of the supplicant's answer and shares the High Priest's confoundment.]

—◆—

November 21—Toby is awake but has yet to rise. He still feels Alley's death like a stone on his chest, as he will for many days and nights to come, but as if it were one with the ascending light, his heart is lifting too because he knows the garden will be waking soon, and that it will open wider today and drink deeper than it has been. For there is nothing that Helena enjoys so much as remembering the end of Fernao Lopez's story, as she does this morning. There is nothing Toby enjoys so much either.

The King and Poklemmit were true to their word. They sent Lopez back to the island, just as he had asked, and he lived out his days there, among the orchards and woods, the streams, the waterfall, and the steep black rock. But now when the tall ships dropped anchor and the sailors rowed to shore, Lopez no longer hid from them. He came out and greeted them. He showed them how their seeds had grown, how the saplings had turned into trees, and he shared their fruit with them. So they brought him more: banana trees, pineapple trees, date palm and fig and pomegranate trees. Fruits and flowers from all the distant kingdoms of the world were brought to St. Helena, in faith that Fernao Lopez would take them and plant them and look after them. And the same was true of animals: Pheasants and ducks, partridges and peacocks were left on the shore there, to find their way inland and nest among the native wirebirds. Turkeys gobbled through the brush. Bulls grazed the same meadows as the goats that grew so fat and shaggy there. St. Helena was a garden in his care, and the passing sailors, when they saw him, did not gawk at his scars or think that he was maimed. They saw how the island flourished for him, and they counted themselves blessed that they could be with him, if only for one day.

And now it was Quinto's turn to be so blessed.

PART VI

LOT, SANDY BAY

CHAPTER TWENTY-ONE

NOVEMBER 21-26

—◦◦◦—

Cockburn serves notice—Betsy recounts the ball—The island is poison—
Raffia and pine needles—Tweedling fifes and drums—Toby's dream

November 21—The rumor which circulated among the guests at
the ball, that General Bonaparte had apparently slipped security at
the Briars to go calling on Major and Mrs. Hodgson, did not sit
comfortably on Admiral Cockburn's pillow.

He goes to pay a special morning visit to the Briars, to revise his
estimation of when Longwood will be ready. He speaks specifically
to General Bertrand, telling him that the chief carpenter up at the
site, Mr. Cooper, sees two more weeks of work. General Bonaparte
and all those whom he intends to bring with him should be prepared to leave their present abodes by December 3.

Bertrand offers no objection, asking only that sufficient time be
permitted for the last applied coat of paint to dry. No one wants a
repeat of what occurred on the boat.

—◦◦◦—

"I see you've put on your little boy pants again."

Betsy hasn't been able to find him until now, late in the day. He
is alone beneath the arbor, Las Cases having just departed.

"Tell me, it was fun?" He looks awfully tired. His eyes are glassy.

The small hairs beneath his forelock are matted, but he rouses to her presence.

"Yes," she says, with a curl in her tone. She doesn't want to make him feel too bad for not being there, and in fact, it wasn't so much fun.

"Did you dance with Gogo?"

"I did. Once."

"Miss Wilkes was there?"

"Yes."

"Did she pay attention to Gogo?"

"She did," concedes Betsy. "They danced."

He waves away her condolence. "J'ai un coeur bronze." *My heart is bronze.* "Tell me, what did the Mesdames wear?"

She tells him. Madame Bertrand's gown was pink and white and cut beneath the shoulders. He knows the one. "But the scandal was Madame de Montholon's jewelry."

"The pearl brocade."

"Yes. Some of the ladies didn't think it was appropriate. They were calling it booty."

The Emperor smirks. "C'est de la jalousie."

"Oui."

"Very good. So the dances?"

"The dances." She shifts. "Let me remember. There was a 'Faine I would.' "

"What is this?"

She suspects he knows very well, but she shows him in any case. She stands. "Well, it's for eight. Man-woman, man-woman, all the way around. And first you change places with the person to your left, like so." She performs the step for him, how the hands are to be held. "Then you switch with the couple across from you, like this." She pantomimes meeting the couple across from her, raising her left hand. "And you keep exchanging like that, it's hard to explain, but at the end you fall back into the arms of the person you were first with, like this." She dips as best she can.

He is not impressed. " 'Faine I would.' "

"Yes."

"A kitchen dance." He scorns. "What else?"

"Well"—she thinks—"there was a 'Friar and Nun.' "

" 'Friar and Nun'?"

"Yes. And some trots."

"Trots? What are you saying to me? I am subjected to all of this endless talk and talk and talk about the ball—'When is it going to be?' 'What are we going to wear?' I see everyone puts on their finest shoes—then they go and dance trots and reels?" He whisks the idea behind him. "Tell me about the dress."

"The dress was fine." She wants to be modest, but she can't. She blushes.

"None was better?"

"No. Well, the women, yes. Miss Wilkes's was very lovely, but among the younger women, definitely I would say that mine was the most . . . beautiful. The others were all in blouses and white skirts. They were all the same."

"Except for you."

"Yes."

"So it's good that I let you wear it?"

"You didn't let me."

"I did." His eyes glimmer, lids descended—he enjoys his mischief—but as she looks at him, his complexion does seem awfully waxy.

———

Dr. O'Meara is summoned from town and arrives midday to confirm that His Majesty has developed a slight fever. The windows and sashes are checked for drafts. The shutters are closed, and for the next three days the Emperor is confined to the Pavilion, no longer eating or sleeping in the tent.

The Emperor himself shows more frustration than concern, once again ascribing the fever to a process of acclimatization. The valets, having observed the same in Moscow, Elba, and Egypt, would concur, but Las Cases is no longer so sure. His Majesty's continued bouts of fatigue are a growing concern, and not just for the Count.

In private conference under the tent this morning, Dr. O'Meara acknowledged certain rumors he has heard concerning the overincidence of liver disease among island residents.

"Are you saying that the climate may not be wholesome?" the Count asks.

O'Meara steers shy of commitment. "It is an idea"—he fumbles his French; a *notion*, he calls it—"that isolated environments are liable to cultivate unusual, specific conditions, which may not be—"

Sensing concern, Gourgaud steps in to offer his impatience. "What is he saying?"

"Oh, nothing," Las Cases sarcases. "Just that the island they've brought us to is poison."

—————

November 22–25—Marie observes no real change in Quinto, but she is not looking for any. She doesn't know who the puppets are or why the Balcombes' gardener hung them outside the window, only that Timu does not want them moved, and they don't seem to bother Quinto.

The days unfold as before. She leaves at dawn; Quinto is on the porch, weaving. She returns after nightfall; Quinto is on the porch, weaving. She knows he isn't there all day. Timu takes him around to help with the chickens, but she has seen how he acts. The chickens gather around the two of them, gobbling and pecking. Quinto hardly seems to notice. He scatters the grit, and when the bucket is empty, he leaves Timu there and returns to the porch, to his baskets. Sunday, Quinto and she took Timu's wagon over to the Old Woman's Valley. There is a grove of raffia trees there, and some pine trees as well, and they spent all day collecting needles and palm fronds. Quinto will still be working on them when she gets back from town, stripping them and twisting them until they're soft like rope. He'll stop when he hears her feet in the leaves, though. He'll take her hand for dinner, and when they are done, she'll wash his face, his hands, and his feet, and they'll lie down. The only difference is that he's finally sleeping through the night again.

Betsy is permitted in to see him once in three whole days—once!—and even then he stayed on the couch the whole time, dosing in and out. She held his hand, but the moment he awakened, they shooed her away again. She is growing very impatient with all of them, and him. How frail he seems. He likes to brag about his endurance. He says he once rode four days straight, without stopping. She doesn't believe it. He is always so "indisposed," complaining about sore throats and sniffles. Of course she wishes for his sake that he felt better, but doesn't he realize? He is wasting *their* time.

"Did he come out today?" Her father joins her at the rail of the veranda.

"No," she says, openly glum. In the distance the drums of another regiment can be heard, marching closer. All day long, she thinks. How many drums and drummers can there be?

"Is Dr. O'Meara there?"

She shrugs. She wishes he'd go and leave her. All her father cares about is his reputation and how it might reflect poorly on him that Napoleon Bonaparte was sick the whole time he stayed there.

"I don't understand why he has to go," she says. "I'm sure he doesn't want to."

"Did he say that?" Her father looks over at her, so suddenly pinched and nervous she hasn't the heart to lie.

"No," she mumbles. She pities him and is embarrassed by him. Marchand has more dignity.

Up on the road the soldiers have come into view, marching double file, with their silly drums and their stupid tweedling fifes.

"I wish they'd just be quiet!" she snaps. "How do they expect him to sleep?"

November 26—Toby tries to go about his days quietly and without expectation. He feeds the chickens, tears out chickweed, and sweeps the paths, all in faith that the invisible sacks of mud that he's been dragging since Alley's death will eventually, task by task, dry and spill out.

He hasn't seen so much of Bony; Bony hasn't been out the last few days. Sarah says 'Scilla saw a goat looking in the pavilion windows the other night; they think it was Kalanoro. Toby does not agree or disagree. He does not want to think about such things anymore. He does not contemplate the flesh of the fruit he collects from underneath the four old fruit trees or peer too long into the white-faced briars. If he hears a foot tread on the path or the moan of a cart wheel, he does not even stand to see who it is, if it is Timu, or Marie, or Quinto.

Then Wednesday night he has a dream, for the first time since Bony came. Finally Winston-Kumar lowers the scarf from Toby's sleeping eyes, and he is not surprised to find himself on the old island, the island Lopez found. Toby recognizes the colors and the pitch of the hills, but most of all he remembers the sense of welcome, the air's reminder that this is not a forbidden place at all. This is the place that waits for them, all of them, whoever chooses to come.

He is standing high on the far side of the Great Ridge, looking down toward Sandy Bay. It is night, but the clouds reflect the moonlight bright enough for him to see: There are no houses or tilled land, just the hillsides spilling fast into one another and the ocean beyond. In the foreground, to the left, is a flowering agave, rising up from the base of a dark sheer hillside, straight and slender, its limbs upturned with golden tufts at the end like little burning flames. In the distance stands Lot, a fallen shard of the moon, and behind him Lot's wife, another smaller shard. They are showing him, calling him down to the bay. This is where he is, they say. This is where he went. And the next thing Toby knows, he is down on the beach, his feet sunk in the cool, wet sand, with a giant sea turtle sleeping beside. The cliffs to the north are bathed in blue moonlight and pitted black with caves the seabirds use to nest—except for one, from which a faint golden light is hueing.

Toby starts up. He climbs to a shelf of black lava stone and freshwater pools, swimming with the red and silver fish, and he remembers even better now. This is where he goes. This is where the boy found him (and in his dream there is no difference between Quinto and the Javaboy, or himself), just up on the next ridge there, in the faintly glowing cave. Toby follows toward it, up a jagged path. The ocean foams and pounds below, the blue cliffs rise above, but Toby isn't bothered or uncertain until he comes right up to the mouth of the cave. He notices three coins shining on the path. Bony's coins. Toby is confused now. Is he wrong then? Are they all wrong? He peers around up over the ledge and looks inside.

The space is very small, smaller than his own room, but there is a lantern in the middle, with a low flame that's casting quick shadows across the walls. Over on the far side, the light is bouncing off something smooth and shiny. Bottles. Toby leans closer, and there is a familiar scent. He isn't sure what it is, though, until he sees: Those are Mr. Balcombe's claret bottles. The scent is Alley. This is Alley's cave, but Toby isn't scared. He knows he must be there, somewhere in the shadows. Still, Toby knows what he must do. He crawls across to the far side. The bottles are lined in a row and empty. He takes them and starts tossing them down onto the rocks and waves below, one by one.

CHAPTER TWENTY-TWO

NOVEMBER 27–DECEMBER 6

———∙∙∙∙∙∙∙———

Betsy is punished again; licorice—The Emperor's revival—
Confronting the Reverend Eakins—Blindman Blove—The date is set—
Idol of the jovi-bara maidens

November 27—Still no sign of him yet today. Betsy is in the sewing room, with pins and scissors and her blue gown over her knee.

"What is this?" Her mother is standing at the door, glaring, but Betsy does not look up.

"Why does he have to make the stitches so tight?"

"What are you doing? Should you not be working?"

Betsy rolls her eyes. She is too tired of this conversation.

"Shouldn't you? Madame Bertrand says you're not doing your lessons."

"I am."

"Not according to Madame Bertrand. Betsy, the reason we agreed to let Madame Bertrand superintend your studies was that we thought you liked her and that you respected her."

"I do."

"It is not respectful to disobey her."

"I'm not *disobeying* her."

"Did she give you an assignment?"

"I don't know. Yes."

"Have you completed it?"

"No. Not yet. Maybe. I don't know. I tried, but I can't find the book."

"What book is it?"

"I don't know, I lost it. I didn't *lose* it, but I don't know where it is."

"Where did you leave it?"

"I don't know. The garden. But why should I have to translate? I speak well enough. Ask the Emperor. Je parle français presque couramment. En tout cas je parle mieux que vous." *I speak better than you.*

"Betsy, don't be smart. Have you looked for it, the book?"

"Yes."

"You have?"

"Yes. Oui."

"What is the title?"

"Je ne sais pas."

"And you're telling me that if I go in your room right now, I won't find it?"

"Je ne sais pas. Je n'ai pas cherché là."

"Betsy, stop."

"I said I didn't look there."

"You didn't look in your room?"

"No."

"You've looked in the garden, but you didn't look in your room?"

"Yes."

Her mother turns and starts for the girls' bedroom. Betsy rushes to follow, leaving her gown behind, with the flower dangling.

Jane is at her desk—reading, of course. And of course there is the book, open on the floor beside Betsy's bed. *Héloïse.*

"Oh, there it is," says Betsy. The Emperor would have laughed, but her mother picks up the book and swats Betsy on the rear with it, quite unexpectedly. Even Jane jolts in her chair.

"You will take this book," her mother says, "and your journal, and you will take them down to the cellar. And I am not letting you out of there until you have completed the assignment that Madame Bertrand has given you. Do you understand? Betsy, do you understand?"

"Yes."

Her mother stalks back out to the veranda, picks up one of the small school desks, and carries it in two hands through the kitchen and down into the cellar. Betsy follows helplessly, silently, contemptuously. Her mother marches down the cellar steps, desk out front, and plants it on the floor.

Betsy says nothing. The cellar will be fine, she thinks, as long as *she* won't be there.

She leaves twice. First to get a chair and some ink. Then to go fetch her blue gown. The light is no good, though. There are only two windows—or half windows, high up on the wall. They open to the ground level outside, so that is where she seats herself, on her chair on a table by the window, with the blue dress spread out on her lap, tugging at stitches with her pin, trying not to harm the flowers as she removes them.

She is once again cursing Monsieur St. Denis—it can't possibly be necessary to sew anything so tight—when she recognizes a pair of feet approaching, in white tight socks and low black shoes, and very cocksure. They walk right up to the window and stop, facing out, as though their owner had chosen here to stand and view the vista, even though there is no vista. Betsy holds her tongue at first; it is a silent contest, but then she sees where the socks have been mended, of the holes torn by the needles of the prickly pear. She cannot help laughing.

"What?" he says, not looking down, but to the air. " 'Oo is there? 'Oo is this geegling?"

She tries to keep quiet, but can't.

" 'Oo?" He leans down and looks in. "Y-a-t'il un rat?"

"Un rat? C'est vous le rat."

"Ah! Is Mademoiselle Betsee." He leans down. He looks well again. "What are you doing down zere?"

"Pas de rien."

"But I thought you don't like this place."

"It's not so bad. In the day."

He takes a seat. There is a stool just outside the window. His back to the wall. She can still only barely see his face.

"Are you feeling better?"

"Who told you I was not feeling well?"

"No one."

"I am feeling better."

He offers her some licorice from a small tin box. Betsy has never liked licorice very much, but she takes some anyway.

"Why are you being punished?"

"None of your business. Because I didn't translate some pages."

"That Madame Bertrand assigned?"

"Yes."

"You should do this. It's disrespectful. What did she assign?"

"*Héloïse.*" She shows him the cover.

"Oh, well. This is very good. And you would do well, a girl like you, to open up your mind to something of quality. Rousseau." He looks down at the gown in her lap.

"Will you help me?"

"Absolutely not." He sees the cover on the sill. "What pages? What is happening?"

She puts down the gown. She hands him the book through the window and gets her pen and ink all ready. Then he reads it to her slowly, stopping every few lines to make sure she has caught up, and also to feed her bits of licorice from his tin box, one by one.

————

November 27–December 1—The Emperor does indeed seem to be feeling more spry, which comes as a great relief to Las Cases. For the first time in weeks, His Majesty is dressing fully again, in his Chasseur du Gard uniform. He has taken to conducting two and sometimes three dictations a day, with all scribes attending, and has also decided he *would* like horses to be brought to the Briars after all, a choice which the Count deems a personal victory. That he should now have to share His Majesty with the others he does not mind as much as he might have before. He and the Emperor have more or less concluded discussion of the Italian campaign, his eyes are still deteriorating, and in fact, the combined presence of all his amanuenses—himself, Bertrand, Gourgaud, and even at times de Montholon—seems to have had an energizing effect upon His Majesty. As blurry as the image may be, Las Cases still finds it thrilling to watch him pace back and forth in front of them, jumping between the various chapters of his history, from Lautzen to Waterloo, from Egypt to the various assassination attempts. Las Cases had no idea, for instance, that the Christmas Eve plot of 1800 was foiled only at the last moment by the worker the Jacobins had hired to block the street with caltrops, so to delay the Emperor's carriage, so to blow him up.

"If not for the instincts of one man"—His Majesty thrusts his finger into the air—"one man! the Consul would almost surely have been destroyed."

Las Cases knows his eyes will scold him later, but he cannot help himself: He dips his pen and writes.

The other men of the suite are not quite as round in their enthusiasm. General Gourgaud has been licking his wounds ever since the night of the ball, which did not go as well as it might have appeared. To him, the Emperor's revival, welcome as it may be, serves only to aggravate his tender state. The weather turns cold on the thirtieth and drives the men inside for the day, all of them, cramped up in that little teahouse. At dinner the Emperor entertains himself by attacking poor Gourgaud, drilling him on first artillery exercises. "Show the second position! Now! Present arms!" Gourgaud fails miserably, reversing the order of several maneuvers. The Emperor is finally so disgusted he gets up from his chair and shows them all himself how it should be done. His form is perfect, needless to say, though all do. "One would think he'd taken the exam only yesterday!" Las Cases exclaims.

De Montholon joins in the applause, but of the present company, he is most alert to the spectacle. Indeed, he has begun to detect in His Majesty's performance the last several days what he fears may be the first sprigs and sprouts of outright dementia. Yesterday, for instance, he chanced, with sinking heart, to witness the Emperor "breaking" one of the ponies on the lawn, on a white tarp which had been laid out, and all before the adoring gaze of the rude blond girl. A more pathetic display of pointless heroism one could hardly imagine. Worse yet is having to listen to him out in the garden paths, wagging his finger at the poor Malay who tends the flowers. "I will buy him, do you know? As soon as I am permitted my accounts. I will buy him and set him free!" As much as the Marquis hates to admit it, his wife may be right. And the others. A book may be his only hope.

As for the Grand Marshal, loyalty and experience advise him to reserve judgment, which is to say that he too detects what he fears may be a wobble of imbalance in His Majesty's current upswing. His Majesty has never been one to waste his energy on hindsight, for instance, but in the last two days he has revisited Waterloo three times. He has the maps taken out after dinner. "If only we had turned on the enemy's right," he says, pointing with a dinner knife to show them, "rather than tried to pierce the center and separate the two armies, we might well have succeeded." But how was he to know that Grouchy was lost, that Ney would seem so bewildered, that d'Erlon would be useless? "If I'd known of Grouchy's position and attacked when we had the chance, who is to say? The reserve was a morning away." He looks up at them all with a strange light in his eye, more fascination than regret. "But the battle turns in a single moment, yes?"

There follows the silence of four men who can no longer tell what the most ingratiating reply would be.

———✧———

December 3—Sunday. The Reverend Boys's sermon this morning took as its inspiration the confrontation at the river Jordan between John the Baptist and the Pharisees who'd come out to test him, the "brood of Vipers!" The Reverend's particular focus, to the surprise of none who listened, was the Baptist's warning to those who would assume their place in God's kingdom on account of birthright alone. "Think not to say within yourselves, We have Abraham to our father: for I say unto you that God is able of these stones to raise up children unto Abraham." Boys left little doubt that such assumptions were hardly confined to Judeans alone. They found harbor in many a familiar heart, and he would even venture that he touched a few this morning, to judge by the expressions in the front several pews. And yet, as he stands out on the chapel steps now and watches the congregation gossiping in their usual cliques—the Hodgsons with the Pritchards, the Brookes with the Reades—he fancies that if his counsel were smoke, he would see it now, drifting from all their ears and noses and blowing away in the endless blue sky.

It is at this same moment, however, that he first notes the presence of his nemesis and predecessor, the Right Reverend Eakins. The two have been trying to steer clear of each other since their summer squabbles—and with some success—but Boys unexpectedly switched venues with the junior Reverend Mr. Vernon today. Vernon took Country Church, while Boys presided in town, judging that his sermon might be better suited to the Jamestown congregation, which tends to be comprised of more island elite. The marina is a better place to see and be seen.

The Right Reverend is at present gracing the Leeches and the Kinnairds with his eminence, short and increasingly stout, of no stature on the whole, but hideously large in every particular. His head sprouts from the middle of his round shoulders like the tumescence of a freak potato, scant hair on top, ample white tufts on the side. His gaggle looks down on him adoringly, nonetheless, and no wonder. Eakins is the one who cultivated in them precisely the false sense of spiritual entitlement which it has been the Reverend Boys's most determined mission, as this morning's sermon testifies, to strip away.

"Ah, and here he is"—Eakins extends an arm of false welcome—"whose latchet I am not worthy to tie."

The party chuckles at the blasphemy.

"Another earnest sermon, Reverend." Mrs. Leech is too kind.

"Yes, the passion is always most impressive." As is Major Kinnaird, if only by way of excusing himself and his wife. And just as well, it's Eakins that Boys wants, as Eakins seems to have gleaned. He bids his flock a good day and turns back to Boys with a kind of feigned bemusement that instantly vindicates every ounce of enmity he bears the man: the rococo splurge of his brow, the pooched lips, used to affect so many different lies—humor, tolerance, the hopeless and exquisite burden of wisdom. "What is it I can do for you, Reverend Mr. Boys?"

"I'm not sure," says Boys, more plainly. "We came across a chest recently, up at Country Church."

Eakins waits, but again with that same boundless, baseless self-satisfaction. "And am I to shed some light on this chest, Reverend Boys?"

"As I say, I'm not sure. I didn't know if it had come into possession of the church during your Reverend's ministry."

Eakins smiles, for patience. "Perhaps if you told me what was *in* the chest, Mr. Boys."

"Puppets."

He bends his ear. "Pumice?"

"Puppets."

He scowls now, pretending to scour the corners of his mind. "The flat ones?"

"Yes."

"Yes. What of them, Reverend?"

"I simply wasn't sure where they'd come from, but I take it that they did arrive during the period of your chaplaincy?"

"They did. Reverend, I'm not sure I understand. Is it that you want them moved?"

"No." Boys remains calm. "We've certainly the space. I was simply curious where they might have come from."

Eakins sniffs and takes a half step back. "Well, Reverend, I may have to think on this. I'm not entirely sure that's your province."

"Perhaps not. If you've established some confidence in the matter, I'd be the last to intrude. Still, they are on premise—"

"Well, there again, Mr. Boys, if your purpose is to have me come collect them, I'll send James this afternoon."

"I'm not asking you to collect them, Reverend." Boys sharpens his tone. "I am asking, as I have asked in several prior instances—

without effect, I am afraid—nothing more or less than to be ap-
prised of all assets and debits which may befall my office. Now tell
me, did they come from the slaves?"

"Well, of course they did. Mr. Boys, this is unseemly!" Eakins's
sudden volume has stirred notice among the lingering congregation,
particularly in regard of the two men's rather public rivalry. The
Right Reverend so notes and therefore calms himself. He assumes
the pose of conciliator and, with an open sigh and one more the-
atrical curdle of his brow, endeavors to humor his successor's mad-
ness. "Very well, let me see." He scratches at the last wisps of hair
still clinging to his forehead. "It was the children, if I remember.
Some of the slave children had been misbehaving during lessons.
They were being disrespectful. I came to understand that the cause
of their ridicule—its origin, I should say—was a story that one of
the elder slaves had been telling them."

Boys understands: Some of the slave children had been mocking
the Right Reverend. "With puppets?"

"Yes." Eakins snorts.

"Who?"

"Mr. Doveton's coachman, if you must know."

"So you took the puppets away from him?"

"I spoke to Mr. Doveton. He was in agreement, but yes, it was I
who intervened."

For some reason, this last admission—and the pride with which
it is offered—sparks a rage in Boys he thinks it best not to tempt any
further.

"Mr. Doveton's coachman, you said?"

"Winston, yes," Eakins answers casually, "but I should think the
point is moot. He died soon after." And that quickly, with a lazy
flick of his wrist, he tosses the matter behind him.

Boys says no more, but as he looks at Eakins now, chuckling for
the benefit of their audience at the apparent absurdity of the exchange, he wonders why he should have bothered. He needs no
sanction from Eakins to do what he knows he should.

Before returning to his home that afternoon, he stops off at
Country Church. He goes straight to the storage room and up into

the loft. He recalls there having been a blue blanket. He recalls the chest's having been somewhat fuller, but he does not let the difference slow him. He lugs the coffer onto his back and down the ladder steps. He hauls it past the pews and the pulpit to his rectory office on the opposite side, where he promptly builds a fire. He locks the church doors, front and back, then slides his chair up to the hearth, and there spends the remainder of the day feeding the puppets to the flame, one after another after another. He opens a window despite the descending cold, to clear the acrid smell of burning paint, leather, and bone.

—◁◌▷—

December 5—"I still say you should have a ball." Betsy is with him in the Pavilion, measuring the space with her eye. "It wouldn't have to be a large ball like the Admiral's. Just for dancing."

He does not answer. He is looking at some pages of his memoir, dissatisfied by something, some turn of phrase he might improve.

"Why not?" she presses. "Why not? Speak to me!"

"Because. It is impossible."

"Why?"

"Because"—he puts the pages down—"even if it were allowed, it would take planning, preparation."

"So?"

"I don't know that I am going to be here much longer."

She collapses on the divan. She knows it's true, but to hear him say it, she wishes she hadn't mentioned the idea. "But you should do *something*." She sinks farther into her seat, and her despair.

"Betsee, no." He rises and rounds the desk. He stands right in front of her. "Tsk. Don't. No tears."

She can't help it.

"Betsee. Betsee, no."

He tucks her chin. "Dites-moi. Que voulez-vous que je fasse, Mademoiselle Betsee, pour vous consoler?" *What would you have me do? What would console you?*

She looks up.

"À part un autre bal." *Other than a ball.*

"The game?"

"What game?"

"The *game.*" He knows. She's been trying to get him to play since he got here. Blindman's Bluff. When he realizes, she can tell he doesn't want to, but he has given his word. He has offered.

At dinner the Emperor informs the guests, including the two Mesdames and the Las Caseses, that they will be playing a game called 'Blindman Blove' as part of the evening's entertainment. As soon as the dessert plates have been cleared, the guests dutifully gather in the drawing room. Betsy explains the rules, which are apparently not so different from a French game called Colin-Maillard. Then she passes out the cards to see who will begin. The blindman's card will be the ace of spades. It goes to her.

The Emperor supplies the scarf, a white one. He ties it around her head and does a suspiciously good job of it, except that it is too tight. She tugs at it.

"Ah-ah!" He spanks her hand. "We must make sure."

"It's too tight."

He waves his hand in front of her eyes and she flinches.

"There, proof. You must not be able to see."

He reties it, and this time she is blind. She can't even lift her lids. He begins to spin her around very quickly. The others scramble, he pinches her nose, and the game has begun. She can hear the other children yelping and laughing. Madame Bertrand screams, and Betsy is drunk with joy. She can hear him, then, cackling over behind the sofa. She reaches out and starts stalking over, feeling for the chair and the table. Their feet all thump across the floor like a litter of puppies, and now his voice is over on the other side of the room. She turns and just then bumps into someone. A boy, her brother Nicholas, who falls to the floor, giggling hysterically dead.

So they tie the scarf around Nicholas this time. Again the Emperor obliges, spins Nicholas around and around, and now it is Nicholas's turn to fumble around the furniture. The players all scatter, but Betsy is watching him, the Emperor. He is not like the other adults. They go find safe places—Las Cases stands in the corner with his hands on his ears; the Mesdames take each other's hands and remove themselves entirely, to the veranda—but the Emperor stays among the children. He runs behind little Hortens and picks her up as Nicholas comes closer, using her as a shield.

"Cheater!" cries Betsy. She desperately wants to see him with the blindfold. She starts over, around behind the tables and lamps. "He's over here, Nicholas! This way! I'll get him for you." And she would have. She was going to grab him from behind and hold him, but just as she is reaching out, there comes a loud knock at the door, and menacing. The room goes silent, all but for Nicholas's giggle, which tapers off. It's dark outside, but Betsy can see two horses on the lawn.

Sarah goes to answer. It is the Grand Marshal and the Admiral, both looking very tall and solemn. The Grand Marshal seems the more embarrassed. He can tell they've interrupted.

"Votre Majesté," he says, bowing slightly, "l'amiral voudrait vous parler."

And that quickly all gaiety is snuffed. The Emperor sets a pillow down on the chaise and exits. The others mutely watch him go.

When the door has closed behind them and the men have descended the porch steps, a throat clears, and Betsy can feel several sets of eyes turned to her, the children mostly, waiting to see if they're going to keep playing, but she doesn't want to look back. Out the window the three generals are nearing the narrow path leading up to the Pavilion. They have to pick an order, single file. He leads, and as the others follow him up, the answer is too obvious. The game is clearly over.

—⬦—

Cockburn sets out the terms of the Emperor's captivity at Longwood in clear, firm language. The move is to take place three days hence, on the eighth. If the prisoner and suite are not prepared to leave by then, two hundred soldiers will be ordered to surround the

Briars and escort them up to Deadwood Plain. From that point forward the prisoner—and this is the word he uses, reading from the order that he himself has composed—the "prisoner" shall at all times be in clear view of a British officer. The Admiral specifies several of their stations: one in the dining room; another in the drawing room. He delineates the various boundaries of the property as well. The Emperor will be permitted to walk freely throughout, provided he remains in view of the sentries. He will be free to ride as well, so long as he is in the escort of an officer.

The Emperor and Bertrand both expected as much. Terms are always more stringent than actions, and more strictly applied at the outset of an assignment. Certainly Bertrand finds the mention of the two-hundred-soldier escort to have been de trop, but the Emperor does not seem to have taken offense. He seems quite composed, in fact. Bertrand has been watching him as the Admiral goes down his list, item by item, and for the first time in a long while he thinks he might see it again, the old sangfroid, the cool implacability from which so many drew so much. Sitting there in his Windsor chair, listening to the brutal tedium of Cockburn's order, His Majesty's expression bears an almost admiring glow, the same as lights the loser's eye near the end of a well-played game of chess, at recognition of the mercilessness—the calculated and necessary mercilessness—of one's opponent.

The light persists. Hours later, when Bertrand and the Emperor have convened with the other members of the suite, His Majesty remains remarkably calm. In conveying Cockburn's order, he puts it that they shall be going "from a cage to a vise," but with that same encouraging detachment. It is the others who cannot help themselves, venting their frustrations.

Las Cases clenches his cuff. "The Spanish Princes at Valencia were treated with more respect!"

"The Pope and Fontainebleau," Gourgaud seconds, and they both are correct. The Spanish Princes were never made to feel their chains. They hunted and gave balls. And the Pope lived in a palace by comparison to this.

But again, the Emperor seems the least bothered among them.

"And yet consider how many soldiers still refused to guard him," he points out calmly, philosophically. "Not that I took offense. I might have done the same."

"Of course," says Las Cases. "And I certainly didn't mean to question Your Majesty's principles. I am only pointing out, in this instance, that there remain matters of respect, dignity."

The Emperor allows with a cool nod. "But there is no use blaming Admiral Cockburn. He is only doing as he has been ordered." He turns to Bertrand. "We'll need to find a gift for Monsieur Balcombe."

December 6—Deep down, Toby believes that Lopez already has returned. He's not sure when it happened or what has made him think so—whether it's the posture of the flowers or the waning simmer in 'Scilla's eyes—but he no longer feels so anxious about seeing Lopez or not seeing him. Maybe Lopez is like food that way, that just to have him on hand somehow keeps the hunger at bay, because now all the questions of the past few weeks seem much simpler to Toby, not so fraught. Lopez left because they forgot, and he has returned because they remembered, and when they remember, it is hard to believe he ever was gone, they know him so well; Toby does. Sometimes Toby feels as if he knows every moment Lopez spent here—of peace and longing, and loneliness and reconciliation. He knows why he hid from the sailors and why he came out. He knows what caused his faith to fail and what restored it; he can still hear it in the trees.

Wednesday morning begins the same as any other. Toby heads down to the coop after his tea. Toby goes about his chores, feeding the chickens, counting the eggs, and loading up a fresh barrow of hay and droppings, all before the masters are awake. He wheels back out to find 'Scilla kneeling in the kitchen garden, pulling at the dirt, and Bony's two servants heading down to the creek with their buckets.

When he returns to the garden gate, he can tell it's been opened and entered. Bony is inside, so Toby takes the low path back to the cottage, not wanting to disturb him. Halfway there he passes by the giant jovi-bara, lounging in a circle, waiting for the sun to crest the eastern hill. Toby is not inclined to look, but a branch lies across the path, fallen from a dwarf oak tree, and leaning down to pick it up, he sees that the great green succulents have lifted their heads already and that their gaze has met, not so far from its usual place, a dozen above the middle of the teaberry. Toby can't help smiling. Did he come back last night then? Or did the full moon fool them?

He tosses the branch on his pile of mulch, but as he stands straight again to take up the handles of his barrow, his glance lands unexpectedly on Bony—the far side of the garden's middle hump, beyond the shadow of the magnolia tree, and framed by the arbor trellis. He is seated in his chair among the spiders, but slumped, one leg straight, one leg bent, a thin forelock riddling his brow, as he glowers at the lone orange on the table in front of him. And Toby would not pause this way and stare, except that the image should seem so strange to him. It is as if he were seeing Bony for the first time, even though what he sees is what has been there nearly every morning since he came.

Bony stirs. He senses someone looking at him and turns, and this is the moment Toby knows for sure that Dom Fernao is back. Not because he has a vision or hears his step, but because he feels him, inside of him, like a shadow in his belly rising up and filling him to his skin, peering through his eyes so he can see him too—the new one. And Toby knows it's Dom Fernao looking, because what he observes in Bony's eye at that moment is exactly what Dom Fernao observed in Toby's so many years ago: no monster; no King; no prisoner; no slave. Just another man who isn't getting off the island alive.

Bony lifts his chin in greeting, and that quickly the shadow subsides.

Good man, Toby.

Good man, Bony.

Toby tosses the branch onto his barrow and wheels on down the path, leaving Bony to his defiant orange and the jovi-bara maidens to their recovered idol.

That evening Toby arrives at dinner to find a stack of new baskets waiting for him on the bench. Sam and Charles are there as well. They've been up at the Briars more often since Alley's passing. From the whoops and shrieks he's heard sputtering from the coop, Toby would guess they brought another rooster from Timu's today, but it's the baskets that mean more. He recognizes the hand; they are made of raffia leaves, soft and tough, stripped and wound tight like rope, and bound with pine needles.

"These are from Timu's?"

The boys both nod, as 'Scilla and Sarah now step out with bowls and black bread.

"Who give them to you?" asks Toby.

"Marie," says Sarah.

Toby keeps looking at the boys. "What did she say?"

Sam shakes his head, nervous and wanting his food. "Said the gardener would know, Ra-Toby."

They all look at him: eight eyes, trained and waiting. Toby looks down at the baskets. There are four of them, all the same shallow shape but ascending in size, from the cup of two hands to a cradle of arms.

Toby nods; he knows. He slides them down to the end of the bench and takes his seat for dinner.

CHAPTER TWENTY-THREE

DECEMBER 7-10

—⊶⫘⊷—

Paint and newspapers—Privilege of the office—The Emperor's departure

December 7—With the move scheduled in just two days, Grand Marshal Bertrand and General Gourgaud made the trip up to Longwood this morning to check on the status of the extension. Their arrival back at the Pavilion coincides with that of the Emperor and Las Cases, returning from their midday walk. Urgency compels that His Majesty excuse himself; Las Cases takes to the moment to debrief.

"So? General Bertrand?" He can already sense their concern. "The rooms are ready, I assume."

Gourgaud nods.

"What is it then? General Bertrand? Not the paint?"

Bertrand barely nods his head, the lid of boiling pot.

"But I thought we'd been clear."

"We were."

"When did they apply the last coat?"

"Two days ago," Gourgaud replies. "So they say, but 'the air,' " he mocks.

"What? I don't understand, 'the air'—"

"The air is very damp up on the plain," Bertrand explains, resigned.

Las Cases sniffs; this is not good, and now His Majesty is returning from his errand. He speaks quickly. "How long before it's dry, the paint?"

"It's difficult to make an estimate." Bertrand keeps his voice low as well. "It depends upon the weather."

"What does?" The Emperor rejoins them, spry and relieved. "Did you see the house? Will it be ready?"

"We did, Your Majesty, and yes."

The Emperor looks at them. "But? What else? What has General Gourgaud so upset?"

Las Cases acts as spokesman. "It seems there is still a smell, Your Majesty."

"Of?"

"Paint."

The Emperor looks up at Bertrand. "When did they apply the last coat?"

"Two days ago, Your Majesty."

"So they say," adds Gourgaud.

"And it still smells?"

His Majesty awaits. The three men are silent, none wanting to mention the climate. Also they are joined at this moment by the Marquis—de Montholon—just arrived from town. He bows in greeting but senses their collective distraction.

"What is the news?"

Again Las Cases answers. "It seems there is still a smell up at Longwood."

"Smell?" De Montholon is surprised. "I was there late yesterday; I didn't notice any smell."

"Paint," says Gourgaud. "It's very strong. You mustn't have gone inside."

"Of course I went inside." He looks at the others. "I didn't notice any—"

"Well, *which is it?*" the Emperor snaps. It is by far his loudest outburst since coming to the Briars. "Does it smell, or doesn't it?" He looks at them, one to the next, by height: from Bertrand to de

Montholon to Las Cases and finally to Gourgaud, not only the
shortest but also the most vulnerable to his sting. "Is it not enough
that I am made to suffer such indignity, but that I am also forced to
rely upon squabbling, mewling children? Listen! We have been here
long enough! We have overstayed our welcome, and there are too
many eyes. It is time we go!" He turns and stalks off in the direction
of the pomegranates.

The men wait until he is safely out of earshot; then General
Gourgaud turns to de Montholon. "Well done."

"What I have done?"

"Do you not have a nose? It is unthinkable that His Majesty
would sleep a night in that house."

"It is unthinkable that any of us would sleep a night in that
house," replies de Montholon, undaunted; encouraged even, as he
regards the Emperor's flare-up to be the first real display of sanity
he's shown since they all arrived.

Gourgaud, not so reassured, stalks off in his own carefully chosen
direction.

De Montholon turns to Bertrand. "Something has upset Monsieur Gogo?" He pats his heart gently.

The following morning Las Cases goes up to Longwood to see
for himself—or smell, as the case may be. There is a faint aroma of
paint, to be sure, but not so noticeable in the Emperor's chamber.
Granting His Majesty's proven sensitivity, it is the Count's considered
opinion that further delay would be far more nauseating than the
smell. He has a worker help him open the windows, then returns to
deliver his report.

He finds that matters, and tempers, have all more or less settled.
The men are in the tent, seated around the dining table, reading
newspapers. The *Minden* arrived today, and some officers have apparently done the kindness of furnishing His Majesty with what
looks to have been at least a two-foot stack of newspapers, half of
which have already been devoured and cast aside.

The Count waits until a page is turned before interrupting. "I
wanted Your Majesty to be assured that the smell of paint up at

Longwood is dissipating and that there should be no problem in proceeding with the plan to move tomorrow."

The Emperor barely looks up from his article.

"Did you read this?" asks Gourgaud, from the far side. He has *Le Figaro*. "It says the duc d'Orléans might be chosen to succeed Louis."

The Emperor scoffs. "They'd sooner *I* returned."

The silence is pregnant with leery confusion.

His Majesty explains. "How many more Napoleons need they fear?" No one ventures, but the answer would seem to be none. "How many more cousins?"

Ah, yes, they nod, a well-taken point, and relievedly turn their noses back to their pages.

⸺✥⸺

December 9—Reverend Boys has asked Lotte to come see him again as soon as she is finished sweeping out among the pews. She takes the seat against the wall. Her womb is a round melon beneath her dress.

"Miss Lotte."

"Rev'ren'." She tucks a strand of hair beneath her scarf. The circles beneath her eyes are even darker today.

"I have spoken with Sarah, who works at Mr. Balcombe's." Boys shifts his eye to the frayed feather of his quill pen. "Am I to understand that the young slave who was killed last week was the father of your child?"

She stills. This is the first time he has mentioned any such thing.

"Am I to understand?"

"Yes, Rev'ren'."

"You have my sympathy and condolence." He marks a note in his book, of nothing. "May I assume he was intending to marry you?"

She looks at him, still frozen, not understanding yet why he should even ask.

"I will assume," he says, "and that the child is therefore due baptism."

Lotte's eyes search, bewildered.

"The child will receive the sacrament," says Boys, more insistently, and only now does she grasp. He is offering.

"Thank you, Rev'ren'."

"No thanks are necessary, Miss Lotte. It's a privilege of the office." He closes the ledger. "Good day, then."

She rises and curtsies quietly, but before she leaves the church, she pauses at the head of the nave, just as Lieutenant Wood did. Boys can see her through the door. She kneels and crosses herself. He isn't sure, but he thinks it's the first time he has ever seen her do so.

—◈—

December 10—That morning Betsy emerges to the sight of the front lawn cluttered with his things, just as it was eight weeks ago, except for the marquee. The night before last a storm tore it down from its posts, and now it lies among the rest: his campaign bed, the globe, his nécessaire, trunks filled with plates and snuffboxes and all the bijouterie, the portraits of his son, all awaiting their place in the wagons.

He is there too, pretending not to notice her, eating breakfast with her father. He is dressed in his green Chasseur du Gard uniform, and it is just the two of them on an open patch of grass—a silver pot of coffee and toast—but Betsy does not join them. She stands on the veranda, watching Marchand and St. Denis easing down the stand for his washbasin, making sure the legs aren't set upon a stone. Right beside is the tea chest with the ivory miniature of Canton inside; she nearly feels sick to her stomach.

Time is so strange. She has grown so used to seeing him, it is as though he has always been there, in the Pavilion. The others come and go, but has he not always been there? She cannot imagine he was not here before, or she can, but she cannot imagine she did not know how drab and gray a place that was. She feels as though she's been shown a whole new world the last eight weeks, lived a whole life, and now that world, and life, were leaving.

Up on the road the islanders are beginning to gather. They know that today is the day. There is Mr. Breame in his hat, and Mrs. Baggett. Gawking, shameless paysans. Betsy cannot look anymore; she goes back inside. She lets the door slam and sits in the parlor, alone and angry.

She doesn't care what they know or think they know—that she pestered him the whole time, that she was spoiled and rude and insolent. He knows, and she could tell them if they were really interested, things he said and did, that when her mother tried to punish her, sent her to the cellar for some reason she can't even remember anymore, he came to her window and sat on the ground and fed her licorice from his box. But she will never tell them that.

Jane is at the door. "Betsy, are you coming? They're ready. He's asking for you."

She wipes her cheeks dry and follows her sister out. He is still out on the lawn, standing with her father and brothers, grinning faintly as she and Jane descend the steps. The sun is high and bright now, and his things are being loaded onto carts and wagons. They are even using the Balcombes' own.

"Look what he's given Father," says Jane.

Her father shows her, proudly. It's a brass monogram, the royal cipher, set in a velvet-lined case. Alexander and Nicholas show off their gifts as well. Coins, from old campaigns.

"Et maintenant," he says, "pour Mademoiselle Betsee." He turns to St. Denis, who produces a small enamel bonbonnière. She has seen it among the other boxes. It has golden bees on it, and it's not that she doesn't like it—it is a very lovely box, in fact—but she doesn't want it. Not now. He sees. "Perhaps one day you can give it to little Las Cases," he jokes, "comme un gage d'amour." *A token of love.*

At this she bursts into tears and runs away, up the steps and all the way back to her room. She flops on her bed. She doesn't want his gifts. She wants everyone to go away. She wants him never to have come. She buries her head into her pillow, and she would gladly keep it there till she was sure they'd gone, but then, between her sobs, she hears some footsteps. Her heart stops, because she knows they're his—she can tell—and they're inside the house. Then comes a knock—on her mother's door. He has come to say good-bye.

"Madame?"

Betsy listens, but her mother's voice is muffled, embarrassed. He does not enter. He speaks through the door, in rehearsed English.

"Madame, you need not rise. I only want to telled you—what a great plaisir it has been . . . to stay with you and your fam'lee, who is most charming, and I regret any imposition, but I shall look upon this time as a patch of sun in what I think now is a gloomy sky. Madame, thank you." He bows, she knows he does, though no one is there to see.

Her mother replies, something brief that Betsy cannot quite hear. He sets down his gift for her, and all is silent for a moment. Betsy wonders if he'll go, but then she hears his tread again. He is coming here. Her face is burning hot. She knows she's red, but now he is standing at the door.

It is the first time he has seen her room. He enters, though she does not look at him. He clucks his tongue, and her head and shoulders shiver. He sits beside her on the bed, their knees aligned, four in a row.

"Why you are so sad?"

She shrugs.

"I am only going up the road, and you will come see me, no?"

"Oui."

"Of course. I will make your father promise." He points to the little box on the pillow. "Did you see inside?"

She shakes her head. He clucks his tongue and presents it to her again. She isn't nervous. She's strangely calm, in fact, now, but her hands are shaking as she opens it. It is a lock of his hair.

"Aha!" he says, as though he did not know.

It is from behind his ear, she can tell. It could just as well have come from the head of his son, though, the King of Rome, it is so soft and fine.

"Mais j'aurais dû vous offrir un cadeau," she says. *But I should have gotten you something.*

He shakes his head. "You will come see me."

She nods. "Oui."

"Oui, see?" He takes her hand. "Everyone must ask permission, except for my Betsee."

She nods.

"You know this?"

"Oui."

He leans down and places a kiss on her forehead, just above the brow. Then he stands.

"Good-bye, Betsee." He turns and leaves.

Outside, the wagons are now all full and waiting, Lewis's cart among them. Even in the brief time that the Emperor has been inside the bungalow, many more people have come to watch. Up the hill they line the inland road on both sides now. The Bertrands have arrived from Hutt's Gate; the de Montholons from town. There is a sizable British escort as well, and Admiral Cockburn stands beside the horse that Bonaparte has chosen, the jet black pony, Hope, which St. Denis has saddled in crimson velvet. As Bonaparte mounts, there is a palpable reflex among all who see, even those up on the road, of reassurance. He turns the pony and walks it out onto the lane of banyans. Cockburn and his mare are a pace behind, and on the other side is Bertrand. The wheels of the wagons all begin to turn, and the procession begins.

It advances five steps into the shade before the Emperor stops. He raises his hand, and all the horses, the wagons, the soldiers, and members of his coterie tug to a halt.

The Balcombes' servants are lined up along the left side of the lane, with gifts.

"Monsieur Tobee." Bony removes his hat and holds it to his chest.

Toby removes his hat as well and steps forward to present the first, and smallest, of Quinto's baskets. No one else can see, but there are two handfuls of seeds inside, on a bed of myrtle leaves.

"What is this?" asks Bony.

"The flowers you like," says Toby. "And yam."

Bony makes a face. He doesn't like yam, as Toby knows, but he accepts the basket just the same. He summons the first valet, the painter, to come and take it.

Sam and Charles now step out together. 'Scilla has lined their baskets with leaves as well. In Sam's is a small pile of salt. In Charles's is rice. They hand them over to the servant, and Bony thanks them each with separate nods, then turns to Sarah. Hers is the largest basket, filled with fresh biscuits. Bony smiles when he sees. "These I do not share." He motions for his servant to keep them safely away from the others.

Finally it is 'Scilla's turn, though she has no basket. She steps out with her head low, but her steely eyes turned up at him, and extends a black iron skillet. A chuckle ripples through the departing company; Bony does not hear it. 'Scilla then removes a small tin from her pocket and sets it on the skillet.

"Matches," she says.

Bony tilts his head in gratitude, and now the second servant attends. The arms of the first are already full.

'Scilla steps back then, to clear the way. Bony dons his hat again, then taps his heels against Hope's belly. The wheels of all the laden carts and wagons groan forward, and so begins the three-mile climb to Longwood.

EPILOGUE

Bonaparte's captivity at St. Helena will last another six years, spent almost entirely within the confines of the Longwood compound. He will never again know company of his choosing, and he will never again be alone. There will be the valets, rubbing him down with lavender water and eau de Cologne every morning. There will be his steward and his chefs, and the rest of the suite, bickering and trying to curry his favor. The de Montholons, the Las Caseses, and General Gourgaud all will be right there in the house; the Bertrands, just down the lane. There will be the sentries stationed at every turn, and the fortress on the hill, pounding the sky three times a day.

He will continue to dress for dinner. The servants will wear livery and take their stations on either side of his chair. He'll keep telling his version. The men will keep writing it down and make note of everything else he does as well, for posterity and personal gain. He'll continue to study his maps and rethink battles, and the rats will be so plentiful throughout the house no one dares set down his hat. Chess and cards will pass the time, and plays will be read aloud after dinner until His Majesty falls asleep. He'll make plans for a new house, of Grecian design, which will arrive in stages from the Continent. He will dig a garden. Chinese carpenters will build him trellises and ramparts, fences and trenches to hide him from view of the guards on the hill. He'll keep tubs of redfish; grow pansy beds, passionflowers, and éternelles, and he will kill any goat or pig or ox that dares trespass.

Betsy will visit him. Not every day, but once or twice a week, she will go up to Longwood with Jane or with her parents, and she will not need to ask permission. She will behave herself not much better than she did at the Briars, and a rumor will eventually find Europe, by way of a Russian aristocrat who briefly visits the island, that the exiled Emperor is having an affair with a very young English girl. When Bonaparte is told of this, he will give Betsy a pair of scissors and tell her to go cut off the Russian aristocrat's ponytail.

In the spring of 1818 the Balcombes will leave the island for good, fleeing suspicions that Mr. Balcombe has been helping smuggle letters out of Longwood. The family will live five years in Devonshire. Then, in 1823, thanks to the influence of his older brother, Robert, Mr. Balcombe will be named Colonial Treasurer in New South Wales. He will die in Sydney in 1829, but most of the family will remain in Australia, in penury. Betsy will marry, not well, and will be forced by financial need to publish a memoir of her friendship with the Emperor Napoleon, under her married name, Abell.

The Briars will remain, and Toby will remain at the Briars. No record survives of his passing, but he will have to live only three more years to see the demise of slavery on St. Helena. All children born of slaves on or after Christmas Day 1818 will be free. Fourteen years later all slaves whatsoever will be emancipated.

Bonaparte will not be so fortunate, and in time, his captivity, the unremitting climate, as well as the bitterness and the treachery of his only companions, will take their toll. He will sleep fitfully, suffer colds, take long baths, and grow fat. A new Governor will be appointed by the Crown, one Hudson Lowe, whose first and foremost charge will be to ensure the prisoner's captivity. He will treat the former Emperor with a far more stern and petty hand than Admiral Cockburn, and many pointless conflicts will ensue, to help distract them from their boredom.

The suite will slowly drift away, by varying degrees and distances. The first to leave will be Las Cases, in the fall of 1816. His notebooks full, he will see no need to suffer any further the insults and insinuations of Gourgaud and de Montholon. Gourgaud will follow fifteen months later, seeing no need to suffer the insults of de Montholon. The last straw will involve de Montholon's mocking Gourgaud's claim to having saved the Emperor's life at Brienne. Gourgaud will challenge him to a duel. De Montholon will accept and then back out, and when the Emperor fails to take sides in the matter, Gourgaud will ask permission to leave. Coincidentally, he will be on the same boat that bears away the Balcombes, the *Winchelsea*.

The following year, July 1819, the de Montholons will strategically split, Albine taking the children with her (now including an infant daughter, Napoléonne), while the "Marquis" will stay behind, for the promise of money. Not long after, the Bertrands will try to leave as well, but when the Emperor forbids the Grand Marshal to go, his wife, Fanny, will decide to stay, but refuse to visit the Emperor ever again, relenting only at the last hours of his life.

These come May 5, 1821. The given cause of death, as determined by the seven physicians who attend Bonaparte's autopsy, will be cancer of the stomach.* A number of his organs will be removed and studied, to try to see what makes a great man great. His stomach will be shipped to England; his heart will be put in a box and sent to his son. Telltale locks of his hair will be distributed among the servants, while sundry other parts, casts, and death masks will be boated off for sale and display in museums around the world.

What remains will be dressed in the uniform of the Imperial Guard, with orders on his breast, cocked hat, and long boots with spurs. Amid his cutlery and other tokens, the body will then be closed inside a tin coffin, inside a mahogany coffin, inside a lead cof-

---

*Many years later, arsenic levels found in Bonaparte's hair will give substance to the rumor that he was poisoned. No evidence exists to implicate any remaining member of his entourage, but it will be observed that only de Montholon had sufficient opportunity and deficient character to undertake such a scheme.

fin, inside another wood coffin. This will be buried in a great stone
crypt alongside the road to Longwood, down by the vale of geraniums. The site will stand for nineteen years; then, in 1840, the
French government will assert its claim and bring the body and its
several casings back to France, to be buried again at the military hos-
pital in Paris, Les Invalides, where it remains to this day.

The tomb remains at St. Helena, though, a black iron fence
guarding nothing, and the one place on the island that all the visitors
are sure to see. Even among the world of others who'll never get the
chance, her name will always be linked to Bonaparte. Many will
think she is in the Mediterranean, confusing her for Elba. Others
will know better, that St. Helena is the second island, the one in the
Atlantic where the Emperor wasted away.

Only those who live there, though—and among these only a
few—will understand the truth: that St. Helena cares no more for
Napoleon Bonaparte than for anyone else who ever lived or died
there—the governors and slaves, merchants, rebels, captains, children, and freebooters. They are clouds passing over. She feels their
shadows, visits their thoughts as she pleases; then they're gone. There
is only one she keeps with her, always: not the first to find her, but
the first to stay, who lost his faith on the far side of the world, and
found it again with her, and who left her only one time after that,
and only so he could return and be with her, and know that he
would be within her when he died.

ACKNOWLEDGMENTS

—◦◦◦◦—

To those readers interested in exploring for themselves the various materials from which the foregoing has been drafted, the author happily recommends:

Recollections of the Emperor Napoleon, by Mrs. L. E. Abell, London, 1844.

A St. Helena's Who's Who, by Arnold Chaplin, London, 1919.

The Life, Exile, and Conversations of the Emperor Napoleon, by the Count de Las Cases, London, 1835.

The Commentaries of the Great Alphonso d'Albaquerque, vol. 3, Hakluyt Society no. 62.

Memoirs of Napoleon Bonaparte, by Louis Antoine Fauvelet de Bourrienne, London, 1885.

St. Helena, 1502–1938, by Philip Gosse, Oswestry, London, 1990.

Napoleon in Exile: or, A Voice from St. Helena, by Barry O'Meara, London, 1819.

"Bernard Gui: Inquisitorial Technique (c. 1307–1323)," in the *Internet Medieval Sourcebook*, edited by Paul Halsall, Fordham University Center for Medieval Studies (www.fordham.edu/halsall/sbook.html).

A variety of maps and images provided by Barry Weaver, including:

Views of St. Helena, by T. E. Fowler, St. Helena, 1863.

St. Helena: A Physical, Historical, and Topographical Description of the Island, Including Its Geology, Fauna, Flora, and Meteorology, by J. C. Melliss, London, 1875.

Tracts Relative to the Island of St. Helena, by A. Beatson, London, 1816.

Extracts from the St. Helena Records, by H. R. Janisch, St. Helena, 1885.

A History of the Island of St. Helena from Its Discovery by the Portuguese to the Year 1806, by T. H. Brooke, London, 1808.

A Description of the Island of St. Helena, anon. (F. Duncan?), London, 1805.

Of less immediate, but no less vital, assistance have been:

The Emperor's Last Island, by Julia Blackburn, London, 1991.
Napoleon, by Vincent Cronin, New York, 1971.
Napoleon Bonaparte, by Alan Schom, New York, 1997.
"The Earliest Exile of St. Helena," by Hugh Clifford, from *Blackwoods Magazine*, London, May 1903.
The Religion of Java, by Clifford Gertz, Chicago and London, 1960.
The Eighth Continent, by Peter Tyson, New York, 2000.
On Thrones of Gold, by James R. Brandon, Cambridge, Massachusetts, 1970.
Chicken Tractor: The Permaculture Guide to Happy Hens and Healthy Soil, by Andy Lee and Pat Foreman, Columbus, North Carolina, 1998.
ABC of Poultry Raising, by J. H. Florea, New York, 1977.

As ever, my more personal thanks and appreciation go first to Paul Elie for the continuing height of his standards; to Sarah Chalfant for the depth of her commitment; to Cecily Parks, Susan Mitchell, Jonathan Lippincott, and Sean Mills for helping turn the manuscript into a book; to Jonathan Galassi, Amanda Urban, and the many generous friends, family members, and institutions that have offered their time, resources, interest, gifts, and criticism, but especially: Jill Dunbar at Three Lives & Co., The New York Public Library, University of Texas at Austin—Perry-Castañeda Map Collection, Stage Left, Esty Foster, Sheila Glaser, Hope Hansen, Peter Hansen, Sam Hansen, Whitney Hansen, Robert Howe, Elizabeth Meryman, Virginia Priest, Yannick van de Velde, Lewis Vogler, and Elizabeth Webb Woodworth.

And finally, to my own primary source, Elizabeth.